LP
FIC
BEAUFORT

8-14

THE MURDER HOUSE

She made one stupid mistake ... and paid a devastating price: a gripping psychological thriller

When PC Helen Anderson takes the files for a forthcoming court case to study over the weekend, she commits a cardinal error. For those files are not supposed to leave the police station – and the moment they fall into the wrong hands, Helen's ordinary, uneventful life begins to spiral out of control. For one small lie will lead to another, then another – culminating in a rendezvous in an ordinary suburban house in an ordinary Bristol street ... the scene of a gruesome and extraordinary murder.

THE MURDER HOUSE

Simon Beaufort

Severn House Large Print
London & New York

This first large print edition published 2014
in Great Britain and the USA by
SEVERN HOUSE PUBLISHERS LTD of
19 Cedar Road, Sutton, Surrey, England, SM2 5DA.
First world regular print edition published 2013 by
Severn House Publishers Ltd., London and New York.

British Library Cataloguing in Publication Data

Beaufort, Simon author.
  The murder house.
  1. Policewomen--Fiction. 2. Detective and mystery stories.
  3. Large type books.
  I. Title
  823.9'2-dc23

  ISBN-13: 9780727897039

Severn House Publishers support the Forest Stewardship Council™
[FSC™], the leading international forest certification organisation. All
our titles that are printed on FSC certified paper carry the FSC logo.

Printed and bound in Great Britain by
T J International, Padstow, Cornwall.

For our favourite policeman:
Commander Ralph S. Riffenburgh

ONE

My name is Helen Anderson, and I'm a murderer. This is my story. It isn't a confession, as those tend not to make very interesting reading. It's my *story* – how I came to do the things I did, and why. For all their diligence, I don't think the police fully understand what happened, and this is my chance to explain – for myself, as much as for anyone who happens to read it.

It won't be easy to write, given that I've learned things that no one should ever have to know: how to kill, how to conceal it, and how to lie to protect myself. There was a stage when I exulted in the power that brought – to offer a hint and watch the police doggedly follow the road I had selected, knowing their efforts would be wasted. But mostly, I was just scared and confused.

I suppose I should start at the beginning. It sounds trite put like that – all stories should start at the beginning. But *when* did mine start? The first time I met James Paxton? Our single, fumbling, sordid date years later? The point when he realized that a friend in the police might be good for more than a few cheap jokes about handcuffs? I think I shall go back to the *very* beginning, when we were still young, although even then there was a sharp distinction between his world and mine.

The distinction became clearer as we grew older, and perhaps that's where the problems started – my ridiculous gratitude at being noticed by the bright star that was James; my pathetic pleasure at being invited into his exclusive world. But, of course, that was before I learned that all that glitters isn't gold.

James and I were at school together in Bristol – or rather, we were in the same school at the same time. He came late, when we were fifteen, but he made his uniform look as if it had been styled in Savile Row, and he quickly became the school pin-up. All the girls were aware of him, whether with the usual adoration for the exotic and handsome, or a sort of fascinated unease, where we pretended not to notice him but were nonetheless flattered when he smiled in our direction.

James quickly became Redlands School's star pupil. He passed his GCSEs with flying colours, was Head Boy, captain of the cricket team, took the leading role in all the plays, and had a set of friends who basked in his reflected glory.

Meanwhile, I worked hard and made respectable grades. I was an average athlete, and a reliable backstop on the rounders team. I took care with my appearance, although photographs show me with no sense of style, and a thatch of fairish hair that would have looked better short. My parents owned a shop. They were good people, who were proud when I scraped through enough A-levels to win a place at a provincial university.

James had a mother with Thatcher hair and the confident attitude of someone used to getting her own way. His father was apparently dead, but he never talked about it. I suppose bad things happen even to boys like James, who had everything he could want and a good deal more besides. He caught the bus to school with the rest of us in the mornings, but sometimes a man would collect him in his mother's Mercedes. We joked that the driver was his mother's lover, and sniggered at the thought of that stiff, uncompromising lady rolling around with the monkey-faced, unshaven fellow in the car.

So, that was James. Destined to go to Oxford, where he continued to excel, while I studied psychology in Newcastle.

One day, when I was in the university careers service – I was there because I didn't have the faintest idea what I wanted to do with my degree – my advisor ran late. To pass the time, I filled in an application for the police. When a letter came inviting me for an interview with the Avon and Somerset Constabulary, I was stunned – I hadn't imagined they'd reply. I went along, and the next thing I knew I'd been accepted and was due to start training. So I became a police constable. I bought a terraced house in the Hotwells district of Bristol and prepared for my new life.

At first, I was assigned to pleasantly rural Midsomer Norton, where we dealt with minor thefts, the odd case of incest, and the kind of vandalism that always happens when bored teenagers have nothing else to do. But the uniform still meant something to the people of that nice country town, and getting the job done wasn't difficult. For the next three and a half years, I was happy.

Then the force decided that more officers were needed in urban areas, so I was re-assigned to the Bristol West district, which covered the main shopping areas, the harbour, and much of the 'inner city'. Bristol West HQ, known as New Bridewell, was a nasty, multi-storeyed affair with grime-encrusted windows set in grey concrete, which had not been updated for years. Home Office reviews, stupid legislation and constant public criticism had demoralized and embittered the people who worked there, and I disliked it from my first day. Time did nothing to make it any better.

In the country, I'd shown an aptitude for handling frustrated farmers and angry motorists, and I'd even demonstrated a modest talent for dealing with bewildered livestock. At New Bridewell, I was lost. I had no 'feel' for the criminal side of the job and found it hard to tell the difference between strange truths and accomplished lies. Moreover, I disliked the confrontational encounters with the rough, violent, persistent offenders who were regular faces at the station.

There was another problem, too. I found myself landed with more boring traffic duty than was fair, given my age and experience – Britain's police forces may have policies on sexism, but that means nothing when there are officers like Sergeant Barry Wright in positions of authority. Wright was what my colleagues generally – and usually admiringly – called 'an old-style police-man'. To me, he was a bigot.

If work was dismal, so too was my social life. Shifts and unscheduled overtime play havoc with relationships, a problem compounded by the fact that not everyone wants a police officer as a friend. It isn't just that we make unreliable acquaintances, who often cancel long-standing arrangements at the last minute, but there seems to be a belief among the public that off-duty officers have nothing better to do than catch them breaking the law.

I had no real friends at New Bridewell, although I always joined the post-shift drinks in a local pub. The men were either married or on the prowl – or both – while the women were either struggling to juggle the job with home life and children, or wanted to party hard. I was at a particularly low point in my life when I stopped James for running a red light.

I'd had a really bad day. I was on an early shift, which meant getting up before four a.m., and my in-tray was full of petty burglaries and thefts to 'investigate'. Cars were in short supply, so I'd had to walk, and I was hot, tired and irritable. I was trudging back to the station in a foul frame of mind when a black BMW shot through a busy exchange after the lights had changed. I leapt off the pavement, arm raised in an imperious gesture for the driver to stop.

I confess I was flattered when James declared himself delighted to see me. He took the ticket I wrote with good grace, then told me about himself. Needless to say, he was successful. He'd left Oxford with a First in law, and a number of high-paying firms had offered him a position. He'd chosen Urvine and Brotherton, where he specialized in criminal law. They had offices in Queen Square, one of Bristol's loveliest areas.

Then he told me he was meeting some old Redlandians at a harbour-side cafe that Saturday. He mentioned several names I recognized – Colin Fairhurst, Gary Sheldick, Frances Moorfield – and suggested I join them. I smiled politely and told him I'd try, in the way people do when they have no intention of trying at all. Such exulted company wasn't for the likes of me.

Yet when Saturday came, and I was settling down for a night of mediocre telly with a bag of Thornton's 'continentals', I realized there was no reason why I shouldn't meet up with them. The harbour wasn't far; I could walk there in less than half an hour. So I went, nervously fiddling with my keys as I approached their table, but relaxing when I sensed that they were genuinely pleased to see an old schoolmate, even if it was only one of the 'average girls'.

I was relieved to find that the youthful arrogance had gone from Gary, Frances and Colin – they were normal people, who talked about mortgages, ageing parents and where to go on holiday. Colin was a computer programmer, while Frances and Gary worked for an insurance company. I didn't feel overawed or bedazzled by them, as I had at school.

I met them several times after that, becoming

particularly good friends with Frances and Gary. They'd been a couple at school, and had kept their relationship going through different universities and demanding jobs. James, meanwhile, was always charming and attentive, and I was foolishly flattered that a good-looking man seemed interested in me. When he suggested a date at a wine bar on Park Street, I accepted, although there was a part of me that wondered, even then, why an ambitious lawyer would want to go out with a plain police constable with scant chance of promotion.

Our date was a disaster. Without the relaxed bonhomie of the others, our conversation was stilted. James took me back to his designer-furnished flat, where our sex was no more satisfactory than our discussions about wine, politics and work, and left us both uncomfortable. I slipped away while he was still asleep, and walked for two hours in the dark to get home. He didn't call me, and I avoided the Saturday night gatherings for several months, opting instead to see Frances and Gary during the week.

And that was that. When I finally returned to the old Redlandians' fold months later, James wasn't there, and enquiries revealed that he'd slipped out of the habit at about the same time as me. The story of my association with James Paxton should have ended there. I wish to God it had.

TWO

Detective Inspector Neel Oakley was used to people misspelling his name. It had been chosen by his Indian mother because she thought it would fit nicely into the two cultures that comprised his heritage. Oakley had never visited India, and with his mother dead and contact long since lost with her family, nor was he likely to. The only reminders of his ethnic background were an olive complexion, dark eyes and a fondness for curry. And the name, of course, which often caused confusion. One such occasion was currently in progress, as he stood in the witness box at Bristol Crown Court to give evidence against one Andrew Brown.

'There appears to be a mistake,' drawled James Paxton, the defending barrister. 'One of the clerks has spelled Neil with two 'e's. That's the disgrace of our education system, My Lord – it teaches people to spell phonetically.'

Patiently, Oakley explained the origin of his name. He disliked Paxton, having watched him in action before, belittling witnesses and using his sharp mind to confuse and undermine them. He knew the remark about his name was an effort to get under his skin, to annoy him and make him incautious.

Brown had already served time for burglary and, if there was any justice, was about to spend a fourth spell behind bars. He had snatched a bag from an old woman, clubbing her to the ground in the process. It had frightened the wits out of her – literally. Mrs Harris was now so confused that Oakley suspected her testimony was going to lose them the case. Paxton obviously thought so, too, because he was already gloating.

Paxton's smirk faded to irritation when Oakley declined to be needled, but returned when Detective Sergeant Mark Butterworth took the stand – the younger man's anger and indignation were palpable, and Paxton soon manipulated him into blurting that, yes, he *would* love to see Brown behind bars, and of course he would use all the methods at his disposal to see justice done.

'We should have hired an actress to be Mrs Harris for the day,' Butterworth muttered, as he and Oakley sat in the corridor, waiting for the verdict. He was from Yorkshire, a small, fair-haired man devoted to his job and his baby daughter in equal measure. 'She was crap, which means Brown's going to walk – Paxton's going to get him off.'

'Very possibly,' sighed Oakley. 'Just like he got Gordon Noble off last year.'

Butterworth glowered. 'Noble! I spent weeks on that case, only to see the bastard go free. I still think Paxton nobbled the jury.'

Oakley didn't. Paxton seemed altogether too sure of his own skills to resort to anything illegal. He had simply given the jury reasonable doubts about Noble's guilt, and that was that.

'Bloody Noble!' muttered Butterworth. 'Still, we'll have him sooner or later. He won't stay clean for long. Nor will Brown – because he *is* going to walk today.'

He was right: the jury returned a verdict of 'not guilty'. With only circumstantial evidence placing Brown at the scene of the crime – and suspicions that Mrs Harris' pension had been planted on Brown by overzealous police officers – the defendant was free.

'Can't win 'em all,' taunted Paxton as he gathered up his folders. 'Better luck next time.'

'There ought to be a law against gloating,' said Oakley to the prosecution barrister, Simon Ingram, as he watched Paxton strut away. He wondered how the man's suit could look so elegant after a day in a humid, stuffy courtroom. Oakley himself felt sticky and soiled, although the sensation had as much to do with the proximity of Brown as it had the heat of the building.

'What goes around, comes around,' said Ingram, dislike clear in his voice. 'Unfortunately, Paxton is blessed with the luck of the Devil. I haven't seen him lose a case yet.'

'What, never?' asked Oakley.

'No – and he's had some tough ones.' Ingram snapped his briefcase closed. 'But no one wins forever. Good morning, gentlemen. The next time you bring me a villain, perhaps you would remember to provide some decent evidence as well.'

'The evidence *was* good,' muttered Butterworth resentfully. 'Brown was in Dean Lane when the old lady was mugged, and her pension was in his pocket. What more does he want? Well, maybe Brown will mug Paxton's mother next time. That'll give the smarmy git something to think about!'

I first heard James' name mentioned at New Bridewell when DI Oakley and DS Butterworth lost the Brown case. In the following months, many more villains were freed thanks to his quick brain and clever words, and although I was tempted to mention casually that he and I had been at school together, I had the good sense to hold my tongue. And thank God I did, considering the way things turned out.

October
New Bridewell's CID had so much work that Oakley was often obliged to beg the uniform branch for help with routine surveillance. Overtime was inevitable rather than optional for his detectives, and the teacher who had been delighted to move in with him six months earlier had moved out, declaring she wanted a relationship with someone who would be home at least *one* evening a week. Oakley knew his life was a mess when he didn't find her letter until three days after she'd gone.

The current reason for Oakley's lack of a personal life was Gordon Noble, a vicious thug with fingers in many illegal pies. Noble had previous convictions for robbery and aggravated burglary – including a time when he had almost severed a security guard's arm with a hatchet. During the previous decade he had eliminated his competitors to become a major player in Bristol's criminal underworld. Although now wealthy, he refused to sit back and supervise his underlings, such as his two heavy-set 'enforcers' – Justin Castle and Mike Gray. Instead, he continued to lead his operation from the front, actively participating in a variety of crimes. Yet, despite being caught several times, he remained free, thanks to James Paxton's courtroom skills.

For months, Oakley's informants had been telling him that something was brewing at Noble's dilapidated row of sheds near the marina. These were ostensibly used for storing engine parts, as Noble's legal business was repairing outboard motors. But Oakley believed his sources, and was convinced something significant was about to happen there.

That 'something' was related to the kids hanging out near one of Noble's all-night pizza joints. Oakley and his team watched money and small packets exchanging hands there on a regular basis and, although he could not prove it, Oakley was sure Noble was a key figure behind the flow of drugs to Bristol's bored and sullen youth.

But Noble wasn't Oakley's only case, and it was a struggle to watch the sheds and investigate Bristol's other crimes at the same time. Superintendent Taylor had been keen when Oakley had first gone to him with the rumour that 'something big' was brewing, but his enthusiasm had waned as days became weeks and nothing happened. Oakley refused to give up, though, and his patience paid off: word came that Noble was expecting a shipment of goods 'one morning soon'. He detailed a young DC to watch the sheds each day, but Oakley was a meticulous, cautious man, and he wanted the place watched 24/7. As no one from CID was available at night, he was obliged to beg uniform's help.

He approached Inspector Blake, whose shift was working nights that week. Blake was a genial but foolish man close to retirement, who was more interested in honing his computer skills than in actual police work. He approved Oakley's request with a casual nod, and said Sergeant Wright would allocate an officer.

Oakley disliked Wright, mostly for the deplorable way he treated his female officers, particularly Helen Anderson. Oakley suspected that Wright was frightened of her, afraid she might use her sharper wits to expose him as a stupid, vain man without two brain cells to rub together. However, Oakley doubted Anderson would do any such thing: she was shy, and so desperate to be accepted by her colleagues that she ignored his brazen favouritism towards the men in his command.

When Oakley made his request, Wright leaned back in his chair and fixed him with rodent-like eyes. Oakley stared back, noting that Wright had plastered strands of hair across his greasy, balding pate and that his moustache was stained yellow with nicotine.

'You can have Anderson,' Wright said eventually. 'She's no good for anything anyway. Head too full of theories to get down to any real policing.'

'Oh?' asked Oakley mildly. 'And what theories would those be?'

'She'd rather ask a villain about his mother than knee him in the bollocks,' sneered Wright. 'Bloody women! They should stick to raising babies and having the tea on the table when we get home.'

'Anderson will do nicely,' said Oakley. Then he couldn't resist adding: 'I don't want a truncheon-happy yob who assaults suspects and provides them with an excuse for charges to be dropped.'

He turned on his heel and stalked out, feeling Wright's hostile gaze on his back as he went. He collected Anderson from the briefing room and told her what he wanted. She nodded agreeably, although he sensed she felt she had drawn the short straw. He sympathized, but he needed a body. She collected a radio, and he drove her to the derelict house CID was using for observations.

'What made you join the force?' he asked conversationally as they turned down a cobbled street from which SS *Great Britain* could be seen in the distance, its masts and spars a spiky mass against the orange sky. 'The fabulous salary? The excellent working hours? The chance to meet charming people?'

'Do you mean the villains or our colleagues?' she asked, laughing.

'Both. Look, I'm sorry about this. I know you'd rather be out with the lads, but I really need someone here tonight.'

She raised her eyebrows. 'Why? Word is that if anything does happen, it will be during the day. We both know watching the place now is a waste of time.'

'I disagree. A lot's at stake here. Three teenagers have died from bad drugs this year, and
more will follow unless Noble's operation is
stopped. It might not feel like it, but being here
is probably the most important thing anyone on
your shift will do tonight.'

'Really?' she asked coolly. 'Then why aren't
you doing it yourself?'

He grimaced. 'Point taken. But I'll tell you
what: if anything does go down, you're the
arresting officer. It'll look good on your record,
and it'll annoy Wright.'

'It's all right,' she said grudgingly. 'It's not as
bad as traffic duty. At least here some kind soul
might bring me a flask of coffee later.'

'Sugar?' asked Oakley genially.

I'd been at New Bridewell about a year and a
half when Wright assigned me to watch the
sheds. It was a pain, and Wright said that if
anyone other than DI Oakley was in charge, no
one would have bothered to stake out the place
at night. Oakley had a reputation for being
thorough.

But at least Oakley was nice about it. He
seemed genuinely sorry that I'd drawn the short
straw, and spent a full thirty minutes pointing out
various buildings in Noble's domain, and explaining why it was important that Noble was
caught. He was clearly determined to nail the
man.

It was just a shame it wasn't likely to happen
while I was there.

Oakley took Anderson some coffee and a bag of chips just after midnight. The sheds were still and silent, and the derelict house bitterly cold. Oakley experienced a pang of guilt, but he wasn't about to let her go early. He gave her his peace offerings, made sure her radio was working, and headed home. It was a little after two o'clock when he was woken by the crackle of the radio he had placed next to his bed.

'Noble,' Anderson whispered with barely suppressed excitement. 'He's just opened one of his sheds, and his two heavies are down by the waterfront. I think they're waiting for someone.'

'Don't do anything, Helen,' said Oakley, reaching for his clothes in the darkness. 'Sit tight and wait.'

He called the station and, within minutes, a carefully formulated plan was swinging into action. Oakley ran down the stairs, pulling on his coat as he went. Remembering not to slam the car door or gun the engine – the neighbours had recently complained about his nocturnal habits – he drove quickly towards the docks.

Butterworth was already there, almost dancing with glee. 'A boat's making a delivery. Tony Johns can see it from the roof, and he's getting it all on camera.'

'Good,' said Oakley. 'Is everyone here?'

Butterworth nodded. 'DI Davis is up with Anderson, and Wright's got two traffic lads nearby, in case things go pear-shaped. Dogs are on standby, and Bristol East CID are listening in.'

Oakley slipped into the derelict building and

went up the stairs to where two dark shapes were outlined at the window: Anderson and DI Clare Davis.

'You were right, Neel.' Davis sounded pleased. 'The rumours about a daytime delivery were a blind, to make sure we knocked off at dusk. How did you know?'

'I didn't,' admitted Oakley. He grinned at Anderson. 'Looks like you'll arrest one of the most dangerous villains in the West Country tonight.'

The operation went smoothly, and before dawn Noble and six accomplices were locked in New Bridewell's cells and ten kilograms of heroin had been seized. The drug squad was delighted – especially when one suspect offered to give up even bigger fish in exchange for a lighter sentence.

True to his word, Oakley made sure the honour of arresting Noble went to Anderson, and he found himself doubly rewarded – by her pleasure and Wright's fury that she should be the hero of the hour. A preliminary interview was arranged for the morning, so that Noble's lawyer could not claim his client had been questioned late at night when he was tired.

Oakley reminded his team that everything needed to be done by the book, then told them to go home and snatch some sleep before the interviews and reports the following day. Mark Butterworth lingered, however, too wired by the night's happenings to go home. After writing up his pocket book, he went to look at Noble through the grille on the cell door, enjoying the look of indignant rage on the man's face.

Noble was wearing white overalls, as his clothes had been taken to see whether the white powder on them could be matched to the heroin that had been found on the smugglers' boat.

'You won't get me,' warned Noble, masking his temper when he saw he was being watched. 'Not for smuggling. I might enjoy a bit of crack now and again, but I don't get involved in dealing.'

'The forensic boys will prove you do,' taunted Butterworth. 'They'll find it on your clothes.'

'Yeah, my personal stash,' said Noble with a shrug. 'It don't prove I had anything to do with the boat. All I did was watch it arrive. I'm an innocent bystander.'

Butterworth closed the grille and went to the property book – a thick tome in which the contents of a prisoner's pockets were recorded before being placed in a canvas bag and stored until the arrested person left the cells. The custody sergeant, Derek Jones, had gone to fetch someone a cup of water, so Butterworth unlocked the cupboard, found Noble's bag, and emptied it on the counter. Sure enough, there was a packet containing white powder. He glanced at the property book and saw its presence was duly noted. The following day, when Noble's lawyer was present, the packet would be sent to the Forensic Science Service, or FSS, for analysis.

Butterworth, tired and edgy, could see the case going up in smoke when the courts decided that any traces of heroin on Noble's clothes originated from his personal supply, not the boat. Noble was right: he might walk free.

Butterworth looked quickly through the other entries and saw that Noble was not the only one with drugs: Mike Gray had had five tablets in a pouch – ecstasy or some similar party pill. Quickly, Butterworth changed the record so that Gray had three of the tablets and Noble had two. He deleted all references to the powder – which went in his own pocket. There, he thought with satisfaction: Noble could not claim any powder traces on his clothes came from his personal stash if he did not have one.

By the time Derek Jones returned the cupboard was locked, the property book was back on its shelf and Butterworth was innocently studying the arrest file. Jones told him he should get off home if he wanted to be any good in the morning, and Butterworth left without a word, feeling as though he had scored a victory for justice.

Butterworth's attempt to thwart Noble was discovered the following morning, when Jones went to collect the pills and powder for forensic analysis. He distinctly recalled that there had been *five* tablets among Gray's possessions, and it was obvious that the number had been changed in the book. As only one person had been in a position to tamper, it did not take long for Jones to guess the truth. He told Oakley, then his superintendent. Oakley was furious. He cornered Butterworth in the canteen – empty at that hour – where the DS was using the coffee machine.

'You might just have lost us the whole case,' he

fumed. 'Tampering with the evidence! Jesus! What were you thinking?'

'That I had to stop Noble from walking,' objected Butterworth, not bothering to deny the accusation. 'He'll say the powder on his clothes was stuff he used himself.'

Oakley was almost beside himself with frustration. 'Blood tests will show otherwise, so his claim won't see him free, but your tampering might! I can't believe you did this.'

'I was trying to help.' Butterworth looked wretched. His face was grey with fatigue, and there were dark circles under his eyes. Having the kind of job that entailed long hours didn't sit well with having a teething baby at home.

Oakley wanted to rail more, but he could see it would do no good. He ran a hand through his hair and stalked out, wondering what they could do to salvage the situation. Butterworth rubbed his temples with shaking hands. He was aware of a faint movement by the door, and saw Barry Wright lurking there. The sergeant was reading the notice board, and Butterworth had no way of knowing whether he had overheard the exchange. He closed his eyes. One thing was certain though: if Wright had, it would be all over the station by lunchtime.

Oakley sat with Clare Davis, discussing Butterworth's actions. He was still angry, but she questioned whether Noble had told Butterworth about his defence strategy specifically to ensure that the evidence *was* tampered with. Oakley cursed himself for not guessing that Butterworth's nervous excitement might lead him to do something stupid.

They met with Superintendent Taylor later that day, and it was agreed that the pills and packet should be put back as they had been before Butterworth had interfered, and an internal report submitted to the Professional Standards Department. Oakley asked to append a note outlining the stress his sergeant had been under, and the fact that Butterworth's daughter had been sleeping badly for months.

Chastened, Butterworth handed over the small packet he had taken, thanking his lucky stars that he hadn't flushed it down the toilet. Jones initialled the amended entries, and closed the book with an air of finality.

'There,' he said. 'Now bugger off, the lot of you.'

Jones was a quiet, reliable man who didn't gossip, and Oakley was sure the affair would lie dormant until the internal investigation began. Butterworth had been granted a temporary reprieve.

'Thanks, Guv,' muttered Butterworth as he followed Oakley along the corridor.

'You might lose your job over this,' cautioned Oakley, in no mood to be conciliatory. 'Take the day off, and get a note from your doctor saying you've been under a lot of pressure. It might help. I'm just grateful no one else knows about this.'

Butterworth decided it wasn't a good time to mention that Wright might have overheard their discussion in the canteen.

THREE

I should mention the mistake I made, which eventually led me to kill. It was only that – an error of judgement. It wasn't a crime or anything dishonest. It was a mistake, and we all make those. Of course, most don't spiral out of control and lead you to do things you could never imagine doing, even in your darkest nightmares.

The incident that started the chain of events leading to murder happened about a year and a half after my horrid one-night stand with James. I'd been at New Bridewell for about two years, and it was about six months after Noble's arrest. Oakley had let me sit in on Noble's interviews, which was nice of him, and it got Wright off my back for a few days. Then the case passed to higher authorities, and I was back to petty crime and traffic duties. Success had been sweet while it had lasted.

I was seeing Gary, Frances, and Colin Fairhurst fairly often by then, although James had long since moved to loftier acquaintances. Colin ran across James sometimes, and told us that he'd been made a partner in Urvine and Brotherton. James was young for such a post, and it showed that he was set for a glittering career.

I heard a different side of things at work, of

28

course, where his name cropped up regularly. Only a couple of months after getting acquitted, Brown was arrested for holding up a post office with a gun. God knows how, but James managed to convince a jury that Brown was innocent on that as well.

As time passed, more stories about James circulated. Police officers often feel a grudging respect for clever lawyers – but not with James. His ability to put violent criminals back on the streets made him someone to hate. Needless to say, I kept my acquaintance with him quiet, and my school days and single night of unsatisfactory lust were tucked away as distant memories.

But none of this has anything to do with my mistake. That happened one pretty spring day in March about a year ago.

March

Paxton was becoming known as one of the best defence lawyers in the city. All the criminals wanted him, and with fame came the opportunity to pick and choose. He preferred the high-profile cases, for which his clients paid heavy fees. Noble's trial for drug smuggling fit the bill perfectly. He had successfully represented Noble before, of course, and Noble had been suitably grateful, not only doubling James' fee, but putting out the word that he was the best.

Paxton had spent the morning in chambers, and was walking past the Crown Court to have lunch in a popular harbourside restaurant when he passed Oakley and Butterworth. Oakley was relaxed and stoical as usual, but Butterworth looked like a cat on hot tiles. He refused to meet the lawyer's eyes, leaving Paxton frowning after him thoughtfully.

'There's no need to *tell* him you've got something to hide,' muttered Oakley, unimpressed by Butterworth's loss of composure.

'What if he brings it up?' whispered Butterworth wretchedly. 'What am I going to do?'

'He won't,' said Oakley. 'He doesn't know anything about it. But you've got to get a grip. He'll have you for breakfast if you don't.'

'That's what my wife said. She sent me to the doctor this morning.' Butterworth reached into his pocket and pulled out a prescription for tablets. 'He said I was depressed and should take some pills for a month. What do you think?'

'Listen to him,' said Oakley shortly. 'Take them.'

'I don't know.' Butterworth studied the form doubtfully. 'These are anti-depressants. Like what they give neurotic housewives.'

'It's what they give perfectly normal people who need a helping hand.'

Ever since 'Butterworth's Blunder', as the incident had become nicknamed to those who knew about it, the DS had been nervous, short-tempered and unreliable. Oakley had tentatively suggested a visit to the force psychiatrist, but Butterworth had responded furiously and the subject had not been broached again.

'So, you think I should take them?' pressed Butterworth. 'But what if they make me weird, and I start saying all sorts of shit I shouldn't in the witness box?'

Personally, Oakley thought it more likely that Butterworth would start saying 'all sorts of shit' without the tablets.

'If you're worried, go back to the doctor and ask him about it.'

'You won't tell anyone, will you?' Butterworth waved the prescription in such a way that Oakley could see his hands were shaking. 'I don't want anyone to know.'

'Of course not,' said Oakley. 'But you've got to sort yourself out.'

He hoped Butterworth would pull himself together by the following Monday, or Paxton would be after him like a fox with a rabbit.

It was half past one on a Friday afternoon, thirty minutes before I was due to finish my shift and be off duty until I began a week of nights the following Monday. I'd worked a lot of overtime that month, which, unlike most of my colleagues, I disliked, as I'd rather have time off than a bigger paycheque. I was tired, and looking forward to having three days away. I was going to Newcastle, to meet some old university friends, and had my seat booked on the three o'clock train.

It was then, just as the weekend was about to blossom, that Sergeant Wright struck.

I could tell that he'd deliberately waited until the very last minute before mentioning that I was due at court on Monday, and that I'd better make myself familiar with the Noble case before I went home. Monday! The day I'd planned to travel back to Bristol on a train that arrived an hour before my shift was due to begin – cutting it fine, I know, but I wanted to squeeze every last moment out of the trip. Wright's piggy eyes gleamed with gratified spite when he saw my dismay.

'It's not going to interfere with your plans, is it?' he asked, casually nasty as he handed me a thick folder. Even with computer technology, the police like their court paperwork in *printed* form. 'Yes? You'd better get on with it, then. It won't take more than a couple of hours. Then you can get yourself off. But be back by ten a.m. on Monday.'

'Why Monday?' I demanded. 'Noble isn't supposed to be up until after the fifteenth of April.'

'Someone cancelled, so he was moved ahead,' replied Wright. 'The court clerk called to make sure it was OK. You hadn't crossed off Monday on the holiday charts, so I said yes.'

'But I *told* you I was going away this weekend,' I protested. 'You knew!'

'Did I?' Wright shrugged. 'I don't recall. But you've got a couple of hours to do here before you knock off. You don't want to be unprepared.'

'I don't need to go through it,' I objected. 'I can remember.'

Wright's expression was unpleasant. 'Even *graduates* should refresh their memories before going to the Crown Court. But it's down to you. I'll tell Oakley that you've got more important things to do. Then if he loses the case because you fuck up, at least he'll know his hard work didn't interfere with your travel plans.'

'That's not—'

'You muscle in on a big case, and this is the payback,' Wright forged on, his resentment that I'd been the one to make the arrest bubbling to the surface. 'You should've stuck to traffic duties if you didn't want to make sacrifices.'

I felt like slapping him as he sauntered away, but when I looked at the holiday records I saw that I hadn't marked Monday as a date when I was unavailable for court. It was my fault, but it felt like his. He gave me a jaunty wave as he headed for the White Swan, a local pub normally called the Mucky Duck, where he intended to spend the afternoon in beery camaraderie with his cronies.

He was right, of course. I *did* need to look over my notes and read my statement so I was up to speed for the witness stand. A clever lawyer could tie an unprepared officer in knots, and cases had been lost for a lot less. Noble was the biggest arrest I'd made, so I had to be ready.

Reluctantly, I found an empty carrel and opened the file so roughly that it tore. I didn't care. I should have been walking to the train station, and now not only was I forced to spend a pretty afternoon in New Bridewell, but I'd miss all my connections and wouldn't arrive in Newcastle until the small hours of Saturday morning. I'd miss the party Caroline had arranged, and everyone would probably be asleep when I got there.

'Good,' came a voice at my shoulder. It was DI Oakley, nodding approvingly. 'CID have been studying that all week, but I've ordered everyone to lay off it for the weekend, so as to be fresh on Monday. We've hogged it, so I hope you don't

33

mind having it now.'

'Oh, no!' I said with bitter sarcasm that made him blink and back away with an uncertain smile. 'Not at all.'

I watched him go, and it was then that the idea came. There was nothing I could do about Monday, except catch a train at some godforsaken hour to be at court at ten. In my limited experience, I knew I could sit around there all day, only to be told that I wasn't needed after all – which made the situation all the more annoying. But I could salvage Friday. Lots of people worked on trains – I would too. The only problem was that court files weren't supposed to be removed from the station – ever – for obvious reasons.

But I would be careful. Wright and the rest of my shift had gone, so no one would miss me. The file wouldn't be missed either, given Oakley's remarks. With a feeling of guilty unease, I shoved it in my bag and ran the half-mile or so to Temple Meads. By three o'clock I was in my designated seat as the train pulled out of the station.

I tugged the folder from my bag and laid it on the table. The carriage was half empty – a testament to the fact that you need to re-mortgage your house to buy a train ticket these days. There was someone at the table in front, but no one behind or opposite, which meant I could work without being worried that someone was looking over my shoulder.

The file was putty pink, with the name 'Noble' written at the top. It looked no more appealing now than it had in the station, and I turned my attention to the brown fields that flashed past outside, letting my mind wander.

'Helen!' came a warm voice. 'I thought it was you.'

I was startled and a little disconcerted to see James standing over me. He looked much as he had when we had parted after our date, but more self-assured. His light grey suit was cut perfectly to show off his broad shoulders, and his loosened tie was carelessly stylish.

There was a man behind him who stirred distant memories. He shoved past James, as though they didn't know each other, but there was something about their body language that suggested he did, and I was fairly sure it was the monkey-faced man who'd collected James from school. Surely his mother's 'bit of rough' wasn't still driving James around? But it was none of my business, so I turned my attention to James himself.

'Have you moved up north?' he asked, sliding into the seat opposite. 'I don't have time for socializing with the old crowd these days, so I don't know any news.'

'Just going to Newcastle for the weekend.' I could see the female student at the table in front looking at him admiringly, and it felt good to be the focus of his attention for a few minutes. 'To see some friends.'

'Nice,' he remarked pleasantly. 'That's where you went to university, isn't it? What did you study again?'

I told him, and we spent a few minutes going over information we'd exchanged before, and that I remembered about him, but he hadn't retained about me. I didn't mind. James was one of those people who went through life pretending to be interested, but the answers went in one ear and out the other. As he spoke, his eyes were constantly scanning the aisles, in the way people do when they're looking for someone more interesting. We chatted for perhaps ten minutes, then he excused himself, telling me that he was supposed to be buying coffee from the buffet car for some colleagues. He went on his way, and I turned back to my file.

The sun poured through the window, making the carriage stuffy. I knew I should move, but that would mean less privacy. I toasted gently in the heat, and gradually felt my eyes close – I'd had to get up at four a.m. that day to be at New Bridewell by six. Just a five-minute nap, I told myself, and then I'd be refreshed enough to spend the rest of the journey studying.

I woke with a start when the guard announced that we were about to arrive in Cheltenham. I rubbed my eyes and stared out of the window, taking a deep breath to banish the floating sensation that waking from a deep sleep often brought. When I glanced at the table, my stomach clenched in horror. The Noble file was no longer there. With unsteady hands, I pawed through my bag, first systematically, then more wildly. It wasn't there. It wasn't on the floor, and it wasn't on the seat. It had gone. I glanced at my watch and estimated that I had been asleep no more than twenty minutes at the most. It had disappeared during that time.

Looking back, it should have been immediately obvious that James had taken it. I hadn't seen him walk back from the buffet car, so it stood to reason that he'd done it while I slept. It had been obvious that it was a court file – at least, obvious to a criminal lawyer. But I wasn't thinking rationally. With a voice that shook with panic, I asked the few people in the carriage whether they had seen anyone take anything from my table, but of course no one had. I'd been pleased with the location of my table precisely because it *wasn't* overlooked by other passengers.

I rummaged in my bag again, sick with worry and remorse. There was no excuse for what I'd done. I'd not only removed the file from the station, but I'd left it where it was vulnerable. For a few minutes I considered a plan where I denied that I'd even seen it, so they'd blame someone else for its loss, but Oakley had seen me with the damned thing. And there was Wright to consider. He'd be the first to put two and two together.

I put my head in my hands, wondering whether I should get off at Cheltenham and go straight back to New Bridewell and confess – make a clean breast of the whole thing. I wish now that I had, even if it meant losing my job. But when the train rolled into Cheltenham, I sat frozen. I needed time to think.

Gradually, I began to ask myself why anyone would make off with a grubby folder but leave my purse, which had been on the seat next to me.

Then I understood – James couldn't have failed to notice the name on the file, and he was Noble's lawyer. *He* had taken it. I was half out of my seat to confront him when it occurred to me that he wouldn't *need* to steal it – he'd have already received a copy as a matter of course. And there was unlikely to be anything else he could use – Oakley wasn't the sort to leave incriminating 'Post-it' stickers all over the place.

Yet James *must* have stolen it, because no one else would have been interested. I wondered why. And what should I do? Confront him, and risk making a fool of myself in front of his colleagues? Or wait for him to come to me?

As it happened, I didn't need to decide. James came to me – going towards the buffet car again, I noticed, which meant he *had* passed while I'd been asleep. With supreme self-control I kept my face impassive as he slipped into the seat opposite again.

'Enjoy your beauty sleep?' There was an edge in his voice that was far from pleasant.

'Yes,' I replied, holding his gaze steadily, although my heart thudded horribly. 'Until I woke up and saw a thief had been by.'

He glanced behind him, then leaned across the table. 'Look, I won't beat around the bush. We both know that removing court files from police stations is a no-no. You'll lose your job – and believe me, it won't be easy for a sacked officer to get another.'

'Your word against mine,' I blustered.

He smiled. 'Yes, but I have the file to support

my claim. You have nothing.'

'If you use it against me you'll have to admit to stealing it,' I countered.

He gazed at me with raised eyebrows. 'But I *found* it on a train. I didn't *steal* it.'

'What do you want?' I asked, trying to sound unconcerned, although my stomach was acid. 'Me to beg for it? To blackmail me into doing something for you? What?'

He smiled again. 'Not blackmail, Helen. Co-operation. I want information, so we shall make an arrangement that'll suit us both.'

'What arrangement?' I felt as if I were in some dreadful nightmare. Under the table, I dug my nails hard into the back of my hand. It hurt, but I didn't wake up to laugh at the tricks the imagination could play.

He glanced around again, although no one was close enough to catch anything he said. The student was sleeping, while the shaven-headed hulk further down had wires dangling from his ears and a dazed expression on his face.

'I want you to help me,' he said softly.

'How?' I asked numbly. 'I'm only a PC.'

'True.' He grinned cruelly. 'Two years ago, I thought a police contact might come in handy, but a lowly constable with scant prospect of promotion was no use. Why do you think I never called you after our evening together? But things have changed, and I'm of a mind to reconsider.'

'Bastard,' I muttered. Was he really so calculating, even then?

He turned his smile on me again, and I felt myself stiffen. 'Unfortunately, the Noble case is pretty watertight as far as I can see. Oakley is a careful man, so I need an edge if I'm to win.'

I was beginning to feel sick. 'An edge?' I asked in what came out as a whimper. He was right: Oakley had a reputation for meticulous attention to detail, and there was no way he'd have made a mistake with Noble.

'Don't worry; I won't demand the impossible. I just want you to clarify something. Then you get your file back, and no one will ever know about our little tête-à-tête.'

'Clarify something?' I repeated stupidly.

'My client tells me there was a commotion concerning his property when he was in the cells. He couldn't hear exactly, but he knows it was something to do with him.'

'I don't know anything about that.' Yet I did – Wright had overheard Oakley giving Butterworth a roasting for tampering with the evidence book, and there wasn't an officer at New Bridewell who hadn't been lured into a corner and regaled with details of Butterworth's stupidity. The sad thing was that the heroin in the packet was completely different from the heroin on the boat – FSS had found both on Noble's clothes – so Butterworth's fiddle wouldn't have made any difference anyway.

'Police stations are no places for secrets,' said James smoothly. 'Now tell me.'

'I don't know what you're talking about,' I insisted. 'I went home as soon as Noble was processed. I wasn't there when he was in the cells.'

'I'm not asking for an eye-witness account,' said James. 'I just want to know what happened.'

He gave that confident smile of his and reached for my hand. I snatched it away. 'Don't be stupid about this. You tell me the rumour, and I'll give you your file back. I promise no one will know the information came from you.'

'Go to hell,' I muttered, looking out of the window so that he wouldn't see the tears that welled in my eyes.

He stood up. 'Fine,' he said, his voice cold. 'As I said, police officers sacked for losing confidential files have a hard time finding another job. I hope you put your Newcastle degree to good use frying hamburgers.'

'Wait!' I said, thinking fast. All I had to do was to invent something he'd believe, get him to give me the folder, and that would be the end of it. I didn't have to tell him about Butterworth. And then he would get his just desserts when he tried to produce some cock and bull story in court. But what could I say? What could Noble have over-heard?

James sat down. 'I know you'll be truthful,' he said, as though he'd read my thoughts. Perhaps he had. I wasn't very good at lying then, although I got better at it later. 'I have a few snippets from Noble, so I'll know if you're spinning me a yarn. I wouldn't make up some wild tale to make me look stupid, if I were you.'

And then, to my horror, I told him the whole sorry tale. I heard myself speaking, but it was as though someone else was saying the words while I watched helplessly from a distance. James' face was impassive, and he heard me out in silence. He nodded occasionally, his eyes never leaving my face. When I finally faltered into silence, he reached out to pat my arm.

'That wasn't too painful, was it?'

'The file.' I hated the pleading tone in my voice. 'Please give it back.'

He reached into his briefcase and removed the familiar pink folder. I snatched it from him, and then I did start to cry, hugging it like a baby as I vowed never to break the rules again.

'There's just one other thing,' James said, standing. 'The smartphone is a wonderful device. I took photos of a few salient documents and emailed them to my office – documents that weren't in the copy I received officially, like the memos from Oakley to his various plods. You know as well as I do that there's no way I could have those without some sort of leak.'

I gazed at him in horror. 'You mean you can still prove you were in possession of a file removed illegally from a police station? But you said it would all be over if I told you what you wanted to know!'

'I lied,' he acknowledged smugly. 'Call it insurance – now you won't go running to Oakley about our little chat. Not unless you want to destroy your future. See you in court.'

FOUR

The horror of what I'd done stayed with me all that weekend, although there were one or two moments when the company of good friends allowed me to forget about it briefly. Since the horse had already bolted, there was little point in locking the stable door, but I did it anyway, keeping the file close to me all weekend, even taking it out to dinner on Saturday. The time dragged, and I was relieved when I was on the train home.

The first thing I did when I arrived at New Bridewell was to put the file back where it belonged. It felt tainted, and I was glad to be rid of it. I went to the locker room and changed into my uniform. When I came back, DI Oakley was sitting in the briefing room with the file open in front of him. I tried to sneak past, but he glanced up and saw me.

'So it was you,' he said with a smile. My blood ran cold, but he went on: 'I was in at eight to read through the file, but you were here before me, working away.'

I nodded stupidly while my stomach churned. 'I wanted to go over my statement,' I mumbled, hoping that no one who'd seen me arrive at nine was listening.

'Good idea,' he said. 'James Paxton's the

defence barrister, so we'll have to make sure we're up to speed. I don't want Noble walking on a technicality. But you look nervous. Don't be. Just tell them exactly what happened. Take your time and don't let Paxton get you riled. You'll do fine.'

I nodded, and felt tears prick my eyes because he was being nice and I didn't deserve it. I'd betrayed him almost as badly as Butterworth had done with his evidence fixing. I turned away and busied myself with my notebook, hoping he'd leave me alone. If he'd been a PC, I'd have walked away, but he was an inspector, so I couldn't.

'It'll be fine,' he insisted gently. 'Really. We've got a watertight case, and the trial's just a formality. Noble knows he's going down, and hiring Paxton is the act of a desperate man.'

'Paxton's not that good,' I said. I hated the way everyone put him on a pedestal, just as they had at school. He was fallible, like everyone else. Worse, he was corrupt and deceitful, and I now suspected that his success had been based on something other than professional skill.

'That's the spirit!' He smiled – a sweet, friendly smile, not one of James' dazzling charmers that was all teeth and no sincerity – and turned his attention back to the file.

I took a deep breath and made a decision. I couldn't go through the rest of my police career – however long that might be – with this hanging over me. It was best to tell him now, and get it over with. It was only fair. Perhaps I wouldn't lose my job. After all, I'd only mislaid a file and allowed myself to be blackmailed. Butterworth

44

had tampered with evidence, which was far more serious, and he was still working. I could claim *I* was tired and desperate, and Oakley seemed like the sort of man who would stand up for his officers. Except I wasn't his officer – I was Wright's.

The thought of Wright's delight in my disgrace made me hesitate. But, no. I wouldn't allow the loathsome sergeant to influence me. I would tell Oakley right now, so he could be ready for whatever it was James planned to do.

'I've got something to tell you.' There. I'd started and there was no going back. There was some satisfaction in knowing James wouldn't get anything out of my stupidity.

But suddenly Butterworth clattered in. His hands were shaking, and he'd cut himself shaving, so red grazes stood out vividly against his white skin. He looked patently petrified. Oakley was obviously exasperated.

'Relax, both of you! We've got a good, solid case. You've nothing to worry about. And I'll buy you both dinner when we win.'

Butterworth slumped in a chair, his eyes haunted. 'But what if—' he began.

'It won't,' interrupted Oakley in the kind of voice that warned him to say no more. I realized then that he had no idea that Butterworth's Blunder was common knowledge around the station.

'It could finish me,' muttered Butterworth. He looked sick, and I knew how he felt. Like me, he'd made a mistake, although at least *he* was able to say that he'd acted in the public interest. I'd done it because I'd wanted a weekend in Newcastle.

'It'll be fine,' said Oakley soothingly. 'You're part of a team – a strong team – and we're all here for each other. That's the good thing about this job – sometimes the only good thing. You've got colleagues who'll back you up.'

Butterworth seemed to cheer up. 'Thanks, Guv,' he muttered.

Oakley turned to me. 'What were you about to tell me?'

'Nothing.' What else could I say after that speech? I wished Wright had heard it – if he'd had the merest morsel of decency and loyalty, he wouldn't have gone around blabbing to everyone about Butterworth's Blunder, and I wouldn't have been obliged to tell James about it. 'I just hope we nail the bastard.'

I wasn't sure which bastard I was talking about.

The courtroom was full that morning, mostly with friends of Noble, Castle and Gray – thuggish, oily men in suits and dark glasses, with mobile phones stuck to their ears, as though business couldn't stop for anything as minor as a trial. There were reporters, too, because Noble was a local celebrity. He donated generously to a children's hospice, and was well known for throwing extravagant events for underprivileged kids.

Outside the courtroom the corridors teemed with waiting witnesses. Besides Anderson, Oakley and Butterworth, there were several officers from the drug squad, and an inspector from Regional Crime, who had charged Noble with a separate list of offences. The policemen had gravitated towards each other, but Anderson stood by a window, staring into a street made wet by a sudden downpour.

The building was Victorian, built to deal with a trickle of malefactors. The trickle had since become a flood, and the old stone staircases, high-ceilinged hallways and wood-panelled rooms heaved with activity five days a week. There was talk of extending it to six so that some of the backlog could be cleared. Ancient radiators belted out heat, and most people had removed coats and loosened ties. The atmosphere was close, sticky and stank of fear and unease.

Noble was neither uneasy nor fearful, however. Oakley watched him stride confidently into the courtroom, giving every indication that he expected to be released. The inspector was bemused – the case was as sound as any he'd ever worked on – there was CCTV coverage of Noble supervising the unloading of the drugs, while FSS had matched the heroin on his clothes to the heroin from the boat.

At Noble's side was James Paxton, resplendent in a dark grey suit and red tie. He, too, appeared confident and relaxed, almost happy. Oakley could only surmise he was looking forward to the intellectual challenge of fighting against poor odds.

Anderson, as arresting officer, was the first to be called. Her face was pale, and Oakley felt a pang of unease. This was the only case he'd ever worked on with her, and he didn't know her well enough to say if she was someone who'd crack under pressure. But he was more worried about Butterworth. The DC had gnawed a fingernail to the point where it had bled, and everything about him indicated that he had something to hide. Paxton was sure to home in on it, and Oakley just hoped Butterworth would keep his head.

Oakley smiled encouragingly at Anderson as she passed, reminding her to relax, and say what she knew and no more. She nodded, gave a tight smile, and entered the courtroom.

I had given evidence in the Crown Court three times previously, and had acquitted myself reasonably well in each. I should not have been worried – all I'd done was call DI Oakley when the drug-boat had arrived, then made the formal arrest when CID had raced in to nab the culprits. But I was so scared that my legs threatened to dump me in a heap in the witness box. My discomfort was even obvious to the judge, who asked if I wanted a glass of water. I said no, and turned to James, wondering when he would ask about the tampered-with evidence at the station. What would I say? Should I acknowledge that Wright had been spreading tales? That would give me a certain satisfaction, as it would dump Wright well and truly in the mire, but it would be nothing compared to the mire Butterworth would be in.

So should I lie? But what if James told everyone about the train? Would that alone be enough to see him victorious? I'd be out of a job, and my downfall would be public and spectacular. I hated to imagine what Oakley would think. He'd been good to me: true to his word in letting me share the glory when Noble was caught, and encouraging and helpful ever since. He was a nice man, a good man. How different might things have been if I'd been working with him, not Wright.

I braced myself, and waited for James to start.

I couldn't believe it was over! It wasn't even James who questioned me – it was one of his juniors, and he asked nothing awkward. Within fifteen minutes I'd been dismissed and told that I was free to go. I was so relieved that I thought I might be sick. I tore out of the building and leaned on the wall outside, my stomach heaving in painful, dry spasms. I took deep breaths of traffic-perfumed air, and gradually the fluttering in my stomach subsided.

Had James decided that the information he had forced from me was too dangerous to use? Perhaps he was ashamed of what he had done, or perhaps he'd realized that exposing me would say nothing good about himself. Regardless, I was just relieved it was over.

I sat for a while near the Watershed, letting the tension subside as I watched pigeons totter and scramble over a discarded bag of chips. Children played some rough and tumble game on the other side of the quay, and there was a contented rumble of voices from a nearby cafe. I told myself that I would learn from this nasty experience. From now on, I would do everything by the book.

It was lunch by the time I arrived back at New

Bridewell, and only three hours before my shift ended. I was back on nights at ten o'clock the following evening, which meant I now had thirty hours to myself. A number of officers asked about court, and I was able to say I'd given my evidence without any problems. The duty sergeant must have seen how relief had turned to exhaustion, because he suggested I spend the afternoon on paperwork, and said that he wouldn't tell anyone if I wanted to slip away an hour early.

I took him at his word, and by five o'clock my in-tray was empty and I was feeling good. I asked whether there was any news from court, and was informed that Oakley had given his evidence, and that Butterworth was in the middle of his. I went home and treated myself to an Indian takeaway, then had a long, hot bath and an early night, during which I slept like a log.

The following day, I went shopping and met Frances for lunch in The Galleries. Then I shopped some more before going home and reading until it was time to go to work.

When I arrived, I immediately sensed an atmosphere – an odd combination of excitement, unease and fear. It had been the same a few months earlier, when poor Sergeant Dowell had died of a heart attack. Clearly, something nasty had happened.

Oakley was on duty, and there was a haunted look in his dark eyes. I felt tendrils of unease uncoil in my stomach. James must have used the tampered-with evidence after all – I had celebrated too soon. I started to walk towards Oakley, but he was talking to Davis, and their faces were so serious that I didn't dare interrupt. Suddenly, Wright was at my side.

'I suppose you won't have heard,' he said, effecting a sombre expression, although I could see he was delighted to be able to impart bad news. It wasn't that he wanted to upset me – he was just one of those people who loves telling others horrible things. 'Did you see the news tonight?'

'News?' I asked stupidly. 'About Noble?'

Wright nodded. 'His defence got hold of the story about the switched drugs. You were lucky they didn't call you back.'

I gazed at him. 'What do you mean? I didn't have anything to do with that. I was at home when Butterworth did it.'

'I know, I know,' he said, offended by the hostility in my voice. 'I wasn't accusing you. I'm just saying that they recalled Oakley after *he* was dismissed, and I thought they might have done the same to you. You were the arresting officer, after all.'

'Well, they didn't,' I said curtly. 'What happened?'

Wright hadn't been in court, and could only have heard the facts second hand, but that didn't stop him telling me the whole gruesome tale. It was much as I'd feared. Right at the end of Butterworth's testimony, just when the DS probably thought he'd got away with it, James had produced a photograph of a page from the property book – the one with the changed entry. I felt my knees go weak. Had it been in the folder

51

James had taken on the train? But it couldn't have been – Oakley wouldn't have put something like that in a file that would go to court. James must have got it some other way.

Butterworth had crumbled and confessed the whole thing. Then Oakley was recalled, and forced to admit that an internal investigation was underway. It couldn't have been easy for him, cornered into agreeing that one of his officers was corrupt, and I could only begin to imagine Noble's delight as he watched the police case fall to pieces. James would have enjoyed it too, of course. So had the press, and the news was full of indignant editorials about corrupt police officers picking on a local man respected for his charitable acts.

I was able to escape from Wright when Paul Franklin arrived. Paul was a stocky man, a bit younger than me and a good officer, but one who Wright was trying to transform into someone in his own image. Paul had resisted so far, although I suspected he would yield before long. Wright was on him like a leech, telling the story a second time in his sly, sanctimonious manner.

Oakley was still with Davis, but I didn't want to talk to him any more. I knew I should confess, because waiting would only make it worse. But he would want to know why I hadn't told him sooner so he could have been prepared, and I had no answer to that. I'd simply been a coward.

I started to walk out, but Oakley saw me and called me over. I went reluctantly. He was grey – the colour people often go when they hear bad or shocking news.

'Did Barry Wright tell you what happened?' he asked.

'Of course he did,' said DI Davis scathingly. 'Why d'you think he's lurking by the door? He's catching people as they walk in, making sure he doesn't miss anyone.'

'He's a gossip,' I said bitterly. I didn't care that I was being disloyal to my shift sergeant by condemning him so bluntly. At least some of the blame for the day's disaster was down to him – if he hadn't chattered about Butterworth's Blunder, I wouldn't have had anything to tell James on the train. 'Is it true? Did Noble walk?'

'Not yet,' replied Davis. 'Professional Standards will take the stand tomorrow, to state that Mark is being officially investigated. But Ingram says that the case is lost anyway. No jury's going to convict when there's proof that the police played around with the evidence.'

'But you put it right,' I objected. 'It was only wrong for a few hours, and it was just a case of a tired man doing one stupid thing.'

'Irrelevant,' said Davis brusquely. 'Mark tampered with the evidence. That means all the forensic tests are out of the window, and there isn't enough left without those.'

'The CCTV,' I said stubbornly. 'We've got footage of Noble unloading drugs.'

'Records show the disk was released to Mark several times,' explained Oakley. 'Paxton will claim that was altered, too, and we can't prove it wasn't. You can do all sorts of interesting things these days, and it's no secret that Mark was a computer buff. Paxton will have it thrown out faster than the forensics.'

The past tense wasn't lost on me. 'Was?' I demanded. 'Mark *was*?'

'He's dead,' said Oakley bluntly. 'Hit by a lorry on his way home.' He must have seen my horror, because he put a hand on my shoulder in sympathy. 'I'm sorry. I thought Wright had told you.'

'He didn't get to that part,' I whispered, fighting the bile that threatened to make me throw up. 'Someone more interesting came along.'

FIVE

Late March

At first, there were whispers that Butterworth's death wasn't an accident – that Noble had taken out insurance lest proceedings hadn't gone according to plan. Then it was claimed that Butterworth had been so distressed by his court experience that he had killed himself intentionally. Oakley dealt with the rumours by making an announcement in the canteen. He deliberately chose a time when Wright's shift was on duty, sensing that both stories had originated with the gossiping sergeant. Anderson was there, standing slightly apart from her colleagues, as was her wont.

Oakley explained that Butterworth had been exhausted by long working hours and the strains of a teething baby. He blamed himself for not staying with him after the courtroom revelations, but Butterworth had wanted to be alone and Oakley had respected that. However, there wasn't a shred of evidence that the lorry driver had been in Noble's employ. The man wasn't local, and had been driving for thirty years without so much as a speeding ticket.

The second rumour was more difficult to dispel when it was known that Butterworth was on anti-depressants. How the gossips should have learned this was beyond Oakley, who had thought that he was the only one who had been taken into Mark's confidence. He skipped over that part, merely concluding that Butterworth had been angry and ashamed but not suicidal, and pointing out that such tales were hurtful to his widow.

As he walked away from the canteen, it occurred to him that they would never know what had really happened. It had been rush hour, and traffic was heavy. The lorry driver claimed that Butterworth had simply appeared in front of him, too late to avoid. They were hoping for a verdict of accidental death, which would allow his wife and child to benefit from insurance that they could not collect had it been suicide. It was a tragedy all round – for Butterworth, his family, the driver, and Oakley, who had lost a valued friend.

Oakley thought Anderson seemed more shaken than she should have been considering she barely knew Butterworth, and he wondered if she was the right kind of person to be a police officer. She was altogether too sensitive. Still, he thought, there was nothing wrong with an officer who was softly spoken, quiet and compassionate. If there was room for men like Wright, then there should be room for women like Anderson.

But he didn't think about Anderson for long. He had work to do – which included finding out how James Paxton had learned about Butterworth's Blunder.

Investigating the leak was frustrating. As far as

he knew, only five people at New Bridewell were aware of what Butterworth had done: Mark himself, Oakley, Derek Jones the custody sergeant, Clare Davis and Superintendent Taylor, who had passed the matter to Professional Standards. Professional Standards could be eliminated as suspects, as it was their job to make sure the incidents they investigated remained secret, and they had no reason to tell anyone else, anyway. That left the New Bridewell people.

Oakley knew *he* had said nothing, while he had known Davis for years, and was certain she wasn't the culprit. So his suspects were Jones, the superintendent and Butterworth himself. The digital photo Paxton had presented of the tampered page had a date in the corner. Oakley checked the duty roster, and saw that Taylor had been at a conference in Leeds at the time, while Jones had been on annual leave.

He thought long and hard about whether Butterworth might have let something slip, but decided it was unlikely. The DS had been deeply ashamed of what he had done, and would not have wanted anyone else to know. Later, it emerged at the inquest that he had not even told his wife. All three were thus exonerated, and Oakley was left with a list of none.

He and Davis discussed the problem over a beer in the Mucky Duck. There was only one conclusion: someone had eavesdropped when the matter had been discussed. Once that possibility was mooted, Oakley knew he was unlikely to find a culprit, although a nagging voice at the back of his head kept reminding him that the biggest gossip in the station was Barry Wright. But there was no evidence to incriminate the sergeant, and Wright was not the sort of man to break down and confess in a fit of remorse.

Then Professional Standards arrived and took over. In the enquiry that followed, every officer in New Bridewell admitted to knowing about Butterworth's Blunder. Wright's name cropped up several times as the source, so Professional Standards grilled Wright relentlessly, but he vehemently denied passing information to outside sources, and as nothing could be proved, their enquiry eventually staggered to a standstill, leaving many questions unanswered and the station uneasy in its wake.

The week that Professional Standards invaded New Bridewell was one of the worst in my life. I was certain they'd know that James and I were at school together, and would conclude that I was the one who'd leaked the information. When they called me in I thought I was going to be sick. My stomach churned and my head pounded, so I could barely hear what they were saying. It took all of my self-control not to look guilty. It occurred to me that this was the time to confess, but I didn't. The whole business had gone too far, and the thought of my colleagues' reproach was more than I could bear.

They asked whether I'd heard about Butterworth's Blunder, and I replied that I had. Then they asked who'd told me, but life was bad enough without having Wright accusing me of disloyalty, so I said nothing. The Professional

Standards men exchanged glances and said that one specific sergeant kept cropping up as a source – I wasn't the first, and probably would not be the last, to name Wright. So I did, and they nodded their thanks and let me go.

And that was it. I'd escaped confessing yet again.

In the following weeks, Oakley often asked for me when he needed a uniformed officer, although I think it was more to put two fingers up to Wright than because he thought I was special. He'd guessed it was Wright who'd spilled the beans about Butterworth, and hated him for it. Wright, meanwhile, embarked on a private mission against Oakley, using every opportunity to point out that he wasn't 'one of us'. I suppose he was referring to Oakley's Indian blood. If I'd been Oakley, I'd have reported him for racism, but then I probably should've reported him for sexism, so I understood why Oakley thought it wasn't worth the trouble.

One day, Oakley asked if I'd known that Butterworth had been so dangerously close to the edge at Noble's trial.

'He looked terrible,' I said. 'Even more scared of the witness stand than me.'

'You were scared?'

I hastened to cover up my near-blunder. 'I'd been in court before, but never for such a major case. I knew how much time you'd invested, and I wanted to make sure I didn't mess up.'

'I knew Mark was nervous,' Oakley said, a little distantly. 'I just didn't realize how much. I let him down.'

'*He* let *you* down, sir. You had a good case, and it was his dishonesty that let Noble back on the streets.'

Oakley stared at me, and I saw I should have kept my thoughts to myself. 'He made a mistake,' he said shortly. 'When he was tired, agitated and unwell. It could happen to any of us.'

He walked away, and I wondered whether he would be so generous about my mistake – the one that led to Butterworth's death.

But gradually, the enormity of what had happened began to fade, and I settled back into my normal life – although wiser, less trusting and more cynical. I went to work, spent my free evenings at home, and enjoyed weekend drinks and meals with Frances, Colin and Gary.

It was about four months after Mark's death when the next thing happened that was to change my life. It started with a series of burglaries in the Westbury area, and a man called Billy Yorke.

July

A damp, gloomy spring was followed by the green and yellow hues of summer. People sat outside on the long, warm evenings, and families looked forward to the school holidays. There was often a carnival-like atmosphere in Bristol's centre, as residents and tourists alike enjoyed its parks, harbour and shopping centres. The air was rich with the scent of takeaway vans, traffic and the tepid water in the docks.

Unfortunately, the fine weather did little to cheer the victims of what the press called the

'Westbury Burglaries'. These were all aggravated, which meant that violence was used during their commission. The stocking-masked culprits were well organized and careful, striking at houses in one of the city's most affluent areas. So far there had been eight attacks, and the thieves didn't care if the occupants were at home – they merely herded their victims into a bedroom, where they were bound with duct tape. Usually the victims were so frightened they did as they were told and escaped relatively unscathed. Anyone who resisted could expect to be hit, however.

As far as New Bridewell's CID could see, the burglaries were random, with no common factor in timing or victims. The villains' team comprised six men who could break through the most sophisticated security devices. A driver stayed outside to make a quick getaway, three dealt with the victims, and the remaining two searched the houses with a ruthless efficiency that suggested they knew exactly what was where. Safes were raided first, followed by jewellery, gold and original artwork. Computers, televisions and other electronic equipment – unless they were very expensive – were ignored.

It was apparent from the beginning that the Westbury Burglaries were the work of experienced criminals, ones Oakley suspected had access to insurance documents that told them what was in each house. However, none of the victims shared the same insurer.

After a while, Oakley began to suspect a villain named Billy Yorke, mostly because they bore his hallmark: ruthless efficiency and care to leave nothing that might later be used to convict. Unfortunately, he couldn't prove it, and Taylor refused to let him search Yorke's various properties until he had something more solid than a hunch.

Yorke was a wealthy man. Once a security guard for a company of architects – most of whom had later gone to prison for fraud – he had financed his climb up the social ladder with serious crime. At the age of fifty-five he owned two mansions and a number of houses that he rented to other criminals, a fleet of cars, and he was a member of the city's most expensive golf club.

'But why him?' asked Graham Evans, the DS who had replaced Butterworth. In many ways, Evans was easier to work with than Butterworth. He was slow and unimaginative, but he followed orders doggedly and with total dedication. He was heavily set, with a princely beer belly, and a shock of fair hair that looked odd with his lined, florid face. Oakley liked him, and the two were on their way to becoming friends as well as colleagues.

'The burglaries have his stamp,' explained Oakley. They were in the CID office, reading witness statements from the most recent attack. The victim was an elderly woman named Emma Vinson, who had resisted the invasion, and had been brutally beaten in return. She was currently in intensive care and it was too early to say whether she would recover.

'They've got Noble's stamp, too,' said Evans

reasonably. 'Theft, violence, fast and ruthless, don't care whether they are seen.'

'Noble's men would have taken the computers and DVD players, too,' argued Oakley. 'And they would have been more violent. The Westbury burglars don't want to injure; they just want the property. They'll only cause harm if they have to.'

'You think three men *had* to hit Mrs Vinson?' demanded Evans. 'They did it because they *wanted* to.'

'She tried to set off the burglar alarm. Their sole aim was to stop her. I agree that they didn't have to hit her so hard, but I don't think cruelty was intended in the attack, just ruthlessness.'

'I don't see the difference, and I'm not convinced it's Yorke. I'm not surprised Taylor won't give you a search warrant.'

'Yorke will be the one who goes straight to the safe,' mused Oakley, ignoring his sergeant's reservations. 'He won't have anything to do with the victims. That'll be left to the likes of Dave Randal.'

'His right-hand yob. Nice man: previous for every violent crime except murder.'

Oakley strongly suspected it was only a matter of time before that particular offence was added to Randal's repertoire.

By the end of July, Oakley's persistence in his investigation of the Westbury burglars had paid off, and one evening he and Evans sat together in the Mucky Duck, celebrating.

'I still don't know how you guessed the

63

Sanderson house was going to be their next hit,' said Evans, leaning comfortably back against the wall. He took a deep draught of bitter.

'Because of holidays,' said Oakley, pulling a face at his warm lager. It was stuffy in the pub, and the open doors and windows served only to let the hot air inside. 'Billy Yorke didn't wait for his *victims* to go away; he waited for the neighbours to go.'

'I understand that now,' said Evans. 'But I don't know how you saw it in the first place.'

'It was obvious once one victim had remarked how odd it was that *he* was burgled, but his absent neighbours weren't. It's easy to take away mobile phones and lock a bedroom door to keep house-owners quiet, but impossible to stop the neighbours noticing something's amiss and phoning us.'

'True. Yorke could control his victims, but obviously controlling nosy neighbours is more difficult. Clever.'

'Who? Him? Or me for working it out?'

'Both. And you predicted which house Yorke was going for next, because Sanderson's neighbours had been talking to him for weeks about visiting Mauritius.'

Oakley had puzzled long and hard over the common factor in the crimes. The burglars knew exactly what valuables were in each house – sometimes ungagging their victims in order to demand a particular item. The link *had* to be insurance, despite the victims having different companies.

Eventually he had found his connection: each

insurance company employed the same photo-copy repair service. This comprised an engineer who did the fixing, and a woman who made multiple copies afterwards, partly to ensure the machine was working properly, and partly as a service to help clients with the backlog that had built up while the copier was out of order.

The repairman was quickly exonerated, but the woman broke down and confessed to photo-copying documents for an ex-boyfriend. Her description of him matched Yorke. Oakley had spotted the holiday connection at about the same time, so it had been a simple matter to visit a few potential victims to determine who had neigh-bours about to go away. The Sandersons were top of the resulting list.

He and his colleagues had spent the best part of a week waiting for Yorke to target the Sanderson house, and even then it had not been easy to snag their prey. The driver was vigilant, and sounded the alarm before the police could act. The gang ran, despite the jewellery and silverware that the police had persuaded the Sandersons to scatter around in an attempt to encourage the criminals to linger. Only one had been caught – a heavy called Keith McInnes – and he refused to give up his accomplices.

In the end, it was a partial fingerprint that had snared Yorke: one of his rubber gloves had split. Yorke vigorously denied the charges, but search warrants were issued and the case began to build. Oakley had arrested Yorke a few hours before and the man was currently on his way to prison, where he would be held until a magistrate determined whether he should be released on bail or remanded in custody until the trial. Oakley was confident bail would be refused, given the serious nature of the crimes and the fact that Emma Vinson was still in intensive care.

'Yorke is a slippery bastard,' said Evans, wiping greasy fingers on his trousers and screwing up his crisp bag. 'Did you see his house? He's got a swimming pool! I wish we could have nicked that smarmy brother of his, too – Michael. He might look and sound like he went to Eton, but he's a villain.'

'Perhaps he did go to public school. Billy has more or less raised him – being twenty years his senior – and he could certainly afford to send his brother to the best of schools on the proceeds of his crimes. He learned from a master.'

'You mean William Pullen, the corrupt architect?' asked Evans. 'That was years ago.'

'Fourteen or fifteen,' agreed Oakley. 'It was a big case at the time, because of the scale of the fraud. They almost got away with it, too.'

'We were lucky to catch McInnes though,' mused Evans, returning to the current case. 'Even if we lose Yorke, the world will be a better place without McInnes on the streets. I only wish we'd got Dave Randal, too. I'm sure it was him who smacked the old lady. How is she, by the way?'

'Not good,' said Oakley. 'Why do you reckon Randal hit her? Why not McInnes?'

'Randal's that kind,' said Evans. 'Pity *his* glove didn't split.'

'I'll settle for nabbing Yorke. Randal and the

others won't stay out of trouble for long without him to look after them. We'll get them. Except Michael – we'd be lucky to catch *him* making a mistake.'

'I can wait.' Evans' expression hardened. 'What was the super going on about before we left? He seemed worried.'

'Bail,' said Oakley. 'By rights, Yorke shouldn't get it, but the word is that Paxton is representing him. The super thinks he's got something up his sleeve.'

'Christ! Not again!'

'He reckons Paxton only takes cases he's sure of winning, and thinks there might be a reason why he agreed to represent Yorke. He's afraid that Paxton's going to pull some stunt that'll see Yorke get bail.'

'A Butterworth's Blunder,' mused Evans. Even though he hadn't known the DS, the affair had become a by-word for well-meaning but misguided actions.

'I don't see how. Everything's been done by the book this time. No one at New Bridewell will pull a stunt like that again.'

Evans thought for a moment, then waved a dismissive hand. 'Taylor's paranoid. Paxton's got nothing on us this time. He's got to lose a case sooner or later, and this will be it.'

'I suppose,' said Oakley, although a vague sensation of unease had settled in his mind, and it was still with him when he bade Evans goodnight and drove home to his empty house.

Tuesday, 31 July

It was evening, and I was sitting outside in a deckchair, enjoying one of those weak French beers that are so refreshing on a hot day. I'd started work at six that morning, and at quarter to two, just fifteen minutes before I was due to finish, Wright had sent me to deal with a juvenile shoplifter.

For once I didn't mind that this forced me to work three extra hours, as I was saving for a trip to Peru. Well, why not? If I didn't see the world soon, I was going to miss it. I was twenty-seven, and it was time I did something interesting.

I'd been in the job for more than five years, and it was obvious that I wasn't going to amount to much. I'd finally yielded to pressure from Superintendent Taylor and taken my sergeant's exams, although it didn't take a genius to see that he wanted my success to look good on his station's statistics, not because he thought I was any good. But, to be honest, the prospect of promotion filled me with dread. I'd started to look for other jobs, and had even applied to do postgraduate work at Newcastle. I'd been happy there, and although I wasn't naïve enough to think it would be the same if I went back, anything had to be better than being pushed around by Sergeant Wright.

When the phone rang I assumed it was my mother. It was half past eight, the sort of time she usually phoned. I went cold all over when I heard James' voice at the other end.

'Hi, Helen,' he said breezily, as though the episode on the train had never happened.

'What do you want?' Time had done nothing to blunt my anger towards him.

'Actually, I wondered whether you'd pop over,' he said chirpily. 'It would be nice to see you.'

'What do you want?' I repeated icily.

'Helen, Helen!' came his mocking voice. 'What makes you think I want anything?'

I hung up.

When the phone rang again a few seconds later, I snatched it up and was about to tell him where to go when I heard my mother speaking. I flopped back in my deckchair and listened to her burbling about my brother's latest sporting success and my sister's newest baby. She talked for a good half hour, without needing much input from me, then rang off. I put down the phone, and answered it without thinking when it rang again seconds later.

'Come over,' came James' voice crisply down the line. 'I was going to do this nicely, but you're being a bitch so I won't. I've still got those photos I took of the Noble file. I heard there was quite a to-do over that. Fur and feathers all over the place. So get off your arse and come over.'

'We had a deal. I'm not going anywhere.'

'You'll do as I say unless you want your colleagues to know that you gave police files to a defence lawyer.' James's voice was frigid.

'You can tell me what you want on the phone,' I said, frightened now. 'I'm not going anywhere, especially your flat.'

'Not my flat,' said James, his tone indicating that he would never again deign to have the likes

69

of me setting foot inside its hallowed portals. 'A friend's house – number nine, Orchard Street, not far from you. Be here in five minutes, or Oakley's going to get a package in the post that'll tell him that the officer he's been nurturing so tenderly is a viper in his nest.'

The phone went dead.

I knew Orchard Street well, as I walked past it most days on my way to work. He was right: it wasn't far.

But should I go there to meet him? Part of me wanted to finish my beer and read my book, just to show him that I wasn't afraid or intimidated. But the truth was that I was terrified. It wasn't just about the Noble file – it was more complex than that. I'd grown to like Oakley, and I didn't want him thinking badly of me. Nor did I want the issue of how James knew about Butterworth's Blunder opened up again.

I took a deep breath and tried to think rationally. I'd have to go, but I wasn't going to march blindly into a situation I didn't understand. For all I knew, Noble might be there, ready to exact revenge on the officer who'd arrested him – or to grin at the camera while James took snaps of us. I took my nightstick, and to protect myself against James' smartphone, I donned a hideous dark red spotted scarf that a friend had once given me for Christmas. I looked like a Russian peasant, but it hid my distinctive hair. I also wore a cheap, dark blue pack-away mac. It came well below my knees, nicely hiding my other clothes.

I walked briskly to Orchard Street, lest my

courage failed and I'd arrive at work the following morning to find Oakley waiting with an envelope from Urvine and Brotherton and an expression of sad disbelief in his dark brown eyes. The area had once been respectable, then down at heel, and was now slowly becoming trendy again in the way of many inner cities – home now to teachers, nurses and managers. Much of it was comprised of Victorian terraces, but some, like Orchard Street, were post-war semis. I preferred the Victorian terraces, which had a certain antique charm with their carved lintels and bay windows. The semis were functional and without character, although still horrendously expensive to buy, given their proximity to the city centre.

I kept my head down when I reached the bottom of the road, then strode up it with exaggeratedly long steps, so that James would have problems persuading people it was me if he was recording my arrival. It was dark – well past nine – and the lighting had never been much good in that particular street, which suited me just fine. I felt slightly ridiculous, like someone in a spy film, but I was angry enough not to care. I realized I should have known that James would be back for more once he'd seen how easy it was to bludgeon me, and I was mad at myself for not anticipating him.

I found number nine, an uninspired semi with nasty black and white mock-gothic decoration. I wondered whether it was divided into flats, but there was only one doorbell, so I rang it, careful to keep my face in shadow. James answered almost at once, and I pushed past him into the hall while he closed the door, keen to be away from public view. He was wearing a suit and a white shirt, but he'd dispensed with his tie, probably because the house was stuffy and hot.

The place stank of strong cleaning fluids, and would have benefited from the windows being opened to air it out. James' hands were in his pockets and so, presumably, was his phone.

'Nice outfit,' he remarked, eyeing the plastic mac and scarf.

'Well?' I demanded. 'What do you want?'

He indicated I was to enter the first room on the right, the lounge. It was sparsely furnished, with a sofa, a coffee table, two armchairs and an empty bookcase. The carpet was functional beige, and I decided it was a rented house. The mantelpiece was its only interesting feature – or rather, what was on the mantelpiece was interesting. A geologist or rock collector must have lived there at some point, because it featured all kinds of attractive or unusual stones. There were several of those purple-blue spiky things that they sell at the seaside, a huge fossil in the shape of a whelk, and a big chunk of something pale and chalky, probably Portland limestone. A football-sized ammonite graced the grate below.

'It belongs to one of my clients,' explained James. 'He lets it to visiting scholars at the university. I use it occasionally for distasteful meetings.'

So I was distasteful, was I? I watched him help himself to a drink from the bottle of Scotch that stood on the table, and shook my head when he offered some to me. Keeping my hands in my pockets, I started to wander around, pretending to be interested in the place, but in reality looking for signs that he was recording the meeting.

'I've got an awkward case coming up,' he said, flopping on the sofa and stretching his legs in front of him. 'I thought you might be able to help me, like you did last time.'

'No,' I snapped. 'You promised we were done when I told you about...' I waved a hand, reluctant, even now, to say aloud what I'd done.

'I lied,' he shrugged, just as he had on the train. 'And you're not in a position to barter. I'm the one with the dirt on you, not the other way around.'

'You'd be in trouble, too, if I told anyone what *you*'d done,' I retorted.

He gave a low, nasty chuckle. 'Wrong. All I did was find a file on a train and photograph a few bits of it. You're the one who left confidential notes lying around, then lied and schemed to cover it up. And you can't come clean with your colleagues now, can you?'

I really hated him at that moment. I stared down at him, wondering what it would feel like to crash my knuckles into that gloating smile. I imagined it would probably hurt – me more than him. Nevertheless, my hands bunched into fists as he continued to grin.

We both knew he had me cornered and that he was going to drag me down even deeper. I can't say how much I wished I'd never taken that damned file, or fallen asleep on the train, or let

James get the better of me in the first place. I should have stormed along to his carriage and arrested him for theft. That would've wiped the smile off the smug bastard's face. But it was too late, and I was stuck in the mess I'd created.

'I'm representing Billy Yorke in court soon,' he said. 'He has links to some very powerful people who want to see the matter dropped.'

'What powerful people?' I demanded. 'Noble?'

'It doesn't matter who. Suffice to say that his arrest is interfering with important business.'

I was repelled. 'What about Yorke's victims? The old lady who's still in hospital with her brains bashed out?'

'Don't be so melodramatic,' he said disdainfully. 'And don't play the pillar of morality with me either. We both know what you're like.'

His words cut deep because they were true. I'd allowed myself to be corrupted, and now I was no better than Yorke and Noble, who also used underhand means to escape justice.

'I can't help you,' I said in a choked voice. 'I—'

'You have to,' he interrupted. 'Don't you know what happens to police officers in prison?' He shuddered. 'Best not dwell on it, really. And you *will* go down if I tell my story. I may even say you accepted money, just to make it more convincing. Everyone knows that you – unlike virtually every other officer in the country – prefer time off to overtime. Then they'll know why: why work overtime when you have money pouring in from elsewhere?'

'You can't prove that.' My voice was unsteady.

74

I'd told him about that particular preference when we'd had our date two years before. He'd remembered it, just to use against me.

'I don't need to prove it.' His expression was so smug that it hurt just to look at him. 'The accusation alone will shatter your little world, and my photos of the Noble folder will raise some serious doubts. Now, I've got a lot to do and I can't waste any more time arguing.' He tossed a couple of sheets of paper at me. 'Put those in Yorke's file.'

They fluttered on to the sofa, and I stared down at them. They were standard statement forms, on which someone charged with a crime tells his own story. Usually, the prisoner dictates what he wants to say, and his words are then signed by him and witnessed by a police officer. This is then entered into his file, where it will be copied and sent to the CPS, the courts and the defence lawyers.

This was Yorke's statement, and was apparently a confession to the burglaries in the Westbury area. It was signed by him, and witnessed by Oakley. I gazed at James in confusion. Yorke hadn't confessed! James saw my bemusement and gave an irritable sigh.

'You're turning into a real plod, Helen. Do try to think for yourself. It's a fake, woman. And you are going to put it in Yorke's file and remove the original.'

I blinked. 'You want me to put a statement in your client's file where he confesses to his crimes, and remove the one where he says he's innocent?'

'Yes.' James started to speak slowly and patronizingly. 'You put the false statement in the file. The file goes to CPS. CPS notices that things don't add up. CPS summons the investigating officers. The officers' pocketbooks and interview recordings show a different story to the statement. I point out that Yorke claims he pleaded innocent. Do you understand now?'

I did. The false confession, which boasted a poor imitation of Yorke's own signature for good measure, would see Oakley accused of fabricating evidence. It would throw the whole case into question, and CPS would drop it before it ever reached court.

James began to tidy up while I read the statement, taking his glass to the kitchen and rinsing it under the tap. I finished and leant against the mantelpiece, hands still in my pockets.

'Take them,' he ordered, nodding at the papers. 'Put them in the file tomorrow.'

'But it will be locked away,' I protested. 'How am I supposed to get at it?'

'Not my problem. And remember that Yorke is relying on you, and he doesn't like being disappointed. We know where you live, so I'm sure we can trust you.'

I felt tears well up. James had me wrapped so tightly in his coils of deceit that I would never escape! He'd be back for another favour after this one, and then another. I'd spend my whole life working to free criminals. And when I was caught I wouldn't be able to tell anyone why I'd done it, because James and his vengeful clients would be waiting. My life was ruined! And all

76

because I'd fallen asleep on a train.

He flicked me a disdainful sneer as he busied himself about the room, straightening cushions and wiping a few drops of whisky off the table. He was so confident that I'd do as he ordered that he wasn't even bothering to persuade me further. I can't tell you how much I hated him then.

He leaned down to pick up a stray piece of fluff from the carpet, and that's when it happened. I don't remember exactly how. One moment I was standing by the mantelpiece looking at his bent head with all the hatred I could muster, and the next he was twitching and juddering on the floor and I had one of those heavy purple rocks in my hand.

SIX

In one single second of blind rage, I'd taken the life of another human being – I'd committed that most vile, filthy and base of all crimes: murder. And the worst thing was I couldn't even remember doing it. I just recall standing there with that stone in my hand. Part of me still thinks it was someone else, and I happened to be in the wrong place at the wrong time, but of course I'm deluding myself. It was me. I am James's killer.

I would have given anything at that point to turn back the clock and make it all turn out differently. I hadn't meant to kill him, of course. I didn't want to kill anyone. I wasn't a murderer, just a normal person, like anyone you pass in the street.

I used to see James all the time in my dreams, shuddering and convulsing on the floor. His handsome face went slack, and a strand of drool eased out of his mouth to pool on the carpet. His eyes blinked for a while, and I'm sure he knew what was happening to him. Sometimes I thought that was terrible, but other times I was glad, as he'd brought it on himself. But these days, I seldom think about him at all. I've done far worse things than dispatching him, and *those* are what play on my conscience.

Anyway, I stood for a long time holding that rock in my hand, watching him twitch. The pathologist said later that James might have lived had he received immediate medical attention, but that he would never have walked or spoken again. 'Irreparably brain damaged' was what he said. But I think James knew that I was watching him as he lay dying.

Of course, it was sheer, blind terror that kept me rooted to the spot while he blinked and twitched. I'm not sure how long I stared – it might have been a minute, it might have been an hour, although I imagine it was somewhere in between. I was paralysed with horror, and simply couldn't believe that I, shy, gentle Helen Anderson, had just hit someone that hard with a rock.

My next reaction was to put it all right again. I dropped the stone, and grabbed his coat in an attempt to make him sit up. I called his name again and again, although the detached part of my mind – the one that had organized the scarf and raincoat – told me that he was a lost cause. I'd seen enough road accidents to know what a serious head injury looks like, and I knew that although James was not yet dead, it would not be long before he stopped breathing.

Wildly, I started to fumble for my mobile, to call an ambulance, but I'd left it at home. James would have one though. I started to reach for his pockets, but then I stopped.

I sat back on my heels and considered. James had stopped twitching and his eyes were glazed. It was already too late to help him, and phoning for assistance would tell everyone that *I* had knocked his brains out. I would end up in prison.

And it wasn't my fault! James had treated me like some brainless bimbo, not even bothering to watch me as he leaned down to pluck the bit of fluff from the floor. He'd been so certain that I'd do what he ordered that he'd already dismissed me from his mind. I was less important than the lint he'd been picking up.

Was that the kind of man I wanted to sacrifice my freedom for? I could imagine what the press would make of it – young, bright lawyer brutally slain by a plain woman; a brilliant professional, universally liked, killed by a dark horse that everyone would say was a little strange, now that they thought about it. I stared at the still form in front of me and made my decision.

I can't begin to describe how much courage it took to turn my back on James. My heart was thudding so badly that I thought it might explode. It hurt, too. No one can know that fear is physically painful – not unless they've been seriously afraid. I don't mean the kind of fear from riding a roller coaster. I mean a deeper, more primal emotion. The kind that our ancestors probably felt when they were stalked through dark forests by beasts with sharp teeth, or that men experienced in the trenches in the First World War. My fear made every nerve tingle in agony, and turned my stomach to acid. A blackness filled my senses and threatened to overwhelm me. It was too enormous a feeling to express with tears, or even a scream.

Walking like a marionette, I forced myself

along the corridor to the front door. It seemed as long as the Blackwall Tunnel, although it was only a few feet. Each step was a nightmare, my feet coming down hard on the floor and sending jarring pains through my body. When I reached the door, I stared at the lock for a long time before reaching out to open it.

Fortunately, the part of my brain that wanted me to survive was working, even if the rest of me was barely functional. My hand dropped. Fingerprints. My life would be over if I left fingerprints. And DNA. It's pretty difficult to commit murder these days and get away with it.

I forced myself back to the lounge and looked around. The only thing I could think of that I'd touched was James, when I'd tried to rouse him. I'd kept my hands in my pockets the rest of the time, probably in a subconscious desire not to touch anything in that seedy little house. The fact that I'd worn a plastic coat would help, as it wasn't going to leave tell-tale fibres, while the scarf would have stopped any hairs from falling out for FSS to find.

I closed my eyes and tried to remember what I'd learned on the course I'd attended on forensics. DNA profiling meant that any blood, saliva or sexual fluids left at the crime scene could be matched to my own unique genetic makeup. Well, I wasn't bleeding, and I hadn't accepted a drink, so my saliva wasn't going to be anywhere. And I certainly hadn't had sex. I'd cried, though. Could DNA be isolated from a teardrop? I couldn't remember.

I stood by the mantelpiece again and scrubbed

with my foot to eradicate any evidence that a tear might have fallen near the body – if indeed one had. My shoes were Crocs, made of hard plastic. It was unlikely that any fibres from the carpet had been caught on them, but I would get rid of them anyway, just to be sure. So, there were no fingerprints and no DNA. Moreover, James wasn't bleeding either – my blow hadn't broken the skin – so nothing could have splattered on me. I was safe there, too.

I don't know if James was dead when I left. I didn't want to see him taking his last breath, and was afraid to look in case I did. I remember a blackbird once flying into my kitchen window. It lay on its side, each breath an agonizing effort. I watched for perhaps ten minutes, breath after heaving breath, slower and slower, until it didn't take another. The leg that had been rigid relaxed, and its eyes closed. The memory had stayed with me for a long time, and I didn't want it replaced by James doing the same thing.

I turned off the lights, covering my hand with the sleeve of my coat to do so. Then I forced myself to wait fifteen whole minutes before leaving, just in case neighbours saw the lights going off and the door opening immediately afterwards. It wouldn't be a particularly suspicious occurrence, I know, but I didn't want to take any chances that I might be seen. Those fifteen minutes were the longest in my life.

After the first couple had ticked past, I started to panic. What if someone arrived and caught me with the body? But it was late – after ten – so it was unlikely that anyone would come now. Then

I thought: what if James had told Yorke that he was meeting a policewoman named Helen Anderson, who would plant evidence to free him because he could control her?

I felt near tears again, and forced them away – I had to concentrate. What I did tonight would determine the rest of my life – and perhaps even whether I lived at all, if Yorke's friends were involved. I considered the last question rationally and concluded that James *wouldn't* have told Yorke my name: a bent copper would be a valuable commodity in his line of work, and he wouldn't want to share such a prize. He'd keep me for himself, so that I'd always be there to foul the cases he wanted to win.

I glanced at my watch, appalled to see that only six minutes had passed. Then another thought occurred: what if someone else was in the house – someone who'd watched me murder a man in cold blood? I'd have to check. It wasn't a big house, and it would kill some time anyway. A distant part of my mind noted that I would never feel the same way about that particular phrase again.

I went to the kitchen first, tiptoeing. It was empty. I picked up a tea towel, and used it to open the cupboard under the stairs. Then I checked the back door, which led to a dismal little concrete yard overlooked by neighbouring houses. No one was in it, and anyway, the door had been bolted from the inside. There was no back way into the house – a garage occupied the space between number nine and number eleven, so there was no side path, while the gardens of the adjoining houses ran along the back.

The upstairs loomed dark and sinister, lit only by the toxic ochre glow from the street lamps outside. I was suddenly afraid again. I pulled out my nightstick.

I began to climb, my heart thudding painfully. My mouth started to water, as it always does when I'm about to be sick. I stopped and took some deep breaths. My DNA would be found for certain if I vomited everywhere. I started to walk again, hoping that the movement would distract my queasy stomach.

There was a tiny bathroom at the top of the stairs. No one was in that. It was next to a bedroom, where I opened the wardrobe and even peered under the bed, but the room was empty. The door to the second bedroom was closed. Was someone hiding there, waiting for me to go before dialling 999? What was I going to do if there was? Brain them, like James? Ask them to forget what they'd seen? Or put up my hands and surrender? Perhaps I should just leave while I still could. The chances were that I hadn't been recognized.

Against my better judgement, I put the tea towel over the handle and began to turn it, wincing as it squeaked. I pushed the door open bit by bit, revealing the darkness within. At first I saw nothing. And then my eye caught the figure standing by the wardrobe.

In a different part of the city, Oakley was standing in the hospital, staring at a diminutive figure that lay surrounded by wires, cables and plastic tubes. A monitor flashed to one side, and even the scented disinfectant couldn't disguise the stench of encroaching death. Emma Vinson, eighty-two years old, and the defiant, courageous defender of her home, was losing her grip on life.

She'd been in hospital since the Yorke gang had left her unconscious four weeks before. At first, the doctors thought she wouldn't last the night, but she'd held on doggedly, and a week previously had rallied enough to give Oakley a few small scraps of information. But it had been a vicious attack, and shock was taking its toll. Her cheeks were sunken, her face was grey, and what had once been a fine head of zinc-coloured hair was greasy and lustreless. Oakley was more than sorry. He'd come to know the feisty old woman through her family, friends and neighbours, and joined them in admiring her tenacity and inner strength.

Her eyelids flickered briefly, and he moved to the side of the bed, ready to push the call button. He was surprised when she recognized him.

'Still here?' she whispered. 'Don't you have a home to go to? A wife? Children?'

'It's late,' he replied softly. 'You should sleep.'

'I've been sleeping all day. And you didn't answer my question.'

He smiled. Dying she might be, but Emma Vinson still had a sharp mind. 'I live alone.'

'But there is someone.' Her eyes were piercing. 'There wasn't, when we first talked, but there is now.'

He didn't hide his astonishment. 'Nothing

escapes you, does it! I met a nurse while I was waiting to see you once. We got talking...'

'So something good came out of this? My inspector found himself a wife?'

'Hardly!' Three dates didn't warrant booking the wedding bells, yet he *was* smitten with Catherine, and was looking forward to building their relationship.

'I've been thinking.' Her expression was distant. 'The man who went to the safe had big ears. They stuck out through his stocking mask.'

'Big ears?' Oakley's pulse quickened. Yorke had extremely prominent ears.

'Big round ears. And the man who hit me had a Bedminster accent.'

'That's very precise.' Oakley had lived in Bristol for twenty years, but he couldn't isolate accents from different areas within the city.

She smiled. 'I taught linguistics at the university once. I wish my grandchildren were interested in linguistics. One was, for a while, but then he went off and became a lawyer. I suppose there's more money in law.' Her eyes began to close, but she gave a tired smile as someone appeared in the doorway. 'Here's someone who'll sit with me. You go.'

Oakley nodded at the man – one of many grandsons – who entered the room, and walked briskly away from the dying woman to where Catherine waited in the brightly cheerful canteen.

I barely stopped myself from screaming, which was just as well, given that the 'figure' was a spare curtain hanging on the wardrobe door. The house was empty – James hadn't wanted witnesses to his sordid business any more than I did. I walked back down the stairs and glanced at my watch. Fourteen minutes had passed since I had switched off the lights. Now I had to go home, making sure that I wasn't seen or followed, especially if Yorke's friends were watching the house.

Stuffing the towel I'd used to open doors into my pocket, I stepped outside, grateful for the cool air against my face. I turned, pretending to lock the door, so that if anyone was watching they'd think I was leaving in all innocence. I glanced around as I strode away, looking for twitching curtains or silhouettes in back-lit windows, but there was nothing. Most houses were dark, and the few where lights showed had their curtains drawn.

I looked into the cars I passed, too, to see if any might contain hidden villains, but all were empty. I reached the end of the road, turned left, then left again, so that I was on the street parallel to The House. No one followed. I turned left a third time and then a fourth, so that I was back in Orchard Street.

My legs faltered, and for a moment I thought my courage would fail, but I forced myself to put one foot in front of the other until I'd passed number nine and reached the end of the road a second time. I passed no one and saw no one. I was safe. I began to walk home.

There was a pub on Cornwallis Crescent, which was about three streets from Orchard, and a man came out of it as I passed. His attention was on a yappy little dog, which had apparently misbehaved itself inside, and he didn't give me the briefest glance, although the dog barked its head off. Perhaps it could smell what I'd done.

I reached home after several more detours, even ducking into someone's garden for a while. Gratefully, I inserted the key into my front door and closed it behind me. Then I only just made it to the loo before the French beer reappeared. I retched until my stomach hurt. And then I retched some more.

When I was done, I took off everything I was wearing – plastic mac, headscarf and shoes included – and shoved them in a black dustbin liner with the tea towel. Then I dived into the shower, putting it on as hot as I could stand. I stood there for a long time, crying and shivering. Eventually the hot water ran out, so I switched it off. I still felt filthy.

I wrapped myself in my favourite dressing gown and switched on the telly, wanting voices in the house. It was the news, so I changed the channel, even though I knew it was far too soon for James's body to have been found.

Inevitably, I began to go over the evening's events in my mind. Could I be sure that James hadn't mentioned me to Yorke? Was someone watching my house right now? I snapped off the lights and went to look out of the window. It all looked quite normal, with my neighbours' cars parked outside. I wondered whether I should have a medicinal drink, but even the thought of alcohol made my stomach churn. I told myself it was going to be all right. Then I told myself that it really hadn't happened, and that my imagination had run away with me. But there was the dustbin liner in the hall, containing my murdering clothes.

Overcome with exhaustion, I fell into a sort of drowse. When I awoke, two things occurred to me. The first was that there was a subtitled film on the telly, because the room was full of what sounded to be Hindi. The second was that all my careful planning had been for nothing, because James had phoned me half an hour before I killed him. The police would not take long to discover this, and then they'd be knocking at my door.

Wednesday, 1 August
I was in a daze at work the following day. I could not believe I was even there. Murderers aren't supposed to go about their daily business as though nothing had happened. Or are they? I listened to Wright summarize what was going on in the division, which didn't include James' murder, but did include that Oakley and Evans were going to remand court the next day to request that Yorke be held in custody until his case came to trial.

Afterwards, Wright assigned me to traffic duty, directing cars and lorries at a busy junction in Broadmead where the lights had broken. The workmen promised they'd have it fixed within an hour, and weren't apologetic when it took them three. I didn't really care, grateful to have something to take my mind off the horrors of the night before. I made a lot of mistakes, though, and more than one motorist shouted abuse at me. Still, I managed to get through the morning.

There was a report of a body on my radio at twenty to one. My stomach clenched painfully, and my senses began to reel. This was it! But it wasn't. The body belonged to an elderly woman who hadn't been seen for a couple of days, and concerned neighbours had peered through the windows to spot her dead in her armchair. I heard no more about it.

The afternoon was spent in Southville. A pensioner who'd had her purse stolen made me some tea, and I felt wretched when she expressed the wish that there were more officers like me. An Indian-run corner shop had had a window smashed. Some washing had been removed from a line in someone's garden. And so on. I could have written the details in my sleep, as I'd recorded these crimes many times before. The only thing that changed were the faces of the victims and, occasionally, those of the culprits.

I walked back to New Bridewell, entered the details on the computer, and lurked in the locker room until it was time to go home. A revving engine in the car park made me peer out of the window to see a council dumpster emptying the station's waste into its cavernous maw. With it went my murdering clothes. There'd been no point finding anywhere clever to dump them, when it was only a matter of time before the phone call pointed the CID in my direction. Still, the clothes had gone now. And if I hired a clever lawyer, then perhaps even the phone call would not be enough to convict me.

SEVEN

That evening the numbing shock wore off and I came out of my daze. In my five-plus years I'd dealt with two 'murderers' – or rather, because I was female, I'd been detailed to sit with them while they were questioned. Both were jittery, terrified women who couldn't believe what they'd done, and were so overwhelmed by remorse that they didn't care what happened to them. In both cases, intolerable husbands and alcohol had been involved. I couldn't claim either of those: James and I had not spent years in an abusive relationship, and one bottle of weak beer was hardly going to drive me wild.

I sat on the sofa with my legs tucked under me, wondering what Wright would say when he learned that I had calmly gone to work the day after killing a man. 'She came in here as though nothing had happened. Talk about callous!'

But I *wasn't* callous, and I *hadn't* gone to work as though nothing had happened. I was only too aware that something *had* happened, and it plagued my every conscious moment. I felt as though I was standing at the edge of a great black chasm, and that if I so much as blinked I'd fall down it. Anyone who's had some really bad news will know the feeling I mean.

I went over the horrible events in my mind yet again. How much evidence would they really have, other than the phone call? I'd been very careful, and unless a witness came forward who'd seen me, there was no way anyone could prove I'd been at Orchard Street. Then my stomach did a painful flip-flop, which almost had me throwing up on the carpet. I went cold all over, and there was an unpleasant buzzing sensation in my head. I suddenly realized that I'd left the murder weapon at the scene. The purple rock would have my fingerprints all over it!

I racked my brains, desperately trying to recall what I'd done with the thing. I didn't remember seeing it when I had thought at the time about what I had touched. Had I left it by the body? Had I taken it with me, along with the tea towel? But no matter how hard I tried, I just couldn't bring it to mind. I supposed I must've dropped it after I'd hit James. Or had the cool, rational part of my mind – the part that had told me to use a cloth to open doors – also made me dispose of the rock? But the truth was that I simply couldn't remember.

I sagged. My fingerprints on the murder weapon *and* the phone call were more than enough to implicate me. With a sick resignation, I saw it would be best to go to Oakley straight away, and tell him the whole sordid story. He would arrest me, of course, but at least he would make sure everything was done properly, and I knew he'd treat me fairly.

But I didn't get dressed and stride to New Bridewell to make my confession. I sat staring at the blank television screen. Perhaps I'd do it tomorrow.

Thursday, 2 August
Oakley and Evans spent all morning at remand court. It should have been straightforward, with the seriousness of the charges and Yorke's previous convictions counting against him. But with Paxton working for the defence, nothing could be taken for granted.

The courtroom was full – Yorke had plenty of friends and family to support him. There was his brother, Michael, looking like an overgrown public schoolboy with his dark floppy hair, summer blazer and loose white trousers, and his chief henchman, Dave Randal, a thick-set man with no neck, a shaven head and the kind of nose that had been hit too many times in brawls. Oakley was sorry he hadn't managed to nab them too, as he was sure Michael had helped to collect the valuables while Randal had dealt with the victims.

He looked at the spectators. There were several high-ranking villains, all wearing smart suits and brandishing mobile phones. There were a couple of respectable middle-aged women whose charities had benefited from Yorke's munificence, and there were men Oakley had seen playing golf at Bristol's most exclusive clubs. Yorke was a gutter thug no longer: his wealth, however obtained, had launched him into outward respectability.

There was a murmur of consternation when the hearing was postponed because Paxton hadn't arrived, and Yorke grimaced when he was led back to the cells. By one o'clock, Paxton still hadn't appeared, and a breathless junior from Urvine and Brotherton respectfully requested that the hearing be postponed. The expression of annoyance on the magistrates' faces was mirrored in Yorke's, and Oakley watched him give the junior a piece of his mind. The hearing was duly postponed and Yorke remanded in custody until the following Monday, much to his outraged indignation.

'Odd,' murmured Evans. 'Paxton doesn't seem like the kind of man to forget a wealthy client.'

'That's what Yorke thinks,' said Oakley, amused. 'Look at him! He's furious that his expensive lawyer doesn't think him worth a few minutes in court. It was worth wasting a morning just to see the bastard inconvenienced.'

I saw Oakley several times that day, but I couldn't bring myself to speak to him, let alone tell him I was a murderer. No one can know what it's like working in a police station when you've committed a terrible crime. It's as if the building is bearing down on you, threatening to suffocate you, and everyone is looking at you accusingly. It was hard not to feel I was going mad.

I'd had to deal with a distressing case, too. The body of a teenager had been found in the river, and Paul Franklin and I were detailed to investigate. The boy's name was Shane King, and he'd been fourteen. The police surgeon said that he'd probably got trapped in the mud that lined the Avon, and had drowned when the tide came in. Footprints higher up the bank and some scraps of rope indicated that friends had probably tried to help him, but the mud was thick and the water more powerful than they.

Shane's death had been late Tuesday or early Wednesday, and I found myself wondering whether he'd died before or after James. It was a gruesome thing to be pondering, but when you've killed someone such considerations play a large part in your thoughts.

Anyway, Shane had been in the river for two days, disguised by the grey-brown mud and un-missed by his family. Although his mother wept when we broke the news, she couldn't remember when she'd last seen him. She thought it was Tuesday, because that was when she got her benefits and he'd been after her money. Shane's father was unknown, and his half-brothers and sisters seemed indifferent to his fate, although they all perked up when the mother asked whether she'd be able to claim compensation for her loss.

Paul and I tracked down Shane's friends, a sullen, uncommunicative horde. They refused to admit that they'd been with him when he'd drowned, although mud still caked the shoes of most of them. There wasn't much we could do, except to point out that they should stay away from the river. Then they threw stones at the patrol car as we drove away. None hit us, and it didn't seem worth going back to take issue with them.

We drove to the station to put in our report. I imagine Paul thought me a dull and uncommuni-cative partner, but my thoughts were in turmoil again about whether I should confess. I just didn't know what to do.

Sunday, 5 August
Five days after the murder, the initial horror had faded. That's not to say that it didn't feature regularly in my thoughts, but I'd come to terms with it. I still had visions of James lying on the floor twitching, but it was more remote, as though I wasn't the one directly responsible. I'd have given anything to talk about it with someone, but as I still couldn't bring myself to face Oakley, obviously that was out of the question.

It wouldn't be fair, anyway, to tell family or friends such a terrifying secret. The law makes it impossible for anyone to have that sort of knowledge and keep it to themselves. It was my mistake, my crime and my sin, so it would be my secret. Then, when I was caught, I wouldn't have the agony of wondering whether it was because of clever policing or a dreadful betrayal.

However, just because I'd killed a man didn't mean I had to sit in every night and dwell on it. I could go out and see my friends without telling them about the thing that had changed my life. I was due to meet my old school friends the following evening for a drink, and I intended to go.

Monday, 6 August
Monday saw a silently furious Billy Yorke represented by Robert Brotherton, one of the founding partners of Urvine and Brotherton. He spoke with great eloquence and conviction, but there

was no convincing reason why Yorke should be released while awaiting trial. The accused man's composure crumbled when he heard he was to remain in prison until the prosecution was ready to proceed, and not even his elegant suit and immaculate tie could disguise the fact that he hadn't risen very far above his origins – he screamed abuse and threats, and even some of his entourage seemed taken aback by his loss of control. Still howling, he was dragged from the courtroom.

His more worldly associates muttered about miscarriages of justice. Michael raised a hand to his brother in a way that indicated the battle would go on, while Randal's face was ugly with rage. Oakley imagined he would be lost without his boss – he didn't have the brains to organize a successful life of crime for himself. Could Michael take up the reins to keep business ticking along? Not the burglaries, as they needed Yorke's expertise and Michael was clever enough to know it, but some other illegal venture?

'I thought Mr Paxton planned to take this case,' Oakley said in a friendly way to Brotherton. 'I'm surprised to see you here.'

'He's on holiday,' replied Brotherton with a tight smile. 'Well, it's August, after all, and he hasn't had a break since he joined us five years ago. He deserves his spell in the sun.'

'He abandoned an important client in his hour of need?' asked Oakley, surprised. 'That doesn't sound like him.'

Brotherton clicked his briefcase shut and

looked hard at him. 'This was only a remand hearing. He'll be representing our client at the trial.'

'Yorke doesn't think this was "only" a remand hearing,' remarked Oakley. 'He was expecting his freedom this afternoon, not a ride in a prison van.'

'Then his expectations were unreasonable,' said Brotherton crisply. 'Good morning.'

He heaved his briefcase from the bench and made for the door, a tall, businesslike figure in the lawyer's traditional pinstripes, dark tie and white shirt. He carried himself with the self-assurance that came from a moneyed back-ground, and exuded a sense of importance. Oak-ley remembered him from long before, however, when he himself was a cadet struggling to make his superiors think a half-Indian would make an acceptable police officer. Then a lowly law clerk, Brotherton had been gauche, brash and naïve – his suave manners had been acquired along the way.

Meanwhile, Yorke's supporters milled around like angry wasps, and Evans wisely suggested that he and Oakley leave before they found themselves confronted. They headed for the door, but Michael intercepted them.

'We're going to appeal,' he said smoothly. 'Just so you know.'

'Fair enough,' said Oakley amiably.

'My brother isn't pleased that you've put him in this position,' said Michael, his youthful face expressionless. 'He wanted me to tell you that.'

'Are you threatening us?' asked Oakley coldly.

'I'm passing a message to the officers in charge of my brother's case,' said Michael, unmoved. 'That's all.'

He walked away, intercepting Randal, who was steaming towards them. Randal's face was murderous, and it was fortunate for him that Michael could control him, because an encounter would have almost certainly ended in Randal's arrest.

'Animals!' muttered Evans in disgust. 'Do you want to do anything about Michael, Guv? We both heard him, so we should be able to make something stick.'

'Nope,' said Oakley, his eyes never leaving Michael as the young man strode away. 'He was just talking. We'll let it go this time.'

'As long as you're sure,' said Evans. 'But I'll jot it in my pocketbook anyway, for the record.'

'There's a missing person's report going around,' said Evans, poking his head around the door of Oakley's office late that afternoon. 'Thought you might like to know.'

Oakley looked up from his computer screen to see Evans' eyes bright with humour.

'Who?' he asked, sensing his DS was itching to tell.

'James Paxton,' Evans pronounced with satisfaction. 'His mother came in last night and said that he failed to show for a garden party yesterday. The vicar was there, apparently, and Mrs Paxton was *most* embarrassed when her son didn't appear.' He chuckled.

Oakley pretended to be sombre. 'You're not

taking this seriously, Graham. The only way a defence lawyer is going to get to heaven is if someone *very* holy intervenes on his behalf. Therefore, I put it to you that Paxton would never willingly miss an opportunity to solicit a Man of God, and we should conclude that one of his clients has slipped a knife between his ribs.'

Evans laughed. 'That's just wishful thinking! But at least we know it wasn't Yorke. I wish we'd got his slime-bag brother, too. It's an offence to decent folk to see *him* walking free. How's the old lady? She still in hospital?'

Oakley nodded. 'It's a shame. The old girl deserved better.'

'Ingram is a cunning bastard,' said Evans consolingly. 'He'll nail Yorke for her. But, back to Paxton, Barry took the missing person's report from Mummy. He managed to prise all sorts of details out of her to give the lads something to laugh about.'

'Like what?' asked Oakley, intrigued.

'Like the fact that he's never had a regular girl-friend, although Mummy claims it's because he doesn't have time, not because he's gay. Like the fact that she knows he wears Y-fronts because she *buys* them for him. Jesus! What sort of man lets his mother get his skivvies, for God's sake?'

'One who can't be bothered to pick them up himself,' suggested Oakley. 'I wish I had some-one to take care of that kind of crap for me.' He saw Evans look disbelieving. 'Where would you rather be on a Saturday afternoon: trailing around Marks and Spencer trying to work out the difference between cotton, cotton rich and polycotton, or sitting in the Mucky Duck?'

'I suppose,' conceded Evans. 'We'll let him slide on that one, then. Wright called Urvine and Brotherton and was informed that Paxton was on holiday. Obviously he booked himself a summer special and forgot to cancel the Pimm's and strawberries under the willows with Mummy and the vicar. He'll be in for some ripe shit when he gets back.'

'Brotherton told me Paxton was on holiday as well,' said Oakley. 'I suppose it's true, then.'

'Of course it's true,' said Evans. 'The smug bastard's in the south of France or taking the waters in Bath bloody Spa. Mummy will make him wish he'd never gone when he gets back, you can be sure of that.'

'So will Brotherton,' mused Oakley. 'Because if Paxton *has* gone on holiday, then he didn't tell his employers. I think that's why Brotherton himself came to remand court today – Paxton went off without asking, and caught them on the hop.'

I wasn't looking forward to meeting Frances and the others at the Watershed that evening. I wanted to sit on my sofa and replay the dreadful scene at Orchard Street again and again, passing the time by imagining scenes where I walked away from James and went straight to Oakley for help. Or called James's bluff, so he was forced to back down.

The more I thought about it, the more I saw I should have held out. James couldn't have *proved* he got bits of Noble's file from me. I wasn't the only one who'd studied it – for all I knew others had sneaked the thing out of the station, too. Oakley might have shoved it in his briefcase at some point. Or Butterworth – he was an evidence-fixer, so what was to say that he hadn't also taken a file home to look through while he rocked his baby to sleep?

James had threatened to tell my colleagues that I'd accepted bribes, but he couldn't have proved that either. And I could have weathered those accusations anyway. Police officers close ranks when one is under attack, and good ones like Superintendent Taylor, DI Davis and DI Oakley would have gone all out to prove me innocent. James wouldn't have got away with it.

Now that I thought about it, I was sure he wouldn't have carried out his threats anyway, as he was likely to have done as much damage to himself as to me, and I simply wouldn't have been worth the bother. I'd allowed his confidence to overwhelm me. For a moment, the blind rage that I'd felt when I'd killed him flooded through me again, and I spent several minutes pounding a cushion, seeing his face in its pillowy curves. I *hated* him! This was *his* fault, and I was damned if I was going to serve time for the likes of *him*!

I was defiant as I donned new jeans and a silk blouse. James' death was too bad. If he hadn't been sleazy and immoral, he wouldn't be dead. And if it hadn't been me who'd brained him, then someone else would have done it. Bristol was a better place without him. Yorke was behind bars, which he wouldn't have been had

James been alive, so at least there was one villain who wouldn't be stalking the streets in search of victims to hurt that night.

Of course, I knew I was trying to build walls around me, to protect myself from the overwhelming shame. It seems odd to say that a murderer feels embarrassment, but it's true. Yes, we feel crushing guilt and revulsion, but I was also embarrassed. Ashamed and embarrassed. That's part of the punishment. For many people, the prospect of the shame heaped on them by their family and friends is one of the things that prevents them from killing in the first place, while embarrassment is an emotion that should never be underestimated.

I was due to meet my friends in our favourite bar at seven o'clock. We were going to have a drink, then Frances had booked a table in a new Italian restaurant. It was a surprisingly nice evening considering it had been such a hot day, and Colin had bagged seats outside. The air smelled of spilled beer, cooking food and the slightly sulphurous aroma of the water in the docks.

Colin told me that Gary and Frances were going to be late, but that was OK: Colin was easy company, and I liked hearing his stories about life in the world of computers – there were even more shenanigans among the anoraks than at New Bridewell. He was a nice-looking man, with that intriguing combination of light hair and dark eyes. He always smelled of soap and clean clothes, and his passion in life was bird-watching.

I was a bit surprised when he suddenly reached across the table and touched my hand.

'I've got this do at work,' he began awkwardly. 'It's this coming Friday, and I was wondering whether you'd come. It'll be as dull as ditch water, probably, but I'll buy you dinner after.'

'Do you need a woman to prove you're not gay?' I asked jokingly. I'd actually used him in much the same way a few weeks before, taking him to the annual shift party, so that Sergeant Wright wouldn't think I was a lesbian. I don't know why I cared what Wright thought, but I did.

'No,' replied Colin seriously. 'I want you to come because I think you're fun to be with, and I can talk to you.' He shrugged. 'I think you're great.'

The tenuous hold I had on my self-control broke. I started to cry. Colin liked me – a murderer who'd killed the brightest star in our school. I didn't deserve it, yet it was a tremendous relief that someone should say something nice. Perhaps I hadn't changed. Perhaps killing James was an anomaly. Maybe I was normal after all.

He put his arms around me, laughing, thinking my tears were because someone handsome and personable should make protestations of affection. Or was I being unfair? Colin was a nice bloke, and it was me who had the problems. In fact, I had so many problems that there was no way I was going to taint him by letting him take me out. He deserved better.

* * *

'I'm sure there's nothing to worry about, Mrs Paxton,' said Oakley kindly, offering a tissue to the woman who sat opposite. She ignored it and took a linen handkerchief from her handbag instead. 'People go missing all the time, and it turns out that they just forgot to mention their plans.'

'James isn't like that,' said Maureen Paxton. She was a determined-looking woman in her sixties, with well-cut grey hair, immaculate make-up and elegant clothes. She was exactly the kind of mother Oakley imagined Paxton would have. 'He's diligent and conscientious. He'd never disappear off on a holiday without telling me. There's Henry, for a start.'

'A dog?' asked Oakley tentatively. Or a lover, he thought, but did not say.

He was due to meet Catherine for dinner. He'd been seeing her a lot recently, and had almost dispelled the myth that policemen made un- reliable partners. He hadn't been late once, although it looked as though he might let her down that night. Superintendent Taylor had caught him just as he was leaving and had asked him to speak to Mrs Paxton, who was demanding to see a senior officer. Apparently, Wright wasn't quite the thing. Unfortunately for her, there wasn't much the police could do when grown men went 'missing'. There was no suggestion that Paxton was depressed, unhappy, or taking medication, so there was no reason to be con- cerned about his safety. That his car was parked outside his house suggested a taxi to the airport.

'Henry is not a dog,' declared Mrs Paxton

haughtily. 'It's a banana plant, a descendant of one brought back from the Caribbean plantations belonging to our ancestors. All the Paxtons have one; it's a family tradition.'

Oakley was not surprised to learn the Paxtons had such disagreeable antecedents. 'And how does having a banana plant infer that James's absence is sinister?'

She sighed her impatience. 'Because it needs to be watered. It was nearly dead when I let myself into his flat this morning. James always brings Henry to me when he plans to be away – which isn't often, as he's devoted to his work and seldom leaves the city.'

'We have his details on file, and every officer in Bristol will be on the look-out for him tonight. Tomorrow, I'll go to his flat myself.' Oakley began to gather the forms together to indicate the interview was at an end. If he left now, he wouldn't be too late for Catherine.

'You'll go to his flat now, to see for yourself that there's something wrong,' said Mrs Paxton angrily. 'Then I want a full-scale search.'

'And what will James say when he returns to find policemen all over his flat and news of his "disappearance" in the local papers?' asked Oakley practically. 'A man in his position won't want that sort of publicity.'

Her eyes filled with tears again, and Oakley felt sorry for her. Unlikeable though she was, she was still a frightened mother, desperate to do all she could for the child she felt was in trouble.

He studied the report that Wright had written while she composed herself. She'd been concerned, but not particularly worried, when her son had failed to show up at a garden party the previous day. She'd tried to phone him at home and on his mobile, but there'd been no reply. The next morning she'd gone to his flat to find it empty.

She'd called several of his acquaintances, but no one had seen him since Tuesday – six days before. But then again, it sounded as though no one had expected to see him, as he tended to be too busy to socialize. Mrs Paxton had then contacted his office, and was surprised to be informed that James was on holiday. The receptionist didn't know where he had gone, only that he must have left on Tuesday evening, as he hadn't come to work on Wednesday.

Oakley rubbed his chin, thinking he wouldn't have time to shave before meeting Catherine. One way his Indian ancestry manifested itself was in a dark, five o'clock shadow. Catherine called it designer stubble; he called it scruffy. He glanced at his watch: eight twenty. He forced his thoughts back to Paxton.

So no one – friends, family or colleagues – had seen him since he had left work the previous Tuesday evening, and it was now almost a week later. *Had* something happened to him? Oakley had been surprised when Paxton had missed Yorke's remand hearing on Thursday. Had he fallen foul of a dissatisfied client? Or had the prospect of a garden party with Mother and the vicar sent him diving for the nearest luxury cruise?

* * *

Colin was wonderful that evening in the cafe with our friends. I'm not sure how it happened, and it was against my better judgement, but I agreed to go with him to his work's do. He was like a schoolboy, all happy and proud. Afterwards he was amusing, attentive and fun, and I even began to enjoy myself. I drank more wine than I should – I wasn't driving – and by the time we left for the restaurant I was feeling better than I had in days. I determined to put James out of my mind for the evening. It probably seems unfair, relaxing in the company of friends while James rotted on the floor of that nasty little house, but even murderers deserve some time away from their guilt. I never used to think so, but I do now.

I was amazed at how a few glasses of wine and Colin could make me feel so much better. He was really good at telling stories. He could transport anyone away from a hard chair and the smell of pizza to his office pranks, or his holiday in Turkey, or wherever else he happened to want you to be. James receded further still.

'Have you heard about James?' Frances asked suddenly, bringing me back to Earth with a thump. We'd been chatting about a school trip we'd once taken to Paris. James had been there, although I don't recall him doing anything special – not like Colin befriending some Russians, or Frances and Gary getting in trouble for staying out late. But it was probably the memory of Paris that brought James to Frances's mind.

My heart started thudding again, although it was nothing like it had been on The Night. I reached for my wine and my hand was unsteady. I didn't drink any, in case I spilled it and drew attention to the fact that I was shaking like a leaf.

'What about him?' My voice was more steely than I'd intended, so I forced a smile. 'I haven't heard anything for months – years. Not since he used to come here and meet us.'

'Nor me,' said Gary. 'The last time I saw him was when we went to see that awful film about the alien invasion. What was it called, Fran?'

They began to debate the name of the film, which led to a discussion about science fiction in general. While they argued, Colin turned to me.

'James once told me that you and he had ... you know. Once.'

'He did?' I asked in panic. Had he bragged to many people? What had he said? That I was a poor and uninspired lover? That it hadn't been worth the price of the meal he'd bought me? The thought was horrible. 'It wasn't a very good night,' I muttered.

'You did, then?' Colin sounded surprised. 'I just thought he was being mean, to get at me because he knew I liked you. He can be spiteful.'

'He can,' I agreed. 'Did he warn you off or tell anyone else?'

'Only me, as far as I know.' If Colin was bemused by the questions, he didn't show it. 'Like I said, he told me because he knew it would hurt my feelings.'

'Well, it was pretty dismal,' I said. It didn't surprise me that James had aimed to wound Colin. He was that kind of person. I went on, remembering to refer to him in the present tense.

'He looks good, but it's all show and no substance.'

I suppose I should have denied having sex with James, so he would think that James's claim was sheer malice. He would have believed me, as he obviously didn't like the thought that James and I had been together. But the wine had taken the edge off my wits, and I hadn't been quick enough to think it through. I changed the subject quickly and started to talk about my pizza, but Colin turned to Frances.

'What about James?' he asked. 'Has he been promoted again? I never see him at Sainsbury's these days. I suppose he's graduated to Waitrose.'

'He failed to turn up for a court case,' replied Frances. 'First on Thursday, then again today. My mum told me. She occasionally temps for Urvine and Brotherton, and she overheard people talking about it. The rumour is he's gone off on holiday to a gay resort.'

'He's *gay*?' asked Colin. 'But I thought...' He couldn't help glancing at me. Fortunately, neither Frances nor Gary seemed to notice.

'It doesn't surprise me,' said Frances. 'I've heard he's a dismal lover, and he's never really been one for girls. Too good looking, that's what my mum says.'

'Well, I don't believe it,' said Gary, shaking his head. 'I'm serious; I really don't. How do you know he's not gone off with a woman?'

'Mum says he doesn't have one,' replied Frances.

'Thanks for the warning,' said Gary, winking.

'It wasn't a warning,' said Frances, rather sharply. 'If he's managed to resist your charms all these years he's not about to jump your bones now, is he? I was telling you because I thought you'd be interested.'

I lifted my glass to my lips, but my hand was steady now. I'd have to brace myself for many more mentions of him in the coming weeks, especially once his body was discovered. I could not go to pieces every time. I'd need to appear puzzled but calm when they confronted me with any evidence they found. I'd need to say that I'd no idea why James should have phoned me, of all people, the night he died. And, as for the murder weapon I'd been so worried about – well, the rock was rough and dusty, and fingerprints don't adhere well to those sorts of surfaces. Perhaps I'd be lucky.

Colin was muttering that he couldn't imagine why a nice, attractive, intelligent and sensitive woman like me had gone to bed with such an arrogant, self-centred bastard. I agreed. It hadn't meant a thing, I said, not adding that it hadn't meant a thing to James, either. The shock of hearing him mentioned had sobered me somewhat, and I wished again that I'd had the presence of mind to deny having a one-night stand. What would happen if Colin told the police that I was one of James' conquests? It would be all over the station in hours, especially if Wright heard about it.

Later, I was to learn that gossip was the least of my worries.

* * *

111

'I'm sorry to bother you at home, Mr Brotherton. It's DI Oakley from New Bridewell. We met this morning in court.'

'Did we?' Brotherton sounded cool and un-interested. 'It's late. What do you want?'

'Just one question,' said Oakley quickly, sensing the 'end call' button was about to be pressed. 'James Paxton's mother is extremely worried. She says he wouldn't have gone on holiday without informing her, and she's asked us to look into it. Will you give us the number of his hotel, so we can put her mind to rest?'

There was silence at the other end, until Brotherton said, 'I don't know it.'

'Did he tell you he was going?' pressed Oakley. 'Or did he just disappear?'

'That's three questions, Inspector. You said one.'

'I didn't realize they were rationed,' retorted Oakley. 'Will you answer them on the phone, or would you rather I came to your house? I can probably be there before midnight.'

There was a gusty sigh. The prospect of a police visit nearly always brought witnesses to their senses. 'He just went. What's this *really* about, Inspector? Has he been caught drink-driving? Or kerb-crawling, perhaps?'

'Not as far as we know.' The police computer had been Oakley's first stop, after he had per-suaded Mrs Paxton to go home in case her son tried to contact her. Phoning hospitals and the mortuary had been the second. 'And I told you what this is about: Mrs Paxton is worried. I hope her fears are groundless, but we're taking them

112

seriously, even so.'

Brotherton was silent, so Oakley waited, too. There was a tendency in people, even self-assured lawyers, to fill gaps in conversations with words, and Oakley had been rewarded with all sorts of information with his wait-and-see approach in the past. Brotherton didn't gabble, but he did start to talk.

'Last Tuesday evening James told his secretary that he would be late the following morning, but he never turned up. I assumed he was making enquiries about one of his cases – he's a partner, and we don't keep tabs on each other's movements. However, he was definitely expected for the Yorke remand hearing on Thursday, and he caught us unawares when he wasn't there.'

'He didn't tell anyone at the office that he planned to go away?'

'No, and believe me, I've asked. I was vexed about him not showing up for Yorke.'

'Where do you think he might have gone?'

'I've no idea,' said Brotherton waspishly. 'But I can tell you that he'll be looking for another firm when he gets back. We can't have unreliable partners.'

No, thought Oakley grimly. Clients like Noble and Yorke were not to be let down. They were powerful men, with the money and connections to make life uncomfortable when things didn't go their way.

'What about his clients?' he suggested. 'Perhaps we could ask them?'

'I couldn't possibly give you names,' said Brotherton irritably. 'We have rules about that

113

sort of thing. However, as you seem to be insinuating that James's disappearance might be sinister I can tell you that Yorke is his only major active case, and *he's* not in a position to do anything – he failed to make bail, as you know perfectly well.'

'No, but Yorke's friends and family are not behind bars,' Oakley pointed out. There was a silence on the other end as the lawyer digested this.

'James disappeared *before* Yorke's remand hearing,' he said eventually. 'So they are un-likely to have harmed him.'

It was a fair point, although it did occur to Oakley that Michael might be pleased to have his brother locked away, thus leaving the way clear for him to take over the family business.

'Is there anyone at the office who might be better acquainted with James? A friend, per-haps?'

'James didn't have any friends, although you could try Tim Hillier. But I'm sure James will turn up when he's ready. Young people do, don't they?'

'Most of the time,' replied Oakley.

Colin insisted on escorting me home that night, which he'd never done before. I was still a little high from the wine, and I was enjoying his company, so I invited him in for coffee, and one thing led to another. I'd never made love to any-one so savagely before. It excited and frightened him, and it astonished me. I didn't think I had it in me. But they say that sex and death are closely related, so perhaps I needed one to counterbalance the other. Or perhaps it was because it had been a while, I was tipsy, and Colin was a good-looking bloke.

We lay in bed afterwards, talking in soft voices, although my walls were thick and there was no possibility of being heard by the neighbours. But it felt right, speaking quietly in the darkness. At first, the room was lit dull orange from the glow of the street lamp outside, but that reminded me of the house on Orchard Street, so I lit a candle and drew the curtains.

'You don't like being in the police, do you?' he asked, running his hand across my hip and down my thigh. He looked as though he liked the feel of it. I certainly did.

'Not much. I'm not very good at it – I don't assert myself enough.'

'I wouldn't mind being stopped by you if I was speeding,' he said dreamily. 'But it would probably be some plod.'

'They're not plods,' I said sharply. 'People are always accusing us of being thick, but we're not. The exams we take are tough, and we *can't* be stupid and survive. And anyway, most have got A-levels and even degrees these days, like bank clerks, nurses and office workers – and *they* don't have a reputation for being dumb, do they?'

'No, they don't,' he agreed. 'I'm sorry.'

'That's OK. It's just something that pisses me off. Plenty of my colleagues are really bright.'

I reached for him and this time our love-making was gentler and kinder. When it was over, I

115

found myself crying again, and couldn't explain why when Colin asked. He probably assumed it was because I'd been lonely, and was pathetically happy now I had a companion. But I really didn't know what made me weep with dry, wrenching sobs, only that it felt really good to feel the stress draining away and to have Colin holding me.

Already extremely late for his date with Catherine, Oakley called her to cancel their dinner in order to be able to contact Paxton's friend, Tim Hillier. Unlike the conversation with Brotherton, Hillier was more concerned than hostile, but although he was obviously keen to help, he knew nothing of consequence, other than the gossipy assumption at the office that Paxton had booked a last-minute gay holiday.

'But I don't think it's true,' he concluded. 'I suspect it was started by Giles Farnaby, who hates him.'

'Oh?' asked Oakley, jotting down the name. 'Why?'

'Giles has been at Urvine and Brotherton longer than James, and the next partnership should have been his. But James got it, basically by putting the word around that he was thinking of defecting to another firm. He wasn't, of course, but it got him what he wanted.'

'And Giles resents it?'

'He certainly does! He still hasn't got his promotion, and seeing James getting all the best cases must be very galling. That's why he started the rumour.'

'*Is* James gay?' asked Oakley.

Hillier shrugged. 'He doesn't seem interested in men *or* women as far as I can tell. However, I don't think he'd have left Bristol for no reason. He isn't the type. He's too ... well, calculating, I suppose. He'd never risk damaging his career.'

'So, where do you think he is?'

'I really don't know,' replied Hillier sombrely. 'But I'm a bit worried.'

Oakley had only ever met Paxton in court, but had found him coolly ambitious and determinedly selfish. That sort of person would make enemies of jealous competitors. Moreover, his work put him in the company of powerful criminals, and Oakley was beginning to have a bad feeling about the mysterious disappearance of James Paxton.

EIGHT

Tuesday, 7 August

The summer was turning into a scorcher. The temperature had climbed to the low thirties, and there wasn't a cloud in the sky. Britain's beaches were crammed with holiday-makers, and when tattooed youths with heavy boots and naked torsos started a small riot on the seafront of Weston-super-Mare, officers from New Bridewell were sent to help restore the peace. Helen Anderson was among them, deemed by Sergeant Wright to be one of three officers he would rather be without – he didn't like the two new probationers either, with their politically correct training still fresh in their impressionable minds.

Oakley went to Paxton's flat, which was in one of the most expensive and desirable locations in the city. Mrs Paxton went with him, to ensure he didn't touch anything. James, it seemed, disliked fingerprints on his metal and glass furniture, and even she was nervous in the shrine to costly minimalism that was his home. Henry was thriving under her care, but she refused to take the plant home. Oakley understood why: it would be like admitting that her son might never be there again to water it himself.

The flat's walls were white, so that carefully

selected artwork supplied the only colour and automatically drew the visitor's eye towards them. The chairs were chrome and leather, and there was a selection of glass-topped tables. The ceilings were high, and large windows afforded pleasing views of the yachts moored along Redcliffe Wharf. Oakley thought the place sterile and unwelcoming, and he couldn't imagine relaxing there with a beer or the paper. The CD stack contained a lot of jazz, which Oakley associated with dull people hoping to make themselves appear interesting. The thick, leather-bound address book was full of clients, but very few friends.

Oakley opened the wardrobe, and asked whether any of James's clothes were missing. Mrs Paxton's face crumpled as she gazed into the cavernous spaces with their neat ranks of expensive suits and laundry-ironed shirts.

'I don't know,' she whispered. 'He has so many that I've lost track.'

'Shorts?' suggested Oakley helpfully. 'T-shirts? Casual stuff like that?'

'You mean the kind of thing he'd take on holiday,' she said heavily. 'I told you – he *wouldn't* go. He doesn't like foreign countries.'

'What, *any* of them?' asked Oakley, amazed that someone could make such a statement.

Back at the station, he and Evans began to dial the phone numbers in Paxton's address book, only to discover that nearly all the information about his friends was out of date – they'd moved on, and either hadn't told him or he hadn't bothered to amend the entries. Meanwhile, while

119

they waited for Paxton's email provider to give them access to his personal account, Tim Hillier helped them look through Paxton's emails at Urvine and Brotherton. Every message pertained to work, and Oakley thought about his own account, which was liberally strewn with personal correspondence as well as official. He began to see Brotherton had been right: Paxton had no friends, and his life centred around work – which meant he was unlikely to risk it by jaunting off on holiday.

The investigation upped its pace. Colleagues were interviewed, and it quickly became clear that Paxton was unpopular. The gay-holiday tale was repeated several times. Unfortunately, Giles Farnaby was also away, so Oakley was unable to question him about his vindictive rumour-spreading. Nor was he able to question Paxton's clients, details of whom were withheld.

Then a three-year-old child went missing, last seen with an uncle who had convictions for sexual assault, and Paxton was forgotten. After the child was found unharmed, there was an armed raid on a post office, followed by arson at the M Shed. The missing lawyer was no longer a priority, no matter how much fuss his mother made.

Friday, 10 August
By Friday, James had been dead eleven days. I tried not to think about what would be happening to him in the intense summer heat. But I took to walking along Orchard Street on my way to work. It wasn't much of a detour, and something

made me want to look at the house as I trudged to and from the station. They say that murderers are drawn back to the scene of their crimes, and it's true, or at least partly true. I didn't mind walking *past* the place, but I felt that wild horses couldn't drag me inside.

I was due to work the two o'clock shift at New Bridewell after three pleasant days doing nothing at Weston-super-Mare – the thugs who'd started the riot soon slunk away when they saw that extra police had been brought in. I strode past number nine, glancing sideways at it out of the corner of my eye, but the house looked the same. The curtains were drawn, and the tiny front garden had an overgrown, unkempt appearance. I wondered again whether the client who had loaned it to James for his shady meetings had been Yorke. If so, it explained why no one had discovered its grisly contents. If Yorke was sent down for life, then maybe James would never be found.

Wishful thinking, I suppose. I knew my period of grace couldn't go on forever.

Oakley was pleased with himself. By interviewing the volunteers at the M Shed, he'd discovered that a gang of youths had taken to hanging around. At first, the volunteers had been delighted that local lads were taking an interest in their heritage, but their optimism had been misplaced, and familiarity had made the kids abusive and cheeky. Eventually they'd been banned from the museum, although they'd continued to lurk around. Then they'd disappeared and hadn't been seen for several weeks.

From descriptions, Oakley had identified one of the boys as Nick King, a twelve-year-old offender from Hartcliffe. Nick had previously confined himself to burglary and joy-riding, although there were a couple of pending charges for suspected criminal damage. His brother Shane had had a brief moment of fame when he had drowned the previous month.

Oakley paid Nick a visit and found him in the garden shed, surrounded by equipment identical to that used to start the fire at the M Shed; there were burns on his hands, and his eyebrows were missing. Nick denied any involvement, but his accomplices quickly cracked. When the boys' homes were searched, a good deal of stolen property was recovered, so that a number of burglaries were able to go down as 'solved' and New Bridewell's crime statistics received a welcome boost.

Only one lad eluded Oakley's net. That was fifteen-year-old Wayne King, Nick's cousin. With sullen spite, Nick told Oakley that Wayne had goods from other crimes, and that he sold them by phoning up different fences. Oakley thought a schoolboy ringing around to get the best offers on stolen equipment was a sad reflection on society.

By five o'clock Oakley decided that he'd put in a good day's work and would treat himself to an early finish. There was a quiz at his local pub that night. He wasn't very good at quizzes, and usually only knew the answer after someone else had given it, but he enjoyed them anyway. He'd asked Catherine to go with him, and was pleased when she suggested a meal afterwards in a new Balti place in Clifton.

He put his head around the door to the radio room to tell John 'Jeeves' Jeavis that he was going home, but that Evans was on duty until eight. Jeeves gestured at his computer screen.

'Fourteen outstanding calls,' he grumbled. 'Eight burglaries, including one that came in at nine thirty this morning. Two disturbances, probably domestics. A missing granny. A dog that's frothing at the mouth. A bad smell coming from a neighbour's house. An abandoned car. And there's nobody free.' He turned hopeful eyes on Oakley.

'I'm going home,' said Oakley firmly. 'But Evans will take a couple of the burglaries. Give him the one that came in this morning. Getting a plain-clothes man might stop the complainant moaning about the long wait.'

'I'll tell you what,' said Jeeves, as though bargaining was an option. 'You've got to drive down the A4 to get home, right? Make a detour up Goldway Road and phone in the registration of that abandoned car. Then it's only a hop and a skip to Orchard Street, where you can put the lid on this neighbour's dustbin.'

'I'm going home,' said Oakley again. 'Have a nice weekend.'

'Come on, Guv,' begged Jeeves. 'We give you Helen Anderson whenever you want an extra body. It's payback time. Do us a favour. Please?'

'Goldway Road?' asked Oakley reluctantly, knowing the radioman was right. 'You just want a registration number? Not a report?' He sensed he was making a mistake, but how could looking at an abandoned car interfere with his night out?

'And then stop off at Orchard Street and have a word about this smell. You call in the details and I'll do the rest. Thanks, Guv.'

Traffic was murderous along the Hotwells Road, and Oakley was relieved to get away from the crawling line of cars and lorries that inched their way along the north bank of the Floating Harbour. The nearby river, with its grey-brown, glistening mud fringes, stank as it always did during hot weather, and the sun beating down on the car made Oakley feel as though he were being cremated. Not for the first time that summer, he wished his car's air conditioning worked.

He found the abandoned car and passed its details to Jeeves, then drove to Orchard Street. A short, officious-looking man in his mid-sixties was waiting. He had a fringe of white hair around a balding head, and large, purple lips, like split plums.

Oakley flashed his warrant card. 'Was it you who made the call?'

'They needn't have sent an inspector,' said the man, aggrieved. 'A constable would have done. I just want someone to break down the door so that I can get into the kitchen. I'm having a barbecue tomorrow.'

Oakley raised his eyebrows. 'And you plan to use the steaks from your neighbour's freezer?'

The man scowled. 'There won't be any steaks in *that* freezer! Meat is expensive, and no one's going to leave it behind when they go. No, all I want to do is empty the bin or the fridge of whatever's causing the stink. I can't have a barbecue with that pong, can I?'

'Have you tried asking your neighbours yourself, Mister...?'

'Smith. Dennis Smith from number seven. And I haven't asked because I can't. A rental agency leases it on a short-term basis to visiting university types – foreigners mostly – only there's no one there now and there doesn't seem to have been for a while. Summer, I suppose: they're all on holiday. I tried calling the agency, but I suppose they've knocked off early for the weekend.'

'So, there's definitely no one there?' asked Oakley, determined not to be caught peeping through the windows if some eccentric academic from Mother Russia was in residence.

'I told you, no,' said Smith impatiently. 'Are you going to break the door down or not?'

'I can't smell anything.' Oakley cursed Jeeves for landing him with this one. The police didn't have the authority to break into houses for the reasons Smith was giving, and it was going to be a case of telling him to call the agency on Monday. He sensed Smith wasn't going to like it.

'It's at the *back*,' snapped Smith. 'I'm not going to have a barbecue out the front, am I? I'd have every Tom, Dick and Harry pinching my sausages. Come with me.'

Oakley recognized the smell the moment he stepped into Smith's kitchen, and it grew stronger when he went into the garden and stood on tiptoe to look over the wall.

'When did you first notice it?' he asked, wondering why Smith had waited so long.

'I've been away – the Algarve for two weeks with the missus. We just got back this morning. She's lying down upstairs, but I wanted to get the smell sorted out before tomorrow. I've got my son coming with his family, and I've invited Mrs Greaves and her boy from number eleven.'

Oakley scrambled over the wall, still cursing Jeeves. Finding dead professors was uniform's privilege, and it wasn't one of the jobs he'd missed when he'd made the transition to CID. He swore when he ripped his trousers on a sharp piece of trellis.

'Been meaning to get that fixed,' said Smith helpfully.

Oakley jumped down and peered through the kitchen window, then backed away hastily at the sight that greeted him. 'Jesus!'

'Break a window,' suggested Smith. 'It's the fridge, is it? Doctor Kovac must've left something in it when he left two weeks ago, and it's gone off.'

'Smells like it's Doctor Kovac who's gone off to me,' muttered Oakley.

I was taking details of a car theft when Jeeves announced on the radio that he needed someone to deal with a body in Orchard Street. I felt as if I was being sucked inside a vacuum, and I couldn't breathe. The man whose vehicle had been stolen continued to talk at me, but I didn't hear a word. Fortunately, he was one of those people who just wanted to rail, and he barely

126

looked at me as he continued to hold forth.

No one answered for a minute, then Wright came on the radio, calling for me. My stomach did a double flip. Dear God, no! Please don't let him give me this one. Not this one. The thought was so appalling that I thought I'd just toss myself on the railway line if he did. It hadn't occurred to me that *I* might be the one to take the call when James was discovered. Not even in my darkest imaginings.

I didn't answer the radio. Wright called again, irritation thick in his voice. The complainant was looking oddly at me, so I went outside and answered, clicking my thumb up and down on the transmit button as I did so, so I'd be difficult to understand.

'Sorry, sarge. Bad connection.'

'PC 7029 will be there in five minutes,' said Wright. 'He'll drop you in Dean Lane, where you can walk to three of these burglaries. They should keep you busy until we knock off at ten.'

He signed off, and I leaned against the wall, legs shaking with sick relief. I was reprieved. But for how long?

A body that was stinking up someone's house was a lot more interesting than the other calls on offer that evening, so Barry Wright decided to take it himself. He hadn't been to a really grisly death for about a year, and another tale of maggots and liquefied brain would be good for his repertoire. He had seen all there was to see, so Oakley's stiff held no terrors for *him*.

He smiled to himself as he drove, wondering if

127

the CID man had thrown up. He hoped so – it would make a good tale to tell the lads in the pub. He felt like the cavalry going to the rescue, as Oakley was obliged to wait before he could do anything – police officers were open to accusations of theft, so it was force policy to enter houses in pairs in such situations. He didn't hurry, although he usually liked an opportunity to use the blue lights. It would do Oakley good to kick his heels.

He arrived eventually and parked in a way that would make passing difficult for other drivers. No one was likely to complain about a police car, despite the doleful look given to him by the pompous little man with the big purple lips.

'What we got, Neel?' he asked, strolling nonchalantly towards number nine. He took a deep breath. 'Do I detect Pong de Stiff?'

'No, that's the river,' replied Oakley, straight-faced. 'The serious smell is around the back. Mister Smith says that the house was last occupied by a Doctor Kovac from Albania. Mister Smith's been on holiday for the last two weeks—'

'The Algarve,' supplied Smith helpfully. 'The missus and me.'

'Prefer Majorca myself,' said Wright jovially. 'Fewer dagos there, if you know what I mean.'

'No,' said Oakley coldly. 'I don't.'

'I don't suppose you do,' said Wright, giving Smith a conspiratorial wink.

It wasn't the time or the place to tackle Wright's bigotry, but Oakley determined to blast the man at the soonest opportunity. 'Apparently,

Kovac said he was going home at the end of July, but Mister Smith is uncertain exactly when, and no one can be sure he went.'

'Nice man, Doctor Kovac,' said Smith. 'Not like some that come here – all snooty and never so much as a wave. But Doctor Kovac always stopped to pass the time of day. He gave me an Albanian sausage while he was here this last time.'

'He stayed here more than once?' asked Oakley.

'This was his fourth visit. It's a pity he's dead. He was all right.'

'Enough talking,' said Wright abruptly. 'Where is the stiff? Round the back? Shall we shimmy over the wall?'

'The *body* is in the kitchen,' said Oakley curtly. 'But I think I can open the front door with a credit card, which means we can secure the house afterwards. And we don't know it's Kovac yet, so let's not jump to conclusions.'

'Of course it's him,' growled Wright, watching Oakley fiddle with the door. 'Who else can it be? We've got a stinking stiff and someone not seen for two weeks. So don't practise your fancy analysis crap on me. Go home, Mister Smith. We'll take it from here.'

Oakley regarded Wright balefully as Smith left. 'You need to work on your people skills, Sergeant,' he said. 'And dispense with the racism, too, if you don't mind.'

'Racism?' demanded Wright indignantly. 'What are you talking about?'

'What are you talking about, *sir*,' corrected

Oakley, deciding that if Wright didn't understand why he was being called a racist, there was little point in discussing it. He turned back to the door.

Wright glowered. 'Nice little talent you've got there, *sir*. Where'd you learn that, then? Calcutta?'

'The gutters. Same place you learned your manners,' retorted Oakley, unable to help himself. 'There. We're in.'

'Bloody Nora!' exclaimed Wright as he followed Oakley along the corridor to the kitchen. 'Jesus bloody Christ!'

'Go outside if you're going to be sick,' said Oakley sharply, noting that Wright's face was pale and sweaty. 'We don't want regurgitated sausage and chips in here.'

'I'm going to open a window,' muttered Wright thickly. 'Shit!'

'Don't touch anything,' snapped Oakley, bending over the shape on the floor and batting away flies to prevent them from landing on him. Wright ignored him and reached for the window latch. 'I said leave it! This is a murder enquiry. I don't want you fouling the scene. And I meant what I said about you throwing up.'

Wright's hand froze mid-air. 'Murder?'

'Use your eyes, man! Someone has wrapped this poor devil in black plastic, and the back of his head is smashed in. I don't think he did it himself.'

Wright turned back towards the window, intending to open it because his need for fresh air was stronger than his training not to meddle with a crime scene. His foot skidded in fluid that had leaked from the body and he stumbled. He put out a hand to save himself and landed heavily on the plastic-clad figure, causing a spill of maggots to sprinkle across the floor.

Oakley sighed impatiently as Wright retched. 'For God's sake! I told you to go outside!'

NINE

Once Oakley had made a call to Jeeves, a smoothly run machine went into action. Scene of Crime Officers – SOCOs – arrived, along with photographers and a police surgeon. Wearing overalls, paper shoes, gloves and masks to prevent contaminating any forensic evidence that might be found, Oakley watched the SOCOs open drawers and cupboard doors, but there was nothing to be found that could confirm the identity of the man in the kitchen – if it was a man, of course. They would have to wait for the pathologist to tell them that.

Like Wright, Oakley had seen more than his share of bodies, but dismissed the much-favoured advice of breathing through his mouth. He breathed through his nose, preferring to smell the stench than to taste it. Wright lurked near the door, and Oakley suspected his unprofessional vomiting would not feature in any story he would later tell his cronies.

While he waited for the SOCOs to finish their preliminary work, Oakley pondered what he had seen of the house. It contained basic furniture, kitchen utensils and clean linen, but nothing else. Surely Kovac would have had clothes, toiletries and other personal items – according to Smith, he had intended to stay at the house for three weeks – so where were his belongings? Had they been stolen by whoever had wrapped him in plastic? And if so, why? Oakley sincerely hoped there would be something in the victim's pockets that would help, because it was clear that the house would have little to tell them.

He peered into the kitchen where the pathologist was kneeling. It was small, with cheap, off-white cupboards and yellow lino, probably chosen in an attempt to brighten what was actually a dismal little room. Underlying the stench of putrification was a sort of mustiness, suggesting the house was damp and underused. There was a stain on the ceiling that told of a leak from the bathroom above. The place was seedy, and he wondered what impression of England its foreign visitors took home with them.

Mr Smith had looked up the name of the rental agency and Oakley had relayed it to Jeeves on the chance that it might be one of the premises protected by an alarm to the police. If so, there would be a key-holder – an employee reachable after hours. Unfortunately, Academic Accommodations had no such contact, and there was little point in leaving a message on an answering machine.

Smith's house was attached to number nine, so he was the one most likely to have seen or heard anything. Unfortunately, as he and his wife had been on holiday when the murder had taken place – it did not need a pathologist to tell Oakley that the victim had been dead for more than the time since they had returned – they could tell the police nothing about the murder itself. Oakley went to number eleven, which was next door but separated from the murder scene – and the smell – by a small garage. The Greaves family lived there – mother and son. A dark-haired, tired-looking woman opened the door in response to his knock.

'It isn't Mrs Smith, is it?' she asked worriedly, standing aside to let him enter a brightly decorated hallway. 'I thought she looked peaky when she got back from the airport, and I told her to lie down.'

'It's a problem with number nine,' said Oakley, showing her a warrant card that she barely glanced at. 'Do you know if anyone's been staying there recently?'

'Doctor Kovac,' replied Mrs Greaves. 'But he went back to Albania at the end of July. There hasn't been anyone since, and the lights have been off.'

'When was the last time you saw lights?'

She looked flustered. 'I don't pay much attention to dates. But there haven't been any for a couple of weeks. Not since Doctor Kovac left.'

'Did you see him leave? With his suitcases?'

'Well, no, but he told me he was going at the end of the month, because his family planned to spend August at the seaside in Albania.'

'Do you have his address in Albania?'

'No, we only exchanged a few polite words when we saw each other out front. Mister Smith might know it, though. Doctor Kovac liked him – he gave him a sausage. Has something happened to him? Is he a drug smuggler? There's lots of that going on these days.'

'Why do you mention drugs?' asked Oakley. 'Did Kovac ever cause you to believe that he was involved in anything like that?'

'No, but it's always the quiet ones, isn't it? Fred West had neighbours who thought he was normal. I read it in the *Daily Mail*.'

'We've found a body,' said Oakley, knowing she would soon see it carried out. 'We think this person died in suspicious circumstances, so anything you can tell us would be very helpful.'

'Doctor Kovac is dead?' she cried. 'Oh, the poor man! He had children. His poor children!'

'We don't know who it is yet,' said Oakley, aiming to calm her by keeping his voice gentle. 'What can you tell me about the last time you saw Doctor Kovac? Take your time, now. Don't rush.'

She sank to a frayed red sofa and began to gnaw a fingernail. 'I think it was about two weeks ago. It was a Monday. Yes! A Monday! July the thirtieth. I know, because Kevin was listening to *Clare in the Community* on the radio, and that's on Mondays. I saw Doctor Kovac and called out to him. He told me he was off in the morning, but that he'd be back in December. He was a physicist. Something to do with partings.'

'A particle physicist?'

'That sounds right.' She smiled. 'You must be clever, to know that. My Kevin would've known, too, before his accident. He doesn't know much now.'

'Your husband?'

She stared down at her feet. 'My son. He was in a car crash two years ago and ... well, he doesn't know much these days.'

'What was Kovac doing?'

'Throwing stuff in the bin, tidying up. You know, like you do when you're leaving a place. He was a nice man, very clean. He said he liked our English baths, if you can believe it! He said he liked to fill them right to the top and lie in them.'

'What about your husband?' asked Oakley. 'Would he have noticed anything?'

'Not unless he could've seen down from Middlesborough,' she said bitterly. 'We're divorced, and I haven't set eyes on him for six years. He doesn't even visit Kevin.'

'I'm sorry to keep pressing you, Mrs Greaves, but you may be the only person who can help us. Are you sure you didn't see Kovac after that Monday?'

She nodded. 'But I imagine he left on Tuesday morning. It's not easy getting Kevin up and dressed, so I never notice much outside, I'm afraid.'

'Would Kevin?' asked Oakley hopefully.

'He's blind,' she said in a low voice. 'It was the glass, you see. From the accident. It went into his eyes.' She swallowed hard. 'Mister Smith was going to have a barbecue tomorrow, and he'd invited me and Kevin. He won't be able to do it now, will he?'

'It might be best to postpone it.'

'Kevin was really looking forward to it. He hasn't been to one since the accident, and—'

She burst into tears, leaving Oakley patting her shoulder in inadequate sympathy.

I heard everything on my radio – Oakley calling for SOCO, photographers, the police surgeon, the works. Wright was quiet, though. I suppose he was looking around the house, satisfying his ghoulish curiosity while Oakley did all the work.

I went to my burglary calls and took down the information, trusting the complainants were giving me all the details I needed because I barely heard what they said. All my attention was on the radio. What had Oakley found? Did he know yet that the body was James Paxton? If not, when would he? Hours? By morning, I was sure. There couldn't be that many missing men in their late twenties wearing expensive suits.

And then what would I do? Carry on as normal, I told myself. The hardest part had to be the actual killing, and I was way past that. All I had to do was sit tight, act as though the body in Orchard Street was nothing to do with me, and everything would be fine. The only things to worry about were the phone call and the purple stone.

I took a deep breath. I'd already decided that the rock wouldn't be good for fingerprints, so I should stop fretting about that. And the phone call? That was easy too – time of death was notoriously difficult to pinpoint, and it became harder the longer a person was dead, so no one could prove that I was the last person to speak to him. But what should I say if anyone asked why he'd called me? That it was a wrong number?

That I'd been out, and he must've got my answer machine?

I decided to go home and think everything out really carefully. I wouldn't make the mistake I'd made with Colin, when I should have denied that I'd slept with James. I'd be cautious and precise and, if there was any justice in the world, it would work out right. After all, James had been blackmailing me – he was the one who deserved to die. I was *not* going to do time for him.

Saturday, 11 August
The previous winter, a man had been stabbed on Park Street in a brawl between rival football gangs. An incident room had been set up while the squad had tracked down the culprit. The case meant that New Bridewell had recent experience of murder enquiries, and the system that swung into operation was smooth and efficient. Superintendent Taylor was to head a mix of local officers and imported experts. Inevitably, uniform was to help with some of the routine house-to-house enquiries.

The first man Taylor chose was Oakley. He needed competent, meticulous officers, and Oakley was probably the most painstaking detective Taylor had ever met. He wanted Clare Davis, too, and a new man named Dave Merrick, who had valuable computer skills. He took Evans because he and Oakley seemed to work well together.

At seven thirty on Saturday morning, Taylor assembled his team in the basement, which was now the Orchard Street Incident Room. He had already heard it called the Kovac Incident Room, and was quick to correct it – he didn't want his investigation to start with shaky assumptions.

He looked around at the men and women he had gathered, and nodded his satisfaction. A good mix of young and keen, and older and experienced. Many had worked on the Park Street stabbing, and knew exactly what was expected.

'I won't speak for long,' he began, 'because we've got a lot to do today. I just want to fill you in on a few details. First, we have a body in a house, wrapped in plastic. The cause of death was a single blow to the head. The pathologist has confirmed the death as suspicious. The house was leased short term to overseas scholars and, as far as we know, the last was one Doctor Marko Kovac from Albania.'

He nodded to Oakley, who took up the tale. 'According to the neighbours, Kovac was due to leave at the end of July, but none of them saw him go. DI Davis and DC Johns will visit Academic Accommodations today, to get a home address for him and to find out who, if anyone, was supposed to move in next. Kovac was in his early thirties, and *could* be the body in the kitchen. We need to wait for the full post mortem and the DNA results to be sure.'

'You and DS Evans can look for the murder weapon,' said Taylor. 'Start with the P.M. Obviously, you'll need some idea of what we're looking for, and the only way to get that is from the pathologist. The rest of you will be on door-to-door enquiries in Orchard Street and at the university. It's the weekend, so people are more likely to be at home than during the week. We've contacted the physics department, and they'll give us a list of Kovac's colleagues later today.'

'So we do think the body is Kovac?' asked Evans.

'It's a working assumption,' said the superintendent. 'Unfortunately, lying in a hot room for two weeks – the pathologist's rough guess – means facial identification is out. As Neel said, we need to wait for DNA and the P.M. However, Dave Merrick can contact Interpol and the Albanian police, so we'll have a head start if it does turn out to be Kovac. Questions?'

Clare Davis raised her hand. 'The body was found in the kitchen. Is that room overlooked?'

It was Oakley who answered. 'There are no curtains on the window, but the garden is enclosed by a five-foot wall that's difficult to see over from the neighbours on either side – and there's a garage between number nine and number eleven. The people who live in the house at the back would be able to see into Kovac's kitchen from their bathroom if their windows weren't frosted and unopenable.'

'Were any blunt instruments of suitable size and shape retrieved from the kitchen?' asked Evans. 'Rolling pins or a domestic fire extinguisher, for example?'

'That's what you and I'll be doing today. I didn't see anything obvious last night.'

'I heard the body was wrapped in bin liners,' said Merrick, a morose man who'd recently transferred from the Lancashire Police to be closer to his ageing mother. 'Is that true?'

'Black plastic sheeting,' corrected Taylor. 'The body was rolled in it, like Cleopatra in a carpet. Perhaps it was a prelude to taking it somewhere and dumping it. Any more questions?'

Dave Merrick raised his hand again. 'Did Barry Wright throw up all over the crime scene?'

The room erupted with a chorus of noises – derisive laughter, expressions of disgust and gratuitous requests for more detailed information.

'Come on, man,' said Taylor irritably. 'That sort of thing isn't going to help.'

Merrick looked indignant. 'I wasn't trying to be funny, sir. I want to know whether samples were sent to FSS – the vomit might have been the killer's.'

From anyone else, the remark would have been made to make sure word of Wright's mishap spread around the station, but Merrick was too dour for malice. The tale had seeped out via the SOCOs, who had fallen foul of the obnoxious sergeant before and had been delighted with the opportunity to hit back. But Taylor did not want trouble between Wright and the murder squad. He dealt with the question briskly.

'Of course. However, I doubt it will lead anywhere, so I advise you to put it out of your minds. Any more questions?'

'What if the body *isn't* Kovac?' asked DC Johns. 'What if he really did go back to Albania and this is someone else? How do we proceed then?'

'It's possible that Academic Accommodations leased the house to someone after Kovac,' said

Oakley. 'We need to find out before we start to speculate.'

'Right,' said Taylor loudly, cutting across the buzz of speculation that followed. 'Thank you, lads and lasses. All I ask is that you keep up the paperwork. Give it to Dave, who'll be running HOLMES 2 – the Home Office Large Major Enquiry System. However, remember: crap in, crap out. It won't help us unless we help it. And be careful of the anonymous rubbish.'

'Sir?' asked Merrick, bemused.

'Unsigned letters, anonymous phone calls or mysterious emails,' elaborated Taylor. 'I don't like them, and I don't want us wasting time on them. If anyone has good information they can damn well tell us about it upfront, not skulk behind a veil of secrecy.'

'I don't think we should ignore them alto-gether, sir,' said Davis uneasily. 'Sometimes such tip-offs give us our best leads.'

'Ask West Yorkshire Police what *they* think of anonymous tips,' said Taylor harshly. 'The hoax-er who made those "Geordie accent" tapes left the Yorkshire Ripper free to kill again. If the tip is genuine then whoever gives it should have the guts to put his name to it.' He rubbed his hands together. 'Now, go out and catch me a murderer.'

'What was all that about?' asked Merrick after Taylor had left. 'I thought we were supposed to take *any* information seriously.'

'Taylor was caught out badly by a hoaxer once,' said Oakley, 'and he's been wary of anonymous tip-offs ever since. He has a point: there are a lot of people who like to see us waste time and resources.'

'And others who get pleasure from seeing us blunder along in the direction they point us,' added Davis. 'I suppose it gives them a sense of power.'

'So we ignore these tip-offs?' asked Merrick.

'Yes, if they're delivered by a youthful voice with a lot of sniggering in the background,' said Oakley eventually. 'No, if it sounds like someone genuinely afraid to give his or her name.'

'Who knows?' asked Davis with a shrug. 'If this investigation starts to flounder – and it might, considering that we have a victim who no one's missed for two weeks – then anonymous tip-offs might be a godsend.'

'I'm sure you've all heard about the Orchard Street murder,' said Wright as he briefed his shift that morning. 'The victim's some foreign geezer named Marko Kovac, who had his head smashed in. Very nasty. Obviously, we've got a lunatic on the loose, so I imagine there'll be plenty of over-time for those who want it.'

I listened in disbelief. Kovac? Who the hell was he? What had happened to James? Had they gone to a different house, and there'd been *two* murders in Orchard Street? Or had they just got it wrong? I was confused, but forced myself to listen.

'It was horrible,' Wright was saying, shaking his head. 'One of the worst cases I've come across – blood all over the floor, trailing under the sink...'

'The sink?' I blurted. What was this? James

143

had died in the sitting room. There was no sink in the sitting room, and there hadn't been any blood, either.

Wright smiled, pleased someone was giving him an opportunity to elaborate. 'The stiff was in the kitchen, wrapped in black plastic. Well, you can imagine what the heat and black plastic do to a stiff.'

What was going on? Black plastic? I hadn't done anything with black plastic! Had someone come along and tried to clear up after me? But why? And what was I going to do? Tell Superintendent Taylor that the crime scene wasn't the one the killer had left? Or was I right with my first thought – that this was a murder in a different house?

'I heard someone was sick,' Paul Franklin said innocently.

'Bloody Oakley!' muttered Wright venomously.

'*Oakley* was sick?' asked Franklin, startled. 'I thought it was—'

'What number in Orchard Street?' I blurted, loudly enough for people to turn and look at me. I hastened to explain. 'I walk to work that way, and—'

'Then go and suck up to Oakley by telling him so,' snarled Wright unpleasantly. 'He wants a uniform to guard the house, so you can tell him you're it. I'm sure we can manage without our *graduate* today.'

'Bastard,' I heard Paul whisper behind me. 'Ignore him, Helen. He's just riled because it was *him* who threw up over the crime scene, so

144

he's taking it out on you.'

I didn't give a toss about Wright's gastric inadequacies, or, for once, the fact that he *always* took his bad temper out on me. I just wanted to find out what the hell was going on with my murder.

Oakley was at the post-mortem, so DI Davis took Anderson to guard the crime scene. Feeling a certain empathy with a fellow female officer, she asked how Anderson liked the job, but Anderson wasn't particularly forthcoming. Davis had seen her around the station, and had been with her during the Noble operation, but this was their first real conversation.

Davis was a pleasant woman in her forties, who had reached her exulted rank without becoming bitter, angry or jaded. She had three teenage daughters who kept her feet firmly on the ground, and a large yellow dog that demanded daily walks, which kept her fit while also letting her mind wander to aspects of life unrelated to criminal investigations.

She glanced at the quiet, unassuming woman next to her and tried again. Oakley, whose judgement she respected, liked Anderson, so she clearly had something to offer.

'I heard you passed your sergeant's exams.' Anderson smiled politely, but still didn't speak, so Davis continued. 'You've been in the job for, what, five or six years? How come you're not on the graduate entry scheme?'

'I didn't want to be in charge of situations I'd no experience of,' replied Anderson in a way that suggested it wasn't the first time she had fielded that particular question. 'It's better to work your way up through the ranks on merit, not because you've got a degree.'

Davis nodded approvingly. 'So why has Barry Wright got it in for you?' she asked bluntly.

'I was born a woman and I went to university,' replied Anderson. 'That's all.'

'You don't have to put up with his crap, you know. You can do something about it.'

'I don't want to be branded as a whiner. Besides, he'd deny any accusations I made and things would be worse than ever. He's been in the job for twenty years, so I don't see my word being taken over his.'

'Perhaps,' conceded Davis. 'But you shouldn't let him get away with it if it bothers you.'

'It doesn't,' said Anderson defiantly and a little unsteadily, so that Davis knew that it did. 'And who knows? Maybe I'll apply for a transfer soon. Anything going in CID?' She gave the DI a quick smile, to let her know the question wasn't serious.

Davis laughed. 'Well, you'll come with plenty of experience at guarding crime scenes,' she said, pulling up outside the house that was surrounded by fluttering blue and white tape, and where marked and unmarked police cars deprived the residents of their usual parking spots.

'It's number nine,' said Anderson in a low voice.

'That's right,' said Davis, climbing out of the car. 'Number nine.'

* * *

146

I couldn't believe it! It *was* the same house. I recognized the unkempt garden and the unruly hedge. And, of course, there was the number. James had invited me to number nine, and I had murdered him in number nine.

I forced myself to get out of the car and walk up the short path to the door, remembering the last time I'd made that trip. It'd been dark then. It was light now, with the golden sun of August beginning to blaze.

The front door was open, like a sinister black slit that led to hell. DI Davis went in through it while I hovered in the garden, not sure what to do. I'd been trained to keep off crime scenes, and warned countless times about evidence lost under curious feet. My instincts were contradictory – to run inside and try to find out what was going on, or to race away from the garden, Bristol and my life in general while I still could. Then Davis beckoned.

'If you're going to join CID, you should take the opportunity to get a bit of experience of the way major crimes are investigated,' she said. 'SOCO worked all night, and they're just finishing. Put these on and don't touch anything. You don't want to do a Wright.'

'A Wright?' I asked stupidly, taking the paper shoe-covers and gloves she handed me.

'Contaminating the crime scene,' she elaborated. I smiled, because she expected me to.

I put the elasticised covers over my feet and donned gloves that were too big. I can't tell you how difficult it was to walk through the door, but I did it, even though my heart was hammering so hard I thought it would explode. Once I was in, though, I found myself relaxing a little. It was so different from the last time I'd been there – now it was light, full of people and business-like voices – that it almost seemed like another place. It occurred to me that leaving a fingerprint here and there might not be a bad idea – it would be assumed that I'd 'done a Wright', and any other trace evidence they found from me would be discounted. I decided to consider it. After all, I was going to be there all day.

Davis went down the hall to the kitchen where the SOCOs were packing up. I could hear them speaking quietly, as though out of respect for the dead. Fortunately, I knew the dead wasn't still there. He was at the mortuary, being pared open with the pathologist's knives. When would they discover it was James, and not the Albanian academic? I anticipated it would not be long now.

I didn't follow Davis to the kitchen, but stopped at the sitting room and took a couple of steps inside. Yes, there was the nasty beige carpet, and the scruffy sofas and chairs. And there on the floor was the fluff that James had been picking up when I'd hit him. I looked around, seeking signs that a man had died there. There was nothing, not even an indentation in the carpet or a stain from the saliva that had dripped from James's mouth. There was no rock either, although I wasn't sure whether or not this was a good thing.

When I'd hit James – as far as I could recall – there was a soggy crack, like an egg dropping on a stone floor, only heavier, deeper and louder. Perhaps an ostrich egg might make the right kind of noise, with its thicker shell and greater contents. But there hadn't been any blood, because my blow hadn't split James's skin. Wright had claimed there'd been blood everywhere. What was right: his observations or my memories?

I rubbed my pounding head. And how had the body gone from the sitting room into the kitchen? Had I done that, in the moments immediately after the murder, when I'd been dazed and frightened? And had I then blotted it from my mind? Had I rolled the body in plastic, intending to return later and get rid of it? If so, my fingerprints would be all over it.

I looked at the mantelpiece, which was grey, white and silver from fingerprint dust. The rocks were still there, sitting in a line, and a police photographer was taking snaps of them. I noticed an ominous gap where one was obviously missing.

'In here, Helen.'

Davis was calling. I reluctantly left the sitting room and made my way to what everyone thought was the scene of the real crime. My legs felt as heavy as lead, and I could smell the stench of decay, even though the body had gone. It hung in the air, like mist, penetrating and polluting everything. I could taste it, feel it scorching my nostrils. I knew it would be seared into my memory forever.

When I reached the kitchen I remembered the characterless little room with its white chipboard cupboards and its cheap yellow vinyl.

There was a small table at one end, with two folding chairs, and the sink was under the window. On the floor near the sink was a long, dark stain, which was a blackish-plum colour, yellow-gold at the edges. It didn't look like blood. Was that what Wright had seen? Had it come from James's shattered head? Or had it oozed from his ears or his mouth as he was moved? I looked closer. It looked sticky, and was set at the edges, like blood mixed with lemonade and left to dry. There were clots of something dark in the middle.

'Bodies leak after death,' explained a SOCO, mistaking my horrified perusal for professional interest. 'Tissues, like the brain, begin to liquefy and gasses cause the intestines to swell. It's like a volcano, with pressure building up, and it's got to come out somewhere, so it does – through various orifices, which I'm sure you don't need me to list.'

'No,' I agreed fervently. 'So, it's not blood?'

'The blow that killed him didn't break the skin, so there wasn't any blood for us to find, more's the pity.'

'Is it?' I asked nervously.

'Oh, yes.' The man was enjoying sharing the secrets of his horrible trade. 'When a victim is hit and the wound bleeds, you get what we call splatter marks. These droplets – which can sometimes be very fine, and other times a real fountain – make distinctive patterns when they land, so we can tell where a victim was killed, how hard he was hit and even the order the blows came in. But we can't do that here.' He sounded disappointed.

'What *can* you tell?' I asked, trying to sound coolly professional.

'It's hard to say at this stage.' The SOCO began to pack small bottles into a bag. 'There are fingerprints all over the place, but that's to be expected in a kitchen. We'll run them all through the computer to see how many belonged to Kovac ... to the victim, and see what we're left with. Since this house is rented to lots of people for short periods, eliminating them and identifying a culprit is going to be a nightmare.'

'What else, besides fingerprints?' I asked numbly. There was no point trying to contaminate the scene if all the relevant surfaces had already been dusted.

'We've found fibres from what will probably turn out to be clothes. We've got cutlery, glasses and cups to test for saliva – DNA, you know. We've taken swabs from every available surface. You name it, we've done it. With a murder, we can't be too careful.'

'True,' agreed Davis, who had been listening as she looked around the room. 'And you lot can do wonders with it all these days. We're placing a good deal of hope on what you find.'

'We'll do our best,' said the SOCO proudly. 'It's not easy to commit murder in the twenty-first century, you know. We *can* now solve crimes that would have been impossible a decade ago.' He gave me a conspiratorial grin. 'We'll get this bastard. I don't have any doubts on *that* score.'

I felt as though I was about to do a Wright.

151

A post-mortem was never a pleasant thing to witness, and one on a body that should have been buried or cremated days before was worse than most. Evans chewed gum in an attempt to combat the stench, but Oakley had visions of molecules of corruption drifting in the air and becoming caught in it. The notion of anything from the corpse entering his mouth was something he didn't like to dwell on. He wore a surgical mask and breathed through his nose as shallowly as possible.

The pathologist was Ben Grossman. Due to retire soon, he was a genial man whom the police liked, as he didn't patronize them or try to distress them with gruesome procedures. He had worked in the mortuary used by New Bridewell for as long as Oakley could remember.

The post-mortem room had recently been refurbished, and boasted gleaming white walls and a hard grey floor with drains, so it could be hosed down at the end of the day. Custom-built lights, a camera and microphones hung from the ceiling, and there were three metal trolleys, each of which held a body; more were stored in large metal drawers in an adjoining room. Stripped of clothes, the Orchard Street corpse was a dark, blackish colour with hints of green. Its stomach was vastly distended, and its lower limbs swollen from the fluids that had pooled there.

'Neel!' cried Grossman, eyes crinkling in a grin that was hidden behind his mask. 'And Mark Butterworth, is it?'

'Graham Evans,' corrected Oakley, uncomfortably aware that Grossman had performed the post-mortem on his friend. How could he have forgotten? Or had he just seen so many bodies that one blurred into another?

'Welcome, welcome,' said Grossman genially. He switched on the spotlights and rubbed his gloved hands together. 'This isn't going to be pleasant, so don't feel obliged to stay. Most will be irrelevant to you, and you can watch the DVD later if necessary. I'll do the head first. That's presumably what you're most interested in. Do you have a name yet?'

'No,' replied Oakley, still discomfited by the mention of Mark.

'He's probably Marko Kovac,' countered Evans. 'He was a visiting scholar at the university.'

'Marko Kovac?' asked Grossman, startled. 'Not the Albanian particle physicist?'

Oakley frowned. 'You know him?'

'I met him, certainly. I teach anatomy at the university, as you know, and attend the occasional science faculty bash. I met him at one last year.'

'Last year?' asked Oakley. 'Not more recently?'

'Christmas. I remember, because I'd never met an Albanian before and I asked how they celebrate the holidays. He was Catholic, and I couldn't decide which of the traditions he described were basic Christian and which were specifically Albanian. That's what happens when a Jew asks questions about Christmas! I should stick to things I know.'

'He was religious then?'

'Not overtly. That was our only discussion, although he told me he visited the physics department a couple of times a year. Dear, oh, dear. Is this him?' He cocked his head and looked long and hard at the body.

'We don't know,' said Oakley. 'Is it?'

'Grossman shrugged apologetically. 'I'm not very good with faces, and you'll appreciate that this one is somewhat changed. You'll have to get me a photo to match to his skull. It could be him: it's the right sort of build, age, hair colour. Eyes have gone, of course, so they won't help.'

'What was he like?'

Grossman considered, pulling absently on the mask that covered his mouth. 'A little arrogant, but that happens when you're good at what you do. Good looking, long eyelashes. I remember those.' He peered at the body. 'I'll have a dig around later, once I've cleared the maggots out, and see if I can find any.'

Evans left the room.

'Was he popular with his colleagues?'

'He seemed a pretty normal sort of fellow to me. Talked about his wife and children, and went on about his work at the university in Tirana and how the Balkan conflicts had affected it. But people at the university will tell you this. I should be telling you about his injuries.'

There was only one: a savage blow to the top of the head that had severely compressed the brain. Grossman peeled back the skin to reveal radiating cracks from a central dent, like craters created by asteroids in deserts. Fragments of bone had been driven into the brain, further compounding the damage. Everything else seemed normal, and Grossman could detect no sign of a struggle.

'Can you tell whether the blow was administered left-handed or right-handed?' asked Oakley.

'Haven't a clue. It might have been done *two*-handed for all I know. However, there was a lot of anger or power behind it. Death would've come fairly quickly.'

'You mean he lived for a while afterwards?'

'Oh, yes. In fact, had he been taken straight to a hospital he might even still be with us. He would never have walked or talked again, of course, but he might still be breathing.'

'Can you describe the murder weapon?'

'Something large and fairly heavy. Not a metal bar or a baseball bat. Something wider and with a flatter surface.'

'Such as what?' Oakley racked his brain for something that matched that description in the house. 'A saucepan? He appears to have died in the kitchen.'

'Possibly, but the bruising is deeper in some places than in others. A very *dented* saucepan would fit the description. I've taken swabs, so we can see if there's any residue from the weapon, but don't hold your breath. If it was metal we won't find anything.'

'A blow of such force raises two questions in my mind,' mused Oakley. 'First, does it suggest a man rather than a woman? And second, why wasn't there any bleeding? I thought scalps bled easily.'

'They do. However, it's not unusual for the first blow in a bludgeoning to break bones but not skin. I often say the first strike is free, and it's the rest that cause the spatter that gives us our clues. But our killer was happy with one. Perhaps it was an accident.'

'An accident?' asked Oakley warily. 'How?'

'He got in the way of some strange sport with dented skillets?' suggested Grossman flippantly. 'Regardless, that's for you to find out.'

'And the force of the blow?' asked Oakley, unamused. 'You said there was a lot of anger or power behind it.'

'Considerable force was used. But there are some very powerful ladies around these days, so I wouldn't like to speculate whether you're looking for a male or a female culprit.'

'But if you *had* to choose?'

'A man, but I'll deny it if you bring it up in court. It's based on good old-fashioned prejudice that men commit more violent crimes than the fairer sex. But look at the victim's skull. It's quite delicate for a man – not abnormal, but it's certainly thinner than yours would be. If the killer had delivered this sort of blow to you, he'd need to follow it up with another to make sure you were dead.'

'Would the culprit know this?' wondered Oakley.

'I doubt it. Most killers don't give their victims a physical examination before launching murderous attacks. It was probably luck – for the killer, I mean. Certainly not for the victim.'

'Lord!' muttered Oakley. The post-mortem was throwing out more questions than solutions.

'When you bring me a body in this state, you reduce the chance of getting definitive answers,' said Grossman. 'For example, I can't tell whether it was bundled up in the plastic straight away or later. I'll need to call in an insect specialist, too. He might be able to give you a more accurate time of death. My guess – which won't go in my report – is the week between Saturday the twenty-eighth of July and Saturday the fourth of August.'

'Kovac was alive on the thirtieth of July because he spoke to his neighbour. That was two weeks ago.' Oakley sighed. 'Of course, this may not be him. Kovac might be the killer.'

'Unfortunately for you, DNA will only give you a name if you've got a sample to match it to. Kovac almost certainly won't be in the criminal database here, and I doubt the Albanian police have access to such modern technology. You'll have to resort to old-fashion identification methods, like dental records. Or perhaps they'll have his fingerprints on file – academics are still regarded with suspicion there, so you may be in luck.'

'Are his clothes Albanian?'

'No, they all have British labels. But lots of Eastern Europeans treat themselves to Western clothes, so you can't read anything into that.'

'Perhaps that's why we didn't find a suitcase in the house,' said Oakley gloomily. 'The culprit wanted his fashionable clothes.'

'Last year we had a woman who was killed for

the four pounds in her handbag,' Grossman pointed out sombrely. 'A suitcase of clothes is an improvement on that.'

When he had finished at the mortuary, Oakley drove to the university. A technician there had phoned New Bridewell to say that he was the one who worked more with Kovac than anyone else, and Oakley wanted to interview him personally. Ron Yates, a tall, cadaverous man in his forties, took him to a spotlessly clean chamber and laid his hand lovingly on a console. Thick cables trailed from it and it looked expensive.

'An SEM with an attached ICPMS,' he said fondly.

'Very nice,' said Oakley. He'd been good at physics at school, and read popular science books, but the humming monstrosity that stood before him looked altogether too complex for his meagre level of understanding.

'It's a powerful microscope that can analyse materials at the molecular level,' explained Yates. 'I've made modifications that make this one the best in the country – perhaps in the world. Doctor Kovac comes here to use it – always in the vacations, as it tends to be less busy then. He's been doing some pretty interesting work.'

'What kind of work?'

'Looking at the chemical structures of the particles comprising specific agents.' Yates sounded impressed. 'Some of his findings are revolutionary, and may have a major impact on nanotechnology.'

158

'What's Kovac like?' asked Oakley, changing the subject before he became too lost.

'Nice,' replied Yates, 'but edgy. He was in Skopje when the war broke out in Macedonia a decade ago, and the experience shook him. He worries about his family when he's here. He's always showing me pictures of them.'

'Could he be suffering from post-traumatic stress disorder?' asked Oakley, thinking that Kovac wouldn't be the first person so scarred by war that he perpetrated his own horrors to compensate.

'He might – his stories certainly scared the shit out of me. But he's not violent.' Yates gave a sad smile. 'He'd never hurt anyone, and I really hope it's not his body you found.'

Oakley left the university to give evidence for the remand hearing of the louts who'd set the M Shed alight. The prosecution wanted them imprisoned until the trial, and the defence was making a routine objection. Oakley fretted while he waited, aware that he had far more important things to be doing. But the ponderous wheel of justice hurried for no man, not even on a Saturday, and he could do nothing except pace with increasing exasperation.

As expected, it was decided that Nick King and his mates should be kept in the juvenile detention centre until their case could be heard. Oakley was just leaving when someone stepped out to intercept him. It was Michael Yorke.

'I'd have thought you'd stay away from places like this,' remarked Oakley.

'I was hoping to catch Robert Brotherton,'

replied Yorke. 'He's looking after Billy while Paxton's on holiday.'

'I don't suppose you know where?' asked Oakley. 'His mother's concerned about him.'

'I was going to ask you the same thing,' said Michael. 'His disappearance when my brother needs him is inconvenient. I don't suppose the police persuaded him to take off, did they?'

'I only wish we had that kind of power,' sighed Oakley. 'Perhaps he realized that the case isn't as straightforward as he hoped, and buggered off before he could make a fool of himself.' Or before he could make an enemy of Yorke, he thought.

Michael still smiled, but his eyes were hostile. 'I wouldn't like to learn that the police had anything to do with it. Neither would my brother.'

Oakley met his gaze. 'I think we'd better end this conversation now, before I feel obliged to arrest you for threatening behaviour.'

Michael backed away, raising his hands in the air. 'See you in court.'

Oakley stared after him thoughtfully. It was the second time the Yorkes had suggested the police had something to do with Paxton's odd disappearance. What was going on?

It was a scorching hot day, the sort when everyone should be at the beach or relaxing with friends. I certainly shouldn't have been standing guard at the house where James had died, trying to find a spot that was in the shade so I wouldn't fry.

160

DI Davis had left when the SOCO had finished his lecture, and the forensics team had gone shortly after that, locking the door behind them. They had really known their business, and it showed that it's getting harder and harder to get away with murder these days. But I was going to be the exception. There were certainly some un-solved murders and James's was going to be one of them. They didn't even know who he was, and the Kovac thing would lead them off in entirely the wrong direction.

But what about the black plastic? I'd been confused and frightened after the murder. Could my horror really have caused me to blank out what I'd done? I closed my eyes and replayed it yet again. I recalled staring at James for some time, watching him breathe. Then I'd started for the door, but had gone back to make sure there were no witnesses. I shuddered. I don't know what I'd have done if I had found someone.

'Are you all right?' Inspector Oakley's voice pulled me so suddenly from my musings that I must have looked like a deer in the headlights. 'I thought you might like this. It's hot out here.'

He gave me an ice cream, chocolate-covered with nuts on the outside. I grinned weakly, trying to look grateful, while wondering how I was going to eat the thing without throwing up. Part of what was making me feel sick was the smell of Oakley himself. I'd been a police officer long enough to recognize the rank stench that clung to him. He'd been at James's post-mortem.

'Nothing's happening here,' I said, pulling off the wrapper and trying to think of something other than James lying naked on a steel table. I could throw the lolly away when Oakley had gone. It would melt, and no one would know. I didn't want to hurt his feelings by telling him I didn't want it, but I certainly couldn't eat the thing. 'SOCO left a couple hours ago.'

'And you drew the short straw and got to stand guard. I wondered who'd land that job. I should-'ve known. How long are you here for?'

'Rest of the shift, as far as I know. I don't mind.'

'Well, I do,' Oakley said irritably. 'I don't want dehydrated officers fainting and letting the murderer get into the house. Or the press. I'll make sure you have a break, even if I can't get you out of a second stint.'

I started to tell him that I didn't want one – that I'd rather be alone with my thoughts than taking burglary reports or arresting smirking juvenile shoplifters at the shopping centre, but he opened the door and went in without listening. He called over his shoulder that I should finish my ice cream before following, indicating that he wanted me to join him there. I estimated the time it would take me to eat it before flinging it in the hedge and stepping inside.

He was in the hall with his hands in his pockets. It was hot enough that anyone wearing a jacket would roast, so he was in shirt sleeves. It was a white shirt, nicely ironed, and he'd loosened his blue tie. He looked cool and relaxed. I noticed for the first time that there was silver in his black hair, and that his teeth always looked so white because his skin was a lovely golden colour. I hoped it would be him who arrested me if the affair turned out badly. Or Clare Davis. Either would be kind and fair.

'What are you doing?' I asked, when he just continued to stand there.

'Trying to get a feel for the place. I couldn't do it last night. First, Wright was all over it, telling me how to catch the killer, then SOCO was here. Now it's empty, it feels different.'

'How?' I asked suspiciously. Did he think he was going to catch me by trying to *imagine* what had happened?

'Well, for a start, I can hear next-door's television. That means the walls are thin, and if our victim was killed after an argument, the neighbours might have heard something.'

'But the ones at number seven were away,' I pointed out, repeating what I'd heard during the morning. 'They only got back yesterday.'

'True. But a screaming row would've been heard all down the street, even with the windows closed. It's a quiet road. There isn't much traffic, and there don't seem to be any noisy kids, even though it's the school holidays. So, I don't think he was killed after a fight – well, not a loud one, anyway. I suppose there are always the quiet, menacing ones to consider.'

Was my last discussion with James a quiet, menacing one? I supposed it was. Neither of us had raised a voice. It had all been normal volume, very controlled, very dignified. All the menace had come from him, of course. None was mine, until the rock came into play. I wondered again where it was. Had I got rid of it? Or

163

did I have someone else to thank for that – the person who had wrapped James in plastic?

Then a blinding realization came to me. I hadn't done that – one of Yorke's friends had. He'd come to see if James had managed to get the false statement put in the court file, found James dead and decided to get rid of the body, lest the crime was traced back to his boss. I suddenly remembered the statement lying on the sofa where James had tossed it. It wasn't there now, and I was certain SOCO hadn't found it, because someone would have said so. I felt dizzy with relief. I wasn't losing my mind after all. Someone *had* been in the house between me and the police.

But was I right to be relieved? After all, Yorke wouldn't be pleased that someone had killed his crooked lawyer, and he was a dangerous man. Yet twelve days had passed since the murder, and I'd been careful to ensure that no one had seen me near the house that night. I knew I hadn't been followed, so I was probably safe. Wasn't I?

'We don't have a precise time of death,' Oakley was saying, 'and we don't know whether our victim was killed here. Enquiries in the street haven't gone well. How can they, if we don't know what dates we're talking about?'

'You have a rough idea,' I said, able to be consoling now. 'You know Kovac was last seen on Monday, July the thirtieth, when he told the neighbour at number eleven that he was leaving the next morning. If he didn't leave that Tuesday, it must have been because he was dead. Therefore, he died sometime between that Monday evening and the next day – probably the first half of the day, as no one leaves to go on a long journey late at night.'

And I knew Kovac had gone by the Tuesday evening, because he certainly wasn't there when I arrived. Obviously, James had waited until the Albanian had left before using the house. I was quite pleased with myself. If I managed to make Oakley believe the killing occurred on Monday or early Tuesday, he wouldn't be looking for an alibi from me on Tuesday night.

'I know there's a body of opinion that thinks we've got a dead Albanian on our hands, but I'm not placing any bets. It might be someone else.'

Damn him! 'A tramp?' I suggested, trying not to sound too hopeful.

'Not wearing a nice suit and good leather shoes.'

'And there was no identification on the body?' I asked. 'No wallet or mobile?'

The mobile, of course, was my biggest worry.

'I wish,' said Oakley. He walked into the kitchen and stood still again, hands in his pockets as he looked around slowly. Then he donned a pair of gloves and began to open various drawers and cabinets.

'What are you looking for?' I asked.

'The murder weapon. It's got to be something heavy with a flattish bottom, perhaps like a heavily dented skillet.'

I joined in the search, grateful that he was so wrong. I suppose he thought James had been killed in the kitchen, and was hung up on the idea that the murder weapon had to be some kind of cooking utensil. I realized then that when the police have little to go on, things like where the body was found start to take on unwarranted significance. I could see how easy it would be to lead an investigation astray by over-interpreting, or drawing the wrong conclusions. If I were ever involved in another, I'd know what mistakes not to make.

I'd heard Oakley was tenacious, and now I saw it for myself. He examined every utensil in the kitchen, working methodically from left to right. When he finished there, he moved to the sitting room, where his eyes immediately lit on the stones that adorned the mantelpiece.

'Ha!' he muttered, as he took one down and turned it over in his hands. 'Something heavy and irregular that won't leave splinters or fibres.' He turned to me, his eyes gleaming. 'I think we've found our murder weapon.'

'That?' I tried to make myself sound dubious. 'It wouldn't be heavy enough.'

'Not this one, perhaps.' He was already picking up the others one by one. The gap where my stone had sat didn't escape his attention. He stared at it for a long time, before moving to the one next to it. When he finished, he turned to look at me. 'Perhaps the killer took it with him.'

He was half right. The killer hadn't taken it – that I knew for a fact – but Yorke's men might have done, along with James's wallet and mobile. What had they been thinking? Had they imagined that there might be something on the rock that would associate *them* with the murder? Had James been alive when they'd arrived, so they'd finished him off, lest his arrival in a hospital raised awkward questions? Still, the absence of the murder weapon was a great weight off my mind.

'Perhaps it rolled under the chairs,' I suggested, trying to sound helpful.

He regarded me doubtfully – we both knew that SOCO would have looked already, but he obligingly got down on all fours and lifted the seat cover to peer underneath. I knelt, too, and raised the skirt of the sofa, confident nothing would be there. I was almost sick when I saw my purple rock, complete with a couple of James's hairs still stuck to it.

TEN

For the second time in that nasty brown and beige sitting room, I was frozen to the spot in horror. My rock had obviously been kicked or bumped under the sofa by mistake, probably by whoever had put James in the kitchen, as SOCO are pretty careful about where they step. It sat there, practically with my name written on it. Suddenly, I wasn't at all sure that you couldn't get fingerprints from rocks. I dropped the cover, aiming to distract Oakley until I could get rid of it. I'd been stupid – I'd trusted a gang of criminals to clear up my mess, when I should have been thinking for myself.

'Well done!' came Oakley's delighted voice. 'You should be in CID! I'll make sure people hear about this.'

He crawled across to pull the sofa cover back up. I scrambled to my feet. I could make an end of him just as easily as I had James. I could hit him with one of the other rocks, then go and stand guard at the front door, with the rock – both rocks – in my pockets as though nothing had happened.

Then I pulled myself together. I wasn't that sort of killer. I'd dispatched James because he'd driven me to it. Oakley was just doing his job, and it had been my fool idea to look under the bloody sofa, although I suspected he'd have found the rock sooner or later, given his careful search of the kitchen. The discovery of the murder weapon might not lead to me anyway, and at least I'd get to know whether the evidence was likely to be damaging. Forewarned is fore-armed, after all.

'I don't know how SOCO missed this,' Oakley was saying. 'Still, there's no harm done, as it's been under these covers. Any trace evidence the killer left will still be on it.'

'Good,' I said weakly.

'I'll get an evidence bag.' Oakley jumped to his feet and hurried out to his car.

I snatched up the stone and rubbed it all over with my gloved hands. At first, I considered wiping it on my trousers, but the fibres from a police uniform would be easy to identify. Nothing would come off rubber gloves – which is why we wear them – and hopefully, they'd smudge and confuse any prints I might have left. James's hairs came off, floating gently down-wards to land on my shirt. Repelled, I brushed them off. When I heard Oakley's footsteps com-ing back, I shoved the stone back and stood innocently by the window.

'There were hairs on this a minute ago,' he said in surprise. 'I'm sure there were.'

'Really?' I asked, crouching next to him. 'Per-haps they blew off when you let the cover down. The draught must have dislodged them.'

'Damn! I thought I'd let it down carefully.' He began writing details on the evidence bag, then took a couple of photographs while I held up the cover. Finally, he picked up the stone and placed it in the evidence bag. It was done. Oakley had his murder weapon.

'I'm surprised at SOCO,' he said. 'They're usually very thorough.'

'They probably concentrated on the kitchen. After all, that's where the murder took place.'

'Not necessarily. It could have happened anywhere. In fact, given what we just found, I'd say it's more likely that he was bludgeoned in here.'

I felt like throttling him, exasperated by his caution and attention to detail. Wright wouldn't have been so difficult to manipulate.

'Look,' I said, lest he wondered why I was trying to mislead him. 'There's a hair. Perhaps that's one of the victim's.'

'It might be,' he agreed, collecting it carefully and putting it in another bag.

He got down on his hands and knees then, and spent a long time going over the carpet inch by inch, discovering another three hairs as he did so. I comforted myself by thinking that if one was mine, then at least I had a valid excuse for it being there. He'd asked me to come in, and people shed hairs all the time. He might even have found one of his own.

He gave me my rock to hold while he went outside and hailed Paul Franklin, who was doing house-to-house enquiries – working all along Orchard Street to ask if anyone had seen anything suspicious – with one of the female DCs. He told Paul that he was taking me back to the station for something to eat, since I'd been on guard duty for five hours already. Had it really been five hours? In some ways the time had gone quickly, while in others it felt as if I'd been there all my life.

Oakley radioed Wright and told him that he'd replaced me with Paul. Wright was furious, and said that standing guard wasn't hard – and that Oakley could get me a sandwich if he was worried. Oakley told him that finding the murder weapon should have some kind of reward. The radio went silent, with Wright doubtless fuming that such a glorious discovery should have fallen to me and that it should be announced publicly on the airwaves.

Oakley seemed almost jaunty as he started to drive back to New Bridewell, and I had the feeling that he was delighted to have riled Wright. There was bad blood between them, and I hoped *I* wasn't going to be used in whatever battle they were waging against each other.

Oakley didn't take Anderson straight to the station. He drove to the mortuary first, to ask Grossman whether the stone was the murder weapon. She followed him through the thick plastic doors of the loading bay where bodies were delivered, and he sensed she was dragging her heels. He knew how she felt – he hadn't been keen to see his first murder victim either. It wasn't the fact that the sight might be distressing – far worse things happen in traffic accidents that police have to attend – it was witnessing how easy it was to snatch away a life. In this case, a

171

single blow.

'It's all right,' he said. 'He'll have been put away by now. You won't have to see him.'

'It doesn't matter,' she replied in a brittle voice.

'The head wound wasn't particularly bad,' he went on. 'The worst part is that he's been left for a couple of weeks.'

'I'll have seen worse,' she said, although her face was pale, and he suspected she hadn't.

As it happened, he was wrong about the body. Grossman was still working on it, and it lay on a table with its chest cracked open and its innards in buckets below. The whole place reeked, and Anderson stopped dead in her tracks.

'It doesn't look like him,' Oakley thought he heard her murmur. He took her elbow, concerned by her sudden pallor.

'Doesn't look like who?' he asked kindly.

'I mean it doesn't look like a man,' she whispered.

'Well, it doesn't look like a woman,' said Oakley, wondering what she was talking about. The body was naked, and it didn't take an anatomy student to tell the difference.

'She means it doesn't look human, Neel,' explained Grossman, looking up from his work. 'Take the poor lass outside and give her a glass of water. This isn't everyone's cup of tea, and you know I don't approve of "who can stomach the grossest corpse" games in my mortuary.'

'Sorry, Helen,' said Oakley as he guided her out. 'I thought he'd have finished by now.'

'It doesn't matter,' she said, although he had never seen anyone so white. 'I'll wait outside.

172

It's hot in here.'

It was actually very cool, a temperature design-ed to suit the dead, but Oakley didn't contradict her. He sat with her on a low wall outside, afraid to leave her until some colour had come back into her cheeks. They waited in silence, until she took a deep breath and smiled wanly.

'Sorry, sir. I'm fine now.'

Back in the building, Oakley presented the bagged stone to Grossman, who compared its ragged surface to the bruises on the body's head. He looked at it from several different angles, muttering to himself. Not for the first time, Oakley wondered whether the pathologist was too old for the exacting work that was required of him. Eventually, Grossman straightened, smiling like a benign grandfather.

'You'd better get young Butterworth to take that to FSS, Neel. I'd say there's a good chance it's the murder weapon.'

Oakley stared at him for a moment before taking the stone. Had Grossman forgotten again about Mark's death? If so, what did that say about his ability to perform his professional duties?

I was furious with myself for nearly passing out when I saw the revolting sight in the mortuary, and even more furious for nearly informing Oakley that it didn't look anything like the man I'd left on the floor on Orchard Street. The only thing that looked familiar was James's dark hair, and even that was stained and matted. I could still smell the body, and taste the stench of it in

173

the air around me. The knowledge that I'd taken a warm, living person and turned him into that vile thing was almost more than I could bear.

As soon as the door closed behind Oakley, I started to cry. Perhaps I wouldn't get away with it after all, not because of the forensic evidence, but because I just wasn't strong enough to carry it off.

The familiar turmoil returned. What should I do? Tell Oakley that it was me who'd turned James into that mess of corruption and fly-blown flesh? I didn't think I could, not now. Surely the worst was over? I'd been back to where the terrible thing had happened, and I'd seen the body of the man I'd killed in all its awful glory. What could be more terrible than what I'd already been through?

'Don't worry about what happened,' said Oakley as he drove me back to the station. 'It was the same for me when I saw my first de-composed body.'

I was unable to suppress a shudder. 'I didn't know it'd be so...'

'It's August,' said Oakley, speeding up when a traffic light turned amber. That particular one had lags long enough that some drivers read their newspapers while they waited for it to change. 'It wouldn't have been so bad in winter. Grossman told me that the heat has accelerated the process, which is why it's going to be difficult to pinpoint a precise time of death.'

'Have you learned anything from door-to-door enquiries?' I asked, eager to change the subject. 'Or from FSS?'

'We've got nothing from the neighbours. Walls, hedges and fences mean no one saw a thing. Also, it isn't a particularly friendly street. The Smiths at number seven are the most social, but they were away. Mrs Greaves and her son from number eleven didn't see much either, although she recalls a woman in a scarf walking down the street two weeks ago on a Tuesday night.'

'A scarf?' I gulped. She'd seen me! Christ!

'A headscarf, like they used to wear during the war. The orange street lights distort colours, but she thinks it was dark and spotted. She remembers, because she says it's unusual to see women in scarves these days. Is that true?'

His question startled me. For one awful moment, I thought he was asking whether *I'd* worn the dark spotted scarf. 'I don't know,' I managed to whisper.

'Come on, Helen,' he pressed impatiently. 'I need the help of a woman here. Have you got such a scarf? How would you wear it? And would you do so in August?'

'No,' I replied tersely. 'I haven't got one. So I wouldn't wear it in August or any other month. Ask DI Davis. Or your girlfriend. I heard you were seeing a nurse from the hospital.'

Oakley gaped at me, almost neglecting to stop behind the car in front when it pulled up at a junction. I wouldn't have minded if he had at that point – a quick car smash would be a merciful end to my nightmare.

'How did you know?' he demanded. 'Is nothing sacred?' His expression hardened. 'Wright! I called Catherine from Orchard Street last night to let her know I couldn't meet her. My God, that man's a gossip!'

'Yes, he is,' I agreed, thinking of Wright spreading the story about Butterworth's Blunder.

Oakley was silent for a while, then said crossly, 'I can't ask Catherine to help me with a murder enquiry. It wouldn't be right.'

'But it's fine to ask me?' I shot back.

'You're a police officer,' he explained, as if that deprived me of my sex. He grinned suddenly. 'Besides, we're still at the stage where she thinks I'm Bristol's answer to Poirot, and I don't want to disillusion her just yet. It's nice, being admired. Do you have a boyfriend?'

I was tempted to tell him to mind his own business, but he was only being friendly. As far as he was concerned, we were just two colleagues, chatting to while away the time it took to travel to the station.

'Yes.' I suppose Colin was my boyfriend. We'd slept together, after all, and there were plans to see each other again. I could see Oakley was expecting more than a single syllable, so I elaborated, trying to put some emotion into a voice that was dead with the shocks of the day. 'He's an old school friend, but it's a fairly recent thing.'

'Like me and Catherine, then,' he said. 'We've not been together long. This is the first major case I've had since we met, so now she's learning what it's *really* like to date a policeman. The last one didn't like it at all.'

'Shift work?' I asked, trying to sound interested. I didn't want to know about his personal life. I just wanted to get away before I blurted out my whole, miserable story.

'Unpredictable hours,' he replied. 'Arranging to meet her, then not showing up. Letting her down on plans made months before. Leaving her alone every night. Expecting her not to mind me falling asleep when I did manage an evening at home.'

'Perhaps you should transfer back into uniform,' I said, aiming for jocular. 'At least shifts are vaguely predictable.'

'I like being a detective. What about you? Any designs on CID? Or the traffic department?'

'Neither,' I said, a little sullenly. 'Midsomer Norton was all right, but I hate New Bridewell.'

He seemed surprised by my vehemence. 'You're the one who needs the transfer,' he said wryly. 'You've let Wright get to you.'

'It's hard not to when he gives me all the crappy jobs and tells everyone that I'm the one he can do without.'

'I know what it's like,' said Oakley. I suspected he did, given that being seen as an ethnic minority wasn't any easier than being a female graduate where men like Barry Wright were concerned. 'You should make a complaint or tell him where to get off. But don't let him decide your future for you.'

'I won't,' I said. He was right. I *shouldn't* let Wright dictate my life. I shouldn't let Oakley decide it either, by confessing to murder as we sat slowly baking in his car. I'd decide for myself when – or if – I wanted to come clean.

'This scarf,' said Oakley, like a dog with a bone. People were right about him. He *was* tenacious. 'If you did have one, how would you wear it?'

'I suppose I'd put it round my head and tie it under my chin,' I replied, recalling that I'd tied it at the back of my neck.

He shot me an uncertain glance. 'You'd look like Nora Batty,' he said rudely. 'Mrs Greaves said this woman had fastened it at the back, and that she walked briskly, keeping her head down.'

'I'd never don a scarf in summer,' I said, aiming to make him believe I was the last person on Earth that the wretched Mrs Greaves could have seen. 'It would be too hot.'

'Quite. So, we can assume this person was trying to disguise herself. The scarf, the fast walk, and the fact that her head was down all suggest that she may have been up to no good.'

'No,' I countered, a little desperately. 'It means she might have just washed her hair and wore the scarf to keep it in place. Or that she *needed* to wash her hair, but had to go out for milk or cigarettes, so grabbed the scarf to hide it. Or that she was walking away from her lover, and didn't want to be recognized by someone who might tell her husband. It could mean all sorts of things.'

'But as we can't be sure it was the right day, it probably doesn't matter anyway,' he said with a despondent sigh. 'We're chasing phantoms. We're almost twenty-four hours into this case, and we don't even have the victim's name.'

'Marko Kovac,' I said.

'Perhaps.' He frowned. 'But it's a funny old case. If our victim was killed in the lounge – as the weapon you found suggests – why was he moved to the kitchen? And why wrap him up if he was just going to be left there?'

I saw an opportunity to discuss all the things I'd been wondering myself, reckless though that might be. I tried to sound as though my first question had just occurred to me. 'The only way out of the house is through the front door – the back one just leads to the garden. So why move the victim to the kitchen, when you'd have to drag him back past the sitting room if you were intending to spirit him away?'

He looked surprised that I was capable of such probing thoughts. He probably believed that a woman who swooned over corpses would be no good at murder solving. But I had lots of questions, and I was certain mine would be a lot more incisive than his. I started to go through them.

'Did the killer intend to bury him in the garden?'

'Only if he had a pneumatic drill. It's concreted over.'

'Then did the killer aim to carry the body away, but something happened to stop him? Or did he come back after a few days, but the body had started to smell, and he realized he didn't have the stomach for it? Or is he still intending to come back?'

Oakley raised his eyebrows. 'All very interesting points. Grossman thinks that studying the insect larvae will tell us when the body was wrapped in relation to its death, and I'm hoping that the plastic and the duct tape will yield fingerprints.'

Duct tape was a forensic dream. It was hard to use wearing gloves, as it tended to stick to them, and criminals often tore them off in frustration, leaving not only their prints, but other trace evidence, too. *I* wouldn't have used it to wrap a body; I would have opted for string or rope. Anyone using tape was either stupid or very skilled. I decided that Yorke's men were probably the former.

I realized at that point that I was the only one that knew there was a connection between the body and Yorke, although it probably wouldn't be long before that was rectified – not once FSS had analysed the duct tape. And I wanted Yorke's people caught, because then they wouldn't be in a position to come after me. I wondered how I could let Oakley know to look in Yorke's direction without incriminating myself. An anonymous note? Oakley should know that James had been aiming to fix Yorke's trial, too – the case that Oakley had worked hard to build. Perhaps my note should include something about a fictitious statement insinuated into the court file, as well.

'What kind of black plastic was used?' I asked curiously. 'I didn't see any bin liners when we were looking through the kitchen.'

'Stuff you buy by the meter from garden centres.' He must have seen my surprise because he added, 'I bought some to make a pond in Catherine's yard last week.'

'You'll be the prime suspect, then,' I joked, feeling a little better at last. The terrors were beginning to ease, although I'd be sure to take a sleeping pill when I went to bed that night, to get through the darkness and back into in the sunshine again.

He grimaced. 'If we get desperate, we'll have to visit garden suppliers and see who bought some recently. If the killer paid by credit card, we may catch him. Of course, if *I* wanted it to wrap around a body, I'd pay cash.'

'Perhaps the killer found it in the shed,' I suggested. 'Mine's full of things I think might come in useful someday. You'll need to see whether there's a lot of dust on it, consistent with being stored.'

Oakley groaned. 'I have a feeling this case is going to run and run.'

I hoped so, given that solving it would mean me in prison.

Sunday, 12 August
When the preliminary results from the forensics tests came though they were difficult to interpret. The problem wasn't that there was nothing to analyse, but that there was so much, resulting in a mass of information that took Oakley most of the day to trawl through. While he worked, Davis looked through witness statements, and by eight o'clock that evening they were ready to present their first tentative conclusions to their team.

The officers began to gather. All had had a busy day, and were hot, footsore, and mostly

181

empty-handed. Morale was high, though, as it had been the first full day, and even inexperienced officers knew that there was a lot of ground still to cover.

Taylor liked to keep all his officers, whether they were working on the case or not, informed of developments in major incidents as he felt it increased the general efficiency of the force as a whole, although there were details that would be kept between him and his inspectors as a precaution against false confessions.

Normally, Oakley approved of Taylor's open-book policy, but the Butterworth incident had made him aware of how dangerous gossip could be, and he wondered how long it would be before sensitive information was leaked to the press. His main suspect for that remained Wright, and he was not pleased to see the sergeant sitting in the front row at the briefing, as if he imagined himself to be a vital participant.

Taylor called the meeting to order. 'This won't take long, then you can all get off home. Unfortunately, progress has been slower than we hoped, but tomorrow is Monday, so hopefully we'll start getting answers as people return to work. Clare will summarize what we know so far about the victim and the circumstances of his death, then Neel will tell us what we've got from forensics. I'll conclude by outlining the leads we need to follow over the next few days. Clare.'

'We still don't have a definite ID, but the most obvious possibility remains Marko Kovac, and we have made initial inquiries as if he were the victim. No one at the university knew him very well, as he tended to spend all his time working with some specialist equipment. No one has come up with a reason as to why anyone should kill him.'

'What about his research?' asked Oakley. 'Nanotechnology.'

Davis looked puzzled. 'Yes – the science of doing things small. What of it?'

'The science of engineering or manipulating matter at an atomic or molecular level,' corrected Oakley.

'Sounds small to me,' muttered Evans.

'There's both an industrial and military demand for increasingly powerful technology using smaller component parts,' Oakley went on. 'Imagine how many circuits you could cram into a mobile phone if each was the size of an atom. It's a highly competitive field because there's huge commercial potential, and money is invariably a good motive for murder.'

'So Kovac's discoveries might have led another scientist to kill him?' asked Davis. 'Or perhaps he killed a rival. Of course, there's also the fact that he was in Macedonia when it was exploding. He may be suffering from shell-shock, or whatever it's called these days.'

'Post-traumatic stress disorder,' supplied the lugubrious Merrick.

Davis shuffled her notes. 'According to the university, Kovac arrived on the ninth of July, and rented a house from Academic Accommodations. We've not managed to contact anyone from the company yet. That's first on my list for tomorrow. Kovac was due to leave Bristol on

Tuesday, the thirty-first of July. Dave will tell you what he's done about that.'

Merrick stood, clearing his throat. 'I checked all flights in and out of Albania for the past three months, but Kovac wasn't on any of them. Trains are cheaper, so he probably travelled overland. The problem is that you just get on them – you don't need to book.'

'You *can*, though,' Oakley pointed out. 'It's the only way to make sure you get a seat.'

'Well, Kovac didn't – not in June, July or August,' said Merrick. 'There's also the possibility that he came by bus. Again, there's no way to tell. I checked with immigration, but Kovac has an open visa for six months, which means he can come and go as he pleases during that time. However, they've got no record of him doing either.'

'What are you saying?' asked Oakley. 'That he never came and so he never left?'

'I'm saying we can't confirm his movements,' said Merrick. 'Passport control may have just checked his visa and nodded him through. I've got an English-speaking officer from Tirana to look into him. I'm going to call him again tomorrow. Interpol have nothing, so Kovac's not on the FBI's most wanted list or anything.'

'Thanks, Dave,' said Davis as Merrick sat down. 'Mrs Greaves from number eleven saw Kovac on Monday the thirtieth, when he told her he was going home the next day. No one saw him after that afternoon, and no one saw him leave the house. However, there was no suitcase or luggage, so we can't dismiss the possibility that Kovac really has gone home and that we've got someone else's body here.'

'Anything else?' asked Taylor.

'Yes, sir. No one heard or saw anything unusual, except Mrs Greaves, who claims a woman walked down the street in a headscarf on the Tuesday night. It was too hot for such attire, so it stuck in her mind. I suggest we put this on the back burner, as it won't be easy to look into, and I'm not convinced it's relevant. But if any of you see a dark spotted scarf, bear it in mind. And that's it. We've got no reports of unusual activity, and no strange cars. Neel.'

'Forensics are slow at the moment – just like they've been since the lab in Chepstow closed down. Everything has to go to Solihull lab, which is overworked and underfunded, thanks to the government's austerity measures. I've been told not to expect anything from DNA for at least a couple of weeks—'

He was interrupted by a chorus of indignant objections. The loudest came from Superintendent Taylor. 'I trust you told them this is a *murder* enquiry?'

'Of course, sir, but it's not the only one, and the rather rude clerk who deigned to speak to me on the phone said it's low priority as our victim has been dead a while and the case isn't politically sensitive.'

'Cheeky bastards,' muttered Taylor. 'So what *did* you get from them?'

'That the house was thoroughly cleaned with bleach, which will have destroyed a lot of evidence. And we've got hundreds – literally – of

185

partial fingerprints that will take someone weeks to go through.'

'What about the time of death?' asked Davis. 'Any progress there?'

'We'll know more when we get the insect report, but at the moment it's been set roughly between Saturday the twenty-eighth of July and Saturday the fourth of August. Obviously, it would be nice to narrow it down, as if it was *before* the thirtieth, when Kovac talked to Mrs Greaves, we'll know he was either the killer or an accomplice.'

'There's another possibility,' said Davis. 'Someone stored the body in the house after Kovac left – a body that might have been dead for several days.'

Oakley shook his head. 'FSS managed to establish that the victim was killed in the house. In the sitting room, to be precise.'

'It was the kitchen,' said Wright belligerently. 'FSS is wrong.'

'The victim was *found* in the kitchen,' said Oakley. 'But he died in the lounge – his saliva was found there in the kind of pool that suggests that's where he breathed his last. However, the pattern of fluids that leaked from the body suggest he was moved to the kitchen not long after he died. The angle of the blow suggests he was kneeling or crouching and was hit from behind. So we have three possibilities: the dead man is Kovac; Kovac killed the victim and abandoned the body; or Kovac left the house as planned and the murder occurred shortly after.'

'Which of these do you favour?' asked Taylor.

'First or third,' replied Oakley. 'I don't see Kovac leaving a body in the house he rented, knowing it will be traced to him as soon as the body is discovered.'

'He might think he's safe in Albania,' Merrick pointed out. 'And he's probably right. The police there haven't been very cooperative yet.'

Oakley looked down at his notes and moved to the next item. 'Fibres: we've got plenty, but they're unlikely to give us any decent leads. What they *will* do, however, is allow us to match evidence from suspects, so they'll come into their own in time.'

'Good,' said Taylor, nodding. 'What about the plastic and the tape around the body?'

'Both commonplace, so it'll be hard to find where they came from. However, there are several partial prints on the tape, so let's hope FSS can give us a list of possible matches in time.'

'Here are our priorities for tomorrow,' said the superintendent. 'First, visit Academic Accommodations to see what they can tell us, and press the Albanian police to check whether Kovac is sitting at home playing with his molecules. Second, start looking through the missing person's file to see if our boy matches any outstanding reports. Third, I want the plastic and tape looked into—'

He was interrupted by Oakley. 'We can try, sir, but FSS said the best we can hope for is to match the jagged edge of our piece to the original roll. But miles of the stuff must be sold every day—'

Taylor cut him off in turn. 'Then we'd better

get going. I want all local garden centres, DIY centres and so on checked out. Fourth, I want the door-to-door enquiries widened to a larger area. I've marked it off on the map. Fifth, I want someone looking into this scientific mumbo-jumbo to find out whether it's worth killing for; I also want someone to investigate Kovac's mental health. Finally, we have someone's child, husband, or brother here, so I want tact and discretion. I don't want sensitive details leaked to the press. Next briefing is at six tomorrow evening. Questions?'

There were none.

'Get off home, then, and be back bright-eyed and bushy-tailed at seven thirty tomorrow.'

That night I went to meet Colin. I was in a strange mood, half elated and half scared, as though I'd somehow weathered a great test. At first, I hadn't been sure whether it was more difficult to know details of the case or to remain in ignorance. Now I knew – I'd rather know. It was the uncertainty that was worst, and each day seemed that much more precious to me because of it. I appreciated my walks to and from work, and I relished the sun on my face. I looked forward to meeting Colin, too. At least until my thoughts returned to that vile thing at the mortuary.

I sat in the bath and scrubbed and scrubbed, but I could still smell James – a thick, rank, filthy stench. It was how I felt inside: dirty, rotten, corrupted. I called my mother and listened to her chat about nothing, silent tears rolling down my cheeks when I realized that sweet lady would become a pile of slimy, oozing flesh one day. The thought stayed with me all evening, and I felt a nagging unease, as though I wanted to take hold of everything I loved and protect it.

Colin was nice. I told him that I'd been at a murder scene, but he must've sensed that I wanted to forget about it, and didn't press me for details. We had a drink in the Hole in the Wall, an atmospheric old smugglers' haunt, then walked hand-in-hand along the harbour.

Being summer, it was busy. Lights twinkled on the black waters, streaming out from the cafes, pubs and art galleries that line it. There was the smell of the water mixed with the aroma of frying onions from a hamburger van, and someone was lighting fireworks. They popped and echoed, sending sparkling rockets high into the sky and releasing them in veils of golden stars. Colin's hand felt warm and dry. I held it a little harder, trying to put away my black thoughts for a while.

'Helen? Is that you?'

I almost leapt out of my skin when I heard Oakley's voice. What was he doing here? Why was he impinging on my few moments of peace? Was there nowhere I could be safe? He was with a woman – Catherine, I assumed. She wasn't pretty, but her face had a lot of character. She wore a loose skirt of some light material, and a white blouse that looked cool and stylish. He was still wearing the clothes he'd worn to work, and I wondered whether she'd noticed the smell. Perhaps that was why they were standing some distance apart.

'Sir,' I said, attempting to appear normal. 'Off duty at last?'

He nodded, and turned to the woman. 'Catherine, this is Helen Anderson, the hero of the day.'

'Hero?' asked Colin, raising his eyebrows. 'She didn't tell me.'

'Too modest,' said Oakley, smiling. I could only stare at my feet while he told Catherine and Colin all about the stone – the one I'd used to murder Colin's school friend. I briefly considered shoving him into the water, just to stop him talking. I hoped he couldn't sense the growing anger in me.

'My hero,' said Colin, hugging me affectionately.

The three of them chatted for a few minutes, and on another occasion I might have suggested going for a drink. Now, I just wanted to go home.

'We should go,' I said, tugging Colin's arm.

'Yes,' agreed Catherine, wrinkling her nose. 'I think there's a broken drain nearby. Or perhaps it's the docks. Regardless, there's an awful smell tonight.'

'*I* had a bath,' I informed Oakley pointedly.

I saw the shock on his face as it registered that he should have done the same before spiriting his lady off for romantic walks in the moonlight. 'God!' he muttered, raising his sleeve to his nose.

'So, that's what it is,' laughed Catherine. 'At least it's not permanent.'

They made their farewells and walked away. I

heard them laughing, seeing the funny side of the whole thing. That was probably one of the advantages of dating a nurse, who'd be used to unpleasant smells. Colin was less stoic, and informed me that he'd rather I was late than appear smelling like something two weeks dead. I told him I'd bear it in mind.

We went to my house and made love until I was so tired I couldn't keep my eyes open. I clung to Colin all night, and whenever I woke with the spectre of the black mess in front of me, he was there, all warm, alive and comfortable. In the morning, I awoke feeling more refreshed than I had done in days. Perhaps it was because I'd faced my nemesis and come through it, or perhaps it was because Colin was there. I asked him if he'd come back that evening.

Monday, 13 August
As far as Maureen Paxton was concerned, the police had forgotten her son. She demanded to see an officer more senior than Oakley and was taken to Taylor, whom she did not like. He told her that people walked out of their lives for all manner of reasons, and that as there was no reason to think James was going to harm himself or anyone else, he could disappear if he wanted to.

Then she read about the body in Orchard Street in the papers. At first they said the corpse was unidentified. Then they said it was possibly an Albanian professor who'd gone missing at the time of the murder. But Maureen felt a gnawing sense of unease. James wasn't likely to have been in such an insalubrious part of the city, but his work did oblige him to meet some unpleasant people. What if he'd been visiting a client? Moreover, his meteoric rise had made enemies of some colleagues – instead of admiring him, they hated him.

Could James be the body in Orchard Street? She couldn't get rid of the niggling fear at the back of her mind. She was shaking when she arrived at New Bridewell and demanded to see Oakley, who had at least listened to her and been polite. She paced impatiently in front of the reception desk until he arrived. In his hand was a book about nanotechnology for DI Davis.

'Giles Farnaby,' she declared without pre-amble. 'Ask *him* what happened to James.'

Oakley regarded her warily. 'Why?'

'Because he's jealous of James. If James leaves Urvine and Brotherton, then Giles Farnaby' – she spat out his name – 'will be promoted.'

Oakley was aware that other people in the reception area were staring at them – a young mother in a tight black skirt that showed rather too much fat white thigh; an Asian bus driver, the knees of his uniform shiny with age; and a businessman with an umbrella. He took Maureen to one of the interview rooms and invited her to sit down.

'Do you have new information about James?' he asked, politely but firmly, so that she would know he didn't have time for speculation and unfounded accusation.

'No,' she admitted. 'But one of his colleagues has done something to him. They're jealous, you see.'

'Done what, exactly?' He saw her hands shaking, and was sorry for her distress.

'Foul play,' she whispered, a quiver in her voice. 'I want you to ask Farnaby what he's done to James. He lives in Bath. Here's his address. I got it from the telephone directory and I gave the number a call, so I know he's in.'

'You *phoned* him?' asked Oakley in astonishment. 'What did you say?'

'Nothing. I hung up when he replied.' Her voice hardened. 'I shall be at home this afternoon, so you can contact me there when you have answers.'

Davis ploughed through twenty pages of the scientific textbook Oakley had given her before admitting that she didn't understand a word. There were too many terms she didn't recognize, and too many assumptions were made about the reader's level of understanding. Oakley had offered to follow the nanotechnology lead, given his layman's interest in physics, but Taylor had assigned it to her instead. With a sigh of frustration, she tossed the book on the table. She glanced up and saw Oakley leaving.

'Where are you off to?' she asked.

'Bath,' replied Oakley, taking his jacket from the row of pegs in the hall.

She blinked. 'You're going to visit this Farnaby on the say-so of Paxton's lunatic mother? Come on, Neel! We've got a murder investigation here! We don't have time for her crap.'

'Actually, I'm going to speak to Professor Jinic

in the Balkan Studies Department at Bath University.'

Davis grabbed her bag. 'Can I come? Anything's better than this boring book.'

Oakley disagreed, thinking a couple of hours reading would be infinitely preferable to the congested roads to Bath. They inched along the A4, sticky and uncomfortable as enforced stops and an unrelenting sun heated the car to furnace levels. Yet again, Oakley wished he'd had the air conditioning fixed, and wondered if he'd have time to stop at the garage that week. Of course, the moment he did, the heat wave would end.

They reached Jinic's office at three o'clock and gratefully accepted a secretary's offer of a cool drink, after which they were shown into a book-lined room. The professor was elderly, with vast curling eyebrows and comfortably shabby clothes.

'You want to know about Albania,' he said, sitting in a large leather armchair and lacing his fingers over a sizeable paunch. There was barely a trace of accent left in his voice, although a clipping of vowels suggested he wasn't a native English speaker. 'Do you have a couple of days to sit here while I answer?'

Oakley smiled. 'Perhaps we could just ask you some questions?'

'Would they concern Marko Kovac? I read his name in the papers.'

'Do you know him?'

'Not well, but no one does – in England, at least. He dislikes being away from his family, and makes his trips shorter than he should, given the amount of work he hopes to do. He spends all his time here working, and socializes little.'

'He's unfriendly,' surmised Davis.

'Not at all. He's very friendly and very polite. He just works extremely hard. I suspect his reluctance to leave his family has more to do with Albania's inherent instability than with him not being able to cope without them. He's a responsible father.'

'You like him?' asked Oakley.

'Yes – as well as I like anyone with whom I have a passing acquaintance. He visited me last year – just before Christmas – to tell me news from the ground, as it were: what people think, what life is like away from government-control-led newspapers and television crews.'

'And what is it like?'

'Grim, but no more so than before. Nothing works very well. Roads, buildings and transport systems are crumbling and inefficient.'

'Yates the technician told me that Kovac had been in Macedonia when there was fighting,' said Davis. 'Do you think that affected him at all?'

'Of course,' replied Jinic. 'It would affect you, too. War is a terrible thing, and anyone involved will remember it forever. But if you want to know whether it affected Marko to the point where he might harm someone, then I'm afraid that's a question I can't answer.'

'Do you know anything about his work?' asked Davis.

'Only that it has great potential, and that several multinational companies are interested.

Industrial espionage is a reality in the world, so it is possible he was killed for his discoveries.'

'So,' concluded Davis, 'Kovac's experiences in the Balkans might have led him to harm someone here, and his work is commercially significant enough for someone to kill him?'

'That's about it,' said Jinic with a beatific smile. 'Have I helped you at all?'

'If we leave now we're going to be stuck in traffic for an hour,' said Oakley as they walked back to the car. 'But Giles Farnaby lives around the corner. We can wait it out while we talk to him, and who knows, perhaps he'll offer us tea.'

Davis sighed. 'All right, if you insist. Just don't tell Taylor.'

'Jinic didn't help much,' said Oakley, opening the car door and flinching backwards as the heat escaped. 'We already knew Kovac might be mentally unstable and that his work has commercial implications.'

'Which do you think is more likely? Kovac as the killer, or Kovac as the victim?'

Oakley shook his head slowly as he drove off the campus, all windows wide open. 'I'm not sure I'm happy with either yet.'

'Come on, Neel! We have a man who's been through a war, working on a lucrative branch of science. The moment he's due to leave the country, a body appears in his house. It can't be coincidence. Kovac *is* either the killer or the corpse.'

'I'll wait until we have more facts before I start guessing,' said Oakley stubbornly.

'I think Kovac is the killer,' said Davis, ignoring his cautionary words. 'I don't think people are murdered for industrial secrets any more. If Kovac's work was that good, some rich company would have hired him.'

'If he's the killer, then who's the victim?' asked Oakley, turning into a pleasantly leafy suburban road that was full of detached houses built from honey-yellow Bath stone.

Davis grinned. 'Even my guessing skills don't extend that far. A colleague, perhaps.'

'None reported missing.'

'That's because most are on holiday. Or perhaps he just snagged someone from the street. If he's gone insane, we can't expect a rational choice of victim.'

'But the victim wore a decent suit and leather shoes. We're not talking about a tramp.'

'Kovac liked shopping. Perhaps dressing his victims in good clothes is part of his ritual. Did you find out whether there are any unsolved murders in Albania?'

'Oh, yes,' said Oakley, pulling on to the driveway of a large house with ivy growing up one wall. The lawn was immaculately mowed, with stripes as precise as any stately home. 'Dozens. It's an uneasy country.'

Davis climbed out of the car and looked around appreciatively. 'Farnaby's doing well for himself. I'm surprised he needs to be made a partner if he lives here.'

'This is his mother's place. There's one behind every successful lawyer, apparently. At least at Urvine and Brotherton.'

The man who answered the door was stocky, with a head shaven to hide the fact that its owner was prematurely bald. He wore loose jogging pants and a polo-shirt with a logo on it that indicated it was probably expensive. He looked familiar, but Oakley couldn't place him. He would have asked, but Farnaby's expression was unfriendly.

'I've already spoken to the police,' he said when both officers showed him their warrant cards. 'So piss off and catch some criminals.'

'We're always on the lookout for criminals, Mr Farnaby,' said Oakley smoothly. 'And we find them in the most unexpected of places.'

'Look,' said Farnaby irritably, 'I don't know where James has gone, and I don't care.'

'If you don't care, then why have you taken the trouble to spread rumours about him heading off to some gay paradise?' asked Oakley.

'Because I saw him going into a gay bar,' snapped Farnaby. 'All right? It was in Clifton – one of those discreet places.' He smiled nastily. 'Old Brotherton is pretty peeved about James vanishing, I can tell you! That'll teach him to favour the little shit. A high-flyer Paxton might be, but there's a darker side to him.'

'And on the basis of seeing him at this bar you concluded that he's taken an overseas holiday with a homosexual lover?' asked Oakley.

Farnaby shrugged. 'I've been trained to make reasonable deductions. James was seen in a gay bar, then he goes missing. There's only one con-clusion that can be drawn – he's come out.'

'Not necessarily,' said Oakley, disliking the

arrogant man who kept them standing in the sun. 'He might have been meeting a client.'

'Well, he wasn't,' said Farnaby sulkily.

'How do you know? Did you follow him inside?'

Farnaby glared at him, caught out. 'Yes, because I thought someone should keep an eye on the bastard for the good of the firm. It was a fellow in his late twenties or early thirties. Dark hair. Suit. Sunglasses. A briefcase. Probably a businessman.'

'Why not a client?'

'Because I can tell the difference between scum like Yorke and Noble and decent human beings.'

'That's a curious attitude to take regarding your firm's clients.'

Farnaby's expression hardened. 'Urvine and Brotherton was respectable until James came along and started to represent lowlifes. Yorke and Noble are *his* clients, not mine. And I bet old Brotherton wishes they weren't on our books too – especially Yorke.'

'Then why did he represent Yorke at the remand hearing?' asked Oakley.

'Because James had already accepted his business. But it's clients like him who damage our image. They may be lucrative, but money isn't everything.'

'So you disapprove of Paxton bringing in new and wealthy clients?'

'Yes. I'm thinking of going to a firm where ethics mean something.'

'Have you seen Paxton since Tuesday, July the

thirty-first?' asked Oakley.

'No,' said Farnaby tightly. 'I saw him that lunchtime, bragging about how he was going to win the Yorke trial. And I saw him in the gay bar after work. I suppose he must have realized he'd bitten off more than he could chew, and buggered off before he made a fool of himself.'

'I thought you said he'd gone off with his homosexual lover,' pounced Davis, the expression on her face making her dislike of the man obvious.

Farnaby made a moue of annoyance. 'I don't know *why* he's gone. All I can say is that the firm is a lot nicer without him, and he can stay away as long as he bloody well likes.'

'And that's all?' asked Mrs Paxton, when Oakley called her to say he'd spoken to Farnaby.

'I don't think he knows anything about James's disappearance.'

She hung up, but the news did nothing to ease the uneasy, sinking sensation in her stomach. When days passed, and there was still no word nor any sign of James, her apprehension increased further still.

ELEVEN

Tuesday, 14 August

I was on duty at the hospital that afternoon, watching Emma Vinson, the old woman who'd been beaten during one of the Westbury Burglaries. She was taking an age to die, and while Oakley was still hopeful that she might remember something useful, I thought he was mad. Still, I didn't mind when he asked me to sit with her, in case she woke again.

He walked with me to the hospital, which was easier than driving in Bristol's traffic, because she'd asked for him the last time she was alert. While we went he told me about the Orchard Street case, and his growing suspicion that the body wasn't Kovac. Naturally, I did my best to argue, given that I didn't want him to start looking elsewhere for a victim, but he remained stubbornly adamant.

'Of course it's Kovac,' I said – almost snapped, in fact. 'Who else could it be?'

'You sound like Clare Davis,' he said, smiling. 'But there's something about this whole case ... suffice to say that I'm keeping an open mind.'

Bloody man, I thought, gritting my teeth. I was about to argue more, but we'd arrived at the ward. He went in and stood for a long time staring at the woman in the bed, but she didn't stir, and eventually he went away. Despite his annoying refusal to accept the Kovac theory, I couldn't help liking him, and I admired him more after seeing him with the old lady. He was a *good* man, and I wished he'd been my shift sergeant, not Wright. Then I'd have been happy in my work and James would almost certainly still be alive.

When he'd gone, I stood in the corridor so I didn't disturb the old lady, but I watched her carefully. I could see her thin chest rising and falling with each shallow breath, while the monitor at her side traced endless wavy lines that became mesmerizing after a while. I felt a surge of rage against the man who'd hit her, and hoped Oakley would make Yorke and his gang pay for what they'd done. I hoped they'd pay for what they'd done to *me*, too – if it wasn't for their crimes James would never have been in a position where he could blackmail me.

Then I recalled the idea that I'd had in Orchard Street, about connecting the Yorke gang with the murder – a link that was likely to be made anyway when FSS finally got round to analysing the duct tape and partials found on the plastic wrapping from James's body.

As I stared at Mrs Vinson, my idea of an anonymous letter pointing at the Yorkes seemed to be an increasingly good one. Oakley was moving away from the Kovac theory anyway, so why not point him in the right direction? I was fairly sure the gang didn't know I was the killer – I'd probably be dead if they had – but there was no question that I'd be safer without them walking free.

Yes, it would certainly suit me to have them arrested. And being hardened criminals they'd never reveal that the body was James, as that would help the police, something no self-respecting villain wanted to do.

I'd do it, I decided. Not only for me, but for Mrs Vinson and her family. And for all the other Mrs Vinsons who'd be hurt if Yorke and his minions were allowed to evade justice. I'd sworn an oath to protect people, after all, and what better way than removing a band of ruthless thugs from the streets? The fact that I'd be safer without them was immaterial. Or so I told myself in my guise as heroic defender of the vulnerable.

Friday, 17 August

'Maureen Paxton wants to see you *again*, Guv,' said Evans, putting his head around the door of the incident room. 'She's been here since seven – well over an hour.'

'What does she want now?' Oakley was reluctant to deal with her. He'd just finished going through more results from the Solihull lab – they'd been unable to match the DNA found in Orchard Street to anyone on the database. It was disappointing, but not unexpected. More sensitive tests had been ordered, but there was a backlog, so he'd been warned to expect nothing very soon.

'To see you,' elaborated Evans unhelpfully. 'She won't speak to anyone else, even Taylor. She says that if she has to deal with plods, then she'd rather have one who doesn't actually *look* like a Neanderthal, even if we all think like them.'

'She thinks she'll get what she wants by being abusive?'

'She has. Taylor says you're to talk to her nicely, then get her out of his station.'

'Great!' Oakley looked at the pile of witness statements, reports, interviews with cashiers from garden centres and reams of badly printed faxes from the Albanian police, most of which comprised accounts of their surveillance on every 'suspicious' academic in their country over the last ten years. Oakley had glanced through a few, and hadn't spotted Kovac's name once.

'I'm due at the mortuary at ten,' said Evans, looking at his watch, 'because that's when Grossman gets in. He forgot to sign his statement – he really *is* losing it these days. But I'm free until then, so I'll read some of that stuff, and highlight the page if I spot anything relevant.'

'I'll be gone ten minutes,' grumbled Oakley, relinquishing his seat. 'Not a second more.'

'About time,' said Maureen Paxton when Oakley entered the room where she'd been asked to wait. 'Are you aware that I've been in this miserable hole for more than an hour?'

Oakley sat in the chair opposite. He folded his hands on the table and forced himself to be patient. She was just a mother worried sick about her missing son. 'What can I do for you?'

She slapped a yellow folder on the table in front of him. 'These are copies of my son's dental records. I want them checked against the dead body in Orchard Street.'

Oakley blinked. 'Why?'

'Because I need to know.' Her voice was more desperate than demanding for once, and the tears in her eyes moved him. 'Please.'

Oakley considered. He didn't believe for a moment that the body was Paxton's, as the haughty lawyer was so unlikely to have been in a place like Orchard Street – if he had, he'd have collected samples from the man's flat and sent them to Solihull for DNA analysis. But Solihull was slow and expensive, and it would take Grossman no more than a minute to compare the records on the table with the body in his morgue. It was old-fashioned, of course, but it would cost nothing – especially as Evans was going over there anyway – and it would calm a frightened mother's fears.

'I'll send them to the pathologist this morning,' he promised. 'But is there any particular reason why you think the body may be James? Did he have friends in Orchard Street?'

'Of course not!' she snapped. A tear spilled, and she dabbed at it impatiently with a linen handkerchief. 'It isn't the kind of road he would frequent.'

'Then why...' He nodded at the file.

'Because I *know* something bad has happened,' she whispered. 'Mr Brotherton said he's on unpaid leave of unfixed duration. Do you know what that means?'

'No,' admitted Oakley.

'It means they assume he's dead.' Her chin

trembled. 'They'd have sacked him by now if they thought he was alive – and they're trying to protect themselves from looking callous when his body is found.'

'Are you sure you're not reading too much into it? Going away without telling your boss is grounds for dismissal by most companies. Perhaps Urvine and Brotherton are actually keeping his job open to give him the chance to explain.'

More tears spilled. 'I just need to know he's all right.'

Oakley took the records and stood up. 'I'll have this done this morning, Mrs Paxton. But are you *certain* there's nothing that's made you think the man in Orchard Street is James? He's never mentioned clients there?'

'No, but you can go to his office, and look at his files. That will tell you.'

'Let's take it one step at a time. We'll see what comes from the dental records first.'

'Thank you, Inspector.' Her voice was still unsteady. 'For taking me seriously, and for not telling me that everything will be all right.'

'I'll be in touch as soon as I hear the results,' he promised. 'Whatever they are.'

Mrs Vinson's plight had moved me, and I'd sent my anonymous note three days before. However, although I took every opportunity I could to talk to the Orchard Street team, I hadn't heard a thing about it. I'd taken a lot of care over it, so I hoped it wasn't lost in the post.

First, I'd bought the paper from W.H. Smith, a cheap and nasty pad for fifty pence. A packet of brown envelopes set me back seventy-five pence. I'd nudged them into the shopping basket without touching them and let the cashier put them in a bag for me. Once home, I wore gloves when I touched them. I used a cheap biro I'd found at work and I'd practised writing using capital letters and pressing quite hard. My own writing is light and flowing, and I never leave an indentation on the paper beneath. It seemed a good idea to make one now, to be certain it was as different from my own writing as possible.

I'd thought carefully about what to say. I wanted CID to know that Yorke was involved in the Orchard Street murder, but not that the body was James, lest it led to me. The Yorke mob would deny murder, of course, but why else would they try to get rid of the body? They'd go to prison, and good riddance.

I'd carefully cleaned the table with a hand-held vacuum cleaner, ridding it of any stray fibres that might be traceable. Then I'd placed the pad on it, and written:

BILLY YORKE KNOWS 9 ORCHERD STREET AND HE KNOWS WHAT HAPENED THERE. ASK HIM ABOUT IT AND HIS GOONS TOO. ASK HIM ABOUT FALSE CONFESIONS WHILE YOUR AT IT AND WHY HE WAS PISSED OF BECAUSE HE DID'NT GET BAIL.

I'd been pleased with the result, which I felt was enough to point them in the right direction without giving too much away. I was particularly happy with the spelling mistakes and poor punctuation, which added an air of authenticity. It wasn't too illiterate, just uneducated enough to have been penned by some thug with a vendetta against Yorke. It crossed my mind that I should hint that Noble wrote it, and thus strike a blow at him, too, but I decided not to push my luck. I could always write another later, if my first try at manipulating an investigation proved successful.

When the murder team started questioning Yorke's louts they'd think they'd been betrayed by a rival gang. The letter would never be traced to me. Again, I'd told myself as I wrote that I was doing the police, Bristol and Mrs Vinson a favour.

When I'd finished, I folded the note with my gloved hands and put it in an envelope, sealing it with a cloth moistened with tap water – I knew better than to lick it and leave my DNA. I addressed it to Oakley, thinking he'd be most likely to read it. Then I'd found that I didn't have a stamp, so I'd had to go to the post office. I put the envelope in a plastic bag, bought a book of second-class stamps, and found a quiet corner in which to don my gloves and stick the stamp on the envelope. I dropped the note in the letter box, still wearing my gloves, and went home.

When it was done I'd felt a curious mixture of apprehension and relief. I felt I'd done something good, yet it had been a risk. Mentioning the false confession was dangerous, as it might lead to James – and if he'd told a friend that he was blackmailing me, or had written anything down I'd have some explaining to do. But I sensed that James had been too wise to leave evidence to

prove he'd been involved in something untoward.

However, it was now three days later, and I
hadn't heard the merest whisper about it. There
were plenty of hoax calls, of course – strange,
self-obsessed souls who wanted to believe that
they had the courage for murder, and who regularly confessed to all manner of crimes. There
were calls about the identity of the body, too,
including one that claimed Marko Kovac was an
Albanian spy. I began to feel sorry for Kovac,
having his life pawed through by policemen,
when the poor chap was probably happily making sandcastles on the beach with his children.

But where *was* my letter? In Oakley's bin?
Lost in the post? Dismissed because it was
anonymous? I realized I should have sent it first
class, because second class was notoriously
slow. Or perhaps I should have shoved it into the
station letter box. Should I send another, or leave
the whole matter alone?

Oakley went back to the incident room after
leaving Mrs Paxton. Evans had gone and Dave
Merrick was in his place, reading the Albanian
faxes and occasionally scoring a page with an
orange highlighter. Oakley began to make tea,
using the kettle in the corner, and told him about
Maureen Paxton.

Merrick was sceptical, believing that she was
only convinced something untoward had happened because she couldn't accept the fact that
her son was in the process of coming out. Glancing around to make sure they were alone,

Merrick explained that becoming aware of one's sexuality was a momentous occasion, and struck different people in different ways. Oakley noted how knowledgeable the man seemed to be on the subject, and he regarded Merrick with new understanding as he poked the teabags around in the hot water.

'Being a gay police officer can't be much fun,' he remarked with increased empathy for his colleague.

Merrick hesitated before answering. 'It isn't,' he finally replied.

'Is that why you transferred?' Oakley had always thought the ageing parent excuse odd.

'There was a Wright in my station,' explained Merrick. 'It just seemed easier to go. But the point I'm trying to make is that this respectable lawyer, who's never been overly interested in girls, suddenly realizes that there's actually nothing wrong with him, and that there are other people who feel the same.'

'Liberating,' mused Oakley, heaping powdered milk into the cups.

'Liberating and frightening. He'd want to do something about it straight away, to test himself. His career, family, friends – all would pale into insignificance, and he'd be desperate to act on his new discovery. So Paxton's sudden disappearance doesn't seem at all strange to me.'

'So you think the office rumour is true, and he'll turn up safe and sound when he's decided he's found the real him?'

'I do.' Merrick regarded the tea Oakley handed him in distaste, and added more sugar.

'Do you have any particular reason for telling me this? For example, have you seen him in one of these clubs? Or perhaps heard that he's been rethinking his life?'

'Yes.' Merrick gave a rare smile. 'I know I can trust you – you know what it's like to be different and have men like Wright all over you. Can you imagine what he'd be like with me?'

'Only too well.'

'I saw Paxton at a watering hole I go to now and then because I've got friends there. It was on a Tuesday evening two and a half weeks ago.' He glanced at the date on his watch. 'It must've been Tuesday the thirty-first, and it was early evening, because I'd gone there straight after work.'

'You're not the only one to have seen him there that day,' said Oakley thoughtfully. 'So did Giles Farnaby. At least, I assume it was the same one. In Clifton?'

Merrick nodded. 'Yes.'

'How do you know he wasn't picked up by a killer?'

Merrick grimaced. 'You probably think gay bars are places where you march in and grab the nearest like-minded man. Well, they're not. This is just a quiet spot where decent, hard-working people go for a drink after work with the kind of friends we don't have to pretend to.'

'Like Paxton?' asked Oakley.

'Perhaps. We don't vet those who come in. It's a low-key place. Folk often pop in and leave again without ever even suspecting that it's different.'

'So, what happened? Did you see Paxton browsing through holiday brochures?'

'No. He was with someone, though. No one I've seen before. He and Paxton sat together drinking. I finished my beer and left as fast as I could.'

'Why?'

Merrick sighed. 'Why do you think, Guv? The last thing I need is for a defence lawyer to see me in a gay bar. What if he brings it up in court? What if he uses it to blackmail me? My personal life is my affair, and I don't want it bandied about. Life's hard enough, and if I decide to come out, then I'll do it on *my* terms, not some slimy lawyer's.'

'So he didn't see you?'

'Damn right he didn't! I was on the other side of the room and he was deep in conversation. It was an amiable discussion though – they were both laughing and nodding, and each seemed interested in what the other was saying.'

'Like a date?' asked Oakley, thinking about Catherine.

'Possibly. But I'd put my money on the holiday theory before him going to some slum house in the city and getting himself topped.'

'Your story fits what Farnaby said. He didn't know the man Paxton met either, so we can assume it wasn't a colleague.'

'I can make a few discreet enquiries,' offered Merrick. 'Tim Hillier – Paxton's only friend at Urvine and Brotherton – was helpful with letting us see Paxton's email. I'll ask him for another look, and see if I can spot anything.'

'Go ahead. Meanwhile, I'll get Graham to take Paxton's dental records to the mortuary. At least she'll know he's not dead.'

'She might prefer it if he were,' said Merrick softly. 'She doesn't look like the kind of woman who'd be supportive of a homosexual son.'

The post had arrived by the time that Oakley finished his discussion with Merrick. He flicked through it quickly, making sure there was nothing urgent before he returned to his paperwork. The cheap brown envelope was sandwiched between two larger ones. From the look of it, it had been kicking around the sorting office for a while, because there was a large footprint on the front. He tore it open and read the message inside with raised eyebrows. He dropped it on the table, not wanting to sully it any further with his fingerprints.

He read it again. Clearly Yorke wasn't involved in the Orchard Street death because he'd been in prison when it happened, but his gang – 'goons' as the note called them – had been free. What sort of word was 'goon'? And to what did 'false confessions' allude? Yorke hadn't made any confession at all.

He was tempted to throw the note away, sensing it was no more than spite, but instead he put it and the envelope into separate evidence bags, then made copies of the message. The original was logged in the evidence book and placed in a box for delivery to Solihull. The whole thing was probably a hoax, but there was no harm in being careful. He pinned one copy on

213

the bulletin board and put another in a filing tray to be scanned and added to the HOLMES database.

He was about to return to paperwork when he saw the dental notes and realized he'd forgotten to give them to Evans. He snatched them up and dashed up the stairs towards the car park, but Evans' blue Volvo had gone. He swore under his breath, then spotted Helen Anderson.

'Busy?' he asked casually.

'We're pretty quiet at the moment, but there's no car for me, so I'm on foot patrol.'

'Anywhere in particular?'

'Nowhere exciting – the lower end of Gloucester Road. How's the investigation?'

He hesitated, unused to giving confidential details to people outside CID, but then carried on. She had found the murder weapon, after all, and deserved something for the contributions she had made. Besides, it would annoy Wright if he confided in her. 'We're not much further forward than we were a week ago. The Albanian police aren't very helpful, and don't understand that all we want is his DNA or fingerprints.'

'They won't go to his house in Tirana?'

'Oh, they've done that, but the family has gone to some unspecified seaside campsite for the summer. No one's seen Kovac since he left for England in early July.'

'Kovac won't have gone camping,' she said with conviction. 'At least not straight away.'

'Why not?' asked Oakley, puzzled.

'Because he just spent three weeks working really hard. He won't take his precious data to the seaside. He'll go home to make sure it's all backed up on the computer or wherever. *Then* he'd go on holiday.'

'Well, no one's seen him there.'

'Then his disappearance is ominous, I'd say.'

'That's what Clare thinks,' said Oakley. 'She believes he's our killer.'

'Not the victim?'

'She doesn't think his research was important enough to see him killed.'

'I thought he was involved in something that might generate lots of money. You can't get a better motive for murder than that.'

'Perhaps. But I think that if Kovac really was on the brink of something big, some company would have made him an offer he couldn't refuse – and I don't mean in the Mafia sense. But this whole case has a peculiar feel to it. There's something we're missing, but I can't pinpoint what.'

'Did you get much response from the press conference?' she asked, changing the subject rather abruptly. 'Any new witnesses or leads?'

'Not really. All we've got is this woman in the scarf seen by Mrs Greaves, which is probably nothing, and the usual hoax confessions and bogus scraps of information.'

'Such as what?'

He shrugged. 'Weird notes, people phoning to tell us their husband, father or son is responsible. Most are rubbish, but you never know, so we've got to look into them all.'

'Weird notes?'

'I had one just this morning, saying that Billy

215

Yorke knows something about the murder. It's on the bulletin board. Go read it. But before you do, I was wondering if you could help us.'

She looked at him suspiciously and he laughed as he handed her the keys to an unmarked Ford Fiesta in the CID car pool.

'Run this down to the mortuary. It's all right – I'll clear it with Wright.'

'What is it?'

'Dental records. It's unlikely to be this particular man, but I promised I'd get it checked out.' He regarded her thoughtfully. 'But you knew him, didn't you? James Paxton.'

She blanched, but he was looking at Clare Davis arriving after more interviews at the university, and was wondering if she'd managed to find anything new.

'What do you mean?' asked Helen sharply.

'You met him at the Noble trial.' Davis was searching for somewhere to park, so Oakley waved to where Evans' car had been. 'His mother reckons he might be our Orchard Street victim, so we'll run it through the system, just to put her mind at rest. Hand them to Graham Evans at the mortuary, then come back here to let me know you did it.'

Anderson took the records and walked towards the CID car while Oakley went to tell Wright that he'd taken the liberty of commandeering one of his officers. The sergeant was in the radio room, burly arms resting on the top of a computer console. He was telling Jeeves a story, chuckling as he did so, and Oakley distinctly heard 'thieving niggers' in the muttered confidence. Oakley

216

stood quietly until they saw him, at which point Jeeves promptly began to take an intense interest in the notes that were scattered across his desk. Wright showed no such discomfiture and merely eyed the inspector with disdainful defiance, returning to his tale.

'A word, Barry,' said Oakley shortly.

Wright ignored him. 'Well, you can imagine what I said to that.' He chortled again. 'I mean, what would you have done? There he was, black as the bloody ace of spades, telling *me* that—'

'Sarge,' interrupted Jeeves, desperately trying to stop him before he landed them in more trouble. 'Can you get the duty rosters? I need someone to take a domestic in Kingswood Road.'

'Send Anderson,' suggested Wright. 'She's doing bugger all, as usual.'

'I want to talk to you *now*, sergeant,' snapped Oakley, walking towards one of the small interview rooms. It was a couple of minutes before Wright deigned to appear, and by then Oakley was fuming. Oakley did not lose his temper very often, but Wright had gone too far. He closed the door with a bang.

'Two things,' he snapped. 'First, I sent Anderson to the mortuary with urgent paperwork for the pathologist. *I* told her to go; she didn't volunteer. If you have a problem with that, take it up with me. Second, it may have escaped your notice, but racism is a sackable offence.'

Wright leaned insolently against the wall. 'Racism? Me?'

'If I hear you use offensive language one more

217

time, I'm going to lodge an official complaint. You're lucky I'm busy or I'd do it now.'

'You wouldn't report me,' said Wright confidently, piggy eyes glittering with malice. 'And even if you did, no one would believe you.'

'No?' asked Oakley coldly, fixing him with an icy glare. 'Let's see whether you're right, then, shall we?'

He hauled open the door and left, knowing that walking away before Wright had had his say would annoy him.

'Fuckin' Paki,' came Wright's furious voice. 'Go back to the jungle where you came from.'

'Were you talking to me, Sergeant?' asked Clare Davis, who happened to be passing. Oakley kept walking, wondering whether Wright was worth the bother of the paperwork that would follow. 'Or was some other officer the target of your eloquence?'

'Fuck off,' stormed Wright, pushing past her and heading back to the radio room.

With great deliberation, Davis made a note of the encounter in her pocket book, and asked the two CID men who were with her to sign the account as a record of what they had heard. The younger one took the pen without hesitation, despising the sort of officer who gave the force a bad name. The older signed with misgivings. He'd known Wright for a long time, and personally thought Davis was over-reacting.

In the radio room Jeeves pretended to be too busy to talk to Wright. The radioman liked Oakley but Wright was his shift sergeant and he owed him his loyalty. He didn't know what he'd do if Oakley did make a complaint and he was called to testify, but he certainly wished Wright would go away at the moment.

Meanwhile, Wright railed and fumed, enraged by the fact that officers he considered inferior imagined they had a right to tell *him* what to do. He'd been on the streets for twenty-five years, and knew more about policing than any minority or any woman could ever hope to know. If the country wanted its streets to be safe, they should get rid of the do-gooders and let solid men like him get on with it. And CID had no right to take his officers without permission either. Oakley might outrank Wright, but he had no right to use uniform to run CID's errands.

'Recall Anderson,' he ordered furiously. 'Now. I want her here right *now*. I don't care what she's doing for bloody CID. Now, Jeeves.'

Jeeves did as he was told, fervently hoping that Anderson wouldn't argue or say that she'd oblige in five minutes after she'd completed whatever Oakley had asked her to do. He heaved a sigh of relief when she merely informed him that she was turning around immediately. From the resigned tone of her voice he could tell she anticipated trouble, and felt sorry for her.

'We'll see about this,' Wright hissed. 'I'm going to make a complaint. Harassment.'

Jeeves blinked. 'A complaint about who, Sarge?'

'Bloody Oakley,' snapped Wright. 'And bloody Davis. They've been after me for months, and I'm going to report them to Taylor. He'll get the bastards off my back.'

Jeeves pretended to busy himself again, wondering how Wright could possibly see himself as the victim in the unpleasant scene that had unfolded. When Wright eventually left, Jeeves dialled Oakley's extension and told him how Wright had started talking to him, not forgetting to mention that he hadn't been comfortable with Wright's stories, but what could he do? He was a sitting duck in the radio room, where anyone could come in and rant – it wasn't as if he could walk away. And Wright was a sergeant. Constables didn't tell sergeants what they could and couldn't talk about. But Jeeves didn't approve at all. *He* wasn't like Wright.

'Now, where have I heard *that* before?' Oakley muttered as he put down the phone.

Dave Merrick sat in the incident room and pondered who Paxton might have been meeting in the Clifton bar. A lover? A friend? A client? He hoped it wasn't a client, given what Paxton did for a living – he didn't want criminals to frequent a place he'd grown to think of as a safe haven. The possibility nagged at him though, and he decided he wanted to know – for his own peace of mind as much as anything else.

Because he was new in Bristol he didn't know many local villains, and to find out if the man with Paxton had been a criminal would mean hours on the computer. Merrick figured he'd be wasting his time, but aimed to try anyway. He suspected Taylor would disapprove of him going off on a tangent when there was work to be done on the Orchard Street case, but a hunch was a hunch, and Merrick decided to follow his gut instinct, which also told him to start with Yorke and his associates. He logged in and entered Yorke's name, scrolling down the list of known associates. There were quite a few, although the most relevant were his brother and his 'business partner', David Randal.

Merrick looked at Randal first, but the thick-featured face that glowered out at him from the screen wasn't the man in the bar, nor was young Michael, who was nothing like the handsome man who'd been with Paxton. Curiously, he clicked the 'more information' button, to see why there was almost twenty years between the brothers' dates of birth. The answer was that their father had taken a second wife, resulting in a baby just as his first son was graduating from juvenile detention centres to adult prisons.

Merrick worked steadily, looking at all Yorke's known associates, and when he finished he pulled up Noble's file and did the same with him. Then he stopped, because there were too many to look at in one sitting. But he had a good memory for faces, and the one in the bar had been a pleasant one. If Paxton had been meeting a criminal, Merrick would find him.

When Oakley presented me the envelope containing James's dental records, I don't know how I managed to stretch out my hand and take it. Was there someone up there who knew what I'd done and was determined to ensure that I played a role in every aspect of this wretched case? Was this the way I was going to be punished – by

221

being forced to deliver the documents that would begin to give the police their answers? And why the hell was he bothering with dental records anyway? Surely they were a bit passé in the age of DNA analysis?

'His mother delivered them,' explained Oakley when I'd asked the last question rather snappily. 'It's unlikely to be him anyway, so no point in wasting valuable police resources with expensive tests from FSS.'

He didn't think the body was James! Well, that was a relief. So why was the wretched man bothering with dental records? My thoughts were in such turmoil that I pulled into a side street and parked, to give myself time to think it all through. I didn't think I'd acted suspiciously when Oakley had given me the envelope, although it occurred to me that he might have heard my heart thumping. I suppose he'd assumed any reluctance on my part was to do with Wright. At least, I hoped so. So what was I going to do? I didn't want him to identify James. I wanted everyone to go on thinking the body was Kovac's. Then, if all went well, communications with Albania would eventually break down, and they'd never know whether the missing scientist was dead or alive. Kovac was a very convenient corpse for me.

I pulled the computer-printed pages from the envelope and studied them. There was a chart with boxes for each tooth, crosses marking off the ones that had been extracted or lost, and black ink marking where fillings were. I did the only thing I could: I took a black pen from my bag and put a cross over James's upper right second premolar and gave him a filling in his lower left central incisor, relieved to see that the ink was a pretty good match.

I was pleased with myself. That should confuse them! Even if they did eventually check the dentist's computer, the delay I'd caused would work to my advantage. Witnesses would become less certain of what they had seen, or would move away, and that could only help me. Clearly the best way forward was to slow the whole thing down: the longer they took to identify James, the more difficult it would be to trace him to me. Mrs Greaves would forget what she had noticed about the woman in the scarf, and there might even be a way I could get at James's phone records. I wondered what more I could do to keep the Kovac line of enquiry going, given that it was the biggest time-waster.

I was glad that my note had finally arrived, but had I done the right thing by sending it? Obviously, the best outcome would be for the Yorke gang to be charged with Kovac's murder. Should I send another, to point them in that direction? I decided I'd have to. I'd also visit the incident room when I got back, to see what I could find out. After all, Oakley himself had told me to go and look at the note.

I started the car and was about to ease back into the traffic when the radio crackled. I answered, and Jeeves told me to return to the station immediately. My stomach did somersaults. Why? Had Oakley read my horror after all, and was waiting to arrest me? Had my letter given

223

something away? But I'd been so careful! Surely a hair or a flake of skin hadn't dropped into the envelope! Had it?

My poor heart was thudding again and I thought I might pass out, but then I realized what Jeeves had said: that *Wright* wanted me back. I closed my eyes in relief. Wright had heard what Oakley had told me to do and objected to me being used as CID's errand runner. Wright was just playing power games. I needed to stop jumping in alarm every time something perfectly normal happened, or I'd end up betraying myself. I had to get a grip.

'I've got a man from Academic Accommodations in the interview rooms,' said Merrick, walking up to Oakley and Davis. 'It's taken me this long to get hold of anyone, as the place shuts down for two weeks in August for holidays. Anyway, he's in number three. His name's Geoff Jessop.'

When Merrick had gone, Oakley turned back to Davis. She'd been telling him that, despite spending the best part of three days at the university, she'd learned little about Kovac. He was polite, worked hard and missed his family. He'd once mentioned a brother in the Albanian secret police. Davis intended to ask Professor Jinic for more specifics about that particular organization, to help determine how such an involvement might bear on the case.

'That's it, really,' she said. 'I wish I had more. But a word before you go, Neel – I'm making an official complaint about Barry Wright. Will you

224

back me?'

Oakley nodded. 'But are you sure? He's not a man to go down quietly.'

'He told me to fuck off. I can't ignore that. Frankly, I'm surprised you aren't doing the same. I heard what he said to you.'

Oakley shrugged. 'He's not worth the paperwork.'

'So it's all right for him to tell senior officers to fuck off, and call them any names that happen to enter the mass of slime that passes for his brain?'

'He's a dying breed, and he knows it. That's his problem – he sees the old order changing and isn't happy with the new.'

'Bullshit!' declared Davis. 'Don't make excuses for him! Have you seen how he persecutes Helen Anderson? Giving her all the bum jobs and running her down in front of her colleagues? I'm surprised she's stayed as long as she has. And you should certainly want to see him on the carpet. You know how he feels about *you*.'

Oakley nodded. 'He started a rumour that it was me – not him – who left his lunch on the floor at Orchard Street. Luckily, everyone knows I don't eat station chips, or people might have believed him.'

Davis pulled a face that registered her disgust. 'I took that photo down. We don't want officers from other stations asking why we've got pictures of vomit pinned up. Who put it there?'

Oakley grinned. 'Not me, although I half wish it had been.'

He strongly suspected Merrick, who, as Oak-

225

ley now knew, had good reason to dislike Wright and his bigoted intolerance.

Geoff Jessop was a burly, confident man in his fifties who wore a tweed jacket, old corduroy trousers and a tie with a small knot. He employed two clerks – one for mornings and one for afternoons – and a cleaner. The company took details from anyone who had a house or a flat to rent, and matched them to visiting scholars who needed somewhere to stay. They had a range of properties on their books, from expensive six-bedroomed houses in Westbury to seedy bedsits in Bedminster. Some owners wanted long-term tenants while others preferred short term. Number nine Orchard Street was in the latter category.

'Its owners live in the Middle East.' Jessop passed Oakley a card covered with handwritten notes. 'There's all the information we have, including a list of everyone who's rented it since it came on to our books last summer.'

Oakley scanned it quickly. 'Three stays by Doctor Kovac, none for longer than three weeks, and half a dozen others, but it's empty a lot. It can't be making much money.'

Jessop took the card, adjusted his glasses and studied it. Then he passed it back to Oakley. 'You see where it says "4wmx"? That means "four weeks maximum". That's not much use for scholars who need to be here for a term or more. The ones who come for the odd week usually prefer our bed-and-breakfast service. Orchard Street won't get many takers by imposing that condition.'

'Why do it then?'

'I imagine the main objective is for us to keep an eye on it,' replied Jessop. 'Our cleaner goes round the day the tenants leave, to make sure all's ship-shape and Bristol fashion. Short-term contracts mean it gets cleaned more often.'

'Will this cleaner have been to Orchard Street after Kovac left?' asked Oakley, his interest quickening.

'Of course. Gail will have given the place a quick once-over on the Tuesday morning, but Kovac usually leaves the place very clean so there won't have been much for her to do. An American is due in next week, but I suppose we'll have to find him somewhere else.'

Oakley nodded that he would. 'I'm surprised you didn't hear about the murder. It was in all the papers.'

'I never touch a paper when I'm away. That's why I go – to escape.'

'I should try that myself,' muttered Oakley. 'Can you tell us anything about Kovac? Has there ever been any trouble with him?'

'None,' said Jessop firmly. 'We wouldn't have leased him a property again if there had been. We can't afford troublesome tenants, but most are no bother – they don't get their deposits back if they misbehave.'

'Did you give Kovac his deposit back?'

'No – he's booked for another visit in December, so we agreed that it would be easier for us to keep it, rather than to fiddle about with cheques each time he comes. I didn't even see him when he arrived in July. We sent the keys to the university.'

'How was he going to get them back to you?'

'I don't know.' Jessop rubbed his forehead. 'No, wait a minute! He was going to leave them on the kitchen table for Gail the cleaner, and close the door behind him so it locked. That's right. That's what he did the last time, too. You'll need to ask her whether he left them or not, because I've been gone since just about the same time that he would have completed his stay, and I've not caught up on such details yet. Here's her address.'

'Is there any more you can tell us about Kovac?' Oakley smiled encouragingly. 'As we haven't been able to get a much of an impression from anyone else.'

Jessop sat back and closed his eyes. 'A family man. Wife and two children. Excellent physicist – he had a paper in *New Scientist* a couple of years ago. He loves England. Well, actually, what I think he likes are the shops. He decks himself out in good suits and takes stuff home for his family. He always comes with a briefcase, and goes home with two suitcases.'

'How does he pay for it? I doubt he earns a princely salary in Tirana.'

Jessop shrugged. 'A grant perhaps. The EU can be generous to promising research.'

'We found no suitcases.' Oakley refrained from telling Jessop they'd found precious little else either – just a corpse in black plastic.

'Then I imagine he took them with him. The killer must've seen an empty house and used it for his horrible work. I can tell you for certain that Kovac didn't do it. He's a physicist.'

Oakley wasn't sure that the two remarks necessarily followed. 'Then what about the possibility that the body might be him?'

Jessop frowned. 'Why would anyone would want to kill him?'

'That's what we're trying to find out. Can you tell us any more about him?'

'He has a brother who's a secret policeman. I believe that's rather more sinister in Albania than it is here. Perhaps that's an avenue you should explore.'

'We are,' he said, thinking that discovering more about the Albanian security services was exactly how Davis intended to pass her afternoon. 'Now what about the house's owners? Who are they?'

'We don't deal directly with them. We work through their solicitors – Urvine and Brotherton.'

I don't think I'd ever seen Wright so angry. His face was flushed an ugly red, and veins stood out in his neck and on his forehead. I could see one of them pulsing. He was sweating, too, and his hands were shaking. I knew straightaway that *I* was in trouble because Oakley had used me to run his errands. It wasn't fair.

'*I'm* your senior officer,' he began in a low, menacing voice. We were in the briefing room – he didn't even have the decency to dress me down in the privacy of an office. 'You do what *I* tell you, not some jumped-up Paki with inspector's pips on his shoulder. So, tell me why you ran his errands when I'd already told you what *I* wanted you to do?'

I could see he expected an answer. 'He asked me, Sarge,' I said lamely, turning James's dental records over in my hands. I tried to keep my head up, not stare down at my feet like some chastised teenager. I couldn't bear the contempt in his eyes, so I stared at his mouth, and his nicotine-stained teeth. 'He's an inspector. I didn't feel I could say no.'

'Didn't feel? Didn't feel?' he mocked. 'We're not paying you to "feel", missy. We're paying you to be a police officer. And that means obeying orders, not sticking your nose up CID's arse. And don't think *you'll* be a detective. Frankly, you're not good enough. You're lazy, unreliable and you just haven't got it in you. If you had any sense of responsibility you'd do the decent thing and resign.'

Tears pricked at the backs of my eyes and I tried to fight them back. I knew that Jeeves and Paul Franklin were listening in the radio room, and several others were doing paperwork nearby, trying to look as though they weren't there. I felt myself go hot all over and the heat blaze from my face. I was embarrassed, humiliated.

'You're useless,' he continued. 'Yes, go on! Blush! You should be ashamed of yourself. You're a disgrace to the uniform. Just because you've got a *degree*' – his voice turned sneering again – 'you think you're better than the rest of us, that the rules don't apply to you.'

I felt his spit hit my face, and I raised a hand to

wipe it away. I was horrified to find that the tears I thought were under control were trickling down my cheeks.

'I've had my fill of your sly tricks. I'm—'

'That's enough, Sergeant,' said Davis sharply.

Oakley was behind her and Jeeves behind him. Had Jeeves gone to fetch them, to put an end to my shame? I felt so embarrassed that I wished the ground would open and swallow me up.

'Helen, go get a cup of tea,' said Davis. Her eyes were hard and cold, but not with me, with Wright. It was awful. She was going to make things worse by interfering. I turned and ran out of the briefing room, unable to stop the sobs that racked me. I hated Barry Wright! He had no right to say all those things. Oakley was behind me, and he caught my arm.

'Wait,' he said. 'This is my fault. I'm sorry. I should've known better.'

I didn't reply, because I just couldn't speak. I stared dumbly at him.

'I'm sorry,' he said again. He rubbed his forehead with the tips of his fingers. 'Look, I'll ask Taylor if we can get you seconded to CID for the Orchard Street enquiry. The thing seems set to run for a while, and by the time it's over things will have calmed down, and we can get you on to a shift with a different sergeant.'

I still couldn't speak. I was aware of Jeeves and Paul standing next to me. Jeeves put a hand on my shoulder and squeezed it.

'Ignore the bastard, Hel,' he said gently.

'We're all going out for a drink tonight,' said Paul with forced cheerfulness. 'Come with us.

It's in the Red Lion, PCs only and no sergeants. You'll have a good time.'

Their kindness was more than I could bear. I pulled away and dashed towards the ladies' loo, just wanting to be on my own. I collided with Dave Merrick as I ran, and the dental records were knocked from my hand. I didn't bother to pick them up. I just wanted to be alone.

TWELVE

'Shit!' muttered Oakley, bending down to retrieve the papers Anderson had dropped as she fled. 'She didn't get these to the mortuary. They're James Paxton's dental records. And as the owners of nine Orchard Street are represented by Urvine and Brotherton, we may have a connection.'

'The Paxton who screwed over Mark Butterworth?' asked Jeeves. 'I heard he was missing.'

He glanced nervously over his shoulder towards the closed door of the interview room into which Davis had hauled Wright. No one could hear the specifics, but her voice was an angry monologue – the sergeant wasn't being allowed to get a word in edgeways. Jeeves exchanged a glance with Franklin, unsettled. Oakley was more concerned with the dental records. He beckoned to Merrick.

'Take these to Grossman – and watch him while he looks at them. He's getting forgetful, and I don't want him telling us he's done it when he hasn't. I'm going to Urvine and Brotherton.'

'Wait, Guv.' Merrick caught his arm before he could leave. 'I've been on the phone to the cleaning lady, Gail Langham. She says the keys *were* on the table on the Tuesday morning, as agreed

233

with Kovac, and he'd cleaned out all his stuff and left the place clean and tidy. She also claims there was no dead body on the kitchen floor. She still has the keys, and intended to bring them back to Jessop now that he has returned and the office is open again.'

'Did you ask why she didn't come forward and tell us all this earlier?' asked Oakley testily.

'She was waiting for us to contact her, and is surprised it's taken so long.'

'Get her statement after you've seen to the dental records,' said Oakley tiredly, the idiosyncrasies of the general public never failing to amaze him. 'And get the keys Kovac left, too.'

'Why?' asked Merrick. 'If he left the keys and took his belongings with him, it means he's gone home and we're looking at a different identity for our corpse.'

'Not necessarily,' said Oakley. 'What's to say that he didn't cut himself a new set of keys and come back after the cleaner had gone? Besides, there might be fingerprints on them that we can use. And get on to the university, as well. Check that Jessop really did send the keys to Kovac there.'

'I'll do that,' offered Davis, who had finally emerged from the interview room. Her lips were compressed into a hard, thin line, and Jeeves and Franklin made themselves scarce, afraid that some of Wright's tongue-lashing might fall on them. 'After I've seen to a female officer who's been unnecessarily distressed.'

'It's a shame,' said Oakley. 'But she needs to be less sensitive.'

'Just because you're immune to his charms doesn't mean we all are,' retorted Davis sharply. 'He'd have upset me, too, going on like that in front of everyone. I'd better find something for her to do, because otherwise Wright will be even harder on her now.'

Oakley was grateful that Davis was dealing with Anderson, as he was keen to follow up on the leads that had suddenly materialized. Without further ado, he left New Bridewell and walked to the offices of Urvine and Brotherton on Queen Square. Their offices comprised a terrace of three Georgian houses that had been knocked into one. The rooms were large with high, carved ceilings, and there was an elegant chandelier in the waiting room. He sat in a plush leather armchair while he waited for Brotherton to see him, taking the opportunity to collect his thoughts.

Anderson's distress preyed on his mind, and he knew he'd been wrong to commandeer her without clearing it with Wright. It was true that he outranked the sergeant, but it would have been polite to ask his permission. The fault being his, he was disgusted that Wright had taken his anger out on Anderson. He'd have to make it up to her somehow. She wasn't right for CID, but there were other departments that might be glad of a quietly intelligent woman.

Meanwhile, what was he to make of the morning's events and discoveries? The anonymous note he'd received had gained significance now there was a connection between the murder scene and the law firm that represented Yorke.

235

He'd have to call Solihull to see if they'd found DNA, fingerprints or other trace evidence on the thing, although he suspected it was still lying in its envelope, untouched.

His mind wandered to Maureen Paxton. Why did she think the body was her son? Was there something she wasn't telling them? And what about Kovac in light of what Jessop had said? Was he camping with his family, oblivious to the stir his absence was causing? Had he returned to the house, intending to sneak a few nights without paying rent, or because he thought he had left something behind, and had died for it? And what of the brother in the secret police? Had Kovac brought some foreign operation to Oakley's patch?

His reverie was interrupted by Brotherton, who marched into the waiting room looking at his watch. He was immaculately dressed as always, although there was a bitterness to his suave exterior that had not been there previously. He carried a stack of files to show he was busy.

'Five minutes,' he said rudely, dropping the files on the table with an authoritative thud. 'Fridays are always busy for us.'

'And us, so I'll be brief,' said Oakley, equally brusque. 'First, have you had any news from James Paxton?'

'None. Next question.'

'Does anyone on your staff have any idea where he might have gone?'

'Not as far as I am aware.'

'Do you mind if I ask them again?'

'If you must.'

At this rate they'd be done in one minute, not five, thought Oakley wryly. 'I understand your company represents the owners of nine Orchard Street. May I have their name and address?'

'Certainly not. That would break client confidentiality.'

Oakley put his notebook away. 'I'll return with a warrant at six o'clock, Mr Brotherton. This is a murder enquiry, and you hold information that may be relevant. If you're not here, I shall send a car to collect you from your home.'

Brotherton sighed irritably. 'Very well. Give me a moment.'

He was gone for more than fifteen minutes, and Oakley was on the verge of going to see what was happening when the door opened and Tim Hillier came in. He shook Oakley's hand.

'Mr Brotherton asked me to give you this,' he said, passing over a piece of paper with a scribbled name and address.

'Too busy to do it himself, is he?' asked Oakley, a little sourly.

Hillier had the grace to flush. 'He was called away to an urgent phone call.'

Oakley took the opportunity to quiz the junior partner. 'He said no one's heard from Paxton since Tuesday the thirty-first of July. Is that true?'

Hillier nodded. 'There've been rumours about where he is – I told you about them. But we've not had a postcard.'

'Where do *you* think he is?'

'I really don't have the faintest idea. Giles Farnaby reckons he saw James going into a gay bar that evening, but even if James *is* gay I don't see him disappearing because of it. Personally, I don't believe Giles. I think he made it up. And even if he didn't, and he really did go inside, I doubt he was there long enough to see much. A dark-haired man in a suit.' He gestured to his own attire. 'How many of those are there in Bristol?'

Oakley supposed he would have to question Farnaby again. 'Now, about Orchard Street. What do you know about the owners?'

'Mr and Mrs George Harton. He works in oil. We did the conveyancing when they bought the property. The oil industry's a bit uncertain, and the Hartons aren't sure when they might come back, so James recommended that they lease it short term, so they won't have to wait long before retaking possession.'

'James dealt with it? I thought he was a criminal lawyer.'

'He represented Mr Harton on a drink-driving charge a couple of years ago. I suppose the family asked for him when they bought the house. Giles did the actual work, but James saw them, and recommended Academic Accommodations.'

'Do you have other clients who rent their houses through this particular agency?'

'A few. I can't tell you how many exactly, but I could look it up if it's important.'

'Thank you. Does Billy Yorke have any houses leased through Academic Accommodations?'

'Billy Yorke?' asked Hillier, startled. 'I wouldn't have thought so. He does own property, but he's not the kind of person who'd use Academic Accommodations. Their tenants come through the university, you see, and scholars aren't usually wealthy, although they *do* tend to be respectable. In other words, they're low risk but low return.'

Oakley nodded to the files that Brotherton had dropped on the table and forgotten to take with him. 'The letter on top of that pile – the one on Avon and Somerset Constabulary notepaper – appears to be in my writing. Yet I've never sent anything to Urvine and Brotherton, so what do you think it's doing here?'

It took a lot to pull myself together after the incident with Wright. DI Davis was sweet, and said she'd ask Superintendent Taylor for a temporary transfer to CID, to help with the Orchard Street case. But that was the *last* thing I wanted – it was bad enough getting involved with the murder on an occasional basis; I didn't think I could stand doing it all day. Also, I didn't want everyone to think that Wright had driven me out, and for him to start telling people he'd got rid of me because I was no good. I told her thanks, but no thanks. She seemed surprised, but was understanding when I explained – the second reason, obviously, not the first.

Wright was coolly hostile when I walked into the radio room an hour later and told Jeeves that I was ready to go out on patrol. Jeeves needed someone to see Mrs Vinson at the hospital, and I left without even looking at Wright. I could feel his eyes on me as I went, though, and I was sure

239

he'd be talking about me as soon as I was out of earshot. It occurred to me that I should double back and catch him at it, but I didn't have the strength to take him on again. Loathsome man!

I tried to put him from my mind while I watched Emma Vinson struggling for breath. She was weaker and frailer than before, and I wondered how much longer she would cling to life. How *could* James have contemplated defending the louts who'd done this to her? And how could he have expected me to live with myself if he *had* forced me to play a part in seeing the bastards acquitted? They deserved everything the law could throw at them, and I hoped with all my heart that Oakley would see the whole lot sent down.

Oakley had used Brotherton's lengthy disappearance to look inside the files he'd left, of course. He was a policeman, after all, and curious by nature. There were several of them, all pertaining to clients of Paxton. There was one on Orchard Street detailing its purchase by the Hartons, complete with printouts of emails between Bristol and Saudi Arabia. The Hartons had only looked at the property once, and Paxton had purchased it on their behalf.

More intriguing was the thicker, fatter file concerning Noble, and Oakley was bemused to find in it several memos from him to Clare Davis, reports of the surveillance on Noble's sheds, and even a shift rota, giving details of officers' availability for court.

A cold horror gripped him. Someone had

copied documents from the police file – documents that should certainly not be with Urvine and Brotherton. Was *this* how Paxton had learned about Butterworth's Blunder? There was someone at New Bridewell whose first loyalty was not to his fellow officers.

But who? Wright, who had spread the rumour about Butterworth in the first place? With a few drinks inside him, and a personable lawyer playing to the man's vanity, who knew what the sergeant might do? But for all his faults, Oakley couldn't see Wright passing police files to lawyers.

He'd studied the documents carefully. They weren't photocopies, but printouts of photos taken on a mobile phone – he could tell by the date in the lower right-hand corner. They'd been taken on the thirtieth of March at 4.10 p.m. He decided to check if Wright had been on duty then.

Then Hillier had come in and he'd been obliged to pretend he'd only just happened to notice the memo from him lying brazenly on the top of the pile. Or had Brotherton left them there deliberately, wanting him to know that Paxton had engaged in underhand tactics – tactics that the old, respectable company certainly wouldn't condone?

'Your clerks probably sent them by mistake,' said Hillier, although he seemed as bemused as Oakley as to how they should come to be there. 'It's what happens when we have a system that's drowning in paperwork.'

'A clerk "accidentally" took photographs of

police memos?' asked Oakley archly.

'I suppose it *is* unlikely,' conceded Hillier reluctantly.

Oakley pulled some evidence bags from his pocket. 'Would you mind if I took them?'

'Why?' asked Hillier suspiciously. 'Surely you already have them?'

'Yes, but I'd like these as well.'

'Very well, but only if I take a photocopy first,' said Hillier. He indicated the machine in the corner.

Evidence bags in hand, Oakley prepared to leave, but Hillier caught his arm, glancing around in a way that could only be described as furtive.

'James is a real wally, and you won't find many here who like him. He's too ambitious, and we hate the way he sucks up to Brotherton. He'll get sacked when he comes back. It's already started to go a bit wrong for him.' He stopped and gnawed his lip. 'He's bent some rules.'

'What rules?'

Hillier nodded to the evidence bags. 'Well, that's the latest unpleasant surprise: God knows how he got them. Brotherton was never happy with the Noble case. He was delighted when we won, of course, but he didn't like the notion that James might've obtained the information under-handedly. Perhaps he was aware of the memos. I heard him say he was uneasy about the whole thing, though I don't know the details.'

He should have been, thought Oakley as Hillier escorted him to the door. Someone was just coming in. It was Giles Farnaby, dressed in a suit and tie rather than the jogging pants he'd worn at his home in Bath. In smarter clothes, he looked familiar, and Oakley struggled to think of where he'd seen him before. In court, perhaps?

'How is your grandmother, Giles?' asked Hillier. 'You shouldn't work if you need more time.'

Recognition came in a blinding flash. Farnaby was related to Emma Vinson, and Oakley had seen him at the hospital. No wonder Farnaby hated Paxton! It was not about losing out on a promotion – Paxton was representing the man who'd hurt his grandmother.

'Why didn't you tell me that you were related to one of Yorke's victims?' Oakley asked him before he could follow Hillier down the hall.

Farnaby scowled. 'And have you accuse me of making Paxton disappear? Yeah, right!'

Oakley regarded him coolly. 'And *did* you make him disappear?'

Farnaby sneered. 'No. But he's a bastard, and if anyone can get Yorke off it'll be him.'

'By resorting to illegal practices?

Farnaby's laugh was harsh. 'Of course! How else could he get such fabulous results? When you have imagination and a bit of criminal flair, you can go a long way in this business. That Noble stunt was a prime example.'

'I know,' said Oakley softly, thinking of his dead friend.

'He persuaded – or perhaps blackmailed – some plod to tell him about an attempt to tamper with police evidence. Brotherton said that was unethical, as the wrongdoing had been discovered and put right. He thought James had perverted the course of justice.'

'Brotherton didn't want Paxton to use the evidence he got from his police informer?'

'He suggested James win by using more conventional means. James said he intended to win, full stop. I think he was going to pull a similar stunt with Yorke.'

'How?'

Farnaby stared at a sparrow that had perched on the railings. 'He was certain he'd get Yorke out on bail, but I'd read the file and I thought the police had a pretty solid case. I couldn't understand why he was so confident. There was no way Yorke was getting bail.'

'He didn't,' Oakley pointed out.

'Because James wasn't there. If he had been, I suspect Yorke would be out. Brotherton told me that Yorke was livid when James failed to appear, and he'd expected Brotherton to get him out, just like James had promised to do. James even bet fifty quid on it. He's a mean bastard, so he must have been sure of winning.'

Oakley thought about the note he'd received, suggesting that he explore Yorke and 'false confessions'. He frowned. *False* confessions? Had Paxton aimed to *create* reasons for mistrials when genuine ones did not exist?

'He was up to something,' Farnaby went on bitterly. 'I wish I'd known what. It wouldn't have pleased Brotherton if he'd pulled another Noble quite so soon. We're a respectable firm, and we don't want a reputation for dragging shabby rabbits out of our hats.'

'That depends. You might if it attracts more

clients.'

Farnaby stared at him. 'Of course! He was trying to attract more powerful criminals who'd want to be represented by him and no one else! He planned to make himself indispensable, so Urvine and Brotherton would have to promote him again. Bastard!'

Oakley studied him thoughtfully. It was obvious that Farnaby loathed Paxton with a passion, but was his hatred strong enough to lead him to harm his dodgy colleague?

'Do you want the bad news or the worse news?' asked Evans gloomily when Oakley returned. He and Merrick were drinking tea in the incident room, sorting through piles of paper. Davis was working in the corner. 'Or the strange news?'

'Strange,' replied Oakley, sitting at a computer and beginning to trawl through his emails.

'I borrowed the keys Kovac left for the cleaner and they don't fit. That suggests he left like he said he would, but then he came back, where either he was killed or he killed someone else.'

'So we're back to where we started,' said Oakley, frustrated. 'We still don't know whether it's Kovac or someone else in the mortuary.'

'Well, it's not James Paxton.' Merrick sounded disappointed. 'That's one of our pieces of bad news: the dental records came back negative.'

'I can't say I'm surprised,' muttered Oakley, thinking that let Farnaby off the hook. 'Is Grossman certain?'

'Paxton's records list a missing premolar, but our corpse has it,' replied Merrick. 'It took him

245

all of ten seconds to eliminate Paxton on the basis of that. He says if the records had listed a premolar as present, but it was missing on the corpse, then that would be different, as teeth fall out. But he said a premolar gone was a premolar gone, and they don't re-grow.'

'What if the dentist made a mistake? Crossed off the wrong tooth?'

'I asked that. Extremely unlikely, apparently.'

'I'd have liked the corpse to have been Paxton,' sighed Evans. 'I phoned his mum and told her the sad news.' Oakley looked at him sharply, and he raised his hands in the air. 'Nicely. I was very sympathetic and kind.'

'Can we trust Grossman?' asked Oakley. 'He did the P.M. on Mark, but keeps forgetting – he's mentioned him twice to me as if he thinks he's still alive.'

'Is that so surprising?' asked Evans. 'Think about how many corpses he sees in a year. He can't remember them all.'

'No, but Mark should have been different,' insisted Oakley. 'He should remember him. And I want a second opinion about the dental charts. Just to be sure.'

'You won't get one, Neel,' said Davis, looking up from her work. 'Taylor's already grumbling about you sending that anonymous note to FSS. He says it's a waste of resources. He's not going to authorise another pathologist just because Grossman has got a bit forgetful. Especially as its just to placate the dreaded Maureen Paxton.'

'What's the other bad news?' asked Oakley, suspecting she was right.

'Wright's put in a complaint against you,' said Evans. 'He says you undermined him by poaching his officers.'

Oakley started to laugh. 'You're joking!'

'I wouldn't joke about Wright,' said Evans in disgust. 'He's complained about you, too, ma'am, and he's put Anderson on report.'

Davis's face was dark with anger. 'The bastard has outmanoeuvred me! I haven't had time to submit my own report yet, and he's effectively made sure that I can't, because now it'll look like sour grapes.'

'I don't have time for this rubbish,' muttered Oakley. 'Doesn't the man have a job to do?' He sat up straight and helped himself to a mouthful of Evans' tea. 'Right. Let's review where we've got today. A lot has come in, and we need to think through it.'

'Well, the body's still unidentified,' said Evans. 'And we've had no luck tracing Kovac in Albania.'

'It's odd,' said Oakley. 'After being so certain it wasn't, I was actually beginning to think it *might* be Paxton. He deals with the Orchard Street house while the owners are away, he goes missing at the right time, and that anonymous note said we should look at Yorke for the murder – Yorke is Paxton's client.'

'But Yorke was in prison when the murder took place,' Evans pointed out.

'He's got friends and family,' said Oakley. He told them what he'd learned at Urvine and Brotherton, and about Farnaby's suspicions. 'The leaked documents were nothing – just the

247

usual junk that gets shoved into any file. But Paxton somehow got them – and it seems reasonable to conclude that whoever gave them to him also told him about Mark.'

'So,' concluded Davis, 'we've got the anonymous note accusing Yorke of murder and "false confessions", and we've got Paxton operating in an underhand manner. We've also got Paxton associated with the house where the murder took place.'

'So Paxton killed Kovac?' mused Evans. 'Then buggered off.'

'No,' said Davis. 'I'm sure Kovac is our killer. First, he left duff keys behind so he could return later. Second, he cleaned the house with bleach, according to FSS. Men aren't naturally hygienic, so he must've had a reason for such diligence.'

'To save his deposit,' said Oakley practically. 'If he'd left the place like a pig sty, he'd lose it – and it represents a lot of nice clothes for his family. And anyway, what's this about men being unhygienic? I'll have you know that my house is spotless.'

'So's mine,' added Merrick sourly.

'All right.' Davis raised her hands in the air. 'I concede the point about the clean house. But there's still the keys to think about. Also, I've been learning more about nanotechnology, and I think it *might* make Kovac rich one day. Patenting some process might see him and his family in clover for the rest of their lives. Perhaps he killed to protect his research. Plus there's the fact that he may have psychological problems over what he went through in Macedonia.'

'Then who did he kill?' asked Oakley. 'If Kovac is our murderer, who's the body?'

'I don't know,' she said impatiently. 'But Kovac is a more plausible culprit than Paxton.'

'True – if Paxton *was* the killer, he wouldn't have disappeared,' said Merrick. 'He'd be here, brazening it out. I looked to see if we had his fingerprints on record, but of course we don't. The body's fingerprints are in the kitchen and the sitting room...'

'But not upstairs,' mused Oakley thoughtfully. 'Isn't that odd? Kovac was there for three weeks, so he'd have gone into the bedrooms.'

'But the house was scrubbed down,' said Evans. 'And we know our body and its killer came in *after* the cleaner had been, or she'd have seen it. But all this doesn't rule Kovac out – especially if he used his keys to come back later.'

'I gave his photo to the press today,' said Davis. 'That should flush him out if he's hiding somewhere.'

'What's happening with the black plastic enquiry?' asked Oakley. 'And the duct tape?'

'What a waste of time!' said Merrick despondently. 'There are partials all over both, but Solihull is too busy to work on them. All they'll say for now is that the tape had collected some fine white dust. Lots of it.'

'You mean drugs?' asked Oakley.

'No – FSS thinks that strips were cut then stuck to a wall, so they'd be ready to use on the body. I do the same when I wrap Christmas presents: cut strips and stick them on the table, so I can just grab one without having to let go of the paper. Our boy hacked strips of tape – four of them – got the body rolled, and then took the pieces as he needed them. Sticky patches on the wall seem to bear this out.'

'Door-to-door?' asked Oakley.

'A big, fat nothing,' said Merrick glumly.

'We got the report on the insects though,' said Evans. 'Time of death has been narrowed to between the night of Monday the thirtieth of July and the morning of Thursday the second of August. It's been more difficult than usual, because of the heat. So we're no better off there, either. We can take the cleaner's evidence and say the body wasn't in the house when she left on Tuesday morning, so we're left with a time of death between ten a.m. on Tuesday and, say, ten a.m. on Thursday.'

'It certainly fits with Paxton's disappearance,' mused Merrick.

'Yes, but the dental records don't,' said Davis. 'So that's that with Paxton. We need to drop him before we waste any more time. What about the anonymous note?'

'The report came back today,' said Merrick, rummaging in a pile. 'They rushed it through for you, Guv. Unfortunately, the news isn't good – no fingerprints, fibres, or saliva on the envelope. They say the writer probably wore gloves, and the paper is cheap, mass-produced stuff that we'll never trace in a million years.'

'Come on, Dave,' said Evans, laughing. 'Tell him the good stuff, too. There was no saliva on the envelope, *but* there was a trace of it on the stamp. The writer obviously stuck down the envelope with water, then forgot himself at the post office, and licked it without thinking.'

'Well, that's something,' said Oakley.

'Not really,' disagreed Merrick. 'He left very few cells behind, and FSS doesn't know whether there's enough to be of use. The heat hasn't helped, either, because it degrades the DNA. So the saliva *may* help, but it may not.'

'Let's keep this to ourselves,' said Oakley. 'It would be a pity to get everyone excited about it if it then it turns out to be nothing. If there's good news then it'll be a nice surprise, and if it's bad news no one needs to know.'

'What did Jinic tell you about the Albanian secret police?' Evans asked Davis. 'Could Kovac have been killed by them? It would explain why they're so damned slow in sending us information.'

'Albania does have a secret police force but they're no longer very effective. Jinic doesn't think they'd have the funds to commit murder on foreign soil.'

'He could be wrong,' said Evans.

'He could,' she agreed. 'But I don't think so. Albania is a poor country and Kovac's visa was due to run out anyway. Why put themselves to the expense of a foreign raid when they could kill him in Tirana? No, this has nothing to do with the secret police.'

'Well, I've had enough for today,' said Oakley, standing. 'I'm going home.'

Saturday, 18 August
'I've got a lead, Guv!' Evans' face was flushed

251

with excitement as he waved a piece of paper. 'It's from someone who lives in Cornwallis Crescent. That's some way away from Orchard Street, and we've just found out about it, because we've extended our house-to-house enquiries.'

'Well?' asked Oakley, when his sergeant paused.

'You remember Mrs Greaves telling us she saw a woman wearing a headscarf walking quickly down the road on the night of the murder? Well, someone else saw her, too.'

'And?' pressed Oakley. 'Does the witness know her?'

'No,' said Evans, 'but he saw her.'

Oakley took the statement from him and scanned through it quickly, trying not to let his face register his disappointment. The witness told them nothing Mrs Greaves hadn't already mentioned, although he was able to say that the time had been 10.10 p.m. because of a football game he'd been watching in the pub. Apparently his dog had disgraced itself in some way, and he'd been asked to leave before the game was over. He'd missed a crucial goal while he'd hurried home, so could be very exact about the time.

'The dog went wild when she walked past apparently,' Evans added. 'Mr Jacobs had a hard time quieting it down.'

'So it says here,' said Oakley. He pushed the paper back across the desk to his sergeant and laced his fingers behind his head. 'Where do you think this takes us?'

'It means a woman was walking very purposefully around the streets near where the murder took place – and possibly *just after* the murder took place – obviously in disguise. I think she could be the killer. Or he.'

'He?'

'If the scarf *was* a disguise, this figure might have been a man dressed as a woman. Why not? It'd be a good way to hide yourself.'

'All right. Greaves and Jacobs clearly saw the same person, so look into it. Get a picture drawn up and show it around to see if anyone else noticed her – or him. Show it at the local shops, and see if they know anyone who dresses like that. Show it to Mrs Paxton, and see if she knows whether any of her son's acquaintances had a liking for scarves.'

Evans nodded enthusiastically. 'Right you are, Guv.'

It was hard to get dressed and head for work that Saturday. I was on early shift and left my house at twenty past five to be in the station for ten to six. As I walked in posters of Marko Kovac greeted me, stuck up in the reception area and the briefing room. He was a nice-looking man, with dark hair and green eyes with long eyelashes. Still, at least the poster didn't say 'wanted for murder' on it.

I'd spent the previous evening working on my second anonymous note, using the pen, paper and envelopes I'd used for the first one. I was just as careful as I'd been then, donning gloves to write, and hoovering the table clear of tell-tale fibres. I'd heard about Oakley's visit to James's work, so it was important that I got the team looking back to thinking that Kovac was the body. I'd written:

IT WAS YORKE'S GOONS WHAT DONE FOR KOVACH. IT WAS FOR DRUGS. I SEEN IT ALL.

My mother had called as I was finishing, so I'd had to shove it into the envelope more quickly than I'd have liked, but at least it was done. Rather than risk the post again, I simply dropped it straight into the station's letterbox on my way in, using the cuff of my sleeve to avoid touching it with my fingers.

I had a pleasant surprise when the morning briefing began: it was Wright's day off. His presence was still heavy around me, though. People were going out of their way to be nice, and I wondered if they'd be doing it if he was there, watching to see who was 'on my side'.

Someone had to guard the murder scene at Orchard Street, and I wasn't surprised to find that Wright had pencilled me in to do it. The other sergeant, Rick Jones, gave an apologetic smile, but didn't have the balls to change it. It was stupid, he said – the night shift had been busy, and hadn't had a man to spare for the task. It had been left unprotected all night, but CID still wanted someone on it that morning. It didn't make sense, he said. But I was still stuck with it.

Jeeves arranged a lift and promised he'd get a car to fetch me at ten so I could have a break. He told me that Oakley planned to come by later so I'd have company for a while, adding that Neel was a good bloke. I pointed out, rather tartly, that it was that particular 'good bloke' who'd landed me in trouble the previous day. Jeeves feigned a sudden interest in his work, so he wouldn't have to get into that particular can of worms.

I arrived at the house and stood in the garden. A huge lorry was at the far end of the road, trying to do a U-turn and making a total pig's ear of it. Why something that size had elected to tackle such a narrow collection of streets was beyond me. God only knew if it would ever manage to extricate itself.

For no real reason, other than that it was there, I pushed the front door, and was startled to find that whoever had been there last had forgotten to lock it. I glanced at my watch. Quarter past six – it had obviously been left unsecured all night. With no one on duty anyone could have walked in. I stuck my head around the door and heard someone moving about. I was reaching for my radio to call for assistance when a figure appeared.

'Sarge!' I exclaimed in astonishment.

'What're you doing here so early?' he demanded, consulting his watch. 'It's only five past six.'

'It's quarter past,' I said, bemused. He ducked inside the sitting room, and I followed. What was he doing?

'Get out!' he hissed. 'Mind your own business. You're in enough trouble without messing around in here. Go outside and do your job, woman.'

'I *am* doing my job,' I objected, watching him drop to his hands and knees and concentrate on the floor. 'I'm guarding the house from people who shouldn't be here.'

'Fuck off!' he snarled. 'I got things to do. *Someone's* got to do a bit of coppering around here. We've not got anywhere with women and Pakis in charge, so I'm giving the investigation a bit of a boost. I don't want *my* station branded as not being able to solve a simple murder – and if my meddling lands Oakley and Davis in the shit, then so much the better. Now get the fuck out, and mind your own business.'

He really was a nasty piece of work, I thought in distaste, as my fingers closed around another of the rocks on the mantelpiece. Like James, he was so arrogant and sure of himself that he didn't even bother to watch as he fiddled with whatever he was doing on the floor.

The rock made a thumping sound when it landed, quite different than with James. When I'd hit him, his skull had sounded like an egg smashing on a stone floor. Wright's bones must have been thicker, or perhaps the stone was lighter, because it didn't sound the same at all. For a moment, nothing happened, then Wright flopped to one side. He looked up at me, but I didn't meet his eyes. I hit him again, as hard as I could. The first blow had been on the top of the skull. The second got him on the side of his head, and blood started to flow from his temple.

Without another sound, Wright slumped down and went limp. I felt for a pulse in his neck, but there wasn't one. His nasty little eyes were half open, and it might have been my imagination, but there did seem to be a rather startled expression on his pudgy face.

* * *

Superintendent Taylor was exasperated with the slow pace of the investigation, and suspected the team had been following too many iffy leads. So when he collected the post and found another anonymous letter, he screwed up the cheap paper in a gesture of annoyance and tossed it into the bin. He was irked with Oakley for taking the last one seriously when he'd expressly ordered against it, and he wasn't having more of his budget squandered on useless tests.

He turned to the next piece of post and saw that a thick fair hair had settled across it. Where had that come from? Impatiently, he flicked it away and grabbed the envelope beneath.

THIRTEEN

Killing Wright was very different from killing James. Perhaps it was because I'd brained a man before and so knew what to expect, or perhaps it was because I really hated Wright, whereas James had been pure instinct. Regardless, there was none of the sick horror with Wright that I'd experienced with James. Until my radio crackled, that was, and Jeeves called me. Then I came back to Earth.

A hundred questions clamoured at me as I stared at the body. Had Wright been alone? Had anyone seen me kill him? I looked around wildly. What had he been doing there in civvies at six in the morning, anyway? And why had he been so keen for me to leave him alone to finish it? I dragged my attention away from my panicky speculations and tried to concentrate on what Jeeves was saying.

'We've got reports of a lorry causing an obstruction at the end of Orchard Street,' came his crackly voice. 'Can you go and have a look?'

'I can see it,' I lied, sounding a lot cooler than I felt. 'It's a big articulated thing trying to do a sixty-eight-point turn.'

'Can you sort it out? I've got three calls about it already. It's waking people up by revving its engine, as well as blocking the traffic.'

'I'm guarding the crime scene,' I said, wanting my objection heard on air, lest someone reported me for not doing the job I'd been assigned. Wright would have done.

'It's been left all night,' Jeeves pointed out. 'A few more minutes won't hurt.'

The lorry was inaudible from inside number nine, so it was the homes at the far end of the street that were bothered by the noise. That was good, I thought. It meant neighbours like the Smiths and the Greaves wouldn't be awake, looking out of their windows to see me leave.

Getting away with killing Wright was going to be a piece of cake. He must have sneaked a key from somewhere, but *I* certainly couldn't be expected to have one. All I needed to do was go out, pull the door behind me to lock it, and no one would ever know I'd been in. I glanced at my watch. Eighteen minutes past six. It doesn't take long to kill someone: three minutes in Wright's case. I left everything just as it was, not even worrying about trace evidence this time. I'd helped Oakley to find the first murder weapon, so any fibres or hairs could have been left then.

I took the stone, though, and put it in a plastic evidence pouch before slipping it in my bag. There wasn't much blood on it – obviously, a ball of Portland limestone was good for not causing really nasty, bloody deaths. I didn't think my fingerprints could be lifted from its chalky, dusty surface, but there was no point in taking needless chances.

I examined the door before I left. Wright had

259

left it on the latch, perhaps aiming to make a quick getaway before I arrived. He couldn't have known the house had been left unattended the previous night – unless he'd taken a radio home, which was unlikely – and I suppose he'd anticipated a gap between the nightshift finishing and me starting. Perhaps he'd put me on duty because he thought I'd dally in getting there on time. Regardless, he'd assumed he'd have ten or fifteen minutes for whatever he'd wanted to do. I wondered what it was. Clearly, something he thought would damage Oakley and Davis, and probably something that would frame some poor innocent who'd earned his dislike by being the wrong sex or colour.

I stepped out and pulled the door behind me. Then I stood in the garden and looked around carefully. I couldn't see a curtain quivering or a head sticking out of a window anywhere. I paid special attention to the Smiths' house, but all was still, so I supposed they were still asleep. The same was true of number eleven. I'd been in and out with no one noticing, and if anyone looked now they'd see me in the garden, where I was supposed to be.

I walked to the end of the road where the noise really was loud enough to disturb the residents. I felt calmly detached as I directed the waiting traffic down another road, then set about extricating the driver from his predicament. Between us we managed to get him turned around without trashing any of the parked cars, and he was able to drive away. The residents who'd been watching in dressing gowns and pyjamas gave me a round of applause.

I walked back to number nine, glancing at my watch as I went. It was almost seven. Wright had been dead for less than an hour, and at least ten people could say they'd seen me during that time frame sorting out the lorry. I radioed in to say I was returning to the house.

'No, stay where you are,' instructed Jeeves. 'Paul Franklin will pick you up in two minutes. There's a fire in one of the old warehouses near the harbour and I need you both there to set up a traffic diversion.'

'He's here now,' I said as the patrol car appeared around the corner.

I spent the next two hours establishing road blocks around a building that belched clouds of white smoke. Later, Paul offered to hold the fort for ten minutes while I got a drink from a mobile cafe that was parked up on the harbour front. I bought a cup of bitter coffee, then walked behind the van and stared at the murky green waters of the harbour. I looked around carefully, but I was alone.

I took the stone I'd used to kill Wright and dropped it in the water. It sank without trace.

The paperwork was mounting up on Oakley's desk but the case had made scant headway. More than a week had passed since the body had been found – and the victim had now been dead for about three weeks – but Oakley felt no closer to finding the culprit than he had on the first day. The team was still working furiously, throwing every ounce of energy into the enquiry, but he knew that would change if their efforts didn't take them somewhere soon.

Evans was following the lead about the woman in the headscarf, juggling it with the black plastic enquiry. FSS had come through on the partial fingerprints at last, and had provided a long list of possible matches. These were prints that were too smudged or fragmented to provide a positive match, but that had a few points in common with prints on record. Merrick was working through them. All needed to be checked and eliminated with alibis. In his spare time he was still trying to identify the man who had been with Paxton in the gay bar. Davis had told him scornfully that that line of enquiry was dead, but he'd started, and a streak of obstinacy in him made him reluctant to give up. Davis was learning more than she ever wanted to know about nanotechnology and trying to liaise with the unreliable and bureaucratic Albanians. Taylor was keeping the media at bay.

Meanwhile, door-to-door enquiries were continuing, although these were yielding little of value, and the British Embassy in Saudi Arabia was contacting the Harton family. Oakley was in charge of coordinating it all, and was also pursuing the anonymous note, albeit without Taylor's blessing – and the superintendent had certainly not bothered to mention the one he'd trashed.

Oakley concentrated from six until ten on the mass of reports, and managed to plough through a quarter of them. Because it was in a basement and windowless, the room soon became stuffy, and after four hours his head ached. He rubbed his eyes and leaned back in his chair.

He'd been reading an account of Kovac from the Albanian police, which had been translated by Professor Jinic. Kovac was a minor celebrity in his country, often invited on national television to talk about subjects as diverse as the Hubble telescope, global warming and dinosaur extinction. His achievements in nanotechnology seemed to warrant less publicity.

Why? Because the public was more interested in 'popular' science? Because Kovac wanted to keep his research secret? Or just because Albanian television had yet to make a documentary on theoretical physics?

Oakley had also learned that Kovac had been arrested in his youth for subversion, although there was nothing to suggest he'd done anything more serious than sit with like-minded students in smoky cafes to discuss politics. His 'insurgency' couldn't have been too bad, because he'd been allowed to travel once he became a professor, and he had made regular trips not only to Britain, but to the United States.

Oakley called for Evans, and pointed out that if Kovac had been arrested in his radical youth, there should be records of his fingerprints, so why weren't they with the information that had been sent? Evans explained that after the collapse of the Albanian communist regime a number of government buildings had been set alight. It was possible that Kovac's records were already lost. He agreed to follow up, but clearly thought it was a waste of time.

'So we're just waiting,' said Oakley, dispirited.

263

'Waiting to see if Merrick can link a partial print to a viable suspect; waiting for Tirana to be more helpful; waiting for something to turn up from the black plastic enquiry; waiting for our body to be matched to a missing person; waiting for FSS to analyse the saliva on our anonymous letter; waiting for a witness to remember something to tell us.'

'We've got the scarf enquiry,' said Evans, irked that his 'baby' had not been mentioned in Oakley's list. 'I've got an artist's impression and I was going to hawk it around Orchard Street this afternoon to see if it jogs anyone's memory.'

He rifled among some papers and produced a rather attractive picture, more like art than evidence. It showed a slim woman wearing a calf-length dark coat with a scarf tied at the back of her neck. She was looking down, her face in shadow. Her hands were in her pockets, and her posture was rather furtive. Oakley thought she looked like a Second World War heroine, about to give vital information against the Germans.

'Is that how your witness recalls the scarf being tied?' he asked, thinking about his conversation with Anderson. 'The ends linked together at the back? Not knotted under the chin?'

'Both witnesses say it was like this,' said Evans. 'Besides, what woman would tie a scarf under her chin these days?'

'It's good,' conceded Oakley. 'Get a copy put up in the reception area, too. Who knows? It might prompt someone. She's too young for that look, anyway.'

'This is a woman in her twenties or early

264

thirties,' agreed Evans.

'I don't think you can go that far,' cautioned Oakley. 'But it's not a pensioner. It could be someone of sixty. It could be Maureen Paxton.'

'Yeah,' nodded Evans. 'I bet *she's* got head-scarves.'

'This could be our best way forward,' said Oakley, sensing there might be some mileage in the lead after all. 'If anyone in Orchard Street is out when you call today, make sure you get them tomorrow.'

'How's the note business going?' asked Evans.

'Nowhere – until FSS gets back to us about the stamp. But I think I'll speak to Yorke's little brother this afternoon. Why not? We've nothing to lose.'

'Want me to come?'

'No, you work on the scarf. I'll take Dave instead. It's about time he met the Yorke clan, and it might be a good idea to have some fresh eyes looking at them. We've known them too long.'

'Give me a mysterious woman over an interview with Michael Yorke any day,' said Evans vehemently. 'He threatened us the last time we met, remember?'

'It was just sabre rattling.' Oakley didn't mention his second encounter with Michael, when the man had again indicated that he thought the police had something to do with Paxton's sudden disappearance.

'You look tired, Guv. You should get a strong coffee before you see Yorke. You need to be at your best or he'll make mincemeat of you.'

Oakley knew he looked seedy. His relationship with Catherine was at the stage where they wanted to spend a lot of time together – preferably awake – and he'd had less than three hours sleep the previous night. She'd gone to work at five so he'd driven her to the hospital, then come to the station. Now he was wondering if it would have been wiser to have stayed in bed. Still, he intended to take Sunday off, when he would doubtless exhaust himself further with Catherine. He hoped she'd be free.

He went to the men's toilet and splashed cold water over his face, then decided to go to Orchard Street to look around again. It would give him a break before seeing Yorke, and might even inspire him to new solutions. The investigation already felt stale.

Merrick arrived, looking fresh, neat and cool in a loose cotton shirt and neatly pressed chinos, and offered to go with him. They had a late breakfast first, ordering the 'station special': fried eggs, greasy sausages, flaccid bacon, black pudding and tinned tomatoes. Two cups of tea washed it down, leaving Oakley overloaded and slightly queasy. He nearly always felt ill after a station special, and wondered why he never learned to stick to the toast.

It was a hot day, and the city was busy with folk out shopping or seeking cool breezes around the waterfront. There were sun umbrellas everywhere, and those cafes with tables and chairs outside were enjoying a roaring trade. Traffic fumes hung in the air like poison, mixed with the sulphurous odour from the harbour. Oakley saw a child sucking desperately on an asthma inhaler while her parents crouched next to her in mute concern. Nearby, two mothers with prams stood chatting as a bus belched exhaust over them all.

Orchard Street seemed pleasantly quiet after the bustle of the city centre. Curtains were drawn to keep out the sun, while gardens wilted in the heat, their lawns yellow-brown.

'Oh, shit,' said Oakley as they pulled up at the house. 'I forgot to bring the keys.'

Merrick jangled them jauntily. 'I didn't. We normally lock them in the filing cabinet, but someone had accidentally left them on the windowsill instead. I happened to spot them as we left, and thought we might need them.'

'We're slipping,' said Oakley disapprovingly. 'I'll have a word about security at tonight's briefing. Come on. Let's see what brilliant insights come to us by revisiting the crime scene.' He stopped dead. 'Where's the guard?'

'Uniform pulled out because they're busy. It's been unguarded since about eleven last night.'

Oakley sighed. 'They should have told us.'

'They did – DI Davis – but there wasn't much she could do about it. If uniform doesn't have the manpower, it doesn't have the manpower.'

Shaking his head, Oakley slipped the key into the lock and opened the door. In the distance, the cathedral bells were chiming twelve o'clock. Oakley walked straight to the kitchen, while Merrick went into the lounge.

'Guv! In here! Quick!'

The suspicious death of a police officer warranted some very specific procedures. The duty superintendent, SOCO and police surgeon were all immediately contacted, and all available officers were assigned to initial house-to-house enquiries – but the investigation into Wright's death would be headed by another station, to eliminate mistakes made by anyone emotionally involved.

The first thing Oakley and Merrick did was make sure there was no one hiding in the house – Wright clearly hadn't been dead long because the blood was still wet. Then they began calling for the long list of services they knew they would need. An ambulance was not among them.

Before they left the house to senior officers and SOCO, Oakley stood over Wright and stared down at the body. As he would not be investigating the murder, it would be the only opportunity he would have, so he tried to fix every detail in his mind. Wright had probably been kneeling when he had been attacked, because both blows seemed to have been delivered from above. There was a piece of paper poking from underneath him: a betting slip.

What had Wright been doing there? Was the betting slip relevant? Did he have a gambling problem? He earned a respectable salary as sergeant, but his clothes were cheap. Did that mean his debts had left him short of money? And if so, had someone at Urvine and Brotherton homed in on it and paid him to photograph confidential police files? Worse, had he accepted money to gossip to them about Butterworth's Blunder? Wright had always been in the frame for that, as far as Oakley was concerned.

He and Merrick were taken back to the station in separate cars and interviewed at length by senior officers from Professional Standards. As the person who 'finds' a murder victim is often also the killer, the visiting superintendents were interested to hear that Oakley had a history of disagreements with Wright. Oakley was grateful that Merrick had been with him.

The death of Wright overshadowed everything else that day. The police surgeon estimated the time of death as between five thirty and seven o'clock that morning, while the cause was two blows to the head from a heavy blunt instrument. It wasn't yet known whether any of the ornamental stones along the mantelpiece were missing but they had been photographed for the first murder, so it was only a matter of time before that was resolved.

Policemen talked, and the death of someone they'd known was inevitably going to be the subject of rumours. There was a short-lived one that Oakley had done it, but it was quickly established that he had alibis at the hospital and then at the station, and the time he'd taken to drive between the two – quickly, because it had been too early for traffic – wouldn't have allowed for a detour to Orchard Street.

Davis was another brief suspect, but she had alibis in her husband and three daughters – a problem with a pet duck had seen them all together from three that morning onwards, huddled worriedly over a basket. Helen Anderson also came under suspicion, but it was quickly established that she hadn't had access to the house keys, and there was no evidence that the lock on Orchard Street had been forced. Moreover, a number of grateful residents were willing to attest that she was innocent of any wrongdoing. They'd seen the patrol car drop her off at number nine, after which she'd gone to help with the lorry. One witness even claimed that she hadn't been out of his sight from the moment she'd arrived – he'd been angry that the police were guarding the house, but hadn't responded to his complaint about the lorry.

So, the rumour-makers decided that the original murderer had sneaked back to the scene of his crime while it was left unguarded for the first time in a week. Wright had caught him and had died fighting him. But there was one question that no one could answer: why had Wright been there in the first place?

For the first time since joining the force, I was given a taste of what it felt like to be on the other side of the table. The three superintendents from Professional Standards were grim, hatchet-faced men, who clearly intended to put the fear of God into me. I knew I'd have to be careful. They introduced themselves. The skinny, bald one with the big hands was Sampson, the short one with the glasses was Parker, and the one with the deep tan and the wrinkles was Kidmore.

'Tell us what happened this morning,' said Sampson crisply. 'In your own words.'

'I arrived at work at ten to six, and was told that I'd been assigned to stand guard at Orchard

Street. PC Franklin gave me a lift, and we arrived at about quarter past six.'

'PC Franklin said it was twenty past,' pounced Kidmore pedantically.

'Perhaps it was,' I said, trying not to sound too eager. That five minutes might see me in the clear. 'The first thing I did was have a careful look around the garden.'

'Why?' demanded Sampson.

'Because there hadn't been a guard since eleven the previous night, and I thought I ought to check it over. There wasn't anything else to do, anyway. Standing outside an empty house isn't very interesting.' I spoke with a spark of defiance. I hoped they'd look at the records and ask why I'd been given so much guard duty when it should have been shared out more equally. It would scream of sexism, and wouldn't do Wright's reputation any good.

Sampson nodded approvingly. 'That shows initiative. Did you notice anything unusual?'

My thoughts raced. Here was an opportunity to make something up, to invent a clue or a happening that would lead them away from me. But I decided against it. The less I said, the less chance there was of slipping up.

'Nothing,' I replied. 'After the garden I pushed on the door to make sure it was locked. You may find my fingerprints on it.'

'We did,' confirmed Parker dourly. 'A whole hand, actually.'

I raised it, fingers splayed, and showed them how I'd shoved at the door. 'It was locked, and I pushed quite hard. Obviously, I couldn't check the back door, because it can only be reached from inside the house. Well, I suppose you could get to it through the neighbours' garden...'

'Quite so,' said Parker. 'Then what?'

'Then I got a call from PC Jeavis, the radio operator, telling me to sort out the lorry at the end of the street because there had been a number of complaints about it.'

'Did you go immediately?' asked Sampson.

'I told Jeeves that I shouldn't leave the house unguarded. He said it'd been abandoned all night, so a few more minutes wouldn't hurt.'

'We have that conversation on tape,' said Parker.

'How long did it take to deal with the lorry?' asked Kidmore.

'I'm not sure. Forty minutes, perhaps? It had got itself into an awful muddle. It wouldn't have taken quite so long if I hadn't had to keep stopping to let the traffic filter past.'

'You were clearly busy,' said Sampson. 'But did you find time to glance up the street, or to have a look at the people who'd gathered to watch you work?'

So they hoped I'd seen the killer. It *really* was tempting to make something up.

'No,' I said after a moment of reflection. 'I'm sorry, but the wagon was huge, and I didn't want it to damage someone's car. It took all my concentration. And anyway, the road bends slightly, and I'm not sure if the house can be seen from where I was working.'

'It does,' agreed Kidmore crisply. 'And it can't.'

Thank God I'd resisted the urge to fabricate! They were trying to catch me out, the ruthless bastards!

'Sergeant Wright put you on report yesterday,' said Parker. He was the nasty one. Or perhaps he was the *openly* nasty one, and the others were just as bad, only they hid it with a veneer of pleasantness. 'Would you like to tell us about that?'

I knew that Oakley, Davis and Jeeves had already been interviewed, so the three superintendents knew exactly what had happened. I wondered how they'd interpreted it – aggressive, sexist Wright picking on a woman yet again, or tough, decent Wright trying to make an officer out of a sow's ear.

'I'd gone on an errand for DI Oakley,' I explained. 'I realize now that I shouldn't have done without checking with Sergeant Wright. But I didn't think, and I set off without calling it in. Sergeant Wright recalled me and dressed me down in the briefing room in front of everyone.'

'You must've been angry,' said Parker smoothly. 'An inspector orders you to do something you weren't in a position to refuse, and you get into trouble for it?'

I was right. Parker *was* the nasty one. 'Embarrassed,' I corrected. 'He shouldn't have shouted at me in public. He should've done it in private. I would've, if I'd been in his position.'

'Would you now,' said Parker noncommittally. 'So you weren't angry?'

'I was embarrassed,' I repeated firmly. 'I still am – about the fact that he went for me in public, and that he made me cry. I shouldn't have let him. Maybe I'll be angry later.'

'Would you say he was a popular officer?' asked Kidmore.

'A number of people liked him,' I replied cautiously.

'Did you?' asked Parker.

'No,' I said bluntly. 'I didn't.'

Why was I telling them I had good reason for killing the bastard? Why couldn't I have kept my mouth shut? Unexpectedly, Parker smiled.

'I like honesty, WPC Anderson, and to be frank, I wouldn't have believed you if you'd said otherwise. I know female officers found Wright difficult, and from what I've heard he was more difficult with you than most. Why didn't you complain?'

'Because I wasn't sure it would achieve anything.'

'I'm sorry to hear you think that,' said Kidmore, sounding genuine. 'We've been working to create a force in which sexism and bullying are things of the past. I'm appalled by what's happened here. I hope you – or anyone else – won't be so reticent in the future.'

I couldn't think of anything to say, so I gave him a sort of half smile and stayed silent. The three men looked at each other, and Parker leaned across to say something in a low voice to the others. Sampson stood up.

'I think that's all,' he said. 'Of course, if anything else occurs to you, please contact us at once. I must ask you not to discuss this conversation with your colleagues. Unproven speculation and rumours do no one any good, and may even hamper the investigation.'

'I know,' I said, managing to inject a note of indignation into my voice that they should consider me a gossip. 'Of course I won't discuss it.'

Wednesday, 22 August
In the days immediately following the murder of Wright a number of facts emerged. Some became general knowledge and some were shared only by those who 'needed to know'. Among the former was the fact that Wright had taken the Orchard Street keys from the incident room and made a copy at a local shop – the bright, shiny Yale had been in his jeans pocket. His colleagues had many ideas about why he would do this, some reflecting favourably on him, most not.

A search of Wright's house revealed things that didn't become common knowledge. One was that he had photocopies from the station's property book, including the page that contained Butterworth's Blunder. It was concluded that Wright had either approached Paxton with the information or had left it in a place where he knew the lawyer would find it, in order to cause the Noble case to fail.

'And you don't need me to tell you his motive,' Davis had told the three superintendents. 'It was to discredit Neel Oakley – just because Neel is half-Indian.'

Another item found in Wright's home was a crumpled prescription form. It was made out to Butterworth for a mild anti-depressant. It was concluded that the sergeant had either seen Butterworth throw it away or he had found it in a bin. Regardless, the knowledge had allowed him to start the rumour that Butterworth had committed suicide when he had stepped in front of the lorry.

Oakley burned with a cold, dark anger. If Wright had had any decency he would have told *him* that Butterworth had not collected the prescription that might have helped him keep things in perspective. He was sure he could have persuaded his friend to take the pills – and Mark might still be alive.

The station divided into two camps: those who wanted to dissociate themselves from Wright's infamous bigotry and those who wanted to remember the good things about him. Jeeves was firmly in the former, painfully aware that *he* might be tarred with Wright's brush if Oakley mentioned the episode in the radio room. Keen to ensure that Oakley knew Wright's views weren't his own – and hoping to curry favour by passing information to him before he told the superintendents from Professional Standards – Jeeves sought out the DI in the canteen.

'I need some advice, Guv,' he said, sitting down. Oakley folded his newspaper and waited. 'Barry Wright told me a few things the night before he was killed. I've been thinking about them, and I don't know what to do. It might be nothing, in which case I should forget about them and let him lie in peace. But it might be something...'

'Let's hear it, then,' said Oakley, when Jeeves

paused.

'He was one of us,' said Jeeves unhappily. 'He had his faults, but I don't want to say things when he can't speak to defend himself.'

'Don't eulogize over him, Jeeves. He wasn't "one of us" as far as I'm concerned. He was a dinosaur, and his attitudes were dangerous and unpleasant.'

'I'm sorry I was listening to him that day in the radio room,' blurted Jeeves, 'when you came in. But what else could I do? I couldn't tell him to shut up, could I?'

'Of course you could,' countered Oakley. 'But don't worry, I won't tell the Three Horsemen of the Apocalypse this time. We'll just let it go, shall we?'

Jeeves nodded in relief, then began his story. 'Barry and me went for a drink after work on Friday – not the Mucky Duck, where we usually go, but a place near Redcliffe Bridge. He said he didn't want to be with a lot of bobbies because he was upset by that Helen Anderson business.'

'He was angry,' corrected Oakley. 'Not upset.'

'Whatever. Anyway, because he was off the next day, he drank a fair bit.'

'So I gather.' The post-mortem results indicated that Wright must have been reeling from the amount of alcohol he'd consumed over the previous eight hours.

'I left him at midnight – I had to get up early, even if he didn't. He was pretty drunk, so I took his car keys. I didn't want him driving home.'

'And I suppose you noticed then that he had his car keys, his house keys, and another key all

277

bright and shiny?'

Jeeves nodded. 'The new one was with his car keys, and he made me take it off the fob and give it back. He wouldn't say what it was for, and there was no reason for me to recognize it. But yesterday I got to thinking. He went to get a sandwich at Asda on Friday lunchtime. There's a key-cutting place nearby...'

'So, you think he took the Orchard Street keys from the incident room and went to copy them during his lunch break?'

Jeeves nodded. 'He insisted on coming back to the station before he took the next call, which was weird, as it meant retracing his steps, but I understand now – it was to return them before they were missed.'

'You should tell the Three Horsemen this,' said Oakley, reaching for his paper. 'I don't see why you need me to encourage you.'

'That's not all. When we were at the pub he talked about the anonymous note on the wall of the incident room. While he did, he was looking right at Michael Yorke and Dave Randal, who were sitting in a corner with a couple of women.'

Oakley was astonished. 'You drink in a pub that's frequented by criminals?'

'It was the Hole in the Wall, Guv.' Jeeves was defensive. 'It's a classy place. It's not our fault that Michael and Randal were there that night.'

'So, the meeting was coincidental?'

Jeeves was becoming agitated, seeing in Oakley's questions the conclusions Professional Standards might draw. 'Of course! You don't think I'd have anything to do with the likes of the

Yorke gang, do you?'

'No,' said Oakley, after a moment. He did, however, think that Wright might. 'Go on.'

'After a while Randal went to the bog, and Barry followed him. When they came out, Barry showed me a betting slip. I think he'd picked Randal's pocket.'

'What did he say when he showed it to you?'

'He just grinned and put it in his wallet. Then he went back to slagging you off, saying that you couldn't catch the murderer, so he'd have to lend you a hand.'

'So he stole the betting slip from Randal and was in the process of planting it when someone killed him,' mused Oakley. 'It fits the material evidence, it sounds like something he would do, and it explains why he was there.'

'It doesn't explain who killed him, though,' said Jeeves. 'It wasn't Randal, because I don't think he knew what Barry had done. I doubt he or Michael even noticed us.'

'You need to report this immediately.' Personally Oakley thought that Jeeves was a fool to have left it so long. It looked furtive, to say the least. 'When they ask why you haven't mentioned it before you can say it's only just made sense to you. That's true, isn't it?'

'It is clearer now I've discussed it with you. Do you think Barry was right? The Yorke clan *does* have something to do with Kovac? Yet why would they kill a foreign physicist?'

'I don't know. But I think it's time we paid another visit to Michael and Randal.'

* * *

Before I went home that day I was pleased to hear that one of my anonymous notes was being taken seriously at last – God only knows what happened to the other one. Apparently Oakley was frustrated because there hadn't been a single strand of evidence for FSS to find. I was pleased. All my care and attention to detail had paid off. He wasn't the only one who could be meticulous.

He and Merrick were going to visit the Yorkes soon, although I overheard Superintendent Taylor telling them that they were wasting their time. Wright had believed my note, though, or he wouldn't have been planting 'evidence' to implicate them. Jeeves told me about it, although he wasn't supposed to. Jeeves is rubbish at keeping secrets.

I thought it ironic that Wright's death should come about as a result of my note, and all I can say is that he must have been really drunk to think that he could introduce the betting slip to the crime scene at that stage of the investigation. Perhaps he'd intended to 'find' it himself – an experienced officer solving the case with a quick and penetrating look around him. I doubt Oakley would have fallen for it, though.

The other thing I gleaned from the grapevine was that Wright had given James the information about Butterworth's Blunder – he'd photocopied the property book. But his bank account didn't show any sudden and inexplicable payments, so it was generally assumed that his motives were malicious rather than fiscal.

I was livid, though, because I saw that I'd

probably told James nothing he didn't already know from Wright about Butterworth's Blunder on that horrible day on the train. He'd merely wanted to put me in a terrible situation, so that he could use my guilty conscience to blackmail me later. He'd played me for a gullible fool.

Still fuming, I went home to get ready to see a play at the Old Vic with Colin. My life was so much better than it had been the week before. Colin and I were still getting to know each other, and I liked him more and more. Wright was gone, and the atmosphere at work had been much nicer, despite the shock at his death. Taylor had ordered Oakley not to waste any more time on James's disappearance, while DI Davis was doggedly bent on proving that Kovac was the killer. And James's murder seemed a lifetime ago. I barely thought about Wright's. Perhaps I was getting used to them.

Thursday, 23 August
The police search for Marko Kovac grew more intense now that the case involved the death of one of their own. His photograph was shown again and again on television, with a bulletin to say he was wanted for questioning.

There were two theories among the murder squad officers. First, Davis led a faction that thought Kovac had murdered either someone connected to his secret policeman brother, or someone trying to steal his research. This scenario had him returning to the house when the guard was absent, so he'd been there when Wright had arrived.

The second theory, headed by Evans, was that Kovac was the victim. He'd been delayed in leaving, and the Yorke gang had found him in a house that should have been empty. He was killed to ensure his silence. The gang had then waited until the police stopped guarding number nine, and had killed Wright when he burst in on them.

The problem Oakley had with both hypotheses was the house – why would Kovac return to a place he had cleaned his belongings out of, and why would the Yorke gang be there at all, never mind going back again later? He also thought Wright's death was more complex than just stumbling across the culprit and paying the price. But he had no better explanation, and Taylor was beginning to lose patience with his refusal to accept the conveniently missing Albanian as a solution to the mysteries.

He visited the university again that evening, but the department was locked up. He was about to leave when he saw Ron Yates carrying two buckets of dirty water.

'Trouble?' he asked, watching Yates tip them down the drain.

'An ongoing problem – a flood in the basement. Any news on Marko?'

Oakley shook his head. 'But I wondered if he'd received any post this week that might help us find him.' He knew he sounded as though he was snatching at straws. 'May I look?'

'Nothing came this morning – I've been keeping an eye on it, like you asked. But there might have been a delivery this afternoon. Come in, and we'll check his pigeon hole.'

Oakley followed him along a corridor and down a flight of stairs, where Yates stepped carefully across a puddled floor that was swathed in black plastic, all fixed together with thick lines of silver tape. A large roll of the plastic lay at the far end of the room, along with a box containing a dozen rolls of duct tape.

Oakley stared at them. 'Did Kovac ever ask for any of this?'

Yates shook his head. 'No, why?'

'Then could he have helped himself?'

Yates shrugged. 'Yes, I suppose so, although I can't imagine why. No one ever comes down here except me. There's a men's loo over there, but most of the staff use the newer ones on the first floor.'

'So he may have come for the toilet and seen this plastic and tape?'

Yates nodded. 'Why? Is it important?'

Friday, 24 August
Wright's murder had taken precedence over the stale case of the unidentified body, and Oakley had been forbidden to interview the Yorke gang until it was determined if they were involved in the sergeant's death. He protested vehemently, but the three superintendents were adamant – he might spoil their chances of nailing Wright's killer if he asked the wrong questions. Oakley disagreed, but an order was an order, so he grudgingly abandoned that line of enquiry.

He sent a piece of plastic and a roll of tape from the university to FSS, and the result had come back surprisingly quickly – the edge of the piece from the university was a perfect match for the piece that had been wrapped around the body. Moreover, dust on both proved they came from the Victorian building that housed the physics department. Kovac was indeed responsible for taking them to Orchard Street, thus supporting the theory that he was the killer. As Davis was quick to ask, why else would he pinch them?

Oakley turned his attention back to the anonymous note, casually ignoring both Taylor's orders and the fact that it was a lead that pointed back to the Yorkes. A handwriting expert told him nothing he couldn't have guessed for himself: the author had used capital letters to disguise his writing and the spelling was eccentric, which suggested either a poor education or a deliberate attempt to mislead. Because the writing was neat, the palaeographer was inclined to opt for the second. This fitted in with the pains the writer had taken to make sure there was no trace evidence.

The saliva test on the stamp didn't look promising, either. There wasn't enough of it, and the hot weather since it had been posted had degraded the DNA. FSS hadn't given up completely, though, and one dedicated soul was working on it just for the challenge.

Oakley sat at his desk that evening, put his feet up, and accepted the mug of the powerful coffee Evans brought him. 'Let's review what we've got – not theories and hunches, but actual facts.'

'All right,' said Evans, pulling up a chair.

'Kovac stole black plastic and tape from the university – and there's no reason why he should do that except to wrap a body.'

'Let's not start with him. Let's look at the Yorke gang.'

'Why? We'll never get to talk to them as long as the Three Tenors are here.'

Oakley ignored him. 'Yorke thought Paxton was going to get him bail – a fact borne out by Giles Farnaby's statement *and* by the anonymous note. But Paxton disappeared two days before the hearing. Now, I know coincidences happen, but I don't like this one and I'm thinking more and more that the body might be his.'

'But he's gone off with his gay pals,' sighed Evans. 'Even his colleagues think so.'

'But his mother doesn't, and she knows him better than they do. Let's assume he hasn't, and something bad has happened to him.'

'Then his disappearance fits with our body's estimated time of death. Moreover, the corpse was wearing a nice suit and a white shirt – lawyer's attire. No tie, though, and Paxton was a man who liked ties, according to Mummy. However, there's one big problem with that theory: our body isn't Paxton, because the dental records don't match.'

'Did Grossman look at anything other than the missing tooth? What about fillings, bridges or whatever? Did he check any of that?'

'There was no point. The lost premolar eliminates him. Full stop.'

'What if someone tampered with the dental records? Such as his mother?'

'Come on, Guv! She *wants* him identified. Why would she try to mislead us?'

'Don't you think it's a bit gruesome, bringing your son's dental records to be tested against an unidentified body? Perhaps she knows it's him, but doesn't want us to know.'

'Now you're in La-La Land,' said Evans firmly. 'Sorry, Guv, but our body isn't Paxton, and if you think it is, then it's just wishful thinking.'

'Let's just make sure,' said Oakley, reaching for his jacket. 'I've had a funny feeling about this for a while. Grossman should still be around. Let's get him to have another look.'

'What, now?' asked Evans without enthusiasm. 'It's gone eight on a Friday night. He will have gone home by now.'

'He's there – I heard Taylor talking to him on the phone about a traffic accident not long ago.'

'He won't like it,' warned Evans. 'He'll think you're questioning his competency.'

'I am,' said Oakley.

Evans was right: Grossman wasn't pleased that Oakley wanted him to go over something he'd already done, especially as he had two victims from a fatal pile-up on the M4. He refused at first, but relented when he realized Oakley wasn't going to leave until he obliged. With bad grace, he snatched up a dental mirror, grabbed Paxton's chart and hauled open the drawer that contained the body.

'Look,' he said, exasperated. 'Paxton was missing a premolar – this fellow has all four present and correct. Paxton had a filling in his lower central incisor – this fellow's incisors are untouched. It's not the same man.'

'Are those the only differences?' pressed Oakley. 'What about that big gold crown at the back? Does Paxton have one of those?'

Grossman studied the record. 'Yes. And a bridge across the lower left seven and eight.' He frowned. 'And a complete veneering of all four upper incisors. Curious.'

'Meaning what?' asked Oakley impatiently.

'Meaning there are two definite differences between this man and Paxton, but there are several similarities, including some distinctive cosmetic work.'

'So what are you saying? Is it Paxton or not?'

Grossman looked furtive. 'Perhaps I should call in a forensic odontologist.'

'How long will that take?'

'I don't know. A couple of days.'

'And in the meantime?' asked Oakley, frustrated.

'I suggest you get a sample of Paxton's DNA. His toothbrush would be best. Or his razor.'

'So it *is* him?' demanded Oakley. 'We've got an ID at last?'

Grossman nodded slowly. 'I can't say for sure, you understand, but I'd be surprised now if it proved to be someone else.'

I finished work at ten o'clock that night and planned to go straight to Colin's place. I'd enjoyed my day, and had impressed Inspector Blake by getting two juvenile shoplifters to confess to a whole string of other offences. For the first time in ages I felt as though I was good at my job. There was no question about it: Wright's absence definitely made the world a better place.

I was humming as I walked out – until I met Oakley and Evans, who were just coming in and looked really pleased with themselves. I asked why.

'We need DNA to be sure,' said Oakley, 'but I think we've finally got an ID for our body. It's James Paxton!'

I felt as though the world had suddenly stopped spinning. I'd just about rebuilt my life, only to have it crashing down around me again.

'I thought dental records indicated otherwise,' I said, with a mouth so dry that it felt as if it were stuffed with cotton wool.

'Some clerk must have cocked up,' Oakley explained. 'A filling and an extraction were mis-marked. We'll check with the dentist tomorrow.'

'Grossman is past it,' said Evans disparagingly. 'He should have noticed the similarities as well as the differences. It's time he retired.'

They walked away, discussing Grossman's incompetence, and leaving me weak-kneed in the doorway. My head was pounding this time, as well as my heart.

How long before they requested James's phone records, and discovered that I'd been the last person he'd contacted? I'd done all in my power to prevent them from learning it was James, and I'd bought myself a lot of time. But now what? I forced myself to walk down the steps, hoping that my shaking legs wouldn't deposit me in a heap on the ground.

FOURTEEN

Saturday, 25 August

It had been a busy night for Oakley and Evans, who proceeded as if the body were Paxton. There were numerous protocols to be followed – forms to fill in, a warrant to seize Paxton's records from the dentist and requests made for specific tests, including a visit from the forensic odontologist. Paxton's DNA would need to be matched to the corpse, and his colleagues at Urvine and Brotherton interviewed again. By the time they had finished it was almost four o'clock.

'Shall we visit Maureen now?' asked Evans, leaning back and rubbing his neck.

Oakley shook his head. 'Let her have her sleep. God knows, she'll be facing a lot of bad nights from now on. We'll do it first thing tomorrow.'

'Today,' corrected Evans. 'I might just kip down in the cells for a couple of hours. It's hardly worth going home and disturbing the missus.'

Oakley couldn't sleep because his mind was racing. He went through witness statements with renewed energy, and by the time Evans arrived back, stupid with sleep and sporting a bad shave, he was impatient to make a start. At eight a.m.

289

they were knocking on Mrs Paxton's door to ask for the keys to her son's flat, so they could collect his comb, toothbrush and razor to test for his DNA. And a cheek swab from her.

Despite Oakley's insistence that nothing was certain until the tests had been run, the hapless Mrs Paxton collapsed on the floor and wept. Oakley radioed for a female officer to wait with her until relatives could be contacted, and it was Anderson who arrived. She didn't offer words of empty comfort, but simply sat next to Maureen and put her arm around her.

'I *knew* something had happened to him,' Maureen sobbed. 'A mother feels these things. You didn't believe me.'

'You also said your son would never be in Orchard Street,' said Oakley. 'There was no reason to make the connection between him and the body.'

'But who would want to harm him?' cried Maureen, not listening as she huddled in her own world of grief. 'He *helped* people. He didn't have enemies!'

'Did he ever mention Marko Kovac?' asked Oakley, unwilling to disabuse her of that notion. 'Had he ever been to Albania? Or did he have clients from there?'

'Of course not!' cried Maureen. 'He was like me. He preferred Britain to foreign places. I don't know about his clients. You'll have to ask Mr Brotherton.'

'Did he ever talk about a branch of science called nanotechnology?' Oakley saw her bemusement. 'Making small machines the size of an atom?'

'No! James knew nothing about atom bombs! He was a barrister.'

Oakley wondered who might be able to tell him whether Paxton had been interested in commercially lucrative science. Perhaps Kovac had hired him to patent his idea, but the lawyer had been greedy with fees, so Kovac had dealt with the nuisance with a rock, black plastic and duct tape. Yet patent law was different from criminal law, and he wasn't sure Paxton was qualified. Perhaps that had been the problem.

'You'll have to look in his diary,' said Maureen in a strangled voice. 'Find out who he was meeting between Tuesday after work and Thursday when he was due in court. Whoever he met will be his killer.'

'He probably met any number of people, Mrs Paxton,' said Anderson gently. 'And he may not have noted them all down.'

Oakley imagined that was true, especially if Paxton had been due to liaise with someone – Wright? – who'd offered to provide him with information to see Yorke a free man. However, he'd been through Paxton's diaries and emails – again – the previous night, and knew that Paxton had nothing booked after 4.30 p.m. on the Tuesday. Any other encounters, including the one at the gay bar, had been off the record.

'Farnaby,' said Maureen suddenly. '*He* killed James because he was jealous.'

Or because he didn't want Paxton to represent the man who had beaten his grandmother, thought Oakley. Indeed, at that precise moment

291

Davis and Merrick were asking Farnaby to accompany them to the station for further questioning.

'We're also waiting for his phone company to send us their records,' Oakley said. 'We'll be able to trace who he called and when. There must be a good reason why James's mobile wasn't with his body. Perhaps the killer took it.'

'He was never without his mobile,' agreed Maureen. 'It was always switched on, except in court. Yes – that might help.'

'We're hoping he made arrangements to go to Orchard Street, and the phone seems a good starting point.'

'Wouldn't you have thought it more likely that he was sent a note? asked Anderson. 'By email or even by hand.'

'Not email – I checked. Moreover, the Orchard Street house was available through James's connections, not the killer's, as far as we know. The chances are that he suggested the venue, not the other way around.'

'I'm not so sure,' said Anderson obstinately. 'The phone seems to be a waste of time to me.'

'Well, we'll see,' said Oakley, wondering why he was discussing it with her. What did she know? 'Murder enquiries are all about following leads, and most transpire to be nothing. But some produce gold, and the phone might be one of them.'

'He was never without his mobile,' repeated Maureen in a fresh welter of tears. Her sobs became wracking and uncontrolled.

Oakley escaped with cowardly relief. Breaking

such news was the part of the job that he hated more than any other. He spent the rest of the day speaking to Paxton's colleagues at Urvine and Brotherton and his neighbours, but learned nothing he didn't already know. They were shocked to hear that Paxton had been murdered, but few seemed particularly upset. Only his mother, it seemed, would really miss him.

It was terrible trying to comfort Mrs Paxton, although at least she didn't recognize me from my schooldays – not that she would've done, I suppose. I doubt she would've thought me grand enough for her golden son, and I'd have been well beneath her notice. Still, it was dreadful to know that I was responsible for her grief.

I'd spent a miserable night, fretting and worrying about what the identification of James might mean for me. Colin asked what was wrong – he was too sensitive not to notice my agitation – so I spun a tale about being upset about Wright. He pressed me no further.

It wasn't until the small hours of the morning that I managed to pull myself together, huddled against Colin and feeling the rhythmic rise and fall of his breathing. He was sweating from having me so close and was sleeping restlessly, but I was chilled to the bone and wanted his warmth.

I'd almost fainted when Oakley said that he'd requested James's phone records. I didn't know what to say. Perhaps I should have stayed mum, so that when he asked me why James had phoned me that Tuesday evening – twice – I could deny it. I could say I'd been out at the time. I was fairly sure my mother wouldn't remember whether I'd been with her or not. I could use her as an alibi.

Even as I soothed Mrs Paxton with meaning-less words, a plan began to form in my mind. It was common knowledge that Wright had hated me, so I'd claim that he must have given James my number as part of some spiteful plot. He'd then taken James's phone after the murder and called me on it, and when I'd answered I'd obviously assumed that it was his mobile and not James's. People would almost certainly believe that. Bitterly, I wondered whether Oakley would have followed the trail to James if he'd received my second note – the one blaming Kovac and drugs. What had happened to the damned thing? It couldn't be lost in the post, given that I'd delivered it by hand. Still, it was irrelevant now.

A murder victim has no privacy, and I knew there'd be nothing about James that wouldn't be probed and investigated. Then it occurred to me that blaming Wright would do me no good, be-cause Oakley would find out what school James had gone to and, if he interviewed Frances, Gary or Colin, they'd mention me. Oakley might even recognize Colin from when they'd met by the Watershed. I'd be Oakley's prime suspect, especially given that I'd advised him to drop the phone angle. That had been a mistake. Being a murderer isn't easy, I can tell you.

I was relieved when Oakley left Maureen's house, but frightened at the same time. What should I do? Leave the country? Spain was a good place to go, as there were a lot of flights in the summer, and Brits could easily disappear there. I felt the net closing in and was disappointed my ploy with the dental records hadn't worked permanently.

I sat with James's mother for a long time, but there's not much you can say to someone who's lost her only son – not that's worth hearing, at least. You can't say it will be all right, because it won't. As far as Maureen Paxton was concerned, nothing would be right ever again. So I just sat with her, and wished her family would hurry up and arrive.

While I was there, I did a lot of thinking. Oakley and the others would assume, of course, that it was the killer who'd wrapped James in plastic. I'd concluded it was the Yorke gang, because James had summoned me to help him with Yorke's case. But what if James had been juggling more than one ball? What if he had something going with Kovac, too? Or what if James hadn't died when I'd hit him? What if Kovac had found him injured and had finished the job?

Maureen told me that James hadn't had many close friends, and I'd looked in his address book when she'd shown it to Oakley. I wasn't in it, thank God, probably because he hadn't considered me important enough. Or perhaps he hadn't wanted to be in possession of evidence that he knew me, in case I hadn't played his game and had turned him in.

James was twenty-eight years old, and school was a distant memory. Oakley wouldn't look that far back yet, and would concentrate on his work and clients. I still had a few days grace, which would be enough to think about what I wanted to do: flee to Spain or try to weather it out. But I didn't reckon with Oakley's annoying attention to detail...

Giles Farnaby sat in one of New Bridewell's interview rooms looking pale and miserable. Robert Brotherton sat with him, and sometimes tried to stop him from replying, but Farnaby claimed he had nothing to hide and wanted to help.

He admitted on tape this time to following Paxton into the gay bar, but he had friends who were prepared to swear that he had spent the rest of the evening with them at a completely different location. Merrick quietly confirmed that this was true: he'd seen Paxton in the bar thirty minutes *after* Farnaby said he had met his friends, and he had not seen him in there.

Farnaby had spent hours at the hospital with his grandmother and taken a fair amount of time off work. He couldn't be sure where he was at specific times, but the staff at the intensive care unit could vouch for a good deal of it because there was a visitor's log. Of course, there were times when he was at home, supposedly asleep, when he could have slipped out and committed a murder, but Oakley became convinced during the course of the interview that he hadn't.

There was little more Oakley could do than ask Farnaby not to leave Bristol without giving a contact address. The lawyer walked away with his head bowed, although his distress had more to do with the fact that Emma Vinson had died that morning than his being a suspect in a murder enquiry. When he had gone, Brotherton turned to Oakley.

'Urvine and Brotherton is a respected company. We have a reputation for honesty and fair dealing.'

'Right,' said Oakley, thinking that his experiences with Paxton suggested otherwise.

'We have an interest in justice, just as you do,' Brotherton went on. 'I disapproved of Paxton's tactics in the Noble trial. Had I known what he'd planned I would have stopped him.'

'Then it's a pity that *you* weren't Noble's lawyer,' said Oakley bitterly. 'Paxton's antics had some serious consequences.'

'I know that. And in the interests of justice I feel compelled to pass you these papers. I wish to stress that neither I nor anyone else at my firm had knowledge of these transactions at the time, and that we have only uncovered them following on from your initial findings after James disappeared. I am passing them to you, at this early stage in the investigation, so that you can be assured that we have nothing to hide.'

The sheaf of pages Brotherton passed him comprised transcripts of phone conversations between Paxton and people Oakley didn't know. He glanced at Brotherton, mystified.

'They were members of the jury in the case against Andrew Brown – the handbag snatcher. You don't need me to tell you that fraternising with them during a trial is against the rules.'

'So he *did* get a verdict by unethical means?'

'I believe so, although you won't prove it with those transcripts – he didn't offer money or make threats. He just chatted, doubtless to befriend them in the hope that they'd be more receptive to his arguments. I suspect this was his first dive into the unethical. He became more careful after, and we haven't found anything in our records since. He must've used a different mode of communication.'

'His missing mobile, I imagine. When did you first suspect he was bending the rules?'

'After Brown, when he began to win rather too often. However, I only started to probe into his affairs when he went missing. What you hold in your hand is the result of my investigations.'

Oakley met his eyes. 'When I visited your offices in Queen Square, did you leave those files behind deliberately – the ones with the photographed pages from the police file?'

Brotherton returned his gaze evenly. 'I don't know what you're talking about.'

Oakley nodded. 'Thank you.'

'My firm does not condone what Paxton did, and I wish I'd listened to young Farnaby's suspicions. I dismissed them because James had been promoted over his head – I didn't trust his motives.'

'But it was Paxton's motives that were suspect?'

'Very suspect,' agreed Brotherton.

Sunday, 26 August
The investigation began to leap ahead again. Oakley arrived at work at six o'clock to go

through the witness statements gathered the previous afternoon. Merrick was also in early, and they worked in silence for a while. Eventually Oakley leaned back in his chair and began to summarise what they knew.

'James Henry Paxton. Twenty-eight. Not married; no steady girlfriend. Seen in a gay bar the evening before his death, leading to speculation about his sexuality. Lawyer to unsavoury characters like Andy Brown, Gordon Noble and Billy Yorke.'

Merrick took up the tale. 'He left work at around four thirty on Tuesday the thirty-first of July, and I saw him at six. We've found no one who saw him later – yet.'

'We'd better visit that bar. I'll take Evans with me – it shouldn't be you. Have you heard from the phone company?'

'No. We had to produce a warrant before they'd deal with us, but we should hear today.'

'That's Paxton's mobile *and* his home phone?'

Merrick nodded. 'And Tim Hillier went through his work email with me again yesterday, and I've ploughed through his personal account. I even retrieved some trashed messages, but there was nothing relevant in either. Paxton was a dull fellow – virtually all his messages pertained to business, and none were social. The man was obsessed with work.'

'Or his private life was so dodgy he didn't keep records.' Oakley stood and leaned against the wall, hands in his pockets. 'Let's try to reconstruct what happened that Tuesday night.'

'We don't know he died then,' warned Merrick. 'He might have died on Wednesday or even later.'

Oakley shook his head. 'You just pointed out that he was obsessed by work. I don't see him not showing up on the Wednesday morning without good cause.'

'All right. So, he left work at four thirty and probably headed to Clifton, where he met this friend. Farnaby saw him at five thirty, and I saw him at six, so it wasn't just some quick sordid drop off or hasty exchange of information. They stayed together for at least thirty minutes, and probably longer. We don't know when he left.'

'He went to Orchard Street, which he knew was empty because Academic Accommodations would have told him Kovac had left that morning. He also had a key, because Urvine and Brotherton look after the property.'

'Why there?' asked Merrick. 'Why not a pub?'

'Because he didn't want to be seen. If that anonymous note is anything to go by – and there's no reason we shouldn't take it seriously – the Yorkes are involved. Paxton probably had some trick lined up to get him bail, but died before he could deliver. That suggests three possibilities. First, a rival gang decided to prevent Yorke getting out. Second, Paxton's plan fell through, so the Yorkes killed him. Third, he did have something lined up, but was killed trying to organize it.'

'I agree that he was meeting someone in secret. Orchard Street isn't his kind of place, so he must've had some sly reason for going there. But

300

I don't think the Yorkes killed him. Even if Paxton didn't manage to get Billy bail, he'd still be his best bet for the trial.'

'And I don't see a rival gang as responsible, either,' admitted Oakley. 'I think we'd have heard something on the street if so. Yet that note must've been sent by someone with a grudge against Yorke.'

'At lot hinges on that,' sighed Merrick. 'Find the writer and we'll have cracked the case.'

'Any ideas? Other than hoping the saliva gives us something?'

'None.'

They looked up as Evans walked in. He held a sheaf of papers, and his beaming face suggested that there was good news at last.

'A big step forward!' he announced. 'I got fingerprints to re-check the partials on the duct tape against Randal. We got two hits.'

Oakley took the report from Evans and his elation turned to disappointment. 'No – two of the partials have *points of similarity* to Randal's, but the probability of them being his is one in ten thousand.'

'That's good enough for me,' said Evans.

'Well, it's not for me. There are four hundred thousand people in Bristol, which means that in this city alone we've got forty people who'll match. Nationally, there'll be six thousand. I don't want to go to court with that.'

'But Bristol's not a population of four hundred thousand criminals,' Evans argued stubbornly. 'Discount kids, grannies and God-fearing citizens, and there'll be a lot less.'

'You're assuming that a criminal murdered Paxton,' argued Oakley. 'However, think about the fact that he had confidential police papers in his files, and ... shit!' He broke off as a dreadful possibility occurred to him.

'Wright?' asked Merrick softly, reading his mind. '*Wright* killed Paxton, because Paxton threatened to expose him for leaking confidential information?'

'It fits, doesn't it?' asked Oakley. 'Find out whether Wright was working on the Tuesday that Paxton went missing.'

A discreet word with Jeeves – as far as that was possible – told them that Wright hadn't been out drinking with the lads that night. DI Davis agreed to speak to Wright's wife to see whether she recalled her husband going off on business of his own.

'Kovac and Wright together?' she asked doubt-fully. 'Sounds like a strange combination.'

'I'm not sure how Kovac fits in,' said Oakley. '*If* he does.'

'Of course he does.' Davis ticked the points off on her fingers. 'He disappears the day that the murder is committed. He steals plastic and tape from the university. He remains missing.'

'It's all very speculative,' said Oakley. 'And there's no evidence that Wright was in the house *before* the Paxton murder. But since he was wearing gloves when he died, I suppose he'd have worn them the first time, too. I wish we had something a bit more concrete. God knows, I didn't like the man, but I don't want him charged with murder on the evidence we've got.'

'You're too soft,' said Davis. 'He wouldn't have given you the benefit of the doubt.'

I was doing a brief spell of duty in the reception area when the package arrived from the phone company. Both clerks who usually ran the 'front desk' were off sick, and we were taking turns to do two-hour spells until they came back. Normally, I didn't mind, as it meant staying in rather than trudging around outside. But I was restless and anxious, and I was even more restless and anxious when the courier delivered the parcel.

I knew exactly what it was. And it was a damned shame, because the rumour was that Wright was in the frame for murdering James, and that solution suited me perfectly.

Paul Franklin signed for the parcel, and dropped it in the CID mail basket on the far side of the room. It sat there like a great, bloated bundle of menace, and my eyes were drawn to it no matter where I stood. It held the record of my guilt, and as soon as Oakley began tracking the numbers that appeared in the details printed there, it would be all over for me.

I stared at it. Should I take it and get rid of it on my way home? But Oakley would just order another set, and I couldn't hope to intercept that as well. Should I open it and remove the bit that incriminated me? No – Oakley would notice it was missing. Should I doctor it then, so that instead of my number, it would show someone else's? But I wasn't sure my forging skills were up to that. Moreover, all those options offered only a temporary reprieve – I needed something permanent.

Then the solution came. I could doctor the *whole account*. I could retype the entire thing, leaving out the parts that incriminated me. There were plenty of computers in the station, and no one would ask what I was doing. I could even reproduce the correct font for the headings, and if the phone company's logo was complex, I'd just have to do a cut-and-paste job with glue, scissors and the scanner. Oakley wouldn't be expecting a forgery so he wouldn't question it.

My mind was made up. My spell at reception would be over in a quarter of an hour, and no one kept tabs on me as Wright had done. I could spend the last two hours of my shift pretending to do paperwork. I watched the last few minutes of my reception duty tick away on the large clock above the door, willing fifteen minutes to become ten, then five, then two, then...

'Good,' said Oakley, walking in and grabbing the parcel. 'I've been waiting for this.'

The time spent questioning people at the Clifton bar had been a waste. Oakley had expected the hostility and antagonism usually encountered when the police made enquiries among threatened minorities, but most of the clientele were very helpful, and no one had refused to talk to him. Many were academics from the university, along with a smattering of businessmen and clerks. The pub was friendly and relaxed, and he was not surprised that Merrick liked it.

Unfortunately, the patrons could tell him

nothing useful. Weekday evenings between six and eight were busy because people stopped for a drink on their way home. Many tables were set in small alcoves, for privacy, so people tended not to notice others. Merrick had seen because he'd been trained to be observant – and because he had a lot to lose by being exposed, he was naturally wary – while Farnaby had been trailing Paxton deliberately.

Only two people recognized Paxton, and one was uncertain, because the photograph Oakley had taken from Urvine and Brotherton's promotional brochure showed him smiling. The other said he had only seen Paxton once – about a month before – with a handsome, dark-haired companion who may have been foreign.

'Was this him?' asked Oakley, showing the picture of Kovac.

The man shook his head. 'Not *that* handsome. I'd have remembered *him*.'

On his return to the station Oakley collected the telephone records and took them to the incident room. He and Evans began the laborious process of looking for patterns. Merrick burst in before they'd been at it for long.

'The forensic odontologist's been,' he said. 'He doesn't get many cases any more, so he leapt at the chance to do this one. He didn't wait for Grossman to give him the dental records – he got his own set from the dentist so he wouldn't have to wait.'

'And?' asked Oakley impatiently.

'And its James Paxton,' said Merrick triumphantly. 'One hundred per cent certain. Everything matches, and he says he's surprised Grossman didn't see it immediately.'

'That stupid old man,' grumbled Evans. 'He should retire.'

Oakley felt scant satisfaction with the news, knowing what it would mean for the lawyer's mother, although Merrick soon had the incident room buzzing with the news, and there was a flurry of activity as some lines of enquiry were abandoned and others begun. Oakley and Evans turned back to the phone records.

'What was the last call he made from his landline?' asked Oakley. 'And when?'

Evans ran his eye down the columns of numbers. 'There are several after he was probably dead, including three to Urvine and Brotherton. I think that was Mummy, trying to find out where he was. I imagine the last call *he* made was on the Tuesday morning, to Mummy's number. Then there was one on the previous Monday, preceded by a long gap. I suspect he didn't use it much. What about the mobile?'

'Not as many calls as I'd have thought, considering Maureen said he was never without it. He probably used his office phone until four thirty – although Dave didn't come up with anything helpful when he went through those records yesterday – but there's nothing after five o'clock here. There are a whole series of calls after Friday the third, though, the most recent being this morning.'

'So it's been stolen,' surmised Evans.

'That's risky. Using a phone filched from a murder victim.'

'Why? A dead man's not going to complain.'

'But his family might. And would *you* take the risk?'

'No,' admitted Evans.

Oakley shook his head, dispirited. 'Damn! I bet he had another phone for his more dubious business – a pay-as-you-go, which could be dropped in the river when it was no longer needed. But we'll have to go through his normal records anyway. Just because he didn't call anyone the night he died doesn't mean that he didn't set the meeting up by phone. He might have done it weeks ago.'

'But these records go back three months,' said Evans, dismayed. He saw his inspector shrug. 'All right. Let's make a start.'

Monday, 27 August

A third witness came forward to say he'd seen the scarf-clad woman, but since the 'suspect' hadn't actually been seen entering or leaving the murder house, the information didn't help much. However, the telephone enquiry was proceeding well, because most of the people Paxton had called were clients. As his clients were criminals, the suspect list was growing exponentially. Meanwhile, the phone company was directed to contact the police when the stolen mobile was next used, and the general expectation in the incident room was that when they'd traced it, they'd have the killer.

Yet Oakley remained uncertain. As far as he was concerned, the only real way forward was to interview Randal, to see what he said about the fact that his partials had been found at the scene of the murder.

Unfortunately, the Wright investigation was stopping them. Professional Standards was taking matters carefully, determined that when an arrest was made it would be rock solid. Although it wasn't actually said, the implication was that while the Wright enquiry might jeopardise the Paxton investigation, the opposite would never be allowed to happen.

I couldn't believe my luck! I'd spent the whole night waiting in sick apprehension, expecting at any moment to hear the loud knock on the door, after which I'd be dragged away in handcuffs while my colleagues swarmed over my house, pawing through my personal belongings. I'd been so convinced that it would be my last night of freedom that I hadn't even bothered to undress for bed. I couldn't bear the notion of being found in my nightie.

I'd looked at flights online, and had gone to the bank and withdrawn as much money as I could. Then I'd packed a bag with my favourite things – a picture of my mother, some family jewellery, a couple of books and various other keepsakes. These lay at the bottom of my case, with hot-weather clothes on top.

But I didn't go to Spain, and Oakley didn't come. I couldn't understand why. I went to work that morning, wondering what the chances were that I wouldn't be going home again. But when I arrived at the station, the only news was that Gordon Noble had been arrested for drunk driving. He hadn't been able to stand up straight when his car had been stopped, so even he wasn't going to evade justice this time.

I offered to deliver a memo to Dave Merrick in order to get into the incident room, desperate for information. I felt the familiar thud of my heart as I went in, but it was the same as usual, with people sitting here and there, reading through mounds of paper that would prove irrelevant, and answering phones. Oakley had James's phone records in front of him. He looked exhausted, and I felt sorry for him. Still, I had to think that his moment of victory was coming.

'You were right, Helen,' he said as I walked past. 'Looking into Paxton's phone calls is a waste of time. He didn't contact anyone the night he died, while in the weeks before he must have phoned every rogue in the city. It'll take months to eliminate them all!'

'You mean like Yorke and his friends?' I asked, hoping to steer him back in that direction. What was going on? Of course James had made calls that night – two were to me!

Oakley nodded. 'But so what? Yorke's case was coming up, so of course they'd be in touch.'

But James *had* called me. Did that mean he'd had two mobiles – a legal one and one for making clandestine calls? If so, Oakley would have no more idea where to find it than I did.

'It's still being used, so Taylor thinks the killer must've swiped it,' Oakley went on. 'I suppose it makes sense. After all, someone emptied his pockets of his wallet, keys, et cetera, presumably to prevent identification.'

'Why would the killer use it?' I asked before I could stop myself. What was I doing? Putting doubts in his mind was hardly wise!

Oakley gave a wry smile. 'I don't think he is, but I'm in a minority. Anyway, whoever had it waited for four days before making a call. Obviously he thought he'd be safe by then.'

He clearly knew nothing about murderers. *I* didn't feel safe, and it was almost a month since I'd killed James.

It was odd, I thought to myself, that I was more concerned about being caught for James's murder than for Wright's. Wright meant nothing to me, and I rarely thought about his death. Perhaps it was because James was the first. Perhaps it was because I didn't feel remorse for what I'd done to Wright. Perhaps it was because the shame and disgust for what I'd done to Wright would come later.

But I'd been reprieved yet again – I was free for another day. My fears about the phone had been unfounded, and unless Oakley found James's second mobile, I was off the hook.

Oakley drove to Mrs Paxton's house to find a shiny red BMW parked in the drive. He was certain it wasn't hers, and wondered if it had belonged to James, liberated from his garage without asking police permission.

'I'm Donna Trembleth,' said the attractive woman who answered the door. She was richly confident and immaculately dressed. 'Maureen's niece. I'm here to keep her company until this nasty matter is over.'

'We're working very hard to catch your cousin's killer, Ms Trembleth, but it might help if we knew more about his personal life.'

'No!' The sharp voice from the hall beyond made Oakley jump. Maureen Paxton's hair was perfect, the cement of her make-up in place, and all traces of hysterical grief eradicated. Only a slight darkness under her eyes suggested she'd been under strain. The police liaison officer was behind her, a middle-aged constable in a scruffy suit.

'I don't understand, Mrs Paxton,' said Oakley. 'We only want—'

'I know what happens when you paw through people's personal affairs. Things get misinterpreted and it damages those who aren't there to defend themselves.' Her chin trembled slightly, but then she regained control.

'You think something in James's life is open to misinterpretation?'

'No, that's *not* what I'm saying,' snapped Maureen, 'although it proves my point. I said innocent things are misinterpreted and distorted. The fact that you immediately jumped to the conclusion that James had something to hide proves that I'm right.'

'We're not trying to do anything like that,' said Oakley gently, although she was right. Wright's wife was going through a similar process, and God knew what they'd dredge up from *his* past. 'But someone was unpleasant enough to kill James, so we know he had dealings with at least one unsavoury person.'

'Of course he did, but through *work*. His

311

clients were unsavoury. But you want to look into his *personal* life. You saw what that horrible Farnaby did when James went missing. He started stories that James was homosexual.' She spat out the last word and Oakley saw the liaison officer regard her with dislike.

'We're just trying to get a picture of—'

'Oh, yes, *now* you are. You're fascinated with him *now*, but you didn't give a damn when I reported him missing!'

'That's not true, Mrs Paxton,' said Oakley quietly. 'We did a lot more for James than we do for most missing adults. But now we're trying to catch his murderer. We can't do that unless the people who loved him, and who want his killer brought to justice, are prepared to do all they can to help. You knew James: we didn't. We need you.'

'Mr Brotherton told me that James had bribed juries.' Maureen's eyes filled with angry tears. 'He said that James was involved in all manner of illegal practices, and that he'd brought Urvine and Brotherton into disrepute. But James would never do anything like that.'

'I'm sorry you had to learn that,' said Oakley. 'We'll try to keep it out of the papers – Brotherton certainly won't want it made public. It may come out in the trial, but only if it becomes relevant.'

'Trial!' she spat. 'What do *they* do but destroy innocent people?'

She turned and stalked away, and Oakley saw her shoulders heaving with sobs. Her opinion of trials hardly seemed to be what he would have expected from a criminal lawyer's mother. But she was right about two things: the police *were* more interested in Paxton now he was a murder victim, and her son's dirty linen *would* be pawed through in detail.

'She's upset,' said Donna. 'She didn't mean to be rude.'

'It's all right. I can't begin to imagine what she's going through.'

Donna hesitated, then forged on. 'This is probably totally useless, but I went to the same school as James – I was a couple of years below him, but I knew his friends. There was a couple he really liked: Gary Sheldick and Frances Moorfield. They probably haven't seen each other for years, but they *were* good pals. They might be able to tell you what James was like.'

'And you can't?'

'Not really. He was always too busy for us, so all I know is that he didn't like peas and I saw him steal ten pounds from his mother's purse when he was twelve.'

'Any idea where I might find these friends?'

She gave an elegant shrug. 'I believe Gary used to live in Redland, and I think he works for an insurance company. But that's all.'

Oakley drove home and looked up 'Gary Sheldick' online. There were two listed in the Redland area. He dialled one, and hit gold the first time. He told Gary why he was calling, and arranged for him to visit the station early the following morning with Frances. He put down the phone and forced the case from his mind, determined to enjoy his evening with Catherine.

Then he spent the whole night talking to her about it.

Frances Moorfield and Gary Sheldick were apprehensive when they arrived, telling Oakley that they'd never been in a police station before, let alone made a statement. They were an earnest pair, conventional and decent. Frances wore a blue suit with a pearl brooch in one lapel. Her engagement ring was discreet, indicating that money hadn't been wasted and was probably being put away for a deposit on a house. Gary wore grey trousers and had three pens of different colours neatly lined up in his shirt pocket.

'This won't take long.' Oakley suspected ancient school friends wouldn't have much to reveal, but was unwilling to leave a stone unturned. 'I'm sure you've heard that James Paxton was found dead earlier this month. We're interviewing friends and family to build up a picture of him.'

'Well, I'm afraid we can't help,' said Gary apologetically. 'We haven't seen him for a couple years now. We used to meet fairly regularly, although I always sensed he'd be away to more illustrious acquaintances once he was on the road to success.'

'You make him sound callous, Gary,' objected Frances chidingly. 'But he was just a social butterfly. We were his best friends at school, and he'll come back to us in time.' She realized what she'd said and flushed. 'Or he would have, if...'

Oakley thought she was being overly generous.

The staid pair who sat holding hands under the table weren't the sort of friends who'd have benefited Paxton, and he imagined the lawyer would have been less likely to deal with them, not more.

'He went to Oxford after school,' Frances went on. 'But he had a year out in the middle of it and worked here in Bristol. I think that was when he decided to go into criminal law.'

'No, he decided that at school,' corrected Gary. 'I remember him talking about it. I recommended contract or industrial law, because that's where the money is, but he said there was money in criminal law if you were good.'

'Do you remember him as dishonest in any way?' asked Oakley. This was blunt, but neither seemed surprised by the question.

'He cheated in school exams,' said Gary reluctantly. 'I often saw him looking at other people's papers, reading what they'd written. But I should not be saying this. It can't have any relevance to his death, and it'll only upset his mother if she hears about it.'

'And he stole purses on school holidays,' added Frances. 'He was arrested for shoplifting from Woolworths, too, but his mother got it sorted out, so you won't find anything in the records. She said James couldn't go into law if he had a criminal record. You can ask Colin Fairhurst about that – he and James were pretty tight at the time.'

'Mrs Paxton said Colin was a bad influence on James.' Gary gave a wry chuckle. 'But it was the other way around. Colin's a really nice bloke.'

He leaned across the table and wrote a number on one of Oakley's statement sheets. 'That's Colin.'

'And Helen Anderson,' added Frances. 'She works here so you probably know her. She was at school with James, too.'

'She was?' asked Oakley, startled.

'Well, yes and no,' corrected Gary pedantically. 'She was in our year but she hung out with a completely different crowd. I bet she and James didn't say more than three words to each other the whole time.'

'But it was James who told her to come and meet us for a drink,' said Frances. 'About two and a half years ago. Maybe less. I can't remember now.'

'Colin will, though,' said Gary with a meaningful smile.

'I think I've met Colin,' said Oakley, recalling that was the name of the man who'd been with Anderson the night he'd bumped into her at the harbour. It was indelibly etched in his mind, because he'd stunk of mortuary while trying to impress Catherine. Such a thing might have made a lesser woman think again, and he felt their relationship had taken a huge step forward that day.

'He and Helen have been an item for a while now,' said Frances. 'It's sweet. I'd no idea he liked her. Anyway, Colin will remember when she first started to join us.'

'So Helen is part of a social circle that includes you two, Colin and James?' asked Oakley, thinking he had better get his facts straight before he went to Anderson and demanded answers.

'Not exactly,' said Gary. 'I think she stopped James for speeding and he asked her to join us for a drink – probably to get out of a ticket, although she gave him one anyway. But James was already going off us by then, so I doubt he and Helen met more than once or twice. But ask her.'

'I hope we haven't got her into trouble,' said Frances nervously.

'Is his father dead?' asked Oakley, changing the subject. He had tried to broach the question with Maureen several days before but she had avoided answering, leaving him uncertain as to whether she was a widow or a divorcee.

'Don't you know?' Frances was surprised. 'I thought Mrs Paxton would've told you.'

'Told me what?'

'You'd better not tell her you got this from us,' said Gary anxiously. 'She won't like it, and I don't want her to make a scene at James's funeral. Colin told us, about two years ago – maybe less – but he asked us to keep it to ourselves, so we have.'

'What?' said Oakley impatiently.

'James's father is in prison.'

I'd celebrated too soon. I thought I was home and dry when the phone enquiry floundered, but I was just arriving for work when I saw Gary and Frances in the station. They were with Oakley.

I did a one-hundred-and-eighty-degree turn and ducked into the briefing room, where a carrel provided a convenient screen. I risked a

317

glance over the top, and saw Oakley shake hands in a friendly manner and open the door for them. What had they told him? That I'd known James? Had they, like Colin, guessed that I'd slept with him, and confided their suspicions? How long would it be before he put it all together? Or would he—

'I understand you knew James Paxton.'

Oakley's voice right behind me made me jump a mile. I'd been so engrossed in my terrified musings that I hadn't heard him coming. I could feel the blood draining out of my face, and my heart was thudding hard. Damn! I wasn't going to have time to decide what to say, and hasty answers were likely to be dangerous. I took a deep breath to pull myself together – my life was on the line, and I *had* to be in control. I forced a smile, and hoped he couldn't see my panic.

He did notice, of course, because he was that sort of policeman.

'You made me jump,' I said in an effort to explain away my unease.

'Why?' he asked. 'Do you have a guilty con-science? Did you kill Paxton because he got better A-levels than you?'

My heart had given a painful lurch at his first comment, so when I saw he was being facetious, I was angry. 'You shouldn't sneak up on people,' I said sharply, then added, 'sir,' because berating inspectors was hardly wise.

'I didn't sneak,' he objected. 'I was walk-ing quite normally. What are you doing here, anyway? Oh, I see – reading *The Sun*. No won-der you're embarrassed. You claimed to be a

Guardian reader, and you've been caught out.'

I glanced down, and saw that someone had left a paper in the carrel. It was open on page three, so he probably imagined I was a closet lesbian, as well as a closet reader of *The Sun*. I closed it quickly and let him think he was right. It was better than the truth.

'I've just spoken to a couple of Paxton's school friends who said you were in the same year as him,' he went on. I glanced at the door. Would he catch me if I made a run for it? Or should I stay and brazen it out? His manner was friendly enough, and he'd aimed at levity. Surely he wouldn't do that if he was about to arrest me? I forced myself to calm down and sound suitably apologetic.

'I was wondering if I should mention it, Guv, but I didn't want to waste your time. I stopped him for speeding some years ago. I can't remember when exactly. He invited me to a gathering of old Redlandians, probably as a way to get out of getting reported, although I gave him a ticket anyway. I still see Gary and Frances, but I haven't seen James for ages.'

'That's what they said. And you *should* have mentioned it. To keep it quiet looks deliberately obstructive – the kind of thing Wright would have done.'

That was an unpleasant thing to say; I wasn't at all like Wright. I went on the defensive. 'Actually, I tried several times, but you were always busy,' I lied. 'And I didn't want to *demand* an interview, because there's not much I can tell you, and I didn't want you thinking I was trying

319

to force myself in the limelight over someone I knew a decade ago.'

'I wouldn't have thought any such thing.'

I forged on. 'But James and I barely acknowledged each other at school, and I only saw him for a drink with three other people years ago. It's hardly information to help you find his killer.'

'No, but you could have told me about Paxton's father,' said Oakley. 'It would have been helpful to know that he's inside.'

I gaped at him. 'Inside? You mean in prison?'

'You didn't know?'

I really hadn't, and I could see from his face that he believed my shock was genuine. No wonder he thought I should've talked to him! That kind of information was certainly relevant.

'Blimey,' I breathed. 'There was never a father around for James at school, so I assumed he was dead. He never said anything to the contrary.'

'Your friends said Maureen Paxton started using her maiden name after her husband's trial, and they can't remember what he was called. They think that whatever happened was just before James came to your school, though.'

'He came late,' I recalled. 'When he was fifteen. And he was always called Paxton.'

'How do you fancy a morning on the computer, going through old trials with a view to finding a defendant with a wife called Maureen?'

I shook my head, but tempered my words with a smile. 'I'm on duty in Broadmead today, and I'd better stick to what I've been assigned to do. We all know what happens if I don't.'

He wasn't pleased, but that was too bad. If I'd

asserted myself earlier then Wright wouldn't have blown up at me, and I probably wouldn't have had to kill him.

'All right,' he said. 'I'll get Dave Merrick to do it. By the way, I'm going to ask your boyfriend to come in later. The other two thought he might be able to fill in some gaps.'

Oakley did call Colin, and arranged for him to drop into New Bridewell the following day. It could have been worse – Oakley could have questioned Colin before I'd had a chance to talk to him myself. Colin could tell Oakley anything except the fact that I'd slept with James. The rest of it – school, reporting him for speeding, having drinks after – was taken care of. Gary and Frances didn't know about my night of so-called passion – or if they did, they hadn't mentioned it to Oakley – and I was sure I could persuade Colin to be discreet.

On the phone, Oakley asked Colin whether he knew the name of James's father. Colin did, and Oakley mentioned it to me just as I was leaving the station. He was in a good mood, and told me that Colin had helped him tremendously – that his information had explained a peculiar reaction on Maureen's part when the mention of trials came up. I had no idea what he was talking about.

Apparently, James's father, William Pullen, was an architect who'd raised buildings with substandard materials, but had charged for the best stuff on the market. That had been in the Midlands, and when the trial was over James and his mother had fled to the West Country to begin a new life. Colin had been a good friend, I thought, to keep that secret for so long.

Oakley was driving to Birmingham to interview Pullen in prison that evening. I asked how he thought it would help with the murder enquiry, and he told me that Pullen could not have perpetrated fraud on such an enormous scale without a large number of iffy contacts. It was Oakley's belief that Pullen had been recommending his son to powerful criminals. I suspected he was right: it would explain why James had had so many high-profile clients clamouring for his services. He was young to have earned such a reputation, but it made sense if he had a powerful backer in the criminal fraternity.

I wished Oakley luck and set off to meet Colin. It had been another baking day, and I felt an urge to be by the sea, to walk along cliffs fanned by a cool breeze. Colin was waiting outside the station so I drove him to Brean Down, a mile-long peninsula that stuck into the sea like a swollen finger. Colin and I strolled along the soft, mossy grass, keeping off the path to avoid other people. The sun shot golden rays across the shimmering sea, and the air was full of the scent of salt, mud and hot vegetation. I began to relax.

Colin and I walked to the very end, and watched the sea surge and heave around the rocks below. We sat for a long time, as the gold of the sun faded across the water. Soon it was dark, and I knew we'd have a job getting back to the car, but it didn't matter. We had all night, and we were both off work the next day. Stars began to twinkle, and I realized we were alone. I slipped under the fence that kept the foolish and reckless from going too close to the edge, and indicated Colin should follow.

'What are you doing?' he exclaimed, half-horrified, half-amused. 'Come back. You'll fall!'

'I won't. There's a grassy area down here. Come on, don't be a wimp! I used to play down here when I was six.'

'Yes, but I'm rather larger than a child – there may not be room,' grumbled Colin, climbing down with great caution. When he reached me I stripped off my shirt and pushed him down on the grass.

'What? Here?' He glanced around uneasily, as if hoards of people were watching.

We fumbled with our clothes, and it was strange to feel the prickle of dry vegetation under my back and clinging to my hair. I felt reckless, wild, and I think he began to as well. Eventually, we lay back, slippery with sweat. I swatted at an insect that landed on me, then gazed up at the stars.

'You're going to see Inspector Oakley tomorrow,' I said. By mutual consent, we hadn't talked about work – his or mine – all evening.

'He asked about James's father, and I thought I'd better tell him, even though I promised James I never would. I don't want to be arrested for non-cooperation.'

I began to dress. 'Unfortunately, we can't arrest people for that. If we could, we'd have half the country locked up.'

'You introduced me to Oakley, if you recall,

and he seemed a canny sort of chap,' said Colin, pulling on his trousers. 'I don't want him thinking I topped James because of you.'

'Because of me?' I asked in astonishment. 'What do I have to do with it?'

'He slept with you.' He grinned at me in the darkness. 'I know you said he wasn't very good, but I didn't think you'd have forgotten about it completely.'

'But it was years ago, and it didn't mean a thing.' I was beginning to have a bad feeling about the way this conversation was going.

'Right,' he agreed. *'You* know it meant nothing and *I* know it meant nothing, but did *James*? For all we know, he might have written in his diary that it was the greatest night in his life. That would make me Suspect Number One.'

'Don't be stupid,' I said impatiently. 'And don't tell Oakley rubbish, either. He's really stumped by this case, and the last thing he needs is information to confuse him even more. There's no point in telling him about me and James.'

'But I'd never lie to the police,' said Colin seriously. 'I couldn't. They'd know I was holding something back, and then I *would* be in trouble.'

'Nonsense. All Oakley wants is a bit of background detail – not a list of who James slept with and who he didn't.'

I felt him stiffen. 'Why don't you want me to tell him about you and James?'

'Why d'you think? Because I could lose my job.'

'I hardly think they'd sack you for that! It's not

your fault James was murdered.'

'No, but I didn't tell them about it,' I explained. 'I couldn't bring myself to – it's not something I'm proud of.'

'I can see why.' Colin gave a short laugh. '*You* didn't top him, did you? For being a bastard?'

I was glad it was dark and he couldn't see my face. 'He wouldn't have been worth the ensuing aggravation.'

'I know about Noble,' he said unexpectedly. 'You arrested him. It was a big case, but James got him off.'

I was puzzled. I hadn't told Colin that I'd arrested Noble because by the time we'd started to go out I'd equated the whole incident with James stealing the file on the train – and poor Mark Butterworth's subsequent death. 'How did you know what I did?'

He started to do a jig as he tried to put on his shoes without untying the laces. In another situation, I'd have found it endearing. Now I wished he'd keep still. 'James told me. He lived near me, remember? We met occasionally at the supermarket and he mentioned it then – along with the fact that he'd slept with you. All because he'd regretted telling me about his dad.'

I blinked, bemused. 'I thought he told you about that at school.'

'He did – after he'd been arrested for shop-lifting. He thought criminal behaviour might be in his genes, and told me why.'

I was getting confused. 'Why should the business with his dad have anything to do with me, our one-night stand, and Noble?'

'He was being a bastard, of course. He knew I liked you and he used it to get something he wanted – namely me never to say anything about his villainous sire. If I did, he said he'd put about the tale you slept around. He knew that would hurt me because ... well, I was falling in love with you, you see?'

'*You* didn't kill him, did you?' I tried to laugh, but the sound that emerged was about as far from humour as you can get. Colin was right: James *was* a bastard.

'I almost wish I had, but I was at a conference at the time.'

'Oh, good,' I said lightly. 'But please don't mention this to Oakley. I'm not kidding – I *will* lose my job.'

'I have to, Helen. He'll find out anyway, and then we'll both be in trouble. He'll find out that James stole files from you, too, including the one that saw Noble walk free, so if you haven't already confessed, I recommend you do it soon.'

'James told you that, too?' I gulped. Damn him! How many other people had he blabbed to?

'He did, although he told me how upset you were, so I've never mentioned it before. But I'm glad it's in the open at last. It'll be a clean start for both of us, with no more secrets to hide. And Oakley will understand – he seems a reasonable sort of chap.'

Yeah, right! Showed what *he* knew about the police, the sanctimonious little prick. This was the twenty-first century, not a novel in which honesty was rewarded with a happy ending.

'It doesn't work like that,' I said, not disguising

the desperation in my voice. 'I'll be finished.'

'Then that's a chance you'll have to take,' he said firmly. 'I can't lie, and neither should you. Not to the police. It wouldn't be ethical.'

Bugger ethics! I thought, standing up and lurching forward. With both hands I gave him a good solid shove in the chest. His eyes opened wide in shock, and then he was gone into the blackness. I crawled as close to the edge as I could and peered over it.

He was there, his face just a foot from mine! He was scrabbling at the grass as he tried to pull himself back up again.

'What the hell are you doing?' he yelled. 'I could have been killed!'

Thank God for rocks. I rejected the first one I grabbed and seized a lump that fitted neatly into my hand. His face filled with terror, and I saw appalled understanding flash, just before the rock came down on the top of his head.

He just slipped away. He didn't scream or flail with his arms; he just vanished. I climbed down a few feet and peered over the edge. The cliffs were sheer there, and I could see rings of white where the surf crashed against their feet.

It was late, and I was getting cold. I started the long walk back to my car.

FIFTEEN

Wednesday, 29 August

Killing Colin was horrid. I'd been fond of him, and hoped that we'd have a future together. I was hurt to learn that he put honesty before my wellbeing, and his silence hadn't been too much to ask, had it? As I stumbled back across the downs, the enormity of what I'd done began to hit me and I found myself weeping, huge, uncontrollable sobs. They threatened to overwhelm me and, when they reached a point where I was finding it difficult to breathe, I knew I had to pull myself together. I couldn't walk along wailing like a banshee or someone would call the police.

I eventually reached the car park. It was well past eleven, and only three cars were left, one of which was mine. I found a place to hide, out of a wind that had actually grown quite bitter – or perhaps it just felt cold because I couldn't stop shivering – and settled down to make sure no one had seen me. I spotted a scrap of paper on the ground near my foot. A cinema ticket. I picked it up and kissed it. It was for the 7.30 p.m. showing of the latest James Bond in Weston-super-Mare. I hadn't seen it, although Colin and I had planned to go together the next week. It would be my alibi.

By the time I'd driven home the Colin incident already seemed unreal. Had it really happened, or was it just another nightmare? I realized I always did this after a murder – wondered whether I'd imagined it all. But, of course, I hadn't, and Colin was dead. Coolly, I called his phone and left a message, telling him that I'd enjoyed the James Bond flick, but where had he been? Why hadn't he met me at the cinema as we'd agreed?

I phoned at one o'clock, too, managing to sound irritable, and asking him to call as soon as he got home. I tried again at one forty-five and said curtly that I was tired of waiting and was going to bed. I informed him I'd call in the morning. Maybe. I was pleased with the 'maybe', because it sounded as though I was cross enough not to shower him with concerned calls every few minutes through the night. As it would be established that Colin had died somewhere around nine o'clock, my irritation developing after midnight would clear me of suspicion.

However, familiarity with murder made me over-confident, because it wasn't until the following day that I realized that there would be marine experts who could probably pinpoint exactly where Colin had gone into the water. Then the police would find the plateau where we'd made love and there'd be fibres, hairs and bodily fluids all over the place. Still, there wasn't much I could do about it now, and I could always say we'd been there the previous weekend. Nevertheless, I got rid of the clothes I'd worn, including my shoes. I shoved them in a bag and dumped them in one of the bins behind my local off-licence.

Then I had the rest of the day to get through. I didn't know what I was going to do as I'd planned to spend it with Colin. I phoned him again and made myself sound weary when I asked where the hell he was.

I was in the garden with a book that afternoon when there was a knock at my front door. I wasn't reading: I was imagining a scenario where Colin had agreed not to tell Oakley facts that could see me locked away for life.

I opened the door and my stomach lurched when I saw Oakley. Dave Merrick was behind him. I wondered what they'd do if I slammed the door and made a dash for the back lane. Would they be able to catch me? I pulled myself together. They weren't there to arrest me. How could they be? They didn't know what I'd done – to Colin, Wright or James.

'Colin didn't come to see me this morning,' Oakley was saying. 'I don't suppose he's here, is he?'

'No,' I said crossly. 'We were supposed to see the James Bond film last night but he didn't show up. I suppose he went out with some of his work friends instead and crashed out at one of their places. I don't mind, but he should've called me.'

'OK,' said Oakley pleasantly. 'It was just a thought, and we were passing anyway. I suppose he'll call us when he remembers, and I don't expect there's much more he can tell us. The important thing was the name of Paxton's father, and he's already told us that.'

I wondered whether I should offer them a cup of tea. Policemen always appreciate tea when they're working, and it seemed rude to keep them on the doorstep. But I didn't want them in my house. I wanted them to go away – permanently. But manners got the better of prudence, and they followed me along the hall and to my sitting room, where the sun streamed through the branches of the apple tree outside, making dappled patterns on the carpet and the suitcase that stood packed and ready for my getaway.

Oakley browsed my bookshelves while I made the tea, and Merrick flopped into a chair and closed his eyes, as though being with the inspector had worn him out.

'How did Birmingham go?' I called from the kitchen.

'Not well,' Oakley replied. 'Pullen claimed he hasn't had any contact with his family since the trial. However, the prison governor said he got plenty of letters from his son, and that Pullen replied to them. Paxton also visited. Pullen lied. Perhaps he just couldn't bring himself to cooperate with the police.'

'Doesn't he want his son's killer caught then?' I asked, a little indignantly.

'You'd think so, wouldn't you?'

I carried a tray with three mugs, milk and a teapot into the sitting room and set them on the table. I didn't have any sugar so they'd have to do without. Merrick grimaced when he tasted his and looked around for the bowl, but apparently decided not to make a fuss.

'Anything else?' I asked. 'Such as a connection between Pullen and Yorke?

Oakley frowned. 'How did *you* know there'd be one?'

I hoped I hadn't made a faux pas. The truth was that I hadn't slept well the previous night so tiredness and strain were making me dull-witted. 'Because of the anonymous note you pinned up, which linked the body in Orchard Street, which was Pullen's son, to the Yorke gang.'

'Oh.' Oakley waved a dismissive hand. 'Not that.' He sat on the sofa and fiddled with the ticket stub that lay on the coffee table. Good. I wanted him to see that. 'The connection is that Pullen employed security guards to protect his building sites, and that's how Yorke started out – a security guard for Pullen. Yorke moved to Bristol at the same time as Mrs Paxton and James.'

'The man with the monkey face!' I exclaimed, remembering the 'chauffeur' who had some-times collected James from school. And, I thought as something else clicked into place, the man who'd been with him on the train to New-castle. The train where all my troubles started. I almost clapped a hand to my head when I re-membered that the Bristol-to-Newcastle train stopped in Birmingham – James had been going to visit Pullen! I'd never seen Yorke that I knew of, but I was willing to bet I was right. I decided to look at his mug shot when I was next at the station.

Oakley was staring at me. 'Monkey face?'

Obviously I couldn't mention the train incident, or even allude to it, lest he started putting facts together.

'There was a man who drove James around occasionally,' I explained. 'We figured he was Maureen's lover, but perhaps he was just looking after the family while his boss was inside.'

'Makes sense,' said Oakley, nodding. 'There's no evidence that Yorke has anything to do with them now, of course, other than James taking his case, perhaps as a favour.'

Wrong, I thought. Yorke had a good deal to do with James. An emotional link between them explained why James had been prepared to go to such lengths to get Yorke bail. I wished I could tell Oakley about the false confession James had asked me to plant, but I couldn't.

'James Bond,' said Merrick, picking up the stub that Oakley had dropped back on the table. 'Any good? I fancy seeing that.'

'It's OK,' I said with a noncommittal shrug. 'Plenty of car chases and gunfights.' That was certainly a safe bet.

'Is there a plot?' asked Oakley.

His Catherine probably wants to go, I thought, but he doesn't seem like a Bond kind of man, so he's wondering if he'll be bored.

'Not one that interfered with the cars and guns,' I replied, hoping the current release hadn't broken the mould and gone for intelligence.

'Good,' said Merrick with relish.

Oakley went to stand at the window with his mug. The light made patterns on his blue shirt, and his trousers brushed against my suitcase.

'The Tirana police have finally sent Kovac's fingerprints.'

'Did they match any in the house?' I was sure they would, because the man had lived there for three weeks. Oakley's reply astonished me.

'Yes – on the tape and the black plastic. On the *inside*, where they couldn't have got just from him pinching the stuff from the university. He'd have had to unfold the plastic and cut the tape for them to be where they were. There were others, of course, all over the house.'

'Really?' I felt myself gaping. I'd had the wrapping down to the Yorke gang. What was Kovac doing in the picture?

'So it looks as if he's our killer after all,' said Merrick. 'He was going to remove the body but ran out of time. Or perhaps he realized that lugging a corpse around wasn't going to be easy and abandoned the idea. It explains why he left duff keys for the cleaner on Tuesday morning – he was going to come back and meet Paxton after she'd gone. Then he killed him there.'

'You've solved the murder?' I asked, stunned. Why hadn't they mentioned it sooner?

'We have other leads to follow first,' said Oakley, although Merrick rolled his eyes. 'The fingerprints alone aren't enough to convict Kovac.'

'But it's looking good,' put in Merrick stubbornly. 'Unfortunately, we don't have an extradition treaty with Albania, so unless the lure of the university's physics equipment becomes too great, Kovac stays free. But we're nearly there, and we know one of two things happened. First,

Paxton was meeting Kovac, perhaps to discuss patenting some aspect of his nanotechnology work; or second that Paxton was due to meet someone else, but found Kovac in the house instead.'

'Or perhaps all this is coincidence, and there's another explanation,' countered Oakley.

As was usual in such moments, I wanted to throttle him. Why couldn't he just jump to a few wild conclusions like everyone else?

'I can't see what,' I said, trying to sound reasonable. 'Of course Paxton met Kovac at the house. Why else would he be there?'

'Quite,' said Merrick. 'DI Davis was right. She had Kovac in the frame from the beginning.'

Oakley shook his head. 'Something about this solution doesn't feel right. Perhaps I'm looking for logic where there may be none, but I believe that anonymous note – that the Yorke gang is involved. Especially if Randal's partials may have been found at the scene.'

Damn that note! I'd implicated Yorke when it had been Kovac all along!

'Superintendent Taylor was never happy with the note,' said Merrick, bless him. 'He told us to ignore it, and he was right. *Kovac* is our killer. He probably killed Barry, too.'

Was this it? Was I finally near the end of all my troubles? I didn't see why not. After all, it had to conclude somewhere. Oakley finished his tea and set the cup on the table, but suddenly reached out to pluck something from my hair.

'What have you been up to?' he asked, showing me a piece of grass that must have been there since Colin and I made love on Brean Down the previous evening. 'Rolling in the hay? I thought you didn't see Colin last night.'

I laughed gamely and he walked away. Damn! Damn! Damn!

Thursday, 30 August

It was evening and Merrick sat in his car outside the Clifton bar, pretending to study a map as he watched people arrive. He had his mobile poised, ready to snap a shot if he saw the man who'd been with Paxton. Superintendent Taylor had dismissed the bar enquiry because Oakley had refused to say where the information had come from. But Oakley didn't like loose ends, and felt it important that they establish the identity of the man. Merrick thought it a waste of time, but he'd gone along with his DI. He owed him that, at least, for being discreet and understanding.

He gave up at half past nine and drove back to the station. He entered the reception area, and waved to the civilian on duty, signalling that she was to push the release button to let him in. She was taking details from a motorist, who'd been ordered to produce his driving licence, insurance, proof of ownership and MOT certificate at a police station. The man happened to glance around as the door snapped open, and Merrick forced himself to keep moving. It was the man who'd been with Paxton in the bar.

Merrick collided with Oakley as the inspector was trotting up the stairs from the incident room.

He blurted out that Paxton's friend was actually in the station, and they dashed back to reception, but it was empty. They raced outside, just in time to see the tail-lights of a car flash before its driver turned towards the city centre.

'Shit!' shouted Merrick. 'I should have grabbed him, not raced off to tell you.'

Oakley hurried back into the station and asked for the details the receptionist had just taken, to be sure of his facts before he told Merrick what he had already surmised. The name was there: Michael Yorke.

'It's just as well you didn't demand to know what he was doing with Paxton that night,' said Oakley thoughtfully. 'That's not the way we should play this.'

'Shit!' muttered Merrick, shaking his head in disbelief.

'Shit, indeed. How come you didn't recognize him? I thought everyone knew Michael.'

'I've only recently transferred here, remember? I don't yet know all the local villains.'

Oakley was unmollified. 'But there are mug shots of him. You told me you'd checked them, and decided that no one in the Yorke clan was your man.'

'I *did*,' insisted Merrick. 'Michael's photo shows a spotty-faced youth with an adolescent pout and a crew cut. No one's bothered to update it. Fuck it! I should have realized that he'd look different now. But where does this leave us? I thought we were happy with Kovac as our killer.'

'I'm not. I *knew* there was something in that

337

note.'

'But Kovac bound the body and prepared to get rid of it.'

'Randal's fingerprints were found on the wrapping, too.'

'Not necessarily – you yourself pointed out that the probability of the partials belonging to Randal is low. You can't have it both ways, Guv.'

'Maybe Kovac *and* Randal wrapped Paxton on Michael's orders. Regardless, I can't believe that Michael meeting Paxton a few hours before his death is innocent.'

'What shall we do about it?'

'I want to question Michael and Randal.'

'You can't, Guv. The Three Horsemen have forbidden it because of the Wright murder.'

'Then let's go and see them now – tell them we can't move on arresting Paxton's killer until we've tied these loose ends together. With any luck they'll see reason.'

Merrick followed him unhappily, wondering how Oakley was going to persuade them to do what he wanted without letting slip that the identification of Michael Yorke had come from a gay police officer.

The first thing I did when I got to the station that evening was to go to the newest computer and pull up a mug shot of Billy Yorke. It had been Monkey Face on the train, all right. I wondered why I hadn't considered that possibility before. I recalled stirrings of recognition on the train, but then James had started with his antics and all my attention had focused on him.

So, where did that leave me? Yorke would have known that James had forced me to help him on the Noble case, as he'd been on the train when it had happened. It must have been a comfort to him to know that James had a bent police officer under his thumb.

So Yorke or one of his gang must have guessed that it was me who'd killed James. Or had they – they'd certainly not paid me a visit, as I imagined they would if they'd known I'd dispatched their lawyer. I rubbed my head. Kovac. He was the spanner in the works – he'd confused everything and everyone from the start. He must have come back to the house for some reason, found James dead, and decided he'd better hide the body in case he got the blame. What other explanation was there?

So, did the Yorke gang know about me or not? I wanted to believe that they didn't, basing my hopes on the fact that it had been a month and they hadn't made a move. It would be ironic, I thought, if I ended up bludgeoned to death, too.

Still, I'd used my wits to get me this far and I wasn't about to give up now. A danger more immediate than Yorke was what would happen when Colin was reported missing. Would the pathologist say he'd fallen off the cliff – a tragic accident? Or would he say that the injury to the top of Colin's head wasn't the kind of thing that happened when a person tumbled to his death?

Oakley was in trouble. Neither the three superintendents from Professional Standards nor Taylor would allow him to risk their chances of solving Wright's murder on the say-so of a source he was unwilling to reveal. Merrick was in an agony of indecision. Was solving the case – perhaps both cases – worth losing his privacy over and enduring years of snide comments and humiliation?

'We can't take risks with this one, Neel,' said Taylor. 'Barry was a friend, as well as a colleague, and I don't want to jeopardize catching his killer for a hunch passed on by some snout who we can't use in court.'

'Sir,' began Merrick. 'I—'

Oakley interrupted quickly. 'A year ago, I was seconded to the drug squad for a couple of months, if you recall. Some of the officers are still out there, working under deep cover.'

Taylor frowned. 'Are you saying your source is a copper?'

'I can't say, sir,' said Oakley, meeting his eyes. 'It might put someone in danger.'

Taylor sighed, and with relief Merrick saw he had swallowed the bait. 'All right, I'll arrange search warrants for Michael's and Randal's houses, and we'll nab them tonight.' He glanced at Parker. 'Right?'

Parker nodded. 'We were heading in their direction for Wright's killing anyway. This is sooner than we'd like to move, but we'll manage. We can't have it said that we prioritized one case over the other.'

'Michael or Randal might tell us where Kovac is hiding,' said Merrick hopefully.

Taylor gave a derisive snort as he reached for the phone. 'Right, lad. And I might dance naked along the harbour with daisies in my hair. We'll have to hit Michael and Randal at the same time. It's ten thirty now. We'll aim for midnight. Any later and their lawyers will be screaming about the inconvenience. You'd better make a note in your records that your witness only gave you this information half an hour ago, Neel.'

'Not a witness, sir,' said Oakley solidly. 'An anonymous source.'

All four men looked up as a clerk came in and passed Taylor a piece of paper. The superintendent read it quickly.

'It's from the Tirana police. Kovac phoned his university earlier today, just to check in. He told his secretary that he's been camping with his family since he returned from the UK, and she told him he was wanted by the police. I expect that's the last we'll ever hear of him.'

An hour and a half wasn't long to assemble the team and appraise them of what was happening. Taylor wanted a uniformed presence as well as CID, so applied to Inspector Blake for help. Unfortunately it was Saturday, the busiest night of the week, so only Blake himself, Paul Franklin and Helen Anderson could be spared.

Taylor was going to lead the raid on Michael's house, while Oakley was in charge of the one on Randal's home. Both men would be arrested, after which their houses would be handed over to SOCO. Oakley glanced at the officers who'd be with him – Davis, Evans, Merrick, and the three uniforms. Two Armed Response Teams were standing by, too, just in case either situation turned ugly.

They left the station quietly, travelling in unmarked cars to the quiet suburban area where the henchman lived. Leaving Evans, Merrick and Blake to watch the back and sides of the house, Oakley, Davis, Franklin and Anderson went to the front door. Lights were blazing from a downstairs room, and the muted rumble of a television could be heard. Randal himself answered the door, wearing jogging pants, a dirty T-shirt and no shoes.

'Sod off!' he said, when he recognized the callers.

When Oakley informed him that he was being arrested on suspicion of the murders of James Paxton and Barry Wright, the henchman's jaw dropped in horror.

'You mean the copper? But I never had nothin' to do with him.'

'We'll discuss it at the station,' said Oakley, noting he didn't deny Paxton's killing. 'Put some shoes on.'

'I wanna change,' said Randal, pathetically defiant. 'I ain't going nowhere dressed like this. I got me image to think about.'

Oakley nodded and watched while Randal donned one of his mafia-style suits and a shiny tie. A pair of dark glasses followed, then he reached for the briefcase at the bottom of the stairs.

'We'll just check that,' said Davis, taking it from him and rifling through its contents. She frowned as she pulled something out. It was a police statement form. Randal sagged.

'Shit!' he muttered.

Wordlessly, Davis handed it to Oakley. It was a signed statement by Yorke, admitting to the Westbury Burglaries, and it had been witnessed by Oakley. Yorke's signature was in a different pen from the one used to write the rest of the statement, and someone had added small but distinct marks under four letters. It was an old trick, one Oakley hadn't seen used for years. The letters were S, T, U, and D, and they meant one thing: Statement Taken Under Duress. In other words, the prisoner had been forced to say something he hadn't wanted to, or that wasn't true.

'What were you going to do with this?' Oakley asked. 'Was Paxton hoping to slip it in the court file so he could claim our case was based on misconduct? Is that why you killed him? Because he couldn't do it in time for Yorke's remand?'

Randal was sullen. 'I never killed no one,' he said again. 'He was dead when we got there.'

'So who did kill him then?' pressed Oakley.

Randal glowered. 'I dunno, but I wouldn't mind getting me hands on the bastard. He made a right bollocks of our plans.'

Oakley watched Davis continue to hunt through the briefcase. 'You're going down for a double murder,' he said. 'And one of those murders was of a policeman. You might want to consider playing this one straight if you want to see your grandkids. Think about it.'

'I never killed James,' Randal insisted. 'I was supposed to meet him at that house so he could tell me what was goin' on, but when I got there

343

he was already topped. All I did was wrap him up – wearing gloves, so you can't pin it on me. I was gonna come back later and get rid of him, but I talked to Michael and he said to leave the body alone.'

'You took his wallet and phone,' surmised Davis, while Oakley shook his head in disbelief at Randal's confused tirade of denial and confession. 'That's why it took us so long to identify him.'

'Michael said I should've left everything as it was, but as I'd already been through James's pockets, he said I should chuck what I'd took.'

'And did you?' asked Oakley. 'The phone was used as recently as this morning.'

'Fuckin' kids,' muttered Randal venomously. 'A gang of 'em was watchin' when I lobbed the stuff in the river. They never got his wallet but I had a feeling one of them phones never went in the water. It went in the mud. The little bastards must've climbed down and got it.'

'*One* of the phones?' asked Oakley. 'He had two?'

'Of course – one personal, one for work,' said Randal. 'Like me. It don't do to mix 'em up.'

'I'm sure it doesn't,' muttered Oakley.

'Shane King!' exclaimed Franklin suddenly. 'The boy who drowned at the beginning of August. Helen and I dealt with it. Remember, Hel?'

Anderson's face was pale in the bright lights of Randal's house, but she nodded. 'No wonder they were reluctant to tell us what they'd been doing there.'

Oakley agreed. If he'd been a child, *he* would not have been keen to tell the police that he'd seen a violent thug like Randal dumping phones in the river either.

Randal's face was ugly with anger. 'You can't pin the kid's death on me. It wasn't my fault the little bastard went after the stuff. Blame his friends. They must've let him drown while they made off with the phones. All I did was lob the stuff and get out of there.'

'I imagine Shane's brother Wayne has been using it,' said Oakley. 'A stolen phone would be useful to a fifteen-year-old fence.'

'Little bastards!' snarled Randal again. 'None of 'em are any good.'

Oakley gestured to the false statement. 'Where did that come from?'

'James,' replied Randal sullenly. 'He was gonna use it to get Billy out. I don't know how.'

'You probably should've got rid of it after you found him dead,' remarked Oakley wryly.

'Michael told me to, but I thought we might still be able to use it.' Randal looked at it rather wistfully. 'It's clever, and we'd never get another – I didn't want to waste it.'

'I'm sure the real killer wrote that anonymous note,' said Oakley to Davis in a low voice, while she continued to root through the briefcase and Randal watched her with resentful eyes. Anderson was near enough to hear, but everyone else was concentrating on securing the scene. '*He* killed Paxton, and he's trying to get Randal and Michael sent down for it.'

'Yeah, if you believe this piece of dirt,' said

Davis contemptuously. 'He wouldn't know the truth if it bit him.'

'But I *do* believe him,' said Oakley. 'Paxton planned to get Yorke released by putting that false statement in the court files to discredit our case. I don't know *how* Paxton was going to have it placed in the files, but it means Randal had every reason to want him alive because Paxton was obviously masterminding this scheme. However, when Randal found him dead, he panicked – before the cooler Michael told him to leave everything alone. Michael thought they were in the clear because Randal had worn gloves, but they were thin latex and tore on the sticky tape, leaving behind a couple of partials.'

'It's possible, I suppose,' conceded Davis. 'But it's easier to believe there was a falling out, and Randal and Michael bumped Paxton off.'

'Paxton was Yorke's best hope for freedom *and* he was an old family friend. Moreover, both Paxton and Wright were bludgeoned, which suggests a single killer. Why would Randal and Michael kill Wright?'

'Because Wright was in the process of planting evidence to see them convicted for Paxton?' suggested Davis. 'The betting slip that he'd pickpocketed from Randal in the public toilets the previous night.'

'Then why did Randal leave the slip behind? It wasn't hidden; it was lying in the open. Randal may not be a rocket scientist but he's not stupid. He would have picked it up after braining Wright.'

Davis waved a dismissive hand and turned to

346

address Randal. 'What did you wrap Paxton in?'

'Some plastic and tape I found in the rubbish bin outside,' replied Randal, almost gabbling in his eagerness to extricate himself. 'I would have used bin liners, but there weren't none. Then Michael said I was a bloody fool to have touched anything. I told him I was wearin' gloves, and he said I should just get out of there.'

'Where are these gloves?' asked Oakley. 'We'll need them for forensics.'

'Yes!' exclaimed Randal. 'Forensics will prove I never done nothing. I've seen it on *CSI*. I'll give you the suit I wore, an' all. It's the blue one, upstairs.'

Oakley nodded to Anderson, telling her to fetch it. She did as she was directed, and he saw her hat was pulled down so low that he could barely see her eyes. He didn't blame her for not wanting Randal to see her face. The man was known to be vindictive. Of course, if there was any justice in the world, Randal wouldn't be intimidating anyone for a very long time to come.

'What about Kovac?' asked Davis. 'Was he there, too?'

'I don't know Kovac,' replied Randal. 'I seen his picture on the telly but I never met him.'

Randal was packed into a police car and SOCO arrived. Radios crackled, police lights flashed, and Oakley received the news that all had gone well at Michael's house, too. Predictably, Michael had demanded a lawyer and was refusing to say anything at all. Oakley phoned Taylor.

'What do you think, sir?' he asked. Now it was

over, he found himself strangely dissatisfied with the result.

He heard a gusty sigh. 'We'll let them cool their heels for a few hours and start interviewing tomorrow morning. You get yourself home now and be back at eight a.m. sharp.'

Oakley knew he should get some sleep before embarking on two such important interviews, but he still felt something wasn't right. If Randal had wrapped Paxton in the plastic sheeting, then why were Kovac's fingerprints on it? Suddenly, as he pondered, the pieces of evidence fell together and he felt he knew exactly what had happened.

'Come with me,' he ordered Anderson, the only one of the original arrest team who was left. 'I want you to witness something. Then I'll drop you at the station on my way home.' He switched off his phone. 'I'm off duty anyway.'

Being there while Randal was arrested was unsettling, but not nearly as bad as it would have been if I'd had to go with Taylor to get Michael. Randal was as thick as two short planks, but Michael wasn't, and he may well have recognized me as the police officer that James planned to use in the plot to get his brother out of prison. For all I knew, James had shown him photos or had even told him my name. Somehow, I didn't think Randal was the kind of man James would have confided in. Nevertheless, I kept my hat on and head down when I was with Randal.

Oakley's reasoning about what happened made a lot of sense to me. I'd been right: one of the thugs in the Yorke gang *had* visited Orchard

Street, hoping to hear that all was in place for the remand hearing and instead found James dead. And now I was sure I'd been right about what had happened to the false statement that James had tried to make me plant.

However, I didn't like Oakley's conviction that Randal was telling the truth, or that he knew James owned more than one mobile. It would only be a matter of time before he tracked it down, and then I would be caught for sure. I wondered what I could do to persuade him he was wrong.

'Where are we going?' I asked as he drove.

'Orchard Street. Mrs Greaves told me that Kovac had a thing about English baths.'

I fought back my irritation with his enigmatic remark. I hadn't had much to eat all day, my stomach hurt, and I needed something to absorb the acid that churned there. And I couldn't stop thinking about Colin, which made me realize I'd been fonder of him than I'd thought. If only he'd been more sympathetic. It was *his* fault that he was dead – and just when I could have done with a friend, too.

'I prefer showers,' I said shortly when he made no effort to explain himself. Now what trail was the wretched man pursuing?

'Well, Kovac liked baths. And when I first went to Orchard Street there was a smell of damp in the kitchen.'

'You're kidding!' I exclaimed. 'The whole place reeked of nothing but decomposing corpse.'

Oakley ignored me. 'Mrs Greaves also said

she'd seen Kovac on the Monday putting rubbish in the bin. I think Kovac liked overfull tubs, but the first time he did it, he spilled the water, which stained the kitchen ceiling. Then I think he filched plastic and a roll of tape from the university to put on the floor, to stop it happening again.'

'Which he pulled up before he left?' I asked. 'That was what the neighbour saw go in the bin?'

'Precisely! It explains why his fingerprints are all over the stuff. Then Randal found it – he'd had to look out there because there were no bin liners in the kitchen.'

'I suppose,' I said reluctantly. Bloody Oakley – was he never satisfied?

'Merrick said he cuts several strips of tape when he wraps Christmas presents – not one at a time – and there were sticky patches on the wall in Orchard Street, where it looked as though this had been done. He was almost right. What happened was that *Randal* peeled the tape off the bundle from the bin and stuck them on the wall. Then he rolled Paxton in the plastic, and used the tape to secure him.

'Poor Kovac,' I said, rather maliciously. 'Half the world thinks he's wanted for murder, and you've set the Albanian police after him. All the time he's probably been at the seaside with his family.'

Oakley grimaced but made no reply, probably because we'd arrived at Orchard Street. He unlocked the door and turned on the light, walking through the house towards the kitchen. It wasn't pleasant being back there yet again. I glanced into the sitting room, half-expecting to see Wright, but there was nothing except a small, dark stain on the carpet. That was odd, as I hadn't remembered any blood. But then Wright's murder had been rather rushed, and I *had* hit him twice. Yes! I thought, as it suddenly came back to me. There had been a little blood.

I glanced at my uniform trousers and saw a couple of dark spots I hadn't noticed before. I moved under the light and looked more closely. Definitely blood. Jesus! I'd sat in front of those three superintendents from Professional Standards with Wright's blood all over me! The mere thought of it filled me with a sort of sick excitement. I'd been lucky, but I couldn't afford to be careless like that in the future. Supposing one of them had noticed?

'Look!' Oakley was calling. 'This is where Randal stuck the tape on the wall, and there are sticky bits in the bathroom upstairs where Kovac taped the stuff to the floor. We'll have to get SOCO here again. I'll put in the request tomorrow.'

'Good idea,' I said. 'They'll be busy with Yorke and Randal's houses tonight. I'm glad you nailed them.'

'But I'm not sure they did it,' said Oakley. 'Who sent the anonymous note that pointed us in their direction? It was a set up, and I'm inclined to think that whoever sent that is our culprit.'

Damn the bloody note! 'Maybe Randal or Michael wrote it,' I suggested. 'It looks like the kind of spelling and grammar that Randal would use.'

'Randal's dyslexic, and Yorke wouldn't have been so stupid,' said Oakley. 'No, the real killer's still out there, laughing at us.'

I wasn't laughing, I can tell you.

'You weren't entirely honest with me yesterday,' he said suddenly. 'About Colin.'

I stared at him in horror. Had he brought me here so he could tell me that he knew what I'd done? That Colin's body had been found, and the pathologist knew he'd been murdered? And because I wouldn't have murdered Colin for the sheer hell of it, Oakley had reasoned that I'd done away with Wright and James, too?

'I don't know what you mean,' I said stiffly. I turned away from him and walked to the sitting room, where I stood near the mantelpiece. He followed and sat on the sofa.

'I mean that I saw Colin waiting for you after you finished work. I happened to look out of the window when you both drove off. You told me you hadn't seen him the night before. Why lie?'

My fingers tightened on a rock, and I quickly slipped it behind my back. His attention was caught by some peculiarity in the old springs in the sofa, so he didn't notice. I took a step towards him.

There was an atmosphere of celebration at New Bridewell that night. Taylor brought a bottle of whisky and the officers who'd been on the raid drank it from plastic cups, sitting around on the desks and generally congratulating themselves. Finding a suspect for a murder was always a relief, but it felt particularly good to have the

352

suspected killers of a policeman under lock and key.

Davis, Evans and Merrick sat together, slightly apart from the others. Davis told the two of them about Oakley's reservations, but Evans was sceptical.

'Then why did he insist we nick Michael and Randal tonight? If he's not convinced they did it, we'd have been better waiting until we've built a stronger case. I'll be pissed off if this pair walk because he moved too early.'

'He didn't know what Randal would admit then,' said Merrick defensively. 'And he still thinks that whoever wrote that anonymous note is the killer.'

'The forensic report came back on the saliva from the stamp today,' said Evans. 'It was addressed to him so I didn't open it. You remember what he said about keeping that particular lead under wraps, because Taylor'd told him to drop it?'

'Then let's see what it says,' said Davis. 'Where is it?'

Evans rifled in the mounds of papers that covered Oakley's desk and dug it out. He opened it and read the result with a frown.

'This can't be right.'

'Why? What does it say?' asked Merrick.

'It goes on about how the DNA was degraded, and says that the result is only an *indication* of the licker's identity. They ran it through the database, and came up with one possible, but it's from the police records – the ones we keep for elimination purposes.'

'Who?' asked Merrick. 'Wright?'

'Helen Anderson.' Evans gave a short laugh. 'Mind you, she's got a good reason for wanting rid of Wright!'

'She was at school with Paxton,' said Davis. 'And she met him for drinks with friends a couple of years ago.'

'You don't think...?' Evans' voice trailed off.

'Where is she now?' asked Davis. 'I last saw her up at Randal's place.'

'She went to Orchard Street with Neel,' said Evans. 'He was going to look at something to do with a leaking bath. Get him on his mobile.' Merrick was already dialling.

'I'll tell Taylor,' said Davis. 'It's probably nothing, but...'

'His phone's off,' said Merrick, snatching up his car keys and making for the door.

Oakley hadn't meant anything particularly significant when he'd told Anderson that she'd been caught out in an untruth. If he'd believed she was concealing anything remotely connected to a crime he'd have tackled her about it with witnesses, as was proper. He was just curious, and wanted to know why Colin Fairhurst hadn't shown up to give his statement as planned.

There was also the cinema ticket. Oakley had seen that particular film, and knew it was one of the more clever Bonds, not a lot of mindless chasing and fighting as she'd claimed. It told him she hadn't watched it, so she'd lied about that, too. He still felt pangs of guilt when he recalled the unpleasant scene in the briefing room with Wright. It had been his fault, and he felt a degree of responsibility towards her. If she was having relationship problems, then he wanted her to know he'd be a sympathetic listener.

Therefore, he was surprised when she came to loom over him in what could only be described as a threatening manner. He stayed sitting, hoping that a non-confrontational pose would reassure her that he hadn't meant any harm.

'I'm sorry,' he said gently. 'Colin seemed like a nice chap, and I hope you're not having difficulties.'

'What do you mean?' she demanded angrily. 'We were perfectly happy.'

'*Were* happy?' he asked. So they *had* broken up, and it was a faltering relationship that made Anderson so moody and ... well, strange, to be honest.

'We *are* happy,' she corrected furiously.

'Then why the anger?' he asked, then wished he hadn't. His kindly concern was turning into an inquisition, which he hadn't intended at all.

He glanced up at her, and suddenly everything became crystal clear when a heavy stone appeared in her hand. It flashed down towards him. He twisted quickly, but it still grazed the side of his head and brought stars dancing in front of his eyes. The sound it made was sickening, as though his skull had broken open. He felt blood gush down his cheek.

'No, wait.' He managed to raise one arm, so the next blow was deflected. He sensed her moving around for a better angle, and tried to stand, but his legs were like jelly. Then the pain hit him. He hadn't felt anything when she'd first struck, but now all his nerves screamed in agony and he began to black out. He fought against it, knowing that if he did, he'd never wake.

'Have you killed Colin?' As he couldn't stand, he rolled off the sofa so that his head was under the coffee table. She'd have to move it if she wanted to hit him again, which might buy him vital seconds. 'To stop him telling us something about you and Paxton? And you'd have had time to kill Wright, too, if he'd left the door open and you were quick.'

'Three minutes,' he thought he heard her say.

'Was Paxton blackmailing you?'

'Shut up!' she hissed, and he didn't recognize her face, twisted as it was with malice.

'*You* gave him the stuff from the Noble file.' How long could he keep her talking? And what was the point? Help wasn't on the way. He persisted anyway. 'The file was missing the morning of the trial, and you said you'd been reading it, but you'd actually taken it to show him. The STUD statement we found tonight would have been no good unless we took it to court. You were going to put it in the file.'

'I wasn't,' she growled. 'I wasn't going to do that.'

'You saw Paxton's body at the mortuary.' He was finding it hard to concentrate and darkness tore at the edges of his vision. 'You said, "it doesn't look like him". Grossman thought you meant it didn't look human, but you meant that he had decomposed and didn't look like Paxton.'

'It didn't,' she said dully.

'The woman in the scarf.' He saw her bend to lift the coffee table. 'That was you. You said you'd fasten it in the front, but that was to mislead me because you'd actually tied it at the back.'

Oakley was fading fast, and speaking was a massive effort. His eyes closed, and he couldn't open them again. He heard the coffee table being pulled out of the way.

I'd just moved the table, to see if I needed to belt Oakley again when I became aware of a movement in the doorway. Two men stood there: Mr Smith from next door and a handsome, green-eyed man whom I recognized from photos as Dr Kovac.

'I have come to help the police,' he said in accented, but good English. He and Smith were looking at Oakley, probably wondering why I was standing over him with a rock. 'I have been away with my family, and I had no idea I was needed to help solve a murder.'

I was fairly sure Oakley was dead. His speech had been strangely slurred at the end, and his movements slow and uncoordinated. It was a shame, because he'd been a decent man. But he'd brought his fate on himself by prying into my business. He'd left me no choice.

'This is the man who murdered James Paxton and Barry Wright,' I announced, drawing myself up to my full height, and knowing my uniform would ensure they believed me. 'I've disarmed him and now I'm going for reinforcements. I won't be long, and if he moves, hit him with this.' I handed Kovac the rock.

'Why not use your radio?' asked Kovac. 'Or your mobile?'

'Poor reception,' I replied briskly.

'That's the officer who came the day I reported the smell,' said Smith. 'He looks sort of foreign.'

'He's an impostor.' I headed for the door. 'Very dangerous. I won't be long, but remember – if he moves, hit him hard.'

I left the house and ran for Oakley's car, but the keys were in his pocket, and I could hardly go back for them. In the distance I heard the wail of a siren. Had they finally worked it out and were coming to get me? Or was the rest of my shift just going to break up some brawl? It wasn't far to my house, so I ran there as fast as I could. I tore off my uniform and donned jeans and a T-shirt. Then I grabbed the suitcase I'd packed. Money and passport were already in it.

There was blood on my hand, but I didn't wash it off. There wasn't time. I snatched up my car keys and drove quickly to Colin's house. Only Oakley knew he was dead, and he wasn't going to be telling anyone. I smashed a window to get into Colin's house, and I knew where he kept his keys, credit card and spare money. I took them all and drove to the airport, where I bought a ticket on the first plane out with Colin's credit card. It was to Alicante, and I'd plan my next move when I landed. I sat back in my seat, and thought with pleasure that the next sunrise I'd see would be a Spanish one.

EPILOGUE

A year later

I decided to stay in Spain in the end. I'd taken Spanish at school – in the same class as James, actually – and I enjoyed the challenge of immersing myself in another culture. At first, I worked in bars and restaurants – the kind of jobs where you're paid cash and no one asks too many questions. I liked it. It's a nice country, and it made a change to live somewhere warm.

I read the Bristol papers online, and learned that I was wanted for murder. The local press screamed that I'd killed a brave police sergeant called Barry Wright, a brilliant lawyer named James Paxton, and a talented computer programmer called Colin Fairhurst – Colin's body was recovered a couple of weeks after he'd fallen over the cliff. But I was oddly pleased that only three pictures appeared, because it meant that Oakley was still alive. Now I was safe, and nothing he could do or say could make any difference, I could afford to be magnanimous.

I know you can't believe everything you read on the internet, but I didn't have any other sources, so I had to make do. I gathered from local Bristol message boards that Marko Kovac had been completely exonerated, and was quoted

359

as saying that he'd learned not to be careless with keys – having accidentally left those from the physics lab at the Orchard Street house – or bathtubs again. Another report said that he'd offered to pay for the stain on the kitchen ceiling to be repaired – and that was after he'd forked out for an expensive plane ticket to rush back and help the police the moment he learned he was needed. Urvine and Brotherton had made no comment.

Kovac talked about his nanotechnology research, too, which might have commercial applications, but those were so far in the future that the notion of anyone harming him over it now was inconceivable. Internet gossip also reported that he'd seen a psychiatrist about the atrocities he'd witnessed in the Balkans. So DI Davis had been right in that sense: Kovac *had* been disturbed by his experiences, but they hadn't driven him to kill.

A few months later, I read that Billy Yorke had been sent down for the murder of Emma Vinson, while Randal had turned informer and given evidence against the rest of the gang. Michael was acquitted, however, because there was no evidence, other than Randal's testimony, that he'd ever been at the scene of any crime.

Meanwhile, it emerged that Pullen, the corrupt architect, was strongly implicated in his son's wrongdoings: he'd been feeding James information that would help set wealthy criminals free. It was discovered that he'd developed quite an operation from his prison cell, which he and James had used to make lots of money. Yorke, however, had been a friend. No money had passed hands to get him off the Westbury Burglaries. James had aimed to do that for love.

Mrs Paxton was photographed with her head down, catapulted a second time into the limelight for marrying a famous criminal. I felt sorry for her. She'd worked hard to earn respectability after her husband's downfall and it had all turned to ashes again. I kept an eye on the obituary sections for a while, half expecting to see her name there.

I learned the search for me was widened to foreign countries when Colin's car was found at the airport. Somehow, Colin's answer machine messages were leaked to the media and played over the airways. It made me sound callous – phoning the boyfriend I'd killed to 'cover my tracks'. I can't imagine who was responsible. Not Wright, obviously, as he was dead. It just goes to show that there will always be an element of spite in the police force, and the fact that someone had taken up where Wright had left off made me sick.

A little later, I read that Dr Grossman was retiring – earlier than anticipated, so I suppose the cock-up over James's dental records had taken its toll. Oakley would be glad, I was sure.

And finally, I read that Wayne King had been caught using James's mobile. He was arrested and charged with theft, along with a good many other offences. The CID wrote off dozens of unsolved cases and Wayne went to prison. I was sure he'd learn a lot from older, more accomplished vil-lains, and would return to the streets of Bristol a far better crook.

I cut and dyed my hair, and applied plenty of tanning lotion until my skin really was brown and local-looking. I lost weight, too, and felt good. The newspapers screamed for answers, as they always do when they only have half the facts, but in the end it died down and I was forgotten. I began to relax.

I met a man who was able to give me a new identity, and my name is now Rina Carlo. Unfortunately he asked too many questions, then showed me a newspaper clipping with my picture on it, so I was obliged to resort to the rocks again. The Spanish police aren't as assiduous as their British counterparts, so his death was put down to a fight between thieves and quietly written off. I got a job in a translation agency and started dating a nice industrial chemist called Alfredo. I now live in a lovely bungalow overlooking the sea. Life is better than it ever was in Bristol. Crime *does* pay.

Billy Yorke didn't have to endure life in prison for long. A few months after he was sentenced he was found dead in his cell, having suffered a heart attack in the middle of the night.

Michael supposed he should feel angry with the police officers who'd put Billy inside. But he didn't. They were just doing their job, and Neel Oakley had his own problems anyway. He was facing a slow recovery, and questions were raised as to whether he would ever be fit enough to return to work. Still, his nurse had stayed with him, and Michael had heard they were getting married. Michael wished them well. It wasn't the inspector who was the object of his slowly festering hatred – it was the brown-skinned woman who lay sunning herself by the swimming pool.

It had taken Michael months to trawl the kind of places Brits went when they didn't want to stand out. Clare Davis and Graham Evans had done the same, but they were under pressure of time and limited money, and didn't stand a chance. Michael didn't care that his painstaking search had gobbled up every penny of the proceeds from the Westbury Burglaries, or that he had barely rested since his quest had started. He only cared that he'd found his quarry at last.

The woman who now called herself Rina Carlo liked a sweet, milky cocktail containing rum and coconut juice. She always had one when the Spanish began their siesta, sometimes at the beach and sometimes by the pool. That day, she was by the pool. She was drowsing, made sleepy by sun and alcohol, and she didn't hear Michael when he slipped up to her table and emptied a packet of white powder into her drink. He stirred it with his finger and walked away.

Michael knew a lot about drugs. They were how his family had earned much of their money. He wiped his hand on a white handkerchief – it wouldn't do to lick it clean – then sat at the pool bar, waiting for Rina Carlo to wake up. When she did, she took a long, deep swallow, thirsty from the heat. He thought she grimaced at a slight bitterness, but then she waved to a waiter for another.

Michael watched her for a long time. She laid there neatly, arms to her sides and legs straight, and gradually her breathing slowed until it stopped. He stayed where he was until her second cocktail began to curdle in the heat. Then he stood, flung his jacket over his shoulder, and took a taxi to the airport.